CORE

A Chronicle of M'gistryn
Book One

ANASTASIA M. TREKLES

Halsbren
Publishing, LLC

CORE

First Edition Printing
(2015)

Zelda23 Publishing
http://www.zelda23publishing.com
All rights reserved.
ISBN-13: 978-0-9964311-0-1
ISBN-13: 978-0-9964311-1-8 (electronic edition)

Second Edition Printing
(2018)

Published By: Halsbren Publishing LLC La Porte, IN. 46350

Cover design and layout by Jay Erickson.
Photography by Anastasia M. Trekles.
Throat chakra design by Arcturian, a creative commons image, licensed for commercial use.

Made in the United States of America

DEDICATION

To my parents and friends, and to all who watched the development of this world − enjoy.

Anastasia M. Trekles
-Author

CONTENTS

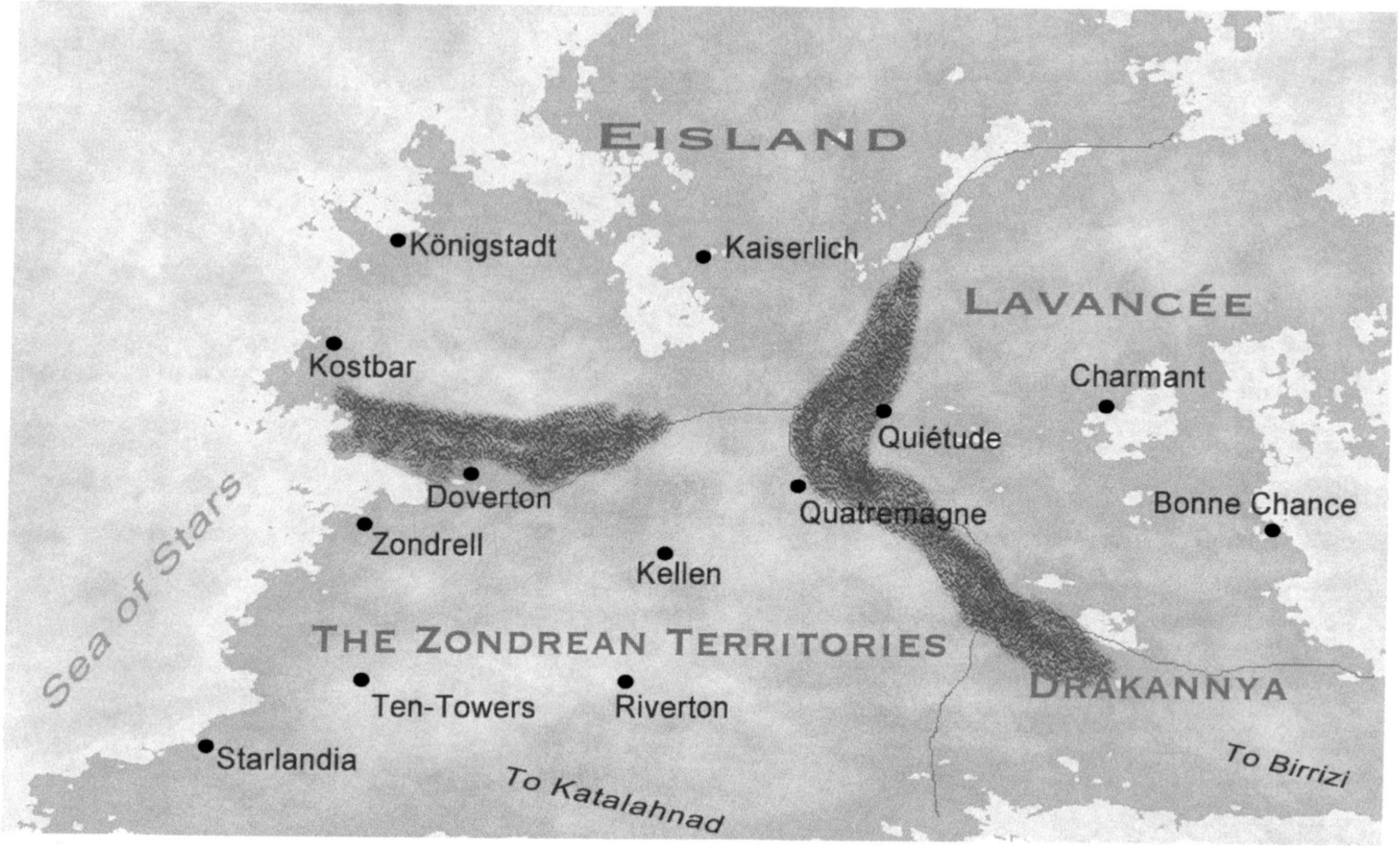
EISLAND
Königstadt
Kaiserlich
LAVANCÉE
Kostbar
Charmant
Quiétude
Doverton
Quatremagne
Bonne Chance
Zondrell
Kellen
Sea of Stars
THE ZONDREAN TERRITORIES
DRAKANNYA
Ten-Towers
Riverton
Starlandia
To Katalahnad
To Birrizi

PROLOGUE

He had never set foot in the city of Zondrell, had never even had the desire despite the wonders it was said to hold. Poised on the edge of the cliffs overlooking the Sea of Stars to the west, many great warriors, explorers, architects, and scholars had left their mark there over its long history. So far, he was neither impressed nor happy to be anywhere near it. He had but one purpose and one destination within those grand walls, and that was all. Yet, he did not fail to notice the budding grasses and flowers of the spring, a much more colorful and pleasant sight than springtime in his homeland. Really, not so far away, and yet so very different of a place... the smells were bright and fresh and airy, reminding him of some of the distant lands traveled in his youth. Lavancée's white sands and green hills, Drakannya's fiery red foliage – these were the things that flashed through his mind as he approached the entrance to Zondrell. Memories of days gone by – not necessarily better or stranger or even worse. Just days that added up into weeks that added up into months and years. Over twenty of them now, by his count, since the last time he had laid eyes on the person he was on his way to visit.

"Nation of origin, sir?" asked the gruff little armed man barring his entry into the bustling streets. Even from the gates, the city was loud, almost deafening. Amazing how the walls could hold in the sound.

Did he really have to tell this stupid, dark-headed cretin where he was from? Upon further consideration he decided that yes, he did, because the man was truly that dense. "Eisland," he spat back.

"Papers?"

Papers? Since when were papers necessary to travel through any part of Zondrea, much less Zondrell where they had hundreds of people in and out every day? Then again, perhaps this place was always such a tightly guarded fortress – he would not have known the difference. And, in a way, it seemed to fit the character of its officious, arrogant, rules-laden people. No man or god could otherwise answer to why anyone chose to come *here* after the War unless there was a rule involved somewhere.

The little man was still staring at him, his displeasure with the situation deepening with each second. "Papers?" he asked again, louder.

The Eislander nodded and reached into a pouch on his belt. There were actually some papers in there, he believed, and... ah, indeed there were. Crumpled and worn and an undetermined number of years out of date, he very nearly threw two sheets of parchment at the guard.

And then he waited. And waited. The guard stepped over to a comrade several times to check on something or make sense of something else. They debated about the authenticity of the King's seal, then proceeded to question the signature. After a while, he became aware of a growing line forming behind him, of others wishing to enter the city. A Katalahni merchant toward the back of the line said something rude that he assumed no one else understood. Under different circumstances, he might have said something back.

Finally, the guard returned. "Brin... er, Br..."

The Eislander cut him off before he could make a bigger fool out of himself trying to pronounce what was obviously far too difficult of a name. "Brinnürjn Jannausch," he said slowly, forming each sound as if teaching a child – *Brin-oor-yin Yaan-nowsh*. It really wasn't that hard, even if the first bit was a little unusual. Actually, it was just old, an ancient name from the ancient dialects of Eisland. How he had gotten stuck with Brinnürjn and his sister had gotten a normal name like Gretchen, he never was able to figure out, but apparently, it had come from a storybook his father had been fond of. Most people, he found, just called him Brin, and that was fine by him. "Can I pass or not?" he asked, his Zondrean perfect despite a rich, lilting Eislandisch accent.

The guard paused for a moment. "Um, yes. Ah, how long will you be staying?"

Did it matter? Nonetheless, he obliged, for the sake of the people behind him. "About a day. I am on business."

"All right. Well, welcome to Zondrell, then, sir."

After that shockingly difficult venture was over, he was on his way once again, beyond the gates and into the heart of one of the biggest cities in the known world of M'gistryn. Far bigger than even the Eislandisch capital of Königstadt, it sprawled out in all directions, a mess of twisting, stone-lined streets that would confuse even the most intrepid traveler under the right circumstances. Brin wondered briefly whether merchants ever found themselves in unforgiving alleys or neighborhoods. Of course, on the other hand, finding one's way to the center of the city was not as difficult as it might have first appeared. He stayed with the wide road, the one big enough for carriages, for several blocks until it became several miles, when eventually the street yawned open and became a great open area, a plaza big enough to engulf an entire small town, dotted everywhere with street vendors of every sort and stripe imaginable.

This was the first time he actually took a moment to look at the people, peering into their eyes and faces as they passed. Few looked back at him. The Zondrell natives were easy to discern, usually small and dark and stately in their way, even the poor ones in their ragged cotton clothes. That was one thing that could not be taken away from the Zondreans – they were proud, almost ridiculously so, and it showed in their manner. They believed that theirs was the greatest civilization, somehow better than others, following in the footsteps of their Lavançaise ancestors. Of course, the Lavançaise were not their only forefathers, but few Zondreans openly acknowledged the Eislandisch heritage that gave birth to their language development and – to some extent – their thirst for war. Cities like Zondrell sprang from moments in time where refugees from various battles sought places to escape their homelands, but as far as any modern Zondrellian was concerned, they had been there since the dawn of history and had the best of everything human culture had to offer. Such arrogance started wars and tore apart families – even twenty-something years after the War of the Northlands, Brin knew this as well as anyone.

The marketplace had almost reached its peak of activity for the day, just after midmorning when the majority of people were up and about. Men, women, and children from all walks of life gathered here, talking, laughing, eating, buying – it was spectacularly loud, and so easy for one to pass unnoticed through the crowds. Wearing a heavy hooded cloak that could cover the weapon on his back and the out-of-place blond hair on his head certainly helped, but the teeming faceless crowd was almost certainly an advantage for one such as he, who had come for only one specific purpose and to meet with only one specific person. But, where to find her? He had imagined it would be a simple affair to find the large, wealthy homes amidst the houses of the rabble, but Zondrell was a much bigger place than even he had anticipated. Heading toward the delicate spires of the palace was probably a safe bet, but he had no plans to wander the city for hours on end, either. If he was wrong, it might not be until well after dark that he came upon his destination, and by then, his patience – and his nerve – would have worn far too thin for his tasks to be accomplished.

He decided the best course of action would be to ask someone. But, it had to be the right person, someone who would attract no attention. One of the market vendors, perhaps. He finally settled on a little booth constructed of wispy cloth and wood, close to the grand fountain at the center of the square. He briefly considered taking a drink from that fountain, but its crystal-clear waters were too perfect, almost suspect. Perhaps magical water was fine for the people of Zondrell, but a few bits of dirt in exchange for something natural was far more trustworthy in his mind.

"Can I get you a cup of tea and spiced beef, sir?" asked the woman inside the booth in a thick, rolling accent. Katalahni –

no one else sounded like that. Their voices were as unique as their looks, dark and rich and beautiful. This one's skin was as bronze as the brazier she cooked upon, the spices filling the air with strange smells. She also dripped with jewels from her neck, ears, fingers, arms- even a ruby stud glinted above one dainty nostril. And, he would have guessed correctly that every single one of those jewels were for sale to the right buyer. It reminded him of different days, traveling through the southern reaches in a futile search for a life beyond war.

"*Ja,*" he said with a nod. "And an extra gold is here for you for some information."

The Katalahni's painted pink lips curled into a slight smile. "I hope that I can give you what you seek." She turned to her brazier again, stirring a small pot of liquid that smelled like oranges mixed with lemongrass. "You look familiar to me, *Habibi*, but I know I have not met you before. Do you live in the city?"

"No. I am here to visit someone." He considered how much to give away, and decided that too much could be dangerous. This woman was obviously not an ordinary poor street vendor, otherwise those jewels would be long gone and she would be selling that svelte bronze body a few blocks further south with the other, less fortunate Katalahni girls. "This person who looks familiar is a friend of yours?"

She nodded. "Perhaps more of a friend of a friend." Obviously, he was going to have to pay for any more than the vaguest bits of conversation, which was fine. The money wasn't the issue, although time was. His cup of steaming tea and small helping of warm stewed beef in a flat circle of bread was exchanged for a handsome handful of gold Royals, the coin that all the Zondrean territories used, which she happily dropped into a pouch at her hip.

"A friend of a friend?" he asked between bites. The intensely spicy, damn-near-heavenly concoction disappeared not long thereafter.

"One of my regular customers has a friend, Eislandisch by blood – partly. Nice men, they are. Generous." She smiled again, sort of a private, inner smile. Her dark eyes danced with the light, or maybe that was Brin's imagination. Maybe. Didn't matter, because it was soon obscured by smoke from a *tsohbac* tobacco stick. She puffed on it slowly, lingering, enjoying it.

"And where do such generous people spend their time in this city?"

She hesitated, with slightly narrowed eyes belying that she thought him some sort of thief, or worse. Their gazes met for a moment, studying each other carefully before she finally gave in. This man meant business, serious business, but in the end, it was not hers to wonder why. Besides, the nobles had guards securing every inch of their territory. Very little left there without someone seeing it, and certainly few would be able to miss this giant of a man in their midst. "Wealth lives on the Gods' Avenue," she replied, the smoke roiling slowly from her mouth as she spoke. "Go north on the Long Road, about eight blocks, turn left toward the palace. The Family estates are all there, all together."

That was all he needed to know. He finished the thick sweet-spiced tea, tossed another few coins at the Katalahni, and disappeared into the crowds once again. Eight blocks north, a little to the west – not that difficult. But yet, with every step and with every building he passed, something did happen. Breathing became more labored, his heart quickened in his chest, nervous energy tingled through his entire body. He was not used to such sensations. Men like Brinnürjn Jannausch did not grow anxious, did not agonize and avoid their fate. But yet, often the greatest foes to be faced are emotions and fears, and have nothing to do with the sword. Such was the case now, and the closer he got to the Gods' Avenue, the more nervous he became. Indeed, he almost did not turn when he saw the signpost. Wouldn't it have been far easier to just let it go, and let Fate take its own course?

Yes, it would have, but whether he liked it or not, he was duty-bound to the people he shared blood with. And coming here, and facing this old – and maybe even silly – fear was part of that duty.

It did not take long to find her, which he also did not anticipate. Anxiety took hold of his throat, made his blood grow ice cold. There she was, a few houses down, kneeling in the dirt and working the soil with slender but strong hands. A pile of blue frost-tip plants lay near her, ready to be planted.

Their blooms were just beginning to pop with spectacular white-blue, speckled flowers. Even though they had been little more than children the last time he'd seen her, he would know her anywhere. Gretchen with the long blond hair, almost always in braids or tied away from her face. Big Sister Gretchen, who some thirty or more years ago used to walk him to his tutor – one of the city elders who liked to take the time to teach the children how to read – every morning, snow, rain, or sun, because he didn't like to walk by himself.

The last thing he had said to her was that she was a whore, and she deserved the *Zondern* she was about to run off with. He was fifteen years old, barely a man, and she about eighteen, enough of a woman to make her own decision. Now, he was almost at a loss for words – almost. "Is it normal for Zondrell noblewomen to tend their own gardens?" he asked, unable to come up with anything better. He said it in Zondrean, thinking perhaps it would startle her less.

In fact, she barely even looked up from her task. "Oh, I enjoy doing this. No one else would do it properly."

At this he couldn't help but smile. "You never let anyone do your work for you." This time, he spoke in Eislandisch, and it definitely got her attention. She looked up with sparkling eyes like the color of the sky, perfect creamy skin, rosy cheeks – she might as well have never aged at all. All the girls from their Kostbar neighborhood would have been insanely jealous to see Gretchen Jannausch today.

"Do we?" Her voice trailed off as she got to her feet, brushing the dirt away onto her apron. Her gaze never left his as she peered at him, into the darkness beneath his hood. They stood together, frozen in time for a moment, before she eventually reached out and pushed the hood away, revealing tousled dark flaxen hair, fresh stubble, and a clean but world-weary countenance. Something familiar and childlike loomed within crystalline eyes, but it couldn't be... "Brin?"

The tears came, for both of them. There was no holding it back, and that was fine- they washed away twenty-four years of pain in but a moment. Suddenly it did not matter that she had once chosen the enemy over homeland, and that he had chosen the sword over his family. That was the distant past, decisions made by youth, immaturity, and pride. None of that changed what was important now – the Jannausch siblings of Kostbar were reunited.

"What are you doing here?" she asked softly, in Eislandisch, stepping away from his embrace but still keeping both hands planted firmly on his shoulders. She could barely believe he was standing in front of her, had to hold on to make sure this was no dream. "*Mein Bruder...* I never thought I would see you again."

"*Ja,* I know." This was all he could think to say. Should he apologize? Perhaps. But he wasn't ready for that just yet.

"I missed you. I worried for you. Brin, where have you been for so long?"

He took her soft hands and held them in his gruff and scarred ones. Such a difference in lives, in lifestyles – it was amazing to him how soft and perfect one's hands could be if she never worked a day in her life, never swung a sword or killed a man. He almost said something about the bits of dried blood still under his fingernails being that of Gretchen's own son, but he held his tongue. Not yet – this wasn't the time. "I quit the army about ten years ago and wandered. I have been all over the world, from Katalahnad to Lavancée. I went back to Eisland – to Kostbar – recently."

Gretchen smiled brightly. "Amazing – I envy you. Did you ever get married?"

"Ah, no." Truth be told, his life had been far too dangerous and tumultuous to invite a woman into it for too long. But, judging by the look on his sister's face, she did not need to hear that part. "Perhaps someday," he added.

If she knew better, she did not indicate as such. Instead, she looked behind her to her home for a moment, feeling proud. "I raised a family here. I have a son. I wish you could meet him but... he serves for the Zondrell army. He is gone somewhere – they will not say where." A scowl clouded her features at this.

Gone "somewhere?" She didn't *know*? This changed things. He had been fully prepared to apologize – for a lot of things – and maybe admonish her and her stupid husband for letting their boy go out to do a job even most men could not handle. But explaining what happened in the first place... well, he didn't know where to begin.

He looked past his sister at the street beyond, realizing that there were a few people milling about. No one paid them much attention, but still, he offered, "Let us find someplace quiet to speak."

"Oh!" Gretchen's cheeks flushed even deeper, almost the color of a splash of wine. "You must be tired from your journey. Come in – we will drink in honor of our family." A drink sounded like a good start to what could be a very difficult afternoon, so Brin was happy to follow her up the steps and through the front door to a more lavish home than he could have imagined. Certainly, he had known that the officer his sister married was a noble, but this was far more elegant than where one might find most regular nobles. Gold and silver accents glinted off of torches and candles set in alabaster sconces. Tapestries displaying proud family memories from generations long past lined the walls, and in between them mahogany shelves held trophies, ceremonial weapons, and other treasures. A servant woman with dark hair mottled by streaks of gray greeted them and offered to take his cloak and boots, and he obliged even though he elected to keep his sword exactly where it was. It made him feel far more at ease knowing that his blade was in handy reach in case things should get out of hand. After all, the man of the house had not yet revealed himself.

As the servant bounded off to find them a bottle of wine, Gretchen led him to a sitting room just as grand as the foyer. Everything was perfectly cleaned and pressed and polished and in its place, making him feel that much more out of place. "Do not worry," she told him as she bade him to sit in one of two well-cushioned leather chairs flanking a small hearth. "Jonathan is not home now."

As the cheerful warmth radiated into his world-weary joints, Brin finally laughed, his nerves easing a bit for the first time. "Worry? I am not worried. But *he* should be." He continued to chuckle, but only because the idea of putting his sister's so-called husband firmly in his place – in his own home no less – was so entertaining.

They toasted over wine to each other and to Eisland as they continued their light banter, reminiscing about what once was and what could have been. Most of the time they spoke Eislandisch, slipping into a strange and garbled version of

Zondrean every so often, and he could only imagine what the servants in the next room were thinking as they surely couldn't help themselves but listen in on their mistress' conversation. There was a lot to say, but it was not really part of Eislandisch culture to dredge through the past, especially the bad parts. He had known Zondreans and Drakannyans who could hold grudges for decades, but the Eislandisch did not do such things. They believed that revenge came in the form of fate, and that the Rivers of time and blood would eventually bring everything into balance, one way or another. So it was that he could sit comfortably in his sister's home and share her wine over twenty years after forsaking her very existence.

Resting atop a little shelf not far from where they sat was a simple but intriguing display, a round piece of engraved silver on a small, cloth-covered stand. The item was slightly askew, as if it had been moved recently, and something beckoned Brin to take a closer look. A trophy, some sort of medal apparently won by the boy. Its tiny script was too embellished to read clearly, especially at a distance, but he could make out the name and the sword and shield decoration at the center. There was also a date inscribed at the bottom, a recent one. "That is the most important honor this place has to give young men," Gretchen told him as he squinted at it. "No one in this family had ever won it before my Tristan. It is a great accomplishment."

"What did he do for it?"

"They have a school where the boys go when they are old enough, to learn to become army officers. He was the best of all of them." There was a note of sadness in her lilting speech. "He was very proud to get that. I think that he fought much for it."

No doubt this was true. No one likes a *Halben* – half-blood – Eislandisch or Zondrean. He imagined Tristan's young life filled with much hatred, discrimination. But rather than lay down and take the abuse, this one rose to the challenge and embraced it. Most certainly, he was his mother's son, at least in that respect. "All for the glory of Zondrell..." he said softly, almost to himself. "Best of the best, I am not surprised."

"What do you mean?" She looked at him, expectant, eyes narrowed a bit in suspicious confusion. Well, at least the ranks of the Zondrell nobility had not affected her quick wit. Unfortunately, now the conversation had turned a corner rather quickly, a bit quicker than he had expected. Brin Jannausch had never been a man of great words, preferring to let his actions do the talking. The next things he said would have to be chosen very carefully if he valued his sister's emotions at all.

"I have seen your son fight," he started, letting the words pour forth so that she could not say anything and ruin his concentration. "He is… remarkable. *Beispiellos*. Worthy of his heritage. But it is for the glory of Zondrell, and I…" He began to lose himself in memories, watching thoughts race across the dimly lit ceiling, its wood and stone casting strange shadows all about. He could see things in those shadows, and they haunted him to the core. "To save him, I had to betray him."

He could still remember the decision he'd made, in a split second, just a few days ago, the decision that led him all the way to Zondrell to seek out a sister he thought he would never speak to again. It was a decision that rippled across time, changed things, forced him to forfeit control over his own fate. He had risked much in making that decision – there was no denying it. But nothing overshadowed the simple fact that blood was the strongest type of bond that people had with one another. "I did it for you, Gretchen, and I am sorry. For many things, I am sorry."

There was silence for a time. She did not understand – had so many questions – but at the same time, knew exactly what had been said. Perhaps she did not need to know all of the details, but she now knew two important things: Tristan had not gone to some benign appointment as her husband had led her to believe, and that her own brother had done something to her only son, obviously quite knowingly. The kind of rage that only a mother can bear began to stir deep within her, to the point where her hands shook as she picked up her wineglass.

"Did you kill my son?" she asked, plain, cool, as if asking how the weather was outside.

Brin downed the rest of his wine. He needed every bit of help he could get. Facing a hundred foes with little more than a cooking knife would have been less stressful than this exchange. He started to question himself as to why he came here at all. Of course, it was because of duty, of family, but oh… a more dangerous assignment he could not have imagined. "I will not lie to you. To be clear, I wanted to kill him. Very much." He would never be able to tell her just how close he'd come to putting his sword through that boy's chest – even after he'd learned his name. "But, I saved his life instead," he told her, and she visibly relaxed somewhat. "He is safe, but the other *Zondern* are coming for him."

"What do you mean?" Her eyes narrowed and her little brow furrowed, revealing tiny lines that gave away her age just a bit. "What did you do?"

He had to stop and think about this for a moment. Usually, he just did whatever came naturally, and said as much. But this was a more delicate situation, and even he had some level of tact. "They will call him Traitor, but as much as I hate the *Zondern*, I would not have put him to that. I just… made it worse. I am sorry."

She shot forward in her chair, sitting so close to the edge that she might have fallen off. The look on her face was focused, intense – almost menacing. "Stop speaking in riddles, Brin. Tell me what happened to my son."

So he did. "I was hired by someone… an old friend. She wanted me to investigate a situation in the borderlands between Eisland and Doverton." *Investigate* was such a simplistic word, but *assassinate* was the last word he wanted to use in front of his sister. At the time, he might have even done it for free, without hesitation, but that's what manipulation does. It warps a man's perceptions and makes him stop thinking for himself.

He realized his hands were clenched in tight fists as he continued, and slowly released them. "We learned from a… survivor, about a camp holed up in the mountain forest, far away from the roads. I would not have thought to look there before," he continued. "But it was, as they say, my lucky day. I knew where to find them, but I only needed one of them, the one the survivor called '*Golddrachen*'. He was the key – without the one who spoke Eislandisch, their entire campaign would be useless."

Most of the color had drained from Gretchen's lovely, proud features. "Oh Holy Mother... You speak of Tristan! What do you mean? Why... What were they doing?"

Brin shook his head and prayed that she believed his feigned innocence. She did, more or less. "Ask your husband. Or his friends. It does not matter what they were doing there. I tracked them down, found him when he was alone. I could have killed him, easily. But a warrior like that – I wanted to know his name. They wear them on their necks, you know. So I looked, and it said Loringham. Of all the names in the entire world, it said Loringham... Amazing how Fate works. I could not do it, so I made him an offer. It was a good offer, a fair one, the *Zondern* would get what they thought they wanted, and then they would leave." He paused, skimming through the pages of memory for a moment. There were parts he wanted – needed – to leave out, things she wouldn't understand anyhow. Hell, he didn't understand them that well himself.

"We had an ambush waiting. I did not think it was needed, but... The *Zondern* did not trust each other. Maybe for good reason. When they started arguing amongst themselves, I launched the attack. I had to. I... I did it for you. To protect your son, Jannausch blood. It was perhaps not right to do. But my choices were limited. Many men died. For Tristan – I made sure it looked good, and would take him out of the battle, so he would be safe. It was not perfect. But it was the only way." He swallowed hard, feeling something odd and constricting within his throat. "I am sorry. Truly. I did not want us to meet again like this."

He looked into her crystal eyes for the first time since he had started talking, and met a face silent as stone, eyes moist but bereft of emotion. Not that the feelings were not there, but she did not know how to express them or what to do with them. They conflicted far too much to make sense. "My son is a good man," she said at length, breaking the heavy silence that had hung between them for quite a while once Brin's story was at an end.

"I... never said anything to the contrary." Had he? He'd tried not to, at any rate. It wasn't exactly easy to do.

"Where is he now?"

"Safe." Again, not quite accurate. He knew the *Zondern* were up there skulking about. They had passed each other as he followed an Eislandisch trade caravan south while a small division of black-and-silver soldiers were marching north. The chances of them actually finding Tristan once they got there were not exactly high, but then again, it depended on where they looked. And perhaps how smart they were.

Gretchen took a deep sigh of a breath. "I want to see him. Take me there."

With a definitive "no," Brin shook his head. "He is not around the corner. You have duties here. You cannot take a trip like that without someone noticing, and I can only protect you so much." Despite her scowl of protest, he sat back with his arms folded across his chest, defiant. The "big sister knows better" routine would no longer go so far when they were approaching middle age.

"Then you need to help him. You need to go back there and help him come home." Her words were pointed and dripping with venom at this point. This was not a request – this was a demand.

"I know." He had a hard time believing that they would let Tristan come home in any other way but at the end of a rope, but now was not the time to worry on that – one step at a time. After all, he was fairly certain that his nephew would sooner try to kill him than follow him back to Zondrell.

They finished the bottle of wine in relative silence. The message he had come to deliver was given, and they had little else to discuss. In a way, it was nice to know that she was well, and that his sister was still as kind-hearted and beautiful as the girl she once had been. Gretchen, too, was happy knowing that her little brother – no longer "little" by anyone's estimation – had grown to become strong and worthy of the Jannausch name. But, they had chosen vastly different lives, and common blood was the only thing left between them. Blood was powerful, though, enough so to keep even the great warrior Brinnürjn Jannausch from striking down his enemies.

At least, so far.

During their entire conversation, Brin had been vaguely aware of a presence in the next room. At first, he'd assumed it was the maid, but then again, what if...? That maid had certainly not been Eislandisch, and the chances of her gaining anything from listening to two people speaking a foreign language seemed low. Finally tiring of the feeling of being watched, he moved to investigate. "If you will excuse me," he said, moving before Gretchen could stop him or even say anything. In one quick and powerful motion, he threw open the door, making a heavy booming sound that reverberated throughout the room, tinkling crystal and wobbling tapestries all over the place. The door very nearly incapacitated the person on the other side.

"Johann! So good to see you!" He *knew* it. Somehow, he just knew that it was no serving woman listening so carefully. He moved in, backing a surprised and wheezing Lord Jonathan Loringham up almost to the next wall.

To his credit, the years had also been relatively kind to "Johann." His face was marred by some extra lines, but not many, and streaks of gray ran through his perfectly groomed brown hair and beard. But, his dark eyes were as clear and bright as they were when he was young. This was the one place where he resembled his son the most, in the shape and tilt of the eyes. The olive-tinged skin tone – a little darker on the elder, of course – was similar, too, but that was about where the obvious similarities ended. The man standing before him was as Zondrean as the gods could make him, and yet his son had managed to get all of the best features of the Eislandisch. Funny how things worked sometimes.

"Good Lady Catherine." Jonathan was squinting hard, trying to place this person who had been conversing – conspiring? – with his wife for close to an hour, maybe longer since before he'd come home. Of course, he only could catch bits of what was said – he was sorely out of practice when it came to the Eislandisch language. He knew enough, though. The worst part was that he knew this giant of a man. Was it? It couldn't be. "Brin?" he asked, his voice almost a whisper.

Brin laughed, but his tone was not so mirthful. Harsh, even venomous, would have been more accurate. "I should be honored that the good Captain Loringham would even remember my name."

The fact that the Eislander spoke nearly perfect Zondrean hardly registered with Jonathan for the moment, although later he would marvel at it. "If I recall, you made quite the impression." Who could forget the half-crazed boy who'd tried on numerous occasions to take out the headquarters the Zondrell army had set up in the middle of Kostbar during the war? Though unsuccessful at doing much real damage then, his acts of rebellion sparked the rest of his brethren to action, helping them realize that it was in fact possible to challenge the Zondrellian occupation. They were forced out within months, but not before Jonathan could propose to the Eislandisch girl he'd fallen in love with. Unfortunately, this did very little to calm that half-crazed boy, since she was his sister. Jonathan could count at least seven separate occasions where Brinnürjn Jannausch had tried to kill him, and now it was appearing that there would be an eighth.

"Stop it now! Both of you!" Gretchen's look was nearly as menacing as her brother's as she attempted to get between them. She knew better than anyone how quickly such a confrontation could escalate.

But, the weapons were already out – or at least, one was. Both Gretchen and her husband watched in horror as Brin produced something thin and glistening from a hidden pocket in his long-sleeved tunic. Before anything could be done, the blade was dangerously close to Lord Loringham's face, forcing him to visibly relax the hand that had been moving toward his own dagger on his belt. Gretchen made a peep of protest but little else, because her voice left her.

"That knife..." Jonathan said, examining the thing held in front of him carefully. He recognized it – would recognize the delicately curved blade and the ruby at the end of the handle anywhere. It had been handed down from father to son in his family for four generations. "Where did you get that?"

"Where do you think? I should have sold it." It was no longer wet or sticky with blood, but he certainly hadn't bothered to clean it either. It was smeared almost tip to hilt in dried, flaky blackness. "Do not worry, most of that belongs to your boy. Most of it."

Now the hand was clenched again, hovering at his belt. "What did you do?" Jonathan growled.

"Tell me what you think I did, and maybe I will you the truth." Brin laughed again – he could hardly help himself. He knew exactly what old Johann would say, because he heard the other *Zondern* say it – the boy was rogue, the boy was a traitor. And here was a family member, so they must have been working together. Ha! Arrogant fools, all of them. This was not the revenge he had envisioned in that mystical someday that may or may not have ever come to pass, but it would suffice. The glee he would get in explaining to Jonathan just exactly how horrible a husband and father he turned out to be was just as satisfying. A part of him briefly felt great sorrow for his sister, who was getting ready to break into tears at any moment. She did not deserve this – not really. Still, if she had stuck to her own kind, things would have been so different.

Jonathan's voice was harsh, angry, hateful. "You did this, didn't you? You tricked him into... something. Tristan was a good soldier, a fine..."

"'Was'? Either you believe him dead or you believe your army's reports. Which is it, Johann? Tell your wife what you believe and what you think you know." The sudden joy of revenge rose with every second Loringham's stammered to answer, avoiding the growing glare of his wife.

"I... Please, don't do this, Brin. I'll talk to you in private, but not here."

Now, he was angry. Very angry. As the knife danced dangerously about in his hands, his shouts could probably be heard two houses away. "She *knows* now, *Dummkopf!* Fucking hell, man, just say it. You sent your boy to do a job beyond most men."

"Brin, I never knew much about the campaign. I..." It was no use, so Jonathan's words trailed off.

"You know something? That boy did *exactly* what he was told. I have watched him – he *lived* for the glory of Zondrell. A fine warrior, too, you are right. You can bet that he did not get that from your side of the family. But this place – *you people* – stole that boy's soul. You should thank me. I might have given it back to him."

With that, he shoved that dagger's ruby handle so hard into Jonathan's sternum that it would stay purplish and bruised for a week afterward. "I used this to protect your boy from his own people," he said. "I would have you hold onto it for him, but I just changed my mind."

As he moved toward the door, he turned back to look at Gretchen. The pain and anger and heartache had exploded in her, pouring out of her eyes now like a wellspring. This was all too much for her – he should have expected that – but it was the way it had to be, the right thing to do. He reached out and took her hands in his one more time, just briefly, and for the first time felt true remorse – for this, for everything. He wanted to apologize to the sister he would leave sobbing in her ornate sitting room, comforted only by a man trying very hard to redeem himself. But, for once in his life, Brin's words failed him.

PART ONE

1

Tristan Michael Johannes Loringham, Second Lieutenant, Fifth Division, Royal Army of Zondrell

It took the better part of a day for me to ride into Zondrell – it was the first time I'd been back in more than four months. Not much changes in such a short time, except seasons, of course. It was spring and the flowers were blooming all across the meadows on my way in; they filled the air with their happy springtime scent, but I gave their efforts little notice. When I got beyond the gates of the city, I knew there would be girls selling those same flowers on street corners, often dressed in tattered clothes, looking terribly forlorn until someone dropped a gold coin into their hands. But, it was better than a few other things they could be selling on the corners, after all.

No, not much can change in four months except nature… at least that's what one might think.

I felt like a stranger in this place, the city where I was born. I checked in at the gates with two guardsmen who looked so young they could have been schoolchildren. They didn't know me and at first they thought I was some sort of mercenary. I shouldn't have been surprised – what sort of person runs around in Zondrellian livery but looks like an Eislander except a mercenary? Really, just me, but they didn't know that. It took a good five minutes to get past them, right after it suddenly occurred to them that I didn't have an accent. Idiots.

I left my horse with the stableman two blocks into town, tipping him fifty Royals to ensure that the horse and my trusted sword latched to its saddle wouldn't be "accidentally" sold by the time I got back. I had little time to worry about anything else. I was sure the funeral visitation was ending and they'd be starting the ceremony soon. As I moved toward Southend, where the Great Temple stood, I was reminded of just how vast Zondrell really was, a sprawling metropolis full of life, the daytime streets bustling with hurried and worried faces. They called it the crown jewel of the Zondrean Territories, the biggest and brightest amongst the seven city-states that shared culture and language and a stretch of land between Lavancée in the east and the Sea of Stars to the west. Being there, though, and looking at the grime and the poverty and the harsh contrast between rich and poor, it was hard to see how it lived up to the rest of the world's lofty expectations. Throughout the city, work was getting harder to find – not many people outside of Southend could afford to just hang around all day in lavish homes and pressed silk, living off of old money. I paid careful attention not to make eye contact with anyone as I worked my way through the cobblestone streets, which gradually turned less dirty and less pocked and cracked with age the further south I got. Normally, I would throw them a gold piece or two as I walked by, but I had little to spare that day. I never brought much with me when I left on campaign because there was no need for it, but people don't know that. They just know that when the nobles look at them and don't offer them some charity, since they have so much to spare, then that's an excuse to get rude. I simply didn't have time for rudeness.

At Center Market, the exact middle of town where the merchants did their business, I stopped at the city's great marble fountain and quickly washed my face, wetted down my hair and slicked it back. The behavior of a street urchin? Absolutely, but what else could I do? The Katalahni girl was selling mirrors and various shiny baubles at her stand nearby, and I couldn't help but go take a look at myself. She said something friendly and I think I said something back, but I can't remember what it was. I was far too entranced by the image staring out at me from that little polished bit of glass.

I really looked like hell. I had more than a day of stubble on my chin and I could feel the little fair hairs poking my palms. My Royal Army uniform – what used to be my good dress uniform, with the buckles in the leather all nicely polished and the black tabard where the silver falcon crest of Zondrell spread its wings – was full of dust and road grime; hell, I hadn't even slept in about a day and a half, but there was no time to deal with any of it. I took a deep breath and straightened my shoulders. I had to get there soon, and if I looked a little primitive… well, Alex would understand.

And I was late, terribly late, as it turned out. It had taken longer than I had thought to cross just over twenty miles of wilderness. The main chapel doors of the Great Temple were never closed during the day unless there was a funeral mass going on behind them, so I knew I was in trouble. For a moment, I froze there with my hand on one of the massive brass handles, staring at the beautiful carvings of doves in the door and having no idea what to do with myself. I felt silly. Now I was going to have to walk in right in the middle of some eulogy or prayer song or something. Alex would forgive me, sure, but what about everyone else? It would be a risk I would have to take.

I took a deep breath and pulled the door open. A young priestess-in-training smiled at my entrance, put a finger to her lips to tell me to be quiet and take a place in the chapel somewhere. Of course, there were no seats free and the whole place was awash in black, white, and gold mourning colors in silk and brocade – it's fascinating how many members of Zondrell's high society there really are when you gather them all up at once. So, I leaned against a wall at the back of the room and felt like a complete and total ass.

Alexander was at the front of the chapel behind the altar with the Book of Catherine opened before him. If he'd actually tried to read from it, I might not have been able to control a chuckle, but luckily he didn't. Right now, though, he was uncharacteristically somber, the sparkle in his dark eyes reduced to an empty gleam. Even from where I stood, a couple hundred feet away, I could tell he was tired. His slender shoulders slumped downward, his olive-tinged skin a bit ashen – perhaps that was just the firelight reflecting off the whitewashed chapel walls. But when he spoke, it was clear that grief weighed heavily on his soul.

"My father used to tell me to be proud of who I am, proud to be a Vestarton." His voice wasn't strong, and it didn't exactly ring through the chapel, but there was deep sadness – reverence – in his tone. "And I am. I always have been. And when I entered the Academy, I was proud to be there and he was proud to see me go. 'You'll be a fine officer someday, Alex.' He told me this a lot of times." There was a long pause – someone coughed, someone else sneezed. Finally, Alex spoke up again. "Even though Lord Xavier wasn't able to watch my whole career, he saw me graduate from the Academy with honors as a Zondrell lieutenant. I'm glad that he at least got to see that."

Again, he stopped to collect his thoughts. If I knew him at all, I knew he hadn't prepared for this and was trying to come up with something intelligent and lordly right off the cuff. What came out, though, was more genuine; poor old Xavier would indeed have been proud if he'd been there to listen. "I guess what I'm trying to say is that I wish he was still here with us, but he is in a peaceful place now, free of pain. No man should have to suffer in death, especially not one as great as Lord Xavier, and I don't think he did. His children were with him, and his wife, and he had a lot to be proud of. My father died an honorable man, and I'll do my best to continue making him proud." Some people applauded, others merely looked on in solemn respect. Up at the altar, his sister, Alice, and his mother grabbed up each of Alex's hands and they all sobbed a little. They were worthy of a portrait standing up there together, three perfect dark-haired, dark-eyed people lit by the altar fire and the sunlight streaming in through the grand, multicolored stained-glass windows lining each side of the chapel hall.

Eventually, it was time for the priestesses to perform the final rituals that would ensure Lord Xavier's soul made it safely to Paradise and the peaceful embrace of the Great Lady. I had only witnessed one other formal funeral in my young life, years ago when I was still just a boy. I didn't understand it then – all I saw was a group of ladies in white standing quietly with their hands together in prayer, while another woman in red-trimmed robes concentrated on the bier until the whole thing burst into flames. This was the Pyrelight, of course, a wizard whose sole duty was to light corpses on fire with magical flame, sending their souls off presumably to a better place, to Paradise, where they can sit alongside Catherine for eternity. If you were Zondrean and cared about your loved ones at all, you called in the local Pyrelight to help you send them off properly when they passed. The service was always quite horrifying to watch, hence the prayer and the dancing and other things designed to divert your eyes and attention... honestly, I always thought that the job of a Pyrelight must be truly one of the worst things in the world. The fragrant oils they'd wrapped Xavier Vestarton's remains in lit like grass in the Katalahni desert, sending up thick black smoke and a smell unlike anything one can fully describe in words. It's a mix of roses, incense, and burning flesh that you simply cannot get out of your mind once you've experienced it – the bittersweet odor of death. Instead of looking away at the priestesses or bowing my head in prayer as everyone else was doing, I couldn't help but watch the flames turn from yellow to gold to white, consuming the body of a man who'd once been so warm and happy and friendly.

I stood there in a mostly blank haze for a good while, as a hot pulsing sickly feeling burned a hole into the pit of my stomach. Alexander's mother spoke a little more, thanked everyone for joining them, and then it was time for the congregation to line up and give their personal regards to the family. The place had so much nobility walking through it that the walls should have bled blue. Alex would have called this a socialite festival, one of those times when you have to watch what you say and do so carefully that you're sure to develop a paranoia disorder by the end of the evening. Somewhere toward the front of the room I caught a glimpse of my own parents; actually, the first person I saw was my mother, because like me, she stood out in any Zondrean crowd. Tall, slender, fair, stately – there was no one else quite like her anywhere near this city, and if there were, they were definitely not welcome here. On the other extreme, my father blended in with the rest of them, a shortish, darkish figure amongst the host of others just like him.

As for me, I stayed right where I was, against the wall in a shadow and hoping I wouldn't get noticed right away. I didn't fit in – I never have, but especially not now. A strange tingling feeling washed over me, and my heart quickened. My breathing grew short and shallow, eventually dwindling to almost nothing at all. I watched people pass up and down the aisle in something of a daze, where images passed before my eyes but my brain didn't process them. I just stood there, frozen in time and wondering what the hell I was doing here.

"I'm very sorry." A small voice near my ear startled me to my senses, and I turned to face it – it was the Pyrelight on her way out, her job here complete. The unmistakable luminescence of magic smoldered bright orange in her eyes, obscuring whatever color they used to be, although I imagined they might be green judging by her wavy auburn hair and rosy complexion. A heartlands girl, maybe from Doverton or Kellen, but much prettier than most I'd seen. Of course, she was young, too, probably my age, or even a few years younger, not quite twenty, still blooming into womanhood. The corners of her mouth turned into the slightest smile when our gazes met. "Ah, for your loss," she said, "I'm sorry for your loss. Peace be with you."

"Thank you, and peace be with you," I replied, not quite knowing what else to say. She smiled a little wider now, offered a polite nod, and continued on her way. I turned my head and watched the way her robes swirled around her slim, diminutive body as she moved, until she was out the door and gone. Girls, especially pretty ones like that, didn't smile at me all that often unless they knew how much money I stood to inherit someday, and I had to admit there was a part of me that wanted to go out and follow her. But then again, another part of me had a strange but distinct feeling that our paths would cross again. I had no idea why, no basis for feeling that way at all, but it was there nonetheless.

"Tristan? Hey, what the f… heck are you doing back there?" I snapped out of my thoughts, looked up toward the source of the voice. It was Alex, peering at me from halfway across the chapel with his arms crossed before his chest. Almost everyone was gone by now – the Great Temple was overwhelming in its emptiness.

"I'm sorry…" was all I could say at first, and all he would let me say before he rushed up, grabbed me and hugged me.

"You have no fucking idea how glad I am to see you," he said as he drew away. Together we both glanced over at the nearest priestess, who eyed him with her little brow furrowed. "I mean, no earthly idea. Sorry."

"I wasn't sure I was going to make it. I came in late. I'm sorry."

Alexander Vestarton – a true friend, very nearly a brother, to the point where he often called me "Brother" as a nickname – shook his head, waving me off with a gesture. He smiled, too, but his heart wasn't quite in the task; he looked so tired, with circles under red-rimmed eyes as if he'd spent the last several days doing nothing but drinking and smoking his prized little paper-wrapped tsohbac sticks. Indeed, after taking a sample of the air around his presence, I was pretty sure that that was exactly what he'd been doing. To be honest, I don't know what's in tsohbac, but the heavy, woodsy scent hangs in your clothes, in your hair, even gets under your skin if you smoke enough of it. Alexander smoked far, far more than enough, and had done so ever since our first year at the Academy. That Katalahni merchant woman had gotten him hooked on it; I tried it myself a few times but never saw the appeal. Must be an acquired taste. "Don't worry about it," Alex said. "Really – I'm just glad you made it at all."

And he was honest in that, but I still felt the need to explain. "I got your message yesterday, around sundown. They wouldn't let me leave till this morning, and it's a long ride."

"Yeah, well it's a good thing these messengers earn their pay, huh? If I hadn't tipped him enough, you probably would have gotten it next week sometime."

By this time, the rest of the entourage had made their way over, and it was time for more hugging and so forth. Mother was the first, of course, fawning over me as if she hadn't seen me in years rather than months, but that was all right. I expected it. "*Willkommen zurück*," she said softly – she often took advantage of the fact that I was the one person with whom she could speak her native language. It had been the one point in raising me that she had been absolutely insistent on.

"*Danke*," I replied. The rest came slower – I really didn't want to see the look on her face once I said what I had to say. "*Ich bin traurig, daß ich nicht länger bleiben kann*." I told her. She smiled but her bright blue eyes turned full of sadness.

"You cannot stay?" She asked, and I shook my head.

At this my father made a low sound at the back of his throat, the typical sound he made when he was interested in saying anything meaningful. "When do you go back?" These were the most pleasant words Lord Jonathan Loringham had said to me in quite a while, even if his glare was still one of disapproval. Maybe if I'd come back with a tan and brown eyes we might have had a more pleasant reunion, but... well, what could I do?

"I need to be back there tomorrow," I told them, and everyone sighed at that. "I'll leave in the morning."

Lady Julia Vestarton smoothed her black dress around her hips. Like her son, she too had dark circles rimming her eyes, but for all the sadness in her face, it never marred her beauty. The wife, now widow, of Lord Xavier seemed just as perfect as always, as if this were a day like any other. "Well, by the Lady," she said, "then we had better get back to the house. We're having a private dinner, just us and our good friends." She smiled and looked at my mother when she said this – she was one of the few ladies within high society who had accepted my mother immediately, and had never once said anything against her. If it hadn't been for Lady Julia and Lady Dona Shal-Vesper, my mother might never have made any friends at all in over twenty years of living in Zondrell.

We walked out of the temple and south toward the estates of the nobility, clustered alongside each other in neat rows, each home embellished and adorned in its own special way. They were massively tall, not like castles but towering buildings nonetheless, each one made of stone and marble with intricate carvings and landscaping – all trying to outshine the house next door. Vestarton Manor lay just across the street from Loringham Manor, the place I called home, and nothing about any of it had changed much. Lady Julia had planted flowers around the entrance to her home, beautiful red day trumpets that were just starting to bloom. Meanwhile, on our side of the street, my mother's blue frost-tips were coming up nicely, but they had little in the way of majesty. Just little, blue flowers with white edges, hundreds of them spreading across the front of the property.

"You really ought to stop in and change," said my father, looking at me the way he always did. "Your room's the same as it's always been."

Given the way I was feeling, going in and washing up was not a disagreeable idea in the least. I practically bolted for the house. Inside the servants were ecstatic to see me again, and I have to admit, it was nice to have someone take my boots and welcome me into a warm beautiful home that smelled of perfume and woodsmoke. And sure enough, my room was completely untouched, left exactly as I left it a few months ago. I peeled off a few layers of dusty uniform and laid back on the bed – a warm, fluffy, actual bed... amazing! I imagined that I was feeling the same thing that convicts felt after their sentences were over. Everything familiar that you take for granted on a normal day all of the sudden has new life, new meaning.

✳✳

I must have fallen asleep at some point, for when I woke it was pitch dark. I also had the distinct feeling that I wasn't in my bed, or in my room. The place no longer smelled nicely of woodsmoke but of temple incense. Incense – why incense? I'd left the church hours ago. I swallowed hard and tasted copper.

Everything seemed blurry and distorted when I opened my eyes, so I shut them again. Had I been dreaming? Must have been... yes, it must have been a dream because I remembered coming back from Zondrell that next day. I had a wicked hangover from staying out with Alex – how could I forget that?

Vague images leaped through my mind, moments in time racing here and there and hiding behind shadows sometimes, just to throw me off their trail. Some time had passed since I came back from Zondrell, I knew that much. Why I was playing my trip back in my dreams I had no idea, but it had definitely been more than a few days ago. Two weeks at the most. But what happened in the meantime? And why couldn't I put the images I was seeing back in order?

I felt sick. My heart raced – I could hear it pounding in my head. Something was not right and I had no idea what it was until I opened my eyes again.

This time it was still dark, but I could make out figures moving around. There was firelight coming from nearby. I was laying down, on my back, face up to the ceiling, a ceiling where the light made shadowy monsters flicker and creep around, like dark ghosts. The panic continued to rise in my heart, in my throat, in my stomach.

"Oh no," I heard a quiet voice behind me, someone unseen and female, unfamiliar.

"What?" There was a blurred figure at my right side. I'd noticed it – her – doing something over there but couldn't figure out what. I still couldn't, but the figure had now stopped whatever she was doing.

"Oh no," the quiet unseen voice said again. "What do I do?"

"What do you mean?"

"He's awake! What do I do?"

"That's impossible."

Oh, it was possible. I tried to squirm, to sit up, to do something, but regardless of how well my brain was working, my body was not cooperating. Desperately uncoordinated, I tried to turn to my side to get up, but that was the most incredibly stupid thing I ever could have done. I cannot put into words what I felt when I put any sort of weight into my right shoulder – real, pure, true honest-to-the-gods pain has to be experienced to be understood. It stole the breath from my lungs so that I couldn't even cry out, but luckily the strange women were there to do it for me.

"Do something, Seraphine!" the one behind me squeaked. I heard the other one – apparently, Seraphine – root around somewhere for something, nervous. Suddenly there was a face before me, and a warm hand on my brow. Even without being able to see well, I will never forget those eyes, bright orange and luminescent and full of tears. "You're going to be all right," she said softly. "Really, just relax."

Relax? Fuck that. I might not have been very coherent, but that one thought stood out in my mind. I don't think I actually said it though, because her expression didn't change. Her hands were so warm, hot and somewhat soothing against my skin.

"I can't believe this... I don't have anything. This isn't exactly an apothecary here, you know." The orange eyes narrowed as they looked away from me and over at Seraphine.

"Well you can't keep going. The pain will be too much."

Seraphine came into view, and I could tell that she was wearing a long white robe, smeared crimson across the front and up both sleeves. "We do what we have to. And pray," she said, taking her seat back at my side. She got close to me and I could see her well for the first time, a plump, pleasant round face with chestnut-colored eyes. "I have to finish patching you up," she said to me. "I want you to lay back and relax. Hold Andella's hand and close your eyes and it'll be over in a few minutes. Can you do that for me?"

Did I have a choice? The woman named Andella took my hand in hers and I looked into her orange eyes. I remember thinking that they looked like two little sunsets bursting across the horizon. This was my last thought, because then there was a tug around my shoulder and an unbelievable sharp pain. The world around me went mercifully black.

2

The night after the funeral was mostly spent with Alex, drinking and talking. We went down to the Silver Mirror, the tavern where all the young nobles tended to spend their evenings, where a lot of drinking and wagering and generally harmless debauchery had been known to take place. But that night was a slow one for the Silver and that was good; neither of us were in the mood for much noise. I remember him still with that quiet, somber demeanor, smoking so much that the whole area around our table actually felt heavy. The barmaid had a coughing fit every time she came to check on us.

"Hey," Alex said, "it's that girl... can't remember her name... that one you had a thing with?" He nodded at someone behind me and I turned, trying to be as nonchalant as possible.

Indeed, I would not have forgotten that lithe, curving figure anytime particularly soon. The girl – I *did* remember her name, it was Dennia, some second cousin twice removed in the Shal-Vesper House – was dressed in layers of green silk that clung to her lovingly, the color perfectly highlighting her smooth olive skin. "Yeah, that's her," I replied, taking one last look before turning back to Alex. "Wouldn't call it a 'thing' though." No, definitely not a "thing" – barely an affair, really. We did have a few very nice evenings together once, a couple of years ago – in fact, she was the first girl I'd ever spent an evening with at all, but that was the extent of it. There was no romance, no love there, just a passing interest in what each other had to offer physically… well, to be fair, *I* was the one with the physical interest, while she was much more concerned with the amount of gold in my family's coffer.

"All right, a couple of drunken nights, whatever. Go have another one. Good for morale, right?"

I shook my head, downed the rest of my ale and pushed it toward the edge of the table, hoping the barmaid would notice it was empty. "Shouldn't I be the one trying to cheer you up, not the other way around?"

"You're too tense. Have a few more drinks at least, relax a bit." He ordered another round before I had a chance to protest. "Hey, by the way, I heard some good news for a change. Just yesterday."

"What's that?"

"Your application went through."

Unbelievable. Teaching at the Academy was something I'd thought I'd wanted to do. It was something I could see myself doing, and I might even be good at it. But after a few years of actually being in the Academy, I had a hard time believing it was possible for them to let that happen. It had taken quite a bit of courage to sign that application and hand it to the Headmaster the day before our graduation ceremony – so much so that I didn't even wait to let him review it before I left his office. I would have been less surprised to hear he had torn it up and thrown it into the fire. "It did? How do you know?"

"Corrin heard it from his father. I don't know if it's official, but when you came back they were going to have you teach the basic swordsmanship classes to the first-years. That's what you wanted, isn't it?"

"Yeah, I guess."

"Sure beats Gatewatch duty. You know that's what they put Corr into, right?" Poor Corr – no one wanted the mind-numbing job of watching the troops collect people's papers at the city gates. I guess someone had to do it, but I certainly never wished it on a good friend like Corrin Shal-Vesper. That explained why he hadn't had time for more than a quick hello a few hours ago before darting off again.

So the night wore on, with bits of idle conversation punctuated by additional pints of ale and the occasional small hit of something harder. It was good, like old times, and Alex was right – I was incredibly tense. It felt good to just sit there and while away the night doing nothing at all of importance. Apparently, though, it didn't matter how much drink I had because I still couldn't relax completely; at one point, I felt a presence nearby, just behind me and out of my line of sight. It made me jump.

"Tristan – good to see you well." Two bright blue-white eyes stared back at me, alien blue and not at all natural like mine, even if the color was close. These were the product of magic, and I knew them well. I think I sneered rather visibly. "Alexander, I'm so sorry about your father," he went on, ignoring me and turning his attention on Alex, who wasn't terribly interested either. However, he was more polite about it.

"Thank you, Victor, I appreciate that." Alex took another drag from his seventeenth *tsohbac* of the evening and stared vacantly past Victor Wyndham, into the bar area where the girls loaded their trays with drinks.

For his part, Victor seemed rather detached. Of course, that was his nature. As a Water mage and the official Royal Army of Zondrell Captain of Magics, he was cold as the ice magic that ran through his veins. His family had also despised mine for generations, so it was all the more a shock when he pulled up a chair and sat down with us. Alex and I both watched his every move, baffled and visibly perturbed. "Look," he said, hunching over the table with elbows resting on the edge, "I've heard some things, and… well, I'm just wondering how my brother's doing, where you're at out there?" He turned to me, and there was genuine concern in his eyes, which used to be dark, almost black. He was a few years older than Alex and me, but not old enough to where I didn't remember when he was just a skinny, awkward kid, with sharp features like his mother, unlike the rest of his family, which was considerably rounder and heavier. I suppose it was lucky for him that he retained that slender figure as he got older, even though to me, he always seemed like a big dark rat.

The barmaid brought us a second round of Drakannyan brandy, and the bittersweet golden liquid did a slow burn as it slid down my throat and settled in my stomach. "He's fine," I replied. "Don't know what you're hearing, but it's not that bad there. Peter's fine."

Victor licked his lips. "I'm a Captain, Loringham. They tell us what's happening up there."

"Yeah, well... Peter's fine. Look, I'll give him your best, all right?" Maybe it was the alcohol, but I started to feel dizzy, weird, almost like I might be sick. My heartbeat got faster and faster and I could hear it like a tremendous pounding at the base of my skull. The world went somewhat blurry – not completely dark, but definitely not right. Lucky for me, I was sitting down and had a table for support, but I also had an extreme urge to get up, to leave and get some air. So I did, without a word – Alex and Victor asked after me and I think I said something back to them, but I don't know what it was or if it was intelligible. I just absolutely had to get out of there before I vomited or my heart exploded... or something. I wasn't about to find out what would happen.

✳✳

I felt like that now again, with the world spinning and swaying wildly around me while I somehow rode it all out. But instead of sitting in silence I started to become of aware of some voices nearby, speaking close by in hushed, urgent tones.

"I think he's going to be all right, but he needs time to recover." This was the one called Seraphine, the priestess. I recognized the lilt in her tone.

"How much time?" This voice was unknown – breathy and a little low-pitched, but definitely female. She had a heavy Lavançaise accent that twisted her words around and slurred them together in interesting ways.

"He's been through a lot. That was a terrible wound. I..."

"How much time?" Very insistent now, and pissed off. Whoever this woman was, I didn't think I wanted to meet her.

"I don't know, m'lady. A few weeks?"

"That is too long."

A door opened and closed. Then I was left in silence, absolute silence. And cold – I'd never felt so cold, and my shivers eventually bumped me into full consciousness. My eyes opened to a whitewashed stone room, with gray-white light coming in from a little window off to one side. Somewhere behind me there was a torch or a hearth, something on fire – the light danced with the shadows around the room in a weirdly rhythmic fashion. I smelled that smoky-sweet odor of temple incense again, but this time it wasn't as strong. I must have been in some kind of sickroom, and a terrible one at that – there was little in the way of furniture or adornment save for a table and the bed I laid on. I might as well have been on the floor. Of course, I probably should have felt lucky enough to still be alive, rather than worry about how comfortable the bedding was, but what can I say? I could hardly move. I was as trapped as a prisoner in a cell awaiting execution – there's only so much to think about in such a situation, really.

Just when I was resorting to counting the number of stone blocks in the ceiling, the door opened again, creaking like something ancient. It was the darkest figure I'd ever laid eyes on in my life. Black hair, black eyes, black clothes – all of it stood in sharp contrast to her smooth porcelain skin. She put her hands on her hips and smiled at me, but this wasn't the kind of smile that meant she was happy to see me. Instead, she looked like she was getting ready to take that dagger off her belt, cut my heart out of my chest, and have a great deal of fun doing it. "*Bonsoir*," she said in a low, gentle, slurring Lavançaise accent. "I believe we have some things to discuss, you and I."

I made a pathetic attempt to sit up, to look a little less like some tragic victim and more like a dignified army officer. The woman in black stared at me unblinking, and I stared back at her. I wanted to ask her who she was, what she wanted, but something told me to wait. I continued to fuss around getting into position, but there wasn't a whole lot else I was going to do to look dignified or at the very least, be comfortable.

She licked her lips and some of the light red stain on them came off. "You may call me Madame Saçaille. It is because of me that you are not dead. You should thank me."

Thank her? Yeah, maybe when I started feeling a little better. Right then and there, I sort of wished that whatever had prompted someone like this to save my sorry life would have thought better of such an act. I continued to stay silent, watching her the way she watched me. She had a thin white scar across her cheek, running from the corner of one almond-shaped eye to the bottom of her small, delicate jaw.

"Tell me something, Monsieur: what business does a Zondrell officer have in this region, hm?"

Right down to business… who the hell was this woman? I shook my head and said nothing. If I was lucky, maybe she would think I didn't speak Zondrean and she'd leave me the hell alone. Whether this one was an enemy or not remained to be seen, but I didn't feel the need to take any chances. Her tall but slender frame didn't seem terribly threatening; nonetheless, something told me not to underestimate her.

After a few minutes of silence she clicked her tongue against her teeth, annoyed, and reached into her shirt pocket, producing a silver pendant on a simple chain. Some of the links in the chain were broken, torn apart, and the flat, falcon-shaped charm, though worn, was clearly stamped with my name and rank. My hand instinctively went to the thin cut on my throat where it had been ripped off a while ago.

"Tristan Michael Johannes Loringham… Lieutenant, Royal Army of Zondrell, fifth division." She tossed it in my lap. "Tristan… rather a Zondrean name for an Eislander, *oui*? Do not sit here and be silent and think I will mistake you, Monsieur. I know who you are. I even know the answer to my question. But I want *you* to tell me."

"Where did you get this?" I asked, taking up the pendant. It was indeed mine, but she wasn't the one who took it from me. The chain was cold as I let it slip between my fingers and fall onto the blanket again.

She got closer, leaned over me so close that I could feel her breath on my neck. It sent a cold chill through my entire body. "It matters not. In some cultures it is considered rude to answer a question with a question. Tell me what you know first, and perhaps – if you are lucky – I may answer you."

A long pause – I was having trouble formulating complete thoughts. I thought I should know what to say, but the memories were tangled and scattered, and I wanted to choose my words carefully. None of this was something *she* needed to know, though, so I looked her straight in the eye. Her pupils were so dark it seemed that if you looked hard enough, you might fall in. "I don't know," I said at last.

Unfortunately this wasn't the answer she was looking for, but her tone and her demeanor remained completely unshaken. "You and I both are aware of what you know. We can skip formalities if you like, but that is really not my… style."

I had a hard time believing that. The way she stared at me, the tone in her voice, the whole situation made my stomach turn and tie itself into knots. Nonetheless, I maintained an outward calm. "I'm sorry – I really don't know what you're talking about."

"No? So you do not want to tell me how you and your people have been burning villages and maiming little girls? All in the name of… well, what exactly? Oh, of course." Her look of utter contempt filled in the words she didn't say.

I eyed her then, brow furrowed and blood cold as ice. If my hands hadn't been formed into such tight fists, they would have been shaking uncontrollably. The memories were still whirling around, not making much sense, but it didn't matter – even at my worst, I still wasn't going to let *this* bitch get the best of me. "You don't know anything about me."

She continued on without acknowledging me in the least. "Many men have died because of you, your mistakes, some might say, weaknesses… you know this? People have said that you are a warrior with no comparison, but I must say to them, that all I see is a frightened little boy." When I said nothing, just sat there staring blankly, her tone grew stern. "To be honest, I expected more."

I looked up at her and met two dark pools, so black one could almost fall right into them. But there was something like compassion there; perhaps I looked miserable and she felt sorry for me, although she didn't look like the type who felt sorry for anyone, ever. "I did what I had to do. That's all I'll say."

She made a low "humph" sound at the back of her throat and proceeded to pull my blanket down, exposing my shoulders and chest. My heart leaped into my throat. I wore nothing except a bandage tightly wound around my right shoulder – and, I suppose, some hair and a few scars. She grabbed my injured shoulder and jerked it toward her without any delicacy whatsoever, and the sickening pain went straight through me in all directions. My vision blurred but I could see that she was looking at something there, examining it closely and for a moment, rather deep in thought.

The dark woman eyed me, an eyebrow raised in interest. "The dragon is a symbol of power, strength... fear," she said softly, never letting go of my arm. "I am sure some do fear you. I do not." Again, that smile; my heart quickened until I could hear it thumping away in my head. Most people don't even know what a dragon is anymore unless you read a lot of books; they've been extinct for centuries. Some debated whether they ever existed at all. The one I had forever scarred into my right shoulder looked ready to pounce, with its glittery gold leathery wings outstretched and tendrils of smoke curling out of its nostrils. That's why I chose it. It wasn't just on the attack – it was on the hunt. In recent months, that point was something I've wanted certain people to remember about me, but how did *she* know that?

Despite the pain I knew it would cause, I jerked myself free of her grasp. Agonizing shock waves traveled up my arm and through my chest. I thought my heart would stop. Hell, at that point I was hoping it would. But I steeled my jaw and my will against the pain anyhow and looked her in the eye again. She straightened and backed up, a slightly shocked look touching her mask-like features.

"Look, I don't know who you are," I said through gritted teeth. Under the circumstances, though, I thought I sounded rather intimidating. And convincing. "I don't know what you want from me, but I don't think you should expect much."

I half-expected her to pull a blade out of her sleeve and gut me with it, but instead she nodded solemnly. "As you wish, Monsieur," she said. "We shall speak again."

The door creaked behind her and she turned, startled.

"Madame Saçaille! I believe you were asked to leave?" A familiar voice, a familiar face – the girl with the orange eyes. Her cheeks were flushed.

"I was just leaving, Mademoiselle." And with that she was gone, disappearing out the door like a shadow, no emotion, no anger, no fear of retribution from the church caretakers, nothing. I fell back onto my pillow with a pained grunt.

"Are you all right?" The girl with the orange eyes rushed over to me, checking my bandage, my pupils, just about anything she could. Her small hands trembled with every move she made, and I could hear her breath coming quick and shallow. "Oh dear... are you all right, m'Lord?"

I made a feeble attempt to sit up a little more but she stopped me. "I'm fine," I insisted.

The brightness in her eyes flickered a bit. What was her name? I remembered hearing it somewhere... Andella. That was it, she was Andella and the other priestess was Seraphine. "No, you're not fine; you're bleeding again." She frowned as she proceeded to unwrap the bandage, carefully, gently, but without a lot of skill. I realized that she was no priestess, but I should have known that already – there are no wizard-priests. It just doesn't happen that way – magic generally hurts, not heals. In fact, I found it a little odd that she was spending so much time in a church at all.

When the stained white wrapping was gone, I craned my neck to investigate the wound, but I couldn't see the entire thing. From my neck to the point where the shoulder began, the flesh was smeared and crusted and bruised with varying degrees of crimson and brownish-black. Just on the edge of my field of vision there was some glistening wetness and a few delicate stitches of silk thread holding flesh together. I reached across and touched it with my left hand, and my fingertips came back wet and crimson.

"Don't! You'll get an infection." The girl – she couldn't have been any older than me – put her hand to her mouth, seemingly embarrassed by what she said. "Sorry. But it's true."

I managed a smile. "I know. You're right." As she reached into the nightstand next to the bed and took out some rags, a small bottle of nearly-clear liquid that was probably vinegar, a new bandage, and another, larger bottle of... well, something, I took the opportunity to introduce myself. I figured the least I could do was offer my name, since I had little else to give her in payment for her troubles. "My name's Tristan. Tristan Loringham."

She looked at me briefly, smiled, and looked back down at her lap. "I know. I mean, we don't know each other formally, but we've met." Her hands shook so much I thought she might drop that bottle as she poured some vile-smelling yellow liquid into the center of the bandage. "At the funeral of Lord Vestarton. I was the Pyrelight."

She *had* looked a bit familiar. "Sorry – I didn't really recognize…"

"Oh, it's quite all right." She began to speak more quickly, as if dreadfully nervous. "I wouldn't expect you to remember that. Actually, we graduated at the same time, too – well, not from the same Academy, of course. I was at the Magic Academy there in Zondrell. My friends used to take me up to the Silver sometimes. I saw you win the graduation tournament." This made her cheeks flush even deeper. "It was, ah… it was exciting. I never went to anything like that before."

I stared at the wall while she started in on my shoulder; every time she pressed on it with a vinegar-soaked rag I could actually feel whatever they'd packed the wound with in there, and it was as gut-wrenching as one would imagine. "I didn't win that tournament."

"Sure you did." Her tone was sharp and insistent, and it made me turn to look at her directly. "That other one, he cheated. Everyone saw." The girl took a deep breath; her eyes were bright and sparkling, like tiny flames. She was actually quite stunning, with small features but large round eyes and high cheekbones, and long auburn hair that hung in wisps and tendrils around her face. She might have had some Lavançaise in her, maybe even some Eislandisch. "My mum used to say that a cheat always gets what's coming to him, even if it takes a lifetime to come back his way…" She trailed off, as if she'd lost her train of thought. She looked away again, coughed a little. "Anyway, my name's Andella, Andella Weaver. My sister, Seraphine, is the priestess here, and I help her take care of the place. I'm one of the only Pyrelights in this area, so I'm not here a lot anymore – just sometimes."

It occurred to me that I still didn't know where I was; I knew I was in a temple and somewhere within Zondrean lands, but after that, I had no idea. "And here… is where, exactly?" I asked. I shifted in my position – I thought I could sit up a little more, perhaps even consider getting out of bed and walking around a bit – but she put a warm hand on my arm.

"We're just outside of Doverton. It's about two miles or so to the city walls," she said, matter-of-fact. "This is probably going to sting a little." I braced myself for the worst, but really, it wasn't all that bad. Her touch was warm and she had to lean in close to wrap the bandage tightly. As promised, the yellow ointment started its work immediately and it did sting quite a bit, but I was too busy focusing on the way her dress moved with her body and the fact that her auburn hair smelled like lemons. The presence of a pretty girl is a pleasant way to divert attention – even the most gallant gentleman will admit to that – and my attention needed some diversion right about then. When it was over she stepped back, wiping her hands on the white apron she had tied around her slender waist. The rest of her clothes were drab and already looking a bit the worse for wear, too – she must have been scrubbing floors recently or something.

I tried to move my shoulder a little, flex out some of the pain while the ointment had me numbed, but it wasn't doing much good. My whole upper body felt like it was made of stone. At least my head was starting to clear.

"Can I ask you something?" I said, and she smiled and nodded. Her eyes never met mine, not once. "Who is that Lavançaise woman?"

Her brow furrowed in confusion. "You don't know her?"

I shook my head. "I don't think I've ever even seen her before in my life."

"Oh. Well, Lady Saçaille is the King's weapon master; she trains our army and things like that. She's basically the right hand of the King. She's told us to heal you, keep watch over you. Said it was important." When she looked down at her hands, she seemed almost a little surprised to see that she was wringing them, rubbing them together idly as if she were worried about something, but she wasn't exactly sure what it was she was worried about. A part of me really didn't want to know, because I could only guess at the possibilities.

"Did she say anything else?"

Andella shook her head, and a little tendril of auburn hair fell in front her eyes. She pushed it back with the back of her hand. "Not really. Not to me. I didn't know what to think when I realized it was you. I mean, what are the chances that we'd meet up again all the way up here? What brings you so far from Zondrell, anyhow?"

"Yeah… I, ah, well, everything's rather fuzzy still." I struggled for something better than that, came up short. I didn't know quite what to say. I really didn't want to lie, and in a way even if I had offered something, I wouldn't have been because I really couldn't remember what happened all that well. I remembered lots of things, lots of images, lots of conversations, but everything seemed strangely out of order. It was not unlike someone had ripped out the pages from a book, dropped them out onto the floor, and then asked me to put them all back in order again. None of that was anything I wanted to share, at least not then, and not to a stranger.

"Oh, that's all right." For a moment she fidgeted with her hair, throwing it back over her shoulders except for that one bit that just wouldn't stay in place. She let it fall to the right of her face and skim her cheek instead. "I should get you some food and some water – you must be starving. I don't know if you'll like everything we have, but…"

I stopped her before her nerves took hold of her. "I'm sure it's fine," I said gently.

"I'll do my best." And with that she hurried off, moving so quickly I was sure she'd rip the door off its hinges if she'd opened it with any more pent-up force. Why was she so nervous? I got the impression that she wasn't used to caring for people here, especially men, and most especially, noble men. Not that I was anyone worth mentioning – all I had was a name and a rank, an inheritance filled with gold and misery back home. But on the other hand, I supposed that all that might be interesting, even exciting, to someone on the outside of it, a common person working hard to make ends meet and keep her family sustained.

✳✳

Graduating rank *and* the High Honor medal were at stake in that final tournament. It was tradition, and had been done the same way for centuries. The long exhaustive tests with paper and pencil we took, the various drills we ran, the reports and speeches we presented, none of it really meant a damn thing in the end. It all came down to how well we conducted ourselves in battle, one-on-one against our peers, fellow cadets who would also become officers, who had made it for four years without dropping out and running home to mum and pop. The honor of every important family in the city hung in the balance that day.

I have to say that I didn't learn much at the Academy. That is to say, I didn't learn anything I didn't already know when it came to what we were really there for – warfare. Sure, we learned history and mathematics and literature and all of that, and there was plenty to know. But I already knew how to use a sword because I'd been training and experimenting ever since I was eleven years old. I had a rusted old blade that used to belong to my father and a quiet space in the garden to practice, so I did, sometimes for hours at a time. Later, I got to use my father's better practice weapons, and he even spent some time training with me. As for battle tactics and leadership and all that drivel, most of it was so simplistic that I found myself daydreaming through a great many of my early Academy courses. Sure, I studied, but only to pass the tests. I took those quite seriously, but I found that much of the time, I knew everything I needed to know. Not that I can say that I'm a great officer – an officer and a warrior were two very different things in my mind. I don't want to lead men into battle and I never really did. I became an officer because that's what noble boys did when they got to be a certain age and their fathers were captains in the military. There's no fighting fate.

No, the only thing I can say with confidence that I truly learned during my time at the Zondrell Military Academy was how to stop feeling sorry for myself.

I almost quit on two different occasions. The first was the first time Headmaster Janus had me whipped because I asked why I'd been given more chores around the Academy grounds than any of the other cadets. It was my second day. No one knew about it – whipping wasn't even on the books as a valid Academy punishment anymore – but I stood for everything Janus hated. He told us during training almost every day, at every opportunity, how he'd killed dozens of blond-haired, blue-eyed fellows back in Eisland during the War of the Northlands. He despised those big ugly hulking men who looked just like me, right down to the square jaw, and he wouldn't be opposed to taking out just one more of them. There was nothing I could do but do my best to stay in his good graces, and after we came to understand each other, I did this successfully for several months.

The second time I almost quit was the day he picked up the whip himself instead of having his soldier henchman do it. Yes, I understood it all, but I'd reached my limit. I was miserable, damned near inconsolable. I had my bags packed; all I had to do was walk out of the gates and leave the grounds forever. But Alex stopped me, said it was a mistake and that my father would disown me and I'd be far worse than miserable forever. He was probably right, but at the time it took more to convince me. That was the first and only time he and I ever fought – between us we had two black eyes, a bruised jaw (his), and a fractured rib (also his). Apparently, it's a real honest-to-the-gods friend who will take a beating from you just to prove a fucking point. Sorry, Alex.

Oh, and I did get whipped for fighting, too, the very next day after I'd unpacked my bags and resolved to see the thing through. But at that point I had learned another very important lesson – feeling sorry for yourself doesn't get you anywhere. It's useless. So, I stopped.

From that day forward, for almost four years, I focused solely on one thing – winning the Final Tourney, graduating first in my class, and watching the mouths of all the Zondrell elite drop when they saw Loringham's half-breed son walk away with the coveted High Honor medal. I never wanted anything else so much in all my young life. Rarely did I go up to the Silver Mirror Inn and drink and cavort with friends after those first few months. I did not take the time to attempt to charm women out of their clothes (not that I was any good at that, anyhow), and I certainly did not go spend every Peaceday back with my family as everyone else did. Mine became the life of an officer and a soldier and a student – for four years, I knew little else.

"You know they're going to call me first," I remember saying to Alex as we stood in the corridor to the tournament arena, all sixteen nervous boys anxiously awaiting their fate on that last day, the Final Tourney. Everyone knew that even though there was a lot more to the Academy than fighting prowess, that last day really was what it was all about. All of those perfect exams, all of those successful practice runs, none of it really mattered. I had studied and worked for quite a lot, but if I couldn't make it here, it was over. Obscurity and a simple life of guarding doors or ordering people around on menial tasks would be my fate if I couldn't get that medal. There was so much energy in that stadium that day, I could almost feel it bristling, making the hair on my arms stand on end and a cold hard lump form in my stomach.

Alex scoffed as he took one last drag on his *tsohbac* before Master Janus came in and caught him. "It's random," he replied, puffing out the smoke and crushing the spent *tsohbac* stick under his boot. "You don't know who'll be first."

"Janus makes the rules, he can break them. He will; you watch."

The tournament worked on a principle of simple elimination: two men enter, one man leaves, the next one comes to take his place, and so forth until there is one left victorious. Everyone knows that this leaves the people called near the end of the tournament at an extreme advantage, but tradition is tradition. The only way to make it "fair" is to call men out randomly, by drawing names from a bowl, which is normally the way it's done. If I thought Janus was an honest, fair gentleman, I would never have entertained the thought that my name would be first. I had a one in sixteen chance, after all. But, I knew that he wasn't fair, nor was he honest – I should have placed money on that wager.

When we walked out into the center of the Grand Stadium, which was nothing but a great stone bowl of dirt at the bottom and lined with tiered seats on all sides, the sun was bright and the heat oppressive. Spring was quick to start that year – it should have been far cooler but the summer sun had already started to show itself. Each of us in our black and silver uniforms, with full sleeves and leather and silk tabards over the undershirt, started to sweat almost immediately. I could only imagine how nasty it would be once we started battling. Throughout the stadium, people whistled and cheered so loud you could barely hear Headmaster Janus present us to the crowd, extolling our virtues as up-and-coming officers. I'd never felt so many eyes on me at one time; it felt strange, almost surreal.

We stood at attention while the crowd calmed down and Janus proceeded to bring out the swords for the duel – blunted, of course, as we were supposed to embarrass, not kill, each other. Then, he called out the first names. I barely flinched when he said my name, and I took my weapon from him without even looking the old bastard in the eye.

My first opponent was Daniel Shilling, the youngest of the seven House Shilling grandsons, and someone who obviously hated the fact that he was first and had to face me, of all people. He stood across from me in that arena visibly shaking, barely able to keep his sword steady in his hand. When the headmaster gave the command, it seemed Shilling was going to burst into tears.

I moved in toward him the way a predator stalks prey; he knew I had no intention of showing any mercy. I never strike first, though, not if I don't have to, and eventually he did make first contact. He swiped at my outstretched sword with his, making a loud *ping* that echoed sharply in my ears. His problem was that he'd struck with the flat of his blade, absorbing more of the blow into his own arm. Amazingly, after years of Academy training he still didn't know not to do that, and when he drew back he was slow, flinching from the encroaching numbness. For a moment, I considered how terrible it would be for him to lose this duel in front of his whole family and this whole huge audience so quickly, before he ever got a second chance to strike. But on the other hand, the opportunity was right in front of me – I'd be a fool not to take it.

I darted in for the "kill," low and wide to the left, as close as possible to Daniel's weapon. In perfect flowing rhythm my sword swept in toward his throat as my left hand grabbed him by the elbow, gripping tight so he couldn't whip around and strike me across the back. It was all I needed to do – as soon as he felt steel on his skin he dropped his sword, letting it fall to the dirt with a dull thud. The crowd made various noises, some happy and others not so much so. Janus made a gruff noise at the back of his throat from his position as observer.

"Do you accept defeat, Mister Shilling?" he barked. Daniel nodded, taking a brief glance up in my direction. He stood fully a head and shoulders below me, and was much smaller and thinner in build. I swear he would have wet himself if I'd made any more sudden movements… and yes, I can admit that I did consider it.

And so it went. Janus called out someone else to take me on, and I crouched into my fighting stance. The crowd, Janus, the stadium itself, they all began to melt away because none of it was important. I wasn't perfect, by any means – I took a smack in the ribs and another good one on the hip, but I barely even felt them. I was always faster than the other guy, smarter and stronger and the better swordsman. If it had been a real battle, with real swords instead of the dulled pieces of steel they gave us, the place would have been awash in someone else's blood.

Eventually Alex – my dearest, truest friend – stepped up to face me. The smile on his face was enormous, uncontrollable. As he walked past me to take his side of the arena, he paused, looked at me with his big dark eyes. "Hey, take it easy on me, okay?" he asked.

I said nothing in return – I wasn't about to make any promises with my blood pounding through my veins and my entire body alive with energy. I felt like nothing in the world could touch me. Of course, I really did try my best to go easy on him, and I let the duel draw out for a while even though I knew his heart wasn't in it. Not only was he not much of a swordsman – and he knew it – but he also had no intentions of winning. This final tournament was nothing but a formality for him. He finally admitted defeat when he lunged straight at me and I ducked right, giving me just enough time to bring my sword around and down across his neck from the back. The blunt edge hit him lightly, but hard enough to give him a start.

"Never saw that coming," he said with a chuckle.

"You need to be more careful."

"Yeah, you do the same."

Alex was my eighth match – I'd gone through more than half my opponents. As Janus picked the next one from the group I had almost forgotten that I was being watched. All I knew was that it was incredibly hot, and it felt like a smith's hammer was pounding out something huge and heavy inside my chest. The sweat seemed like it was just pouring out of me, down my brow, into my eyes – my hair was wet like I'd just bathed, but I sure as hell didn't smell like I had. My breathing came deep and sharp, stinging in my lungs, and even though I knew how undignified it would be, I had to do something about it. While my next opponent joined me in the arena I pulled my sweat-dampened tunic and tabard off and tossed them in a heap, leaving my torso naked to the world. I heard women gasp in the crowd – such a thing was just *not* done – but it was so hot and that heavy black uniform was going to be the death of me. Let them gasp and talk about how terribly rude the Loringham boy was.

The matches and the sights and the sounds all stopped being distinct from one another, just a big blur. I remembered fighting another good friend, Corr Shal-Vesper, but I didn't feel too bad about sending him back to where the rest of the cadets watched. He probably didn't care much, either – like Alex, he wasn't there to win. The arena stunk of sweat and dirt and the despair of battles lost. I stopped thinking about what I was doing; by that point, I was as automatic as the drip of a water clock. To this day I don't know how long we were out there, but the sun was starting to set by the time the final name was called to the center of the arena.

Peter Wyndham.

The Wyndhams and the Loringhams have always hated each other – it was a tradition as longstanding as the tournament the two of us were preparing to end. So, as a result, Peter and I never got along. Up until that day, we never exchanged anything but some off-color remarks, and honestly, I never expected that to change. He didn't have the manhood for anything else. However, as with a number of things in my life, I would end up being quite mistaken.

Peter sauntered onto the battlefield, the last one called, all his energy intact and just waiting for an opportunity to be unleashed at full force. He waved at the crowd, parading his shortish barrel-shaped form around and smiling with big round dark eyes like obsidian teacups – girls from every corner of the place swooned and waved back. It was disgusting.

Meanwhile, I put my sword into the dirt and leaned on it, breathed deep and wiped some of the sweat off my brow. A few feet away from me, Peter was dancing – literally, hopping and back and forth, swinging his blade around, and basically looking like an ass. It took everything I had to refrain from spitting on him.

"How you feeling, Tristan?" he asked, his voice low so only I could hear. "A little tired, eh? You look tired. Actually, you look like hell."

"Fuck you." I started to take up my blade, and right about at that moment I got the nastiest surprise of my life.

My mouth filled with the sour coppery taste of blood; I reeled back a few steps, doubled over in agony. When I looked up I noticed the hilt of Peter's sword sprayed crimson. As he bent over me, a self-satisfied smile blossomed across his round little face. "Sorry, man, but it has to be done. This is the High Honor we're talking about here, and it can't be won by half-breed scum like you." I looked up at him, and he was still smiling. I wanted desperately to take that expression and shove it down his throat. "You'd think you'd know your place by now… guess it's true what they say about the Eislandisch and their mental capacities, yeah?"

Around us, the crowd was in an uproar. I did notice some angry voices coming from the contingent of defeated cadets, and then I heard Janus, near me, right at my ear.

"Can you continue, boy?" he asked without a hint of concern. I put my hand near my mouth and drops of crimson fell into my palm like the first herald of a spring rain. I found myself momentarily fascinated by this phenomenon – my head was spinning so much that it was the only thing I could focus on. Janus repeated himself a few more times and eventually I looked up at him.

It took me a while to answer. I could have wailed on about unfairness, that Peter broke the rules and should lose by default, but that was the same as feeling sorry for myself, and I already knew that was worthless. I could also have admitted defeat and decided he'd played the smartest match of the day, but I had no intention of such an admission – not to Peter-fucking-Wyndham.

I spat a wad of thick viscous blood onto the ground, and more rushed in to take its place. I tasted and smelled nothing but copper but I really didn't care. As I straightened, I brought my weapon to bear, aimed straight for Peter's heart. "I can continue," I growled, feeling the warm blood ooze down my chin when I spoke.

Never one to be caught off guard, Peter stopped nonchalantly fiddling with the hem of his uniform and moved into his fighting stance. "You don't look so good, Loringham," he said. "You sure you want to do this?"

Oh yes, I was sure. I lunged in with my sword leading the charge, but Peter was fast enough to parry. The clang of metal on metal rang out loudly across the arena. We stepped to our lefts in an arcing pattern, then I charged in again, with the same result. One more would get him – I was convinced of this. So I feinted right and swung to his left – he was swift to dodge but not enough to get out of the way. He would have a nasty bruise on his thigh for days.

"You'll have to do better than that," he said, trying hard to look unaffected, but I could see the pain in his eyes. I wanted to see more of it, so I moved in again, fast and low so that hopefully he wouldn't be able to dodge it. But under all the heat and the stress and the noise, I was slowing – my mind was slowing. I was bound to make mistakes… and I did.

Peter stepped out of my way on that low charge so that he was at my shoulder while my sword sliced into nothing but air. As I stopped myself to recover and try to turn back around, I heard an awesome *thwack!* before I actually felt any pain. The flat side of his blade connected straight across the small of my back so hard and fast it might as well have been a whip. It took the wind out of my lungs and even though I struggled for breath my body refused to stop. Instinct took over and I launched my elbow as powerfully as I could straight into his face. Cartilage snapped and tore as blood shot out of his nose like a geyser.

"You prick!" His voice went up an octave as he covered his face with his free hand, trying to stop the bleeding mess. The advantage had suddenly turned around, and I was all too happy to use it to the fullest. I swung around wide with my blade and struck him in the sword arm – panicked and trying not to drop his weapon, he wheeled backward a few paces. I followed him.

Tired, injured people make mistakes. I knew this but I didn't learn my lesson from a few minutes beforehand. I should have waited him out; instead I charged in with full fury, thinking I had the battle won. If only I had been able to recover more quickly.

Peter dodged me again – at the last second – moving out of my reach just in time. My blade swung out high and wide and I wasn't ready for it. I stumbled, and the next thing I knew was total darkness.

It probably only lasted a few seconds but it felt like an eternity. I dreamt an insane dream of battling hordes of enemies while trying to have a conversation with someone who wasn't there. There were voices and flashes of light and forms moving all around me. When I opened my eyes, the sun was so bright I thought that perhaps I was entering Paradise. I sat up with a start, coughing up an amazing amount of blood and spit – at least that meant I wasn't dead.

"Hey, are you okay?" It was Alex. He was kneeling by my side, cheeks bright red and eyes wide.

I didn't say anything. I wanted to stand up. There was a fight still going on, wasn't there? I looked for my sword but it wasn't nearby. I started to my feet and the world wavered around me, dimming and brightening again like someone had just blown lightly on a torch. My head throbbed mightily, especially around my left temple, and when I put my hand there it felt wet and slightly swollen, very much not like it should have felt. I think I said something but everyone looked at me a little curiously – it must not have made much sense.

"Wyndham struck you down," Alex said, speaking very slowly and deliberately at me like one might speak to a child. "He hit you in the side of the head, but I think you're going to be okay. You… you know where you are, right?"

I nodded as I again attempted to get on my feet. Halfway there I almost lost my balance, but Alex was there, shouldering my weight as best he could. Squinting across the arena, I could see Peter Wyndham's stocky little dark form out there, bowing to the crowd under the proud eye of Lord Janus. People were cheering – the noise from the crowd was deafening. My head blazed like the worst hangover one could ever possibly experience, and at that moment I just had to get the hell out of there. It took a few tries to move without the need for Alex's support, but eventually I was making my way toward the arena entrance.

"Hey, where are you going?" he called after me. I didn't answer. In fact, I don't remember too much after walking – well, stumbling – out of there. I do remember looking at myself in a mirror in the dim corridors somewhere within the Academy complex, and thinking that I hardly recognized what I saw. I was scarred and dirty and bloodied, looking more like a wandering beggar than anything befitting a military or family rank. Luckily, I still had all my teeth, but there was a cut on the inside of my lip that bled every time I thought about it, and would for the next two weeks afterward. I also remember that I cried – I couldn't help it. I leaned against a wall, buried my face into the cool unforgiving stone, and yes, I cried like I was a five-year-old boy. The tears flooded out and they wouldn't stop – I couldn't stop them even if I'd had the will of the gods themselves.

"Where did I go wrong?"

The words echoed through the white chamber and my heart jumped in my chest. I hadn't meant to say them aloud. But as I lay there on that uncomfortable bed in a temple outside the remote town of Doverton, I had to ask myself that one question I've asked myself time and time again, ever since that fateful tournament that had both opened and slammed shut every door of opportunity – of fate – for me from that moment on. They'd given me everything I wanted in the end, everything I'd struggled for, and all I had to do was keep following along… so where did I go wrong?

1

Alexander Marcus Xavier, Forty-Third Lord of Vestarton

I should have known something was wrong a couple of weeks ago, the day of my father's funeral. And I *did* know, really – I think – but I was too busy feeling sorry for myself. Yes, that's right – for myself, not for my family, not for my mother or my sister or even for the man who'd spent so many painful weeks sick and dying in bed. How could he leave me there, the head of a family, a fucking Lord? Why couldn't Alice do it instead? I actually asked my father that – on his deathbed, I asked him why I couldn't pass off my duties on my older sister. Of course, looking back, that was really an asshole thing to say. I remember him smiling weakly, chuckling a little despite the fact that he couldn't breathe well anymore.

"You're the only man left in this family," he told me. "Vestarton House must go to you, boy. Just don't let them see your weakness. It doesn't matter what you do in private, but it will matter what you do in public. From now on, appearances are everything."

Appearances are everything. He'd been telling me that for my whole life, but now it was starting to mean something. So I stood up tall in front of the other nobles and smoked and drank outrageous quantities when no one was looking for the entire week between the day my father died to the day of his funeral. I didn't sleep. I didn't eat. And when the big day came, I was as calm and strong as my mother and my sister needed me to be – as strong as the family needed me to be. That day I gave a speech that sounded eloquent and smart even though I'm neither of those things, particularly when drunk, and I shook a lot of hands and kissed a lot of cheeks. In front of all of those false mourners, while I watched my father's soul burn off into Paradise, I stood there silent and reverent – the picture of high nobility.

Then I saw him. From the altar I couldn't see the doors too well but it's rather hard to miss a six-foot tall Eislander walking into a church full of dark little Zondreans. He looked like someone had just dragged him tied to the back of a fast carriage into Hell and back a few times. And for that I could understand why he hung back in the shadows and didn't join everyone else in kissing my ass for the next half an hour or so after the ceremony. Besides, the day Tristan Loringham kisses anyone's ass openly and willingly like that is the day I give up wine and women for life – not going to happen.

He was more like a dusty stone wall than a man when I hugged him. I wondered if his mum had felt the knives holstered under his shirt or not. "I'm sorry," he said. This is what he says to me after nearly four months of being off in the great wilderness somewhere? Sorry – yeah, you and the rest of Zondrell are sorry for my loss. I was so sick of hearing those words I almost said something rude. At least Tristan was actually apologetic, and genuinely wanted to be there – no one goes into a church for a nobleman's funeral looking like that if they didn't *really* want to be there.

"You have no fucking idea how glad I am to see you," I said, then realized a priestess was watching. Oops. "That is, no earthly idea. You know what I mean."

"I wasn't sure I was going to make it. I came in late. I'm sorry."

I was done with apologies. Sorry is a silly word, anyhow – it never seems to amount to much more than just speech. "Don't worry about it. Really – I'm just glad you made it at all," I told him, waving it off. He looked like he had enough problems without worrying about how I felt at the moment. This was especially evident once we got out into the light of day – his blue eyes were slightly bloodshot and dead-looking, like his trip from Hell had also sucked the soul right out of him. I wondered what they were making him do on his little country tour of duty. It's not like anyone was willing to tell me, not even the Lord and Lady Loringham, who surely must have known... you don't send someone's kid off to gods-know-where without telling them about it, right?

Right?

When we got back to the house, Jonathan made Tristan go change, clean up a bit. Fair enough, I supposed, but the rudeness in his tone about it was notably John Loringham. In the meantime, we all sat in the parlor – *my* parlor now, not my father's. That would take some getting used to.

"Dinner's on soon," Alice said, staring at the wall and distant as she'd been known to be for the past few months. Her words broke our little veil of silence as easily as if she'd knocked a vase off the mantle.

Lord Loringham made that *humph* sound in his throat. "Alex, go get Tristan, will you? It's been a while."

"He is tired," offered Lady Loringham in her beautiful Eislandisch accent. Say what you will about the Eislandisch people, but I have no problem with any race that can speak as beautifully as they do. As a child I always enjoyed listening to her talk, about anything – I could certainly see what made old John turn her into his personal war trophy.

"Don't worry," I said, shooting up out of my chair. "I'll go find him. Feel free to start the drinks, first course – whatever. Make yourselves at home." Going anywhere would have been better than sitting under the silence in that room any longer.

Loringham Manor was staffed by a few dedicated servants, including Lissa, who answered the door for me. As a kid, Tristan had an outrageous schoolboy crush on her, and no wonder – great body, pretty dark eyes, long silky hair. Plus, she always gave us candy and things when we were growing up, and everyone knows you just can't go wrong with a woman who constantly supplies you with sweets. Even as an older woman with a little gray at her temples and a little less of a spring in her step, Lissa was still just plain lovely.

"The Young Master's in his room, m'Lord," she said. I made my way to the private bedchambers in the house, did the right thing and knocked first. No answer. I knocked again, louder, called through the door. Nothing. The handle moved easily, so after a moment I barged in, completely unapologetic, and found him asleep on the bed, half dressed and dead to the world. I felt rather badly at having to slap him on the chin to wake him up.

Actually, what really felt bad was the moment directly after doing that, because before I had time to think, he had me pinned on my back with a knife on my throat. I put my hands up, eyes and mouth wide open – a lesser man might have lost control of important bodily fluids. "Take it easy!" I yelped, trying hard to get the wind back in my lungs.

"Oh…" He got up in a flash and tossed the dagger aside. The big red gem on its hilt caught the dying sun through the window and cast some patterns of light on the bedspread. He rubbed his paling, sweat-beaded temples, looking away.

I sat up slowly. "So this is how they greet people in the Army now? I didn't get that message, I guess." Then again, I was never actually *in* the Army. What the hell did I know? I felt stupid the minute I said it, truth be told. Went through all of that Academy training just to have my father get sick and leave me his fortune. Not that our Army did much in the way of actual battle, these days – this was *supposed* to be a time of peace. No one should have been on edge about much of anything.

"I'm sorry, Alex… I was having a dream or something. I don't know. Really, I'm…"

"Sorry, right. Yeah. Don't worry about it. Listen, are you all right?"

He had to think about this one. "Yeah, yeah. Fine," he said at length. "I just need to shave and get myself together." So I sat on the edge of the bed and let him get ready. He pawed through his closet, slowly, deliberately, feeling all the fabrics like he hadn't felt silk or clean cotton in years. I watched him take off his uniform shirt, slightly tattered and grimed up with dirt and sweat, and noticed the various new scars on his chest and back. There was a really nice one cutting a perfect straight line down his left side, across the ribs – it looked fresh, still glistening. Then there were the old ones, the Academy bumps and cuts, the one really nasty whiplash across his back that had never quite healed. It made me cringe just to look at it. Once cleaned up and dressed properly he'd look just as polished and noble as me or anyone else we knew, but now he looked... well, he looked like a common soldier, or maybe something worse than that. At least he seemed healthy – he still had that muscled athlete's physique, the kind most full-blooded Zondrean men like me can only dream about, but now he was even bigger, more powerful-looking than before he left. Whatever they had him doing out there, it was no doubt a bit more challenging than chopping wood and cleaning armor.

I lit a *tsohbac* and watched him go to the washbasin to get the grime off his face and out of his yellow hair. I waited for a conversation, for something to be shared, as something clearly weighed on him, something very, very heavy. But rather than speak, all he did was pause to look at his image in the mirror, staring like the dead. No surprises there – some things never change.

"Hey, Brother," I said, "are you sure you're all right?" He gave a noncommittal shrug, and I knew for sure that something was wrong, but I also knew when to shut up. I put the whole thing out of my mind because it was time to feast, to talk with family and friends, to go out to the Silver and get so drunk we wouldn't be able to stand up straight the next day... but yet something was wrong, and I didn't even try to figure it out.

✱✱

No, the really bad, cold, numbed-out kind of feeling I should have felt then would come and hit me hard, much later, dropping directly on top of my idiot head like the biggest rock falling down from the tallest mountain in the world.

I don't remember large parts of that emergency Council meeting they called me into, not because I wasn't paying attention, but because I was struggling to avoid saying something really stupid… or really rude. I didn't even want to be there, but it was time to conduct myself like a Lord, to keep up appearances and the Vestarton name and whatnot.

When I got to the King's Palace, I couldn't help but notice how huge it was, overwhelming. This King, Kelvaar V, of Blackwarren House, had half the Palace rebuilt about fifteen years ago. I remember it causing rioting in the streets because all the poor people insisted that if Kelvaar had money enough to build himself the world's biggest and most expensive palace, then he sure as hell had money to give them for cleaner, safer streets. Kelvaar obviously disagreed with that logic; instead, he built his huge temple to himself full of gilded carvings and gems and tapestries and as conciliation gave the people a really nice new fountain in the center of town. Certainly *that* would keep the crime down.

As I was led through to the Council chamber, I paused to take in the scenery. I'm no artist or fine collector by any means, but the place was garish. Marble everything, statues of pretty girls and horses and things inlaid with jewels and gold – the whole thing was just too much. I'm sure all the old men in the Council loved it, though. Opulence was what noblemen – especially those of the highest station in the city – did best, after all.

All of the Lords sat at our designated chairs with the little family crests on the backs and everything seemed normal enough. Then Victor Wyndham walked in with his father, both of them resplendent in fur trim and blue silk. I didn't realize it was a formal party instead of an everyday Council meeting, but then again, appearances *are* everything. Ancient Lord Percival took his seat but we all sort of stared at Victor – what in Catherine's name was he doing in a Council meeting, anyhow? He couldn't wait till his father finally gasped his last? And not only was he here, but he was running the thing. He stood at the head of the long table with his alien blue eyes and his irritating thin-lipped scowl, arms folded across his chest.

"Gentlemen," he said in his commanding sort of way, "we have a situation. This young man came into the city early this morning from the North border, scared and covered with blood." On cue, a timid little boy of a soldier walked in from the back antechamber, looking like a cow being led to slaughter. His skin had gone a sort of sickly yellow color instead of a normal healthy olive, and the little chap was quivering. Flecks of iron-red blood were smeared across his cheek – presumably for effect, since they'd obviously let him change his clothes and take a bath at some point today. His red tabard was pristine and freshly pressed, and his buckles were good and polished – a picture of the consummate soldier. "Tell them what you told me and General Torven, Private. Don't be frightened."

"Sure, right." A deep breath, a pause – the kid looked like he was going to break down and cry at any second. "Well, when we entered the town of Südenforst – about two nights ago – it seemed pretty routine. We had no trouble, really; this was a small town. Few men – mostly women and children. He led us there, from a tip extracted from a prisoner."

Wyndham interjected. "As in 'he,' you mean Lieutenant Tristan Loringham, correct?" A few mumbles and whispers broke out of the assembly. The cold hot tingling feeling began creeping in; I could feel it starting in my brow and working down through my temples. I'm sure I went three shades of pale.

"Yeah… uh, yes, Sir. He leads – led – a lot, most of those sorts of missions, especially at night. This was a big one, too, I guess – I don't normally go on patrols. That's for the more experienced guys, you know, because they have better battle skills."

Battle? I thought he was translating for people crossing the fucking border or some such. As I sat there listening, watching this nervous, scared little boy tell his tale, I felt the sensation of something awful crawling around under my skin. It's the sort of feeling that makes you want to scratch at yourself, claw away your skin in the hopes that it'll stop. And it's also a feeling I knew all too well. I reached into my shirt pocket, pulled out a trusty little brown paper-wrapped *tsohbac* stick and shoved it into my mouth. Around the table, various faces glowered at me, but I didn't care. I took my flint and hit it against the inside of one of my rings – the spark hit the Katalahni tobacco stick and lit it with a cheerful comforting glow. The pained tears in my eyes immediately dried up; my body stopped shivering and tingling the way it always did after not having a smoke for a little while, and the crawling, tingling pain subsided. Things were back to normal again... whatever that meant.

"Is the good Lord Vestarton quite ready for us to continue?"

I didn't realize the place had fallen silent, but the annoyed stares from those around the table brought it to my attention quickly. "Sure, yes. Sorry... ah, continue, please."

Victor Wyndham scowled with those bizarre eyes – the eyes of a Water mage. I could actually feel a chill in the air when he looked at me. "So, you were there at Südenforst, during a search of the town based on a tip from Lieutenant Loringham's investigation, when an argument began. Is this correct?" he asked the timid soldier, brow furrowed. A few muffled sounds came from the assembly.

The youth nodded. "Yes, Sir."

"Go on."

"Well, after we had all the townspeople rounded up, Captain Shilling, Lieutenant Loringham, and Lieutenant Wyndham." He stopped, looking wide-eyed at Victor as if he'd just committed some sort of blasphemy, but the mage was expressionless. You would think that would be hard to do under the circumstances, but Victor pulled it off surprisingly well because he had no damned soul. All right, maybe that was a bit unfair, but he'd never proved otherwise from where I was sitting. Even his father at his side seemed relatively unaffected, but then again he wasn't known to have much of a soul either – must have been a Wyndham family tradition.

"Go on, soldier," Victor said, and the boy did.

"Yes, Sir. So, they were talking for a while, sort of huddled and quiet for a bit. I couldn't hear everything they were saying but it started to get... well, they were shouting. I heard Lieutenant Loringham say something about abandoning the mission, and Lieutenant Wyndham said that was the talk of a traitor." He stopped for a moment to collect himself. He happened to glance at me for just a second, then pulled his gaze away as if struck.

I had to say something. "Why? Why would he say that?" Everyone, including Tristan's own father, looked at me like I'd just thrown water on a Pyrelight's flame.

"I don't know, m'Lord. That's just what they were saying. There was a lot of talk, shouting."

Lord Andrew Miller, the current Head Councilor, cleared his throat and leaned on the table with his fat meaty hands folded in front of him. Good thing it was a big, sturdy mahogany table, I thought. "Had you noticed any events like this prior to this particular mission?" he asked. "Any arguing amongst the officers in your troupe?"

"Not really, m'Lord. Oh, maybe sometimes during a game of Five Stars. Nothing serious, though. I mean, we all know they don't like each other, Wyndham and Loringham, but they got along all right. Everyone gets… got along there all right." The youth looked toward me, but only for a second. "And I never noticed anything strange about Lieutenant Loringham, either. Not till then, anyway."

"How do you mean?" Victor asked.

"He never once spoke against Captain Shilling before, Sir. Not once. I'm not even sure he ever raised his voice to any of us."

"Sign of panic, one might say." Wyndham's expression continued to show little emotion, but there was something in his voice – mirth, maybe – and this sparked something in me. I took a sharp breath inward and straightened in my chair.

"This is an impartial Council, Victor," I snapped, feeling the heat in my face, the little beads of sweat forming on my brow, the dozen pairs of eyes staring me down and thinking I was going mad. "You do know what 'impartial' means, don't you? Well, what does it matter, you're not even on the Council." I looked down and noticed my hands were trembling. Evil tingling sensations started walking around under my skin again, even in spite of the *tsohbac*. I took it in deeply, quickly, burning it down nearly to the end in a single breath. When it was gone, I nonchalantly dropped it under my seat and stepped on it when no one was looking directly at me.

"Let the boy speak, Lord Vestarton," someone – probably Old Man Wyndham – said gruffly, to which I really wanted to respond, but I managed to stay silent. Instead, I sat back and started tapping idly on the bottom of my chair.

The young soldier sat silently through this, wringing his hands together and continuing to stare at the floor. His story was getting to the bad part, I guessed. "Sh-… should I continue?" he asked, so quietly that at first no one else heard him. It was a big room and the men were starting to whisper and grumble more now. The boy asked his question again.

"Yes, please continue, son," Miller said, successfully ignoring the rest of us. "I'm sure you'd like to go home and rest, wouldn't you?"

"Yes, Sir." He took another deep breath, coughed a little, then continued his story. "So, the officers were all yelling at each other, you know, and some of us started to get nervous. It, ah, got a little physical after a bit and I didn't do anything but stand there... they were arguing and I think they had their swords out, and then the fire started... It was getting bad, you know?"

"Bad" hardly seemed like a strong enough word for this little tale. John Loringham made the low growling sound at the back of his throat he always made when he was irritated or deep in thought – I didn't know which state he was in then. "What happened?" he asked. The solider continued to wring his hands, harder now, more deliberately, and remained silent. "I asked you a question, solider." Still, the boy couldn't seem to find his words.

I couldn't take it anymore. "What fucking happened?" I growled, standing up, leaning over the table, staring into the yellow-skinned soldier's dark eyes. If he'd been closer I think I would have reached out and strangled him. I knew for sure that my cheeks were as red as a bottle of Lavançaise wine – the heat in my blood was intense. I reached into my pocket, grabbed another *tsohbac* and lit it in one fluid movement. It was a practiced motion, I was good at it, and it calmed me down. A little. My smoke billowed over the table, hanging over the Council like a stormcloud. A couple of the Council members told me to put it out but I ignored them.

The boy's voice was very thin now, trembling and frightened. "Look, they were fighting, and arguing about the townspeople and the whole mission, and I don't know what all was said and I don't know what happened because the next thing I knew I was... I was trying to get out of there." He paused, looked away from us and toward the wall. "The Eislandisch... they were everywhere."

The room turned silent as the stone surrounding us. Everyone was hanging on this kid's words, but he was now almost in tears. Victor pressed him further. "You were attacked?"

"Yes, Sir. They came from… from nowhere. They figured out where we were, I guess. I don't know… Lieutenant Loringham said they knew where we were, but if we left those women and children alone there, we'd be all right. How he knew that, I don't know, but I think he was right." The boy looked down at his feet, avoiding our gazes because water was welling up in his eyes. "We should have left in peace, like he said."

"So you ran off to escape the enemy ambush?"

Despite the water rimming his eyes, the boy's expression hardened. "There were so many of them. What was I supposed to do?"

"Did anyone else make it away safely?"

"Maybe. People scattered all over. Some might be coming back. I don't know… I was only worried about myself. I'm sorry, Sir… I can't lie to you."

There was a long pause. All the Lords looked around, stared at each other, looked at the floor. As for me, I took long breaths and tapped the bottom of my *tsohbac* stick against the table, picking it up to take a drag from it every fifth tap. It would have been an ingenious strategy for keeping myself calm if the tapping didn't gradually keep speeding up.

Eventually, it was Alastair Shilling who stood up. Amazingly, that spindly elder had been quiet the entire time, listening to all this in silence even though I heard the young private mention his own brother earlier. "Thank you, soldier. You've been very helpful. Go on up to the temple and make sure you're in good health and so forth, then go find a commanding officer at one of the south barracks. Understood?" The boy stood slowly, placing his right fist against his left shoulder in salute before rushing out of there.

Victor snorted derisively. "Damn cowards, these kids we let into our army today. The General's right."

"What would you do if you were face to face with a hundred scum barbarians wanting to drink your blood?" replied Miller, successfully ignoring the sneers from Loringham and myself as he spoke. "For your brother's sake, I hope they were all that smart."

"Peter is no coward."

I couldn't help it. I shouldn't have said it but the words came out before I ever thought to keep them to myself. Sure, I was a little taller – *just* a little – more muscular that he was, and I could easily kick his skinny ass in a fair fight. But, a fight with a mage is never fair, especially that one. "Yeah, of course he isn't!" My words tumbled right out of my stupid fucking mouth. I was probably halfway to being impaled on a spear of ice or something right in front of all the other Lords. "I wonder if he showed the same 'bravery' up there that he showed during Final Tourney?"

Those blue eyes grew very bright as they turned on me. "Oh, go fuck yourself, Vestarton," he said, the staccato words flying out of his mouth along with plenty of spittle. "My brother could be dead, and it's all because of your barbarian idiot friend, so you can just go fuck yourself." Those eyes were blazing and whirling now – the magic was building to the surface. You can always tell when a mage is going to strike if you watch him close; high emotion makes it boil up to the surface, and once it's there, watch out. And sure, I knew how powerful he was; for the Lady's sake, he wouldn't ever let anyone forget it if they wanted to. That didn't mean I was going to let him intimidate me. Honestly, I didn't think he had it in him to do anything here, not in front of all of his father's friends. So, I got up, walked over to him, stood eye to eye with him. His eyes narrowed, his sharp little nostrils flared. "I don't think you heard me," he hissed.

I took a long drag on my *tsohbac* and blew it right in his face. I knew it would sting and it did. He started clawing at the air and coughing, so I did it again. "You know, I don't think I did hear you. Say it again."

Just then I felt a strong hand on my shoulder, drawing me back a few paces before the situation got any uglier. It was the big man, Lord Miller, and he gave me a far more disapproving glare than my own father ever could have given me before he spoke. "Gentlemen, please. We have slightly bigger problems right now," he said, before turning his back on us to face the rest of the council. "Look, we need to investigate this, find out what happened before we bring it before the King. What do we need to do?"

Old Man Wyndham chimed in right away. "We need to hunt Tristan Loringham down like the animal that he is and kill him. What else is there to debate?"

I thought for sure John Loringham would say something, but he didn't. Instead he sat there motionless, a statue, detached from the whole thing. I don't think I'd ever seen him like that before – quiet, yes, emotionless, sure, but not like this. I didn't understand it but I also couldn't have cared less how he was feeling – he of all people should have been speaking up, doing something, but he just sat there, and it made me sick. I wanted to slap him.

"We know nothing until we go there and find out for ourselves," I said, suddenly with a tremendous amount of resolve. "I'm going. Anyone who wants to come with can come."

At this, Victor literally spat in my direction. How disgusting. "You? You're his friend – you'll hide him, cover for him, something. The General won't approve."

"And what will *you* do with him? There's this thing we have today called a fair trial. You should look it up. It's what civilized people do in these sorts of situations. And as for the General, he answers to me, to this Council. So fuck him."

There were a lot of mumbles and grumbles and curses flying around now – the Council room was alive in spite of the angry old men occupying it. I put my *tsohbac* out on the Council table (later I would be accused of being no better than some street vagrant for this and all the cursing, although if I remembered correctly, I never spoke a foul word in that particular situation – admittedly, a rarity), and left without another word. I think some of them were calling after me but I didn't care, didn't look back. I was a Lord, equal with them now. I could do whatever I wanted and damn them all. *Appearances*, yeah... I was done with appearances. I had more important things to do now.

I rushed out of the Council chamber, out of the palace, across the drawbridge... and promptly bent over and vomited in the street. My head spun as I tried to make sense of what just happened in there, but I was at a loss. I must have been standing there for a while, doubled over and miserable, because eventually I noticed footsteps coming closer and closer.

"What the hell is wrong with you?" It was Loringham, hands on his hips, obviously irritated. I straightened and looked him straight in the eye – if he wanted me to be scared of him, he was going to be sorely disappointed.

"I might ask you the same question," I replied curtly.

Old Man Loringham shook his head and started rubbing his temple with one hand like he had a splitting headache. He wasn't the only one, to be sure. "Look, Alexander, your father was my friend the way Tristan is yours. I understand – truly, I do. But you need to start conducting yourself like a Lord – a real one. There's a time and a place for outbursts, and that was *not* one of them."

"What do you mean? If I didn't say something in there then Catherine only knows what they would have decided to do. You can't even speak up in defense of your own son?"

He stood there in silence for a long time, not really sure what to say... I had him. He made that gruff *hmmph* sound he often made – I knew well what that particular sound meant because I heard it so much growing up. If it wasn't directed at Tristan, I was generally the next likely candidate. Finally, he cleared his throat and spoke. "There's nothing I can say until I know the truth. The truth – the real truth – isn't yet known. Don't forget that."

My mouth dropped open. "You don't honestly believe any of that business in there, do you? You're talking about someone who would pledge his soul to the Army if they asked him for it. Shit, they basically did. There's no way any of that is true."

"I told you, we don't know the truth yet. I'll decide what I believe when I know the facts, and you should do the same. This is much bigger than you think it is."

I stared at him, into dark eyes that were clear but obviously had seen a great deal in their day. The tiny lines at each corner were slightly more pronounced now, his jaw clenched tightly. By all the gods, he was completely fucking serious. He was willing to at least entertain the notion that his own son – his own flesh and blood – was a traitor and apparently a murderer as well. Now, I have learned that people will often disappoint you if you set your expectations too high... I know this because I've done enough disappointing in my young life and I was sure to cause more in the future. But you don't go from expecting someone not to cheat on a game of cards to expecting them not to stage the slaughter of several hundred men without making a hell of a lot of assumptions in between. "What do you mean by that?" I asked. "What the hell kind of 'border patrol' were they running up there, anyhow?"

Again, more silence. Then, he said, "Alexander, neither one of us knows everything about what happened there. I know he's a good solider, but people do a lot of things under stress." His cheeks turned a little pale as he looked at me – really, looked through me as if I weren't there. He had a lot on his mind, I guessed.

"Yeah, well, I need to go pack my things and figure out where I'm going," I told him, but got completely ignored. I grunted and walked away, moving quickly down the street and back toward home. I had a lot to do in very likely even less time than I thought I had. Along the way I said very little to anyone, but I thought a lot. Tristan a traitor? Never, not in a million years. Sure, maybe he'd been through a lot recently, and was smart enough for something like that... but not Tristan. No, it wasn't possible; I was sure of that. No one takes that much abuse and continues to take it unless he was willing to take it his whole life. Tristan was willing, and I knew it because it was, at least in part, my fault.

2

I rolled over and gradually opened my eyes. Something evil crawled beneath my skin – I needed a smoke bad. As I fumbled for my silver *tsohbac* case, I knocked a half-empty bottle of wine on the floor. Dennis would clean that up, I thought. The stinging tears in my eyes dried up the moment my flint struck and that comforting familiar glow sent smoke into the air; my body stopped shivering and the insects under my skin calmed the hell down. Of course, it hadn't actually been all that long – a few hours, maybe?

I lay there for a while staring up at my vaulted stone ceiling, enjoying the *tsohbac* and the warmth of my bed. All of it would have been better if there were a lady there, but there wasn't and that was all right. There wasn't any time for that anyhow. I let out a long sigh... I had a feeling I wouldn't see any action like that for a long time.

"Lord Vestarton? My Lord? May I request your presence, Sir?" It was Dennis, politely knocking in the way only a good butler can, and I was still naked. Damn – what did he want now?

"It's early, Dennis. What do you want?"

Dennis cleared his throat. He was so good at being kind, even when I knew he was doing everything possible not to tell me to go fuck off. "Actually, it's not that early, Sir. It's almost time for your departure."

I hopped out of bed and peeked past velvet drapes to see a bright golden sun sitting high in a cloudless sky. A great Spring's Dawn day, I thought as I hurried to get myself in order. Shirt, pants... my short dark hair was sticking straight on end and that wouldn't do at all. Thank the gods I'd remembered to shave a bit recently, so I didn't look like some complete vagrant. Close, but not quite. The last thing I did was check my eyes in the mirror – still a little cloudy, but nice and dark. I'd pass.

Dennis' knocks came a bit more incessantly for the next fifteen minutes or so until I was finally presentable enough to open the door for him. When the door flung open, Dennis didn't flinch, just folded his withering old hands in front of him and bowed. "Sir, are you feeling well?"

"Fine. Great!" I pulled out another *tsohbac* stick and lit it on a torch as we went downstairs. The brown paper it was wrapped in crisped up with a satisfying crinkling sound as I drew in a long, deep breath. Pleasant brownish smoke whirled around my head. "Why do you ask?"

"Well, Sir – if I may – you're not looking like you're feeling quite yourself."

I shrugged. "Well, this trip isn't exactly to the shores of Birrizi."

"Certainly, Sir. Ah, you did just miss your dark-skinned friend. I paid her eighty Royals, and her delivery is in the kitchen for you."

"Eighty? I usually tip her to a hundred, old chap." Zizah was the Katalahni girl I met in Center Market who sold me my smoking habit, and she was going to give me a hell of a time next week for getting shorted. Not that she didn't usually give me a hell of a time regardless, but *that* didn't have much to do with money. I liked Zizah because she was essentially the perfect woman – her Zondrean wasn't very good so we didn't talk much, and she always came to see me with a box of *tsohbac* sticks under her arm. "Can you go hit Center Market later and get her that twenty?"

"Of course, Sir. I've taken the liberty of packing your things for your trip. And, the Lady Loringham is here to see you, before you take your leave."

Definitely the very last person in the world I wanted to talk with. I cleared my throat. "Really?"

Dennis nodded. We got to the bottom of the staircase and Dennis started examining me, checking whether all my shirt buttons were done and such. What was I, twelve years old again? "Lady Loringham is waiting for you in the parlor."

I sucked down the last of my *tsohbac* and crushed it on the nearest wall – Dennis would clean that up, too. My hands started shaking so I shoved them into my pockets. Maybe there *was* something wrong with me. Was I sick? All of the sudden, I'd never felt so badly in my entire life. I wished that my father were still alive – even if just to talk me through this whole business, to reassure me, to say something encouraging. Although, if he was there to watch me fumble around and acting like an idiot the way I was, he'd probably just rap me across the forehead and tell me to calm down.

Dennis smiled his knowing smile – the one he used when he knew I was in trouble or about to get into it. You hang around with a person through his adolescence long enough, you start to pick up on things like that. "Sir, I'm sure everything will be fine. Not to worry."

"You really believe that?" I snorted derisively as he helped me on with my black wool jacket – the thin one with the gold buttons I liked – and my boots.

"You do not?" The knowing smile got just a tad softer, and a hint of something very sincere and honest touched his old, slightly hazy eyes. "My Lord, I have known you and your friend for many years. Young Master Loringham has always been, for better or for worse, an honest and trustworthy individual. He is also a very competent young man, much like yourself. I am certain that all will be well in the end."

I had to admit, I liked Dennis' attitude, but I couldn't quite share his upbeat sentiments.

Tristan's father and I had never had much to say to each other; that's what happens when you're a "bad influence" on a man's son, I suppose. But there had been days where I could have talked to his mother for hours. She was just that kind of person. She didn't care whether I was the Lord of Vestarton House or the boy who used to follow her around asking how to say naughty things in Eislandisch – the whole nobility thing never really registered with her.

"Alexander," she said in that deep, throaty accent, "I wanted to give you something, before you leave."

The shaking weird feeling came back now – why, I had no idea. Well, I did have *some* idea, and looking into her sky-colored eyes made me realize just how badly I felt about this whole mess, how frightened I was, how painful it was to think about all the things they'd said at that Council table. I'm sure I went pale because she put a hand on my shoulder to steady me, but that wasn't quite the kind of comfort I needed. I fished into my jacket for a *tsohbac*, pulled one out and lit it – soothing smoke filled my lungs, and the skin-crawling trembling feeling subsided a bit.

Lady Loringham patted my shoulder gently. "You should not do this trip if you are not feeling well."

"I'm fine... I'll be fine. It's, um, just that..."

"I know." Her gaze dropped to her hands, where she gripped a silvery, round object. I didn't even have to see it to know what it was. "Alexander, you should take this. Take this to Tristan." She reached for one of my hands and pressed the High Honor Medal hard into my palm. "Take it to him, or send it to sea with him."

I straightened up, tried to look confident and insistent. "He's not dead. I know that... I'm sure it'll be all right. Really. You should keep this." I tried giving it back but she stepped away, put her hands on her hips.

"I hope you are right, but..." She trailed off for a moment, and a sour look passed across her sharply chiseled features. "Just promise me that if he is gone, that he does not get treated like a *Zondern*. Do not let them... set him on fire the way they do. Please."

The very thought of any kind of funeral, Zondrean, Eislandisch, or otherwise, made me sick to my stomach all over again. I looked down at the silvery High Honor Medal with its tiny delicate inscriptions on it, the image of a sword and a shield, a little place at the bottom for Tristan's name and title. After everything, after trying so hard *not* to give him the most valued prize in all of Zondrellian nobledom, they gave up and handed it over in the end. They even did it during the graduation ceremony and everything. People were a bit stunned, I think, but no one in the history of... well, in the history of *history*, had ever worked harder to earn it. The catch – and there's *always* a catch – was that he had to go out to some assignment far from home, straight away.

After considering the medal for a time, I tried one more time to give it back to her. She hesitated, but I was insistent. "It'll be safer here. He'll be back for it, I promise you." Maybe it was the way I said it or the logic of keeping it safe, but she relented, tears beginning to stream out of her eyes as she did so.

**

Things were so much simpler when we were younger. When I was eighteen years old I was running around with a bottle of liquor in one hand and a girl in the other most days of the week. At different times we would sit around speculating about what life would be like after graduation, and it was usually the same answer. He was going to teach swordsmanship at the Academy because that's what he was good at – and later, because he wanted future cadets to have someone else to deal with besides that asshole Janus. Me, I figured I had a whole life of useless barracks duty and ordering kids around to look forward to till it was time to do responsible things like get married and have a few kids to get the Vestarton name stamped on them properly. Life would be... normal. Fun, even. For Tristan, I imagined things would be no different. Why should it? We lived across the street from each other in some of the best and richest homes in the city – we could have and be whatever we wanted at any time. There really wasn't much that distinguished us from each other, either, except for that one thing.

I think it first started to hit me the day we were admitted into the Academy just how big a difference looks and a bloodline can make. They have to take you into a room, about four cadets a time, and inspect you for physical problems, illnesses, that sort of thing. It's a standard procedure, not that big of a deal. You take your shirt off and they check you over, joke with you for a minute while they sign off on a piece of paper, and you're on your way. Well, Tristan and I went to

Registration Day together, and did the inspection thing at the same time. We did the standard shirts-off thing, answered a few odd questions about general health and such. I was ready to go within a few minutes, but they were still poring over Tristan like he were some sort of livestock. They asked a whole lot of pointless questions about fitness and training and how many drinks he had in a week. It was ridiculous. If I hadn't needed to get properly admitted to the Academy I would have walked over there and told them to get fucked – preferably by the biggest Eislandisch tundra girl this side of the mountains. I should have said it – obviously Tristan wasn't going to. He was calm, "yes, Sir" and "no, Sir" the entire time. I couldn't believe it.

When we walked out of there with our signed papers in our hands, I turned around and stopped him in the corridor, jabbed him in the chest. "What the hell is wrong with you?"

"What?"

"Seriously, what the hell is wrong with you? Since when do you let people talk to you like that?"

He shrugged and looked down at the floor. "What am I supposed to do? Didn't you get that speech from your father about how important this place is? I'm not going to ruin it before they even let me in the damned door. Besides, I'm sure it'll be better once we get settled in and all."

It actually got *worse*. Our Headmaster, the one who ran all of our practices, announced to all of us on our first day of training that he had a medal at home in a cabinet that said he'd killed forty-nine Eislandisch soldiers during the war. And, he was still looking for his fiftieth. This didn't seem to bother Tristan, though – nothing he'd admit to, anyhow. He had gotten Catherine knew how many lectures from his father over the years about being the better man and whatnot. Any talk about his heritage tended not to make a dent in his demeanor... most of the time. And when we got assigned our chores, Headmaster Janus gave him the worst and most painful duties – cleaning stairs and floors, chopping wood, all the things that were mind numbing and hard on the body. And this didn't bother Tristan much either, although eventually the whole thing took its toll. One night, about three months into our first year, I came in from my kitchen duty and found him packing his things.

"What are you doing?" I asked.

He shoved another shirt into his bag so hard the whole bed it sat on shook with the force. "I quit. I can't do this."

Tristan is my best friend, don't get me wrong. But, sometimes he can be incredibly frustrating. Wasn't *he* the one telling *me* how important this place was and all that shit? I rolled my eyes. "Why not?"

"Look, don't worry about it. You're fine here."

I stood there bewildered. Fine? I suppose I was "fine," but so was he. Right? He won all the sparring bouts in every single one of our swordplay practices – he was unstoppable with that blade, and everyone knew it. It was already getting to the point where some of the other cadets were refusing to practice with him, and not because they didn't like him. And he got good scores on his exams – far better than mine. Of course, studying would help, and this is something I generally didn't do, but whatever the case, he was doing well – more than just fine. At that pace, with his record, they'd be throwing awards at his feet and begging him to teach there by the end. Why go now?

Then he stripped his black uniform tunic off to change into normal clothes. He had his back to me, and I stared at it for a solid minute in horror. Finally, I opened my mouth; I had to know. "What the fuck is that?" Tristan turned to face me. He had this look he gave when he thought I'd just said or done something incredibly stupid – he sort of squinted at you so all you could see was a little peek of blue, and his brow furrowed up a little in the center – and this was the look I got then. Okay, so I was stupid. "What *is* that?" I asked again.

His voice was very low and quiet. "Are you daft? What the fuck do you think it is?"

Well, I thought it was a big, bleeding, nasty wound across the massive span of his back but I didn't *know* what it was. I'd never seen anything like it before. "I don't know, Brother," I said. "It looks bad – you should see the healer for that."

"Already have." He shook his head as his eyes rolled skyward. "Haven't you ever seen a whiplash before?"

Obviously, I hadn't. I don't make it habit to whip people or get myself whipped – besides… "They don't do that anymore."

"They do if they don't like you and you ask too many fucking questions." As he pulled another simple black shirt over his head, he winced visibly.

The consequences if he quit the Academy were dire and any noble boy in Zondrell knew it. If you skipped the Academy and failed to do military time, you were basically an outcast for the rest of your life. People had done it – we never heard from them again. I didn't know which was worse, going through that or going through the unnecessary "discipline" and the long, painful days studying and chopping wood and the gods only knew what would come along a year from then... essentially, it was a question of how much misery one man could take. I could have let him go, pretended like I knew nothing about it – a part of me really wanted to. A part of me still wishes I could go back and do exactly that. But instead I did what any good noble-born Zondrell military brat would do for another. I went over to his bed, grabbed the bag full of his things and tossed it into a corner of the room. He gave me the are-you-stupid look again.

"I might ask what the hell is wrong with *you*," he said softly, moving to get past me and get back to his business. But I stood there tall and firm with my arms folded across my chest, thinking I was some sort of immovable object. "Get the hell out of my way, Alex."

"Make me." This was enough to turn his expression to the rarer you-*must*-be-stupid look; he grabbed me by the shoulders and pushed, hard enough to throw me off balance but not enough to give completely. I took a step back and that was all.

Tristan took a long deep breath, looked me straight in the eye, and spoke so softly I had to concentrate to hear. "Please get out of my way, Alex. I can't do this. They don't want me here and I don't want to be here."

"You do know what life would be like if you left now?" I asked. "Your father will disown you; you'll never be able to live your life here, in the city. You'd have to go."

He shrugged. "Doesn't really sound that bad."

"Your life will be *over*, man. Do you get that?" Whether he did or not, he gave no indication. "What would you do for money? Where would you live? You've hardly ever been outside the city walls. I know I sure as fuck wouldn't know what to do with myself out there, anywhere. Don't you dare try to tell me you'd be any better off. You've got everything to gain by staying and everything to lose if you leave – hell, you're the one who told *me* that. I'm not going to let you throw your life away just because they don't like how you look and who your parents are. Rise above it, Brother – they're just going to keep treating you like shit your whole life unless you show them you can take it."

He thought about this for a few minutes. I thought he might have agreed with me, but instead he tried to shove past me again, quite a lot harder this time and I stumbled backward into the wall. It hurt, and now I was pissed. I can't say I actually decided to do what I did next because I didn't think about it too much. I can, however, say with great certainty that it was one of the stupidest things I'd ever done in my whole life… and I couldn't even turn around later and say I was proud to have done it.

Thinking I was some sort of barroom brawl hero instead of an eighteen-year-old kid who had never with actual malice hit anyone in his whole life, I made a tight fist and struck my best friend across the cheek as hard as I could. His head turned violently to the side and he paused there for a while. I couldn't believe what I'd just done; was he hurt? Was I capable of injuring someone with just one punch?

Not really, as it turned out. In fact, all I'd succeeded in doing was getting us both very, very pissed, and I was at a severe disadvantage. He was bigger and stronger, and it took nothing for him to retaliate in kind. Outrageous pain and heat filled one side of my face – it felt like I was on fire. I think I tried to make another move but then I found myself moving backward rapidly, until I met up with the wall again and all the air went straight out of my lungs. Vision was no longer something I took for granted, and my breathing came in fits and wheezes. Suddenly the other side of my face lit up in the most excruciating pain I'd ever experienced, followed by something even worse. My bottom rib snapped with a terrible sickening noise and I doubled over, collapsing on the floor in a useless heap. I think I lost consciousness for a while.

The next thing I remembered was waking up to a lot of pain, and Tristan sitting on the floor across from me, staring vacantly at nothing. The area around his left eye was steadily turning a rich shade of purple. "You're right, you know," he said. There was no conviction there; whether he believed that or not, I'll never know.

I struggled up to a sitting position. It felt like someone was jabbing a spear in my side and twisting it. "You're fucking right I am," I replied, wincing with every word. "And something else... you're a fucking prick. You know that?"

Our eyes met for just a moment, because he quickly looked away and to the stark stone floor. "Yeah, I know. I'm sorry."

He was, genuinely sorry. And he did stay, and seemed to change the way he thought about the Academy. Seemed to, anyhow. My fractured rib healed up within a few weeks, and we never spoke of that night again. All I knew was that none of the torment seemed to matter anymore; he did everything Headmaster Janus and the other officers told him, absolutely without question. He made it his personal mission to be the best soldier, the best tactician, the best leader the Zondrell military had ever seen. He strove for the High Honor like no other man in the Academy's history – he *bled* for that thing.

I was sorry too, but I never got to tell him that, and here was his mother four years later trying to hand me the Medal he worked so hard for, thinking he might be dead. By the gods, I was *such* a bad friend.

Outside, I heard the clipclop of horse hooves, along with the creaking of wood and metal. "I think I need to go," I said, for lack of anything better or intelligent to say. She nodded, and that was that. My bags were in the carriage and I was stuffed inside, and we were off in a whirlwind of soldiers and horses and activity all around. The sense that everything else was moving around me while I stayed perfectly still, somehow locked in time, was with me for a good portion of the way. I don't even remember leaving Zondrell. I just remember looking out the window at some point and seeing nothing but trees and grass and rocks instead of buildings and people. Looking down, on the battered wooden floor at my feet were fourteen spent *tsohbac* sticks, each one burned down to a nub and crushed flat. A fifteenth joined the rest – I let out a long satisfying breath as I put it out under my bootheel.

"Good Catherine Almighty – can you *please* stop with those things?"

I looked at Victor Wyndham, sitting across from me in the ridiculously small and rickety carriage we had ridden all the way from Zondrell to... well, I didn't really know where we were at that point. If my rear hadn't felt so numb from all the bouncing about I would swear by looking at the barren, uninteresting surroundings that we hadn't moved at all for at least an hour. I looked out the window one more time to confirm that we were still traveling through nothing, then turned back to Victor and silently lit another *tsohbac*.

"Fucking insolent..."

"What's that?" I don't think he thought I heard him but how could you not in a carriage this size? I leaned forward and blew my smoke directly in face. "Sorry, I didn't hear you."

Victor coughed a bit, trying to fan away some of the smoke with his bony little hand. It did him little good – the place was filled with the stuff. All I could really see in the haze were his eyes, a deep throbbing bright blue and rimmed red like he had an awful cold. But if he lost it and did something unfriendly and magical in here, it would be the last mistake he ever made. He knew it – you don't go around killing lords no matter how irritating they are. I knew this, too, and I took full advantage of the fact.

"You should relax, Victor," I said between puffs. "It's not healthy, you know?"

If he'd had a drink in his hand he would have thrown it at me. "You're relaxed? You've been smoking constantly for the past four hours – you call that relaxed?"

"It's too early to dive into a flask just yet," I replied with a snide grin that only served to make Victor huff in annoyance and look away out the window. That was fine – it meant he was done talking to me for a while, and that was always a good thing. I let out a long smoky breath and rapped my knuckles against the wooden wall of the carriage behind me. When it didn't stop, I rapped again, louder. "Stop this thing, Driver!" I shouted, and eventually we rattled to a halt. Victor watched my every move as I got up, bent over because the roof was rather low in the rickety little carriage, and hopped out the rear door. Our driver, a young solider trimmed out in black and silver with the buckles polished to a blinding gleam, was out there to meet me, looking concerned.

"Everything's all right, m'Lord?" he asked.

I tossed the nearly spent end of my latest *tsohbac* far out into the brush. "Just need to stretch my legs for a moment." I could have told him what I really needed to do but he'd figure it out in a minute anyhow. I looked around for some trees, some coverage of some kind, but there was nothing but dirt and grass and rocks nearby. A modest man might have tried to hold it till some better scenery came along, but Lord or no Lord, when you have to piss, you have to piss. Besides, any of the twenty or thirty guardsmen riding behind us could probably have cared less – they were taking the opportunity for a break, too.

As I put myself back together I couldn't help but marvel at the huge expanse of land all around us, in all directions. I had never been this far away from the city before, had never seen a landscape not broken up by spires and rooftops. Out here, you could see *everything* – in the near distance, trees and grass and flowers, and further out, almost disappearing into the clear blue sky, was a huge expanse of white-capped mountains. They floated across the entire northern horizon, a great natural barrier into the lands of the North. Most people called them the Mountains With Two Names, because neither the Zondreans nor the Eislandisch could agree on one, and we were heading steadily straight into them. What a joke, I thought – the one time, perhaps in my entire life, I would be allowed to leave Zondrell, to see an actual *mountain* and smell clean country air, and I wouldn't even be able to enjoy it.

"We should be there by nightfall." I whirled around so fast I almost tripped, but it was only Victor. His face soured even more than was usual. "But not at this pace. Are you quite ready?"

To get back into that carriage with *him*? "You know what? I think I'll walk."

Victor dismissed me with a wave of his hand. "Suit yourself," he said, heading back to the carriage, and soon we were moving along once again, toward what could only be described – at least by me – as the Great Unknown.

"You're smart to start now, m'Lord," one of the soldiers said, moving up so that he could walk alongside me. I smiled and nodded at him, not really knowing what else to say. "The road gets rockier as we get further north, too much for carriages. We'll all be walking soon enough."

Now I paid him a little more attention, noting the way the age lines splayed out from the corners of his eyes, and the strike across his jaw where stubble wouldn't grow. Battle-worn, as my father probably would have called him. "You've been up this way before?"

"Aye, Sir, just came back from there, about a month ago. I just wanted to say, for what it's worth, I..." He trailed off for a minute, and when he continued his voice was much softer, as if someone might be looking over our shoulders or something. "I was honored to have the opportunity to fight with Lord Loringham. He was a good soldier."

I almost stopped walking because I thought I might vomit – again – but my new friend put a hand on my arm, ready to drag me onward if necessary. I lit off another *tsohbac* with trembling hands and breathed deeply from it. It wasn't helping the way I would have liked. "Sorry," I said. "My nerves are just completely... fucked. What did you say your name was?"

"It's Delrin, Sir, Sergeant-at-Arms. I don't mean to trouble you, my Lord, I just know that you and he are friends – that's why I wanted to tell you that." Delrin offered a friendly smile and began to walk a little faster, breaking away from me to give me some space, but that wasn't what I wanted just yet. No, I *had* to know more.

"You say you fought with Tristan?" I asked, moving a little quicker to keep pace with him.

"Yes, Sir, out on patrol, many times. Honestly, I'd probably be up there still if my wife didn't give me a third daughter a couple months ago. I'll tell you, she's pretty upset I'm going back again." The soldier chuckled in spite of himself.

Against all better judgment, I pressed on. A nagging voice deep in the back of my head told me not to, to keep my questions to myself, insisted that I didn't actually want to know any of this, but I was already out here. I was going to find out sooner or later, whether I liked it or not. "And do you think he's really... dead? I mean, I don't know what you've heard about what's happened, but..."

"No, I've heard, m'Lord. I talked to the lad who went before the Council yesterday. He told me everything." He swallowed hard, looking ahead at the ground with a certain coldness spreading into his gray-brown eyes. "Anyone who wasn't up there, didn't live it, they won't understand. But I do. You know, I'll be thirty-seven this month. I've seen things, been places – had experiences. You can't put young men like that into a situation... like that... and not expect something bad to come of it. To affect him somehow."

"What do you mean, Sergeant?"

Now Delrin looked straight at me, brows raised, trying to silently ask a question. The problem was, I didn't know what the question was, so I just looked right back at him. We did this for quite a while, maybe several minutes. Surely, he must have thought I was shockingly uninformed – or just plain stupid. Either way, eventually he said, "You don't know, do you? You don't know what we were doing up there, what we were going through for Zondrell?" Well, when you put it like that... I really didn't know *what* to say, but I didn't have to say anything. He knew. "Apparently it wasn't important enough. Then you'll have to forgive me, my Lord, but I have no idea how much blood has to be spilled for the rulers of Zondrell to take notice."

I dropped my half-spent *tsohbac* stick to the ground, feeling a bit like I'd just been slapped across the face. When he started to pull ahead of me again, I rushed to catch up, this time grabbing him by the arm as forcefully as I could. "Look, Sergeant, I'm new at this whole Lord thing. I don't know much of anything right now."

Delrin glanced back toward his comrades, who were laughing and chatting and not paying us much attention. His eyes were devoid of emotion when he turned back to me. "We were looking for something, something big, important. You ever heard of the Kaeren?" I nodded. Of course I had; it's a good faery story, ancient weapon of the gods or some such nonsense. He didn't just say that they were actually out looking for such a thing, did he? "Sure, so I guess according to the mages at the Magic Academy, it was supposed to be in the area, and the King wanted it. Loringham was supposed to help us find it, because he was a good warrior and spoke the language up there." He stopped in his tracks, and in the afternoon sunlight the crags in his weathered face seemed that much more deep, more intense. "I'd be willing to bet all of that... *searching* finally got the best of him. And you know, I wouldn't put him on trial if my life depended on it – I'd defend him to the death. No one that young should be put through what they put him through. Hell, no one at all."

He waited for me to say something, maybe to ask another question, but I found that I couldn't speak. I tried, but nothing happened. My mind seemed to stop working then, completely confused. Was he saying what I *thought* he was saying? No, I didn't even know what I thought – I couldn't begin to wrap my mind around it. Slowly my gaze wandered around, searching out the individual faces of the armed and armored men around me, marching along as if they had no cares in the world. And then there was Victor, secure in his little carriage, enjoying a sip of wine perhaps as we plodded along... Did *he* even know? Likely, he did, and yet he was willing to condone this idiocy – even with the prospect of his own brother dead and bleeding all of his precious Wyndham blood out on a rock somewhere, he seemed all right with all of this. But this wasn't a time of war, so why were we – my fellows, the other officers, the other nobles – sending men off to strange lands to fight, to do things that civilized people aren't supposed to do to each other? What, for a thing, some trinket someone read about in a book and decided to go tear through the countryside to claim? Was that what was really going on here? It was insane, utterly and completely insane.

If I'd known some four years ago... I would have told Tristan to get as far away from the Academy and the city as humanly possible. Go to Katalahnad or Eisland or Drakannya or something. Hell, I'd have gone *with* him! I shut my eyes very hard, clenched my hands into fists. I wanted to scream or yell or do something. I felt dizzy and strange – and not the good kind of dizzy and strange, either.

"My Lord? Are you all right?" There was now some emotion, some caring in Sergeant Delrin's expression. He reached out and steadied me with a strong hand.

"No… No, I'm not." And I wasn't sure I would be "all right" ever again.

1

Tristan Loringham

I had never felt so miserable. At once I was dead tired, but restless; I wanted nothing more than to get up and move about, but at the same time all I wanted to do was sleep. The problem was, I couldn't do much of either, so most of the time I lay there, staring at the whitewashed stone ceiling with a million thoughts racing through my mind. Every once in a while Andella or Seraphine would come in to talk to me, bring me something, prod at me for a bit, but truth be told, I wasn't very good company. Concentrating on conversation, no matter how idle, gave me a furious headache – I didn't talk much and listened even less. I found I couldn't keep my mind on anything for very long, and I was anxious and irritable and generally unpleasant to be around. So, I was left to my own a good portion of the time, drifting in and out of a state that wasn't conscious, but wasn't quite sleep either. Hours, entire parts of days would just become lost. I could wake up in the morning and the next thing I knew it would be almost sunset – nothing was in between, not even time itself. Or, so it seemed to me.

After three full days, dreams started to fill up the time between wakefulness, and suddenly things became much worse; I didn't even think such a thing was possible. I was used to nightmares because they had plagued me for months, but these were different. They felt so real. Indeed, had I put much thought into it, I would have realized much earlier that they felt so real because they were *memories*... the mind's way of putting broken pieces of a puzzle back together. Several times, I managed to escape, to wake myself up before the dream unfolded too much. But the third night into my stay there, deep into the night when the sisters and the world outside were safely in bed, I remember lying still but wide awake for a long time, staring into the nothingness of a pitch-black room so quiet I could hear each individual drop of rain splashing against the window outside. It was starting to storm – thunder rumbled off in the distance like a sleeping dragon waking from a long nap. As I listened, the sound of water rushing along grew louder, more like I was standing next to a riverbank than sitting in the middle of a rainstorm. From somewhere there came the smell of wildflowers, faint but distinctive. How such a thing could waft in from outside two solid panes of glass, surrounded by stone and mortar, I had no idea, but it was there all the same. I shut my eyes tightly – maybe I was dreaming, and there was no water or wildflowers at all.

When I opened my eyes again it wasn't dark anymore. It wasn't light either, just somewhere in between. Water, though... I was distinctly aware of the fact that I was partially wet, and there was a small amount of water all around – I could see light reflecting off of its surface. But it was still – no rain, no waterfalls, nothing disturbed it. A cluster of little blue flowers hovered just over the pool, very close to my face, and I looked at them for a while, trying far harder than it seemed necessary to bring them into focus. They swayed a little in the breeze, and I noticed that they were tipped with white – frost-tips, like my mother used to plant outside the house. Of course, they weren't all the right color, and some were dotted with bright red spots, irregular shapes and smears that seemed quite odd, not at all natural.

Perhaps it had something to do with the fact that they were sitting not near a puddle of clean water at all, but a darkening pool of blood.

Slowly, my eyes traced the viscous flow of crimson, searching for where it was coming from, why there was so much of it. It didn't take long to find the answer – a dagger lay deeply buried in my chest, close to where the arm meets the shoulder. It sat there glistening in the weird light glowing and flickering around me, its silver hilt with random scratches and smears of blood resting just at the edge of my vision. It seemed as if I should have felt it, should have felt extraordinary wrenching agony, but I didn't. My entire body was numb – I could only look at this thing in sheer awe, trying to figure out how it got there.

Sounds flared into being then, as if someone had just opened a window in a quiet and tightly sealed room. At first, there was only a low rumble, a deep thundering noise like a coming storm, but this had nothing to do with the weather. No, this was something very different, because eventually it was accompanied not by the sound of rain but the sounds of people, men shouting, metal clanging on metal... of battle, and there I was in the middle of it.

My heart began pounding so hard that I thought it might burst out of my throat. *Don't look. Don't listen.* These were the only coherent thoughts I could manage. *Don't look. Don't listen.* Because I knew what I would see and what I would hear if I stopped to think about it... and I didn't want to do that.

Don't look. Don't listen. Get away – now.

It was less a conscious thought than an instinct, a will to get up and get the hell away. Where would I go? What would I do? That wasn't important. The only thing that was important at that one moment was to get up, to move. But first... I craned my neck to look down at the dagger. I could barely lift my head, much less my arms, but it had to come out – had to. My breath came in quick, shallow bursts as I willed my left hand up, forced my fingers to clasp around the hilt so tightly I could hear the tendons in my knuckles flexing and stretching under my skin. Then, before I could think much about it, I pulled – hard – and suddenly I was staring not at the sky but at my own ruby-handled dagger, dripping with blood.

And then, the pain began. It radiated out from the wound in all directions, to every corner of my being, washing away the numbness and forcing all the warmth to pour forth. This was nothing like any battle wound I'd ever had – this was a feeling with no counterpart, no explanation, no words to describe it. It felt like... like my soul was trying to claw its way out of my body. I fought it with everything I had – which wasn't a hell of a lot – but it was enough to get me to roll over to my side, to pull myself up to hands and knees. The whole process seemed to take an eternity with no coordination, no balance, and no strength, but I did finally lurch to my feet, clutching at my right shoulder in an attempt to stem the torrent of blood.

The world around me was ruined. Flames danced in every direction, burning everything they touched, crippling the nearby little buildings and threatening to send the bodies that littered the ground straight up to Catherine. There were too many of them, their armor dented and ripped apart, their weapons tossed aside like the neglected toys of a child who's grown a bit too old for them. Those still alive were in retreat, scurrying away while their enemies pursued them, shouting loudly and incoherently.

I started to sink to my knees, my legs no longer able to support me, and my vision blissfully blurred. There was nothing there that I wanted to see anymore, and I had no strength left, *nothing*. But the moment I felt myself fading away, there were strong hands at my back, and a gruff chuckle that very much made me wish that I was joining the dead on their way to the gods.

"Remember," he said in a low voice with deep Eislandisch inflections, "I told you if I wanted you dead, you would be dead. But today is a lucky day – the gods are not done with you." I turned to look at a pair of concerned yet watchful eyes, clear and bright and blue. That was the last thing I saw – everything else seemed to fade away, washed out by blackness.

✳✳

The sound of lightning shooting down from the heavens was accompanied by a terrific peal of thunder, jolting me awake again. The whole building shook with the impact, just a tiny bit, but enough to notice… or perhaps that was just my limbs quivering, or my heart beating far too quickly. The storm was right over the temple now, pelting the building with everything it had. I lay in my sweat-soaked bedding listening to the rain bounce against the glass, staring at nothing and thinking of nothing but the rain and my aching wound. The drops pelting the roof almost measured in time with my heartbeat and throbbing ebbs and waves of pain; in a way, it was soothing. After my breathing steadied I shut my eyes and tried to concentrate on the sound of the rain to put myself back to sleep, but after quite a while I realized it would never happen. My limbs tingled, restless from disuse, and I'd had enough of memories and nightmares for one evening. What I really needed was to just get up and move around, take a walk and get away from my thoughts – from myself – for a while.

It took a bit of effort to get up and on my feet, but it was far better than the first time I'd tried it. This time I actually stayed upright. After a few days of solid rest, I felt far closer to normal – I could even move my bad arm around without tearing up. I wasn't exactly ready to climb a mountain or wield a weapon, but it would get better soon enough. It would have to, because surely I'd go insane if I had to be bedridden much longer. My choices for reading were the Book of Catherine, a scattering of poetry, and a theology textbook, and I could only entertain myself with that kind of a selection for so long.

Quietly, I pulled open the door and stepped into the hall outside for the first time since I'd arrived. Everything was shrouded deep in nighttime's darkness, and I had to keep a hand on the wall to find my way through without running into something. The absolute last thing I wanted was to knock something over, or trip, or otherwise make an ass out of myself while in the process waking everyone up. The tiny cloisters that passed for bed chambers and storage rooms in this church, I discovered as I felt my way along, were very close to one another, with each of the four heavy oak doors just a few feet apart from the next. Luckily, it wasn't far to the only source of light in the corridor, some faint grayness creeping in from the wide opening just ahead. Gradually, I headed in that direction until I wound up in the main chapel of the temple.

It wasn't a huge room by any means, certainly nothing like the great cathedral at Zondrell. The pews were simple and unadorned, just wooden benches running the length of the room with an aisle in center, leading up to an altar covered by a white sheet – nothing surprising or special here. A tall brass incense brazier glowed cheerily at the back of the room, behind the altar where the priestess kept her various trappings and equipment for conducting masses and funeral rites and so forth. The spiced smell it wafted across the room tickled my nose, making me want to sneeze. There was a gold candelabra with several candles burning away in it, a long white robe, an alabaster bowl and pitcher for blessing water for healing rituals, and a beautiful leather-bound, gold-trimmed copy of the Book of Catherine sitting inside a little niche, at waist level, cut into the wall. It was laid open to a page somewhere in the middle, and something compelled me to go over to it and read what was there. I limped my way to the shrine and touched the parchment.

The Goddess of Peace holds the gentle man's heart in sweet embrace – return Her embrace and receive the gift of Catherine. She forgives all men their trespasses, if they release their sins and give of themselves to Her. When a man acts as the Goddess and forgives his brothers and sisters, and accepts the path he walks as truth, Peace reigns in his heart for Catherine is pleased.

It could not have been a more appropriate chapter.

Another massive thunderclap echoed through the high-ceilinged temple, causing me to jump to attention. I looked behind me, through one of the panels of stained glass that lined the east and west walls, but saw nothing beyond them. There was hardly any light on the other side save for whatever moonlight was pushing through the clouds – it was just enough to brighten the windows and reveal more deeply the colorful images burned into them, beautiful images of the goddess Catherine in a green field with bright blue skies overhead, and white birds hovering all around her. The pictures were simple and showed no facial features or particular ornamentation, making them almost abstract, like one might see in paintings from the Ancient Age. I concluded that this must have been a very old temple, perhaps standing here for hundreds of years.

As I looked around I noticed the doors, wide double-doors with heavy brass pulls, at the opposite end of the room. Even though the rain continued to fall outside with reckless abandon, I walked to them, placed my hand on one of the big round pulls and grabbed it firmly. The door moved – unlocked. Energy pulsed through my chest, anticipating... well, something. Taking a walk in the rain was not only rather a silly thing to do, but it was also a really silly thing to get excited about. Nonetheless, I couldn't stop myself. I looked around the chapel for a moment, just to make sure I was alone, and then I slipped out the door as quietly as I could.

As soon as I got out from under the chapel roof's overhang I was instantly soaked from head to toe. The water was cold but it was a good rain – a cleansing rain. I lifted my head and let it pelt my face, closing my eyes and just standing there like that, feeling the individual drops of water run down my cheeks and neck and back. The black cotton shirt the sisters had found for me clung to my skin in various uncomfortable ways, but it didn't really seem to matter. The fresh air, wind whipped up by the storm, filled my lungs and coursed through my body. I felt... *alive*. I could imagine that the rain sounded just like a flowing stream, a fast-running one that crawls through mountains and foothills ceaselessly, fed by melting snow and ice somewhere far away. I concentrated on that image for a while, imagining the mountain stream that I knew so well just a few miles from here. The cold water against my skin was no longer just rain, but that little waterfall, cascading over my head and down my back. I could look down at the pool of water that came up to my navel and see trickles and clouds of bright crimson in the otherwise crystal-clear liquid. It would come from my arms and hands, and I would tear at them to wash it all off as best I could. No matter how hard I worked, though, it seemed like it never would go away, not completely. Looking at it made me sick to my stomach, so I would close my eyes – just as I did in that rainstorm – and just let the water rush over me, the intense chill of it both cleansing and punishing.

I don't know how long I stood there, but eventually I heard something approaching – footsteps, very soft but slightly out of rhythm with the falling raindrops. It was just enough to make me open my eyes and snap back into reality. I looked around slowly, even though I didn't need to see to know someone was there.

"Not a good night for walking. But it is funny – I was just thinking to come by for a visit. And here you are."

Behind me, leaning against the door of the church, was the very last person I thought I'd ever see again. Hanging low on his belt was a dagger sheath, and he began idly pulling out the weapon it held, then sheathing it again, quickly in smooth, simple motions. Each time the blade was whisked in or out, it made a screeching, ringing noise, a sharp contrast to the steady rainfall. The darkness and his heavy cloak covered his face, but I knew who it was – I knew that voice. I felt stuck in place, brought back in time to not that long ago. Two or three weeks, maybe? I couldn't remember when and time had sort of abandoned me at that point anyhow. But it might as well have been yesterday.

Back at the camp where I was stationed, I used to go to a certain place when I felt like being alone, much like the same feeling that had drawn me out into the storm. We called it the Slope. It wasn't much, just a small grassy embankment jutting out over the deep ravine that helped shield our camp from wandering scouts and unwelcome visitors. Early on, I was told, it had served as a lookout, but the fact that you could not see much of the camp from atop the Slope made it a poor vantage point. But, at its center was a single great tree, ancient, rising up out of the rocks for apparently no reason at all – there wasn't another tree like it for miles. It was as if someone had purposely placed it there, or perhaps it was just so stubborn that it would stay there, defying nature and logic, for all eternity. It must have been the latter, because no matter what abuse it took, it never flinched, never withered and died. When I first arrived there, I noticed that some of the men had used it for swordplay practice – there were chips in its bark and small gashes taken out of its great trunk here and there. By the end of that first day, I very much wanted to add some wounds of my own to the tree's thick hide. So I did. I struck from every possible stance, from a million different angles, high and low, slash and thrust. I practiced until my arms were so sore I could barely lift them, until trickles of blood ran out of my nose because of my exertion in the cold, thin air, until the blade needed to go back to the camp smith for sharpening. The next evening, I was there again, doing the same thing, compelled to it as if it were calling to me. It was the perfect sparring partner – here was something that never got tired, never called it quits for the day, never complained if I struck too hard. Practicing there against that tree made me forget about everything else, made my whole body ache in a painfully liberating way.

After a week it had become second nature, part of my normal routine. Sometimes I used an old sword no one had claimed, and sometimes I used my own. After a month, people would purposely avoid going up there at certain times, to give me my turn. After three months, into the dead of winter, the mountain snow would crunch under my weight as I practiced, each time my sword striking the tree trunk with a heavy *thwack*, rhythmic and almost soothing. Eventually my arms and legs grew so heavy I could hardly move anymore – pain shot through them as I sat – almost fell – to the ground and simply stared up at the stars, huge and bright, not like they were back in Zondrell at all. The light and the smoke from the city choked them but here, here in the dead wilderness of the Northlands, very little could stop their pulsing fury.

One night they entranced me with their dancing and subtle winking for a long time, until I heard a noise, not so far off in the distance… perhaps. It was hard to tell where sounds came from out there. I strained to hear, to make sense of what was happening, for far too long, and I should have known it as soon as I felt the pinprick against the side of my neck, right against the vein. It was so soft, almost gentle, that I didn't respond right away. It could have been the wind, or just my imagination, or… and there it was again, this time, a little more insistent. I silently cursed myself for not paying more attention to my surroundings.

"*Bewegen und sterben, Zondern,*" a deep voice said in my ear. I decided it was best to do as he said and not move, sparing my life for the moment. *"Gut. Jetzt, Hände herauf."* I lifted my hands as commanded, nothing else. I didn't dare turn to look at the Eislander accosting me, not that it mattered much. It could have been anyone – it would have been naïve to think that I didn't have the highest price in all of Eisland sitting directly on my head. The foul taste of copper and bile stung my mouth as I could feel my pulse throbbing against the cold steel of the stranger's sword.

"Morden Sie mich," I told him in Eislandisch, surprised by my own composure. But I was done, there was nothing I could do to defend myself. Let it happen. Kill me. Go for it. Honestly, I really didn't deserve any better a death anyhow. And for a moment, I was certain that he was going to honor my request – the blade dug a little deeper into my skin, and a sharp rush of air filled my lungs. I closed my eyes. I thought about home, about my parents and all the people I knew. I thought about the comforts of the city, about warmth and good food and good women. I thought about where I would go when the end came... certainly, not to Paradise.

"Morden Sie mich," I bade him again – just fucking get it over with. And I got my wish, as I felt something sharp pull across my throat with great force, then cease abruptly with a loud metallic *snap!*

It took a second to realize that I wasn't dead, and I started to breathe again. Without thinking, I reached for my neck, felt thin droplets of blood there. There was a light stinging sensation, too, like a bad turn of the knife while shaving.

Behind me, I heard a chuckle, boiling up into a deep, hearty laugh. The sword was no longer dangerously pressed into my flesh so I turned around to face the bizarre stranger, and saw he was holding my identification pendant on its now-broken silver chain. He shook his head as he looked at the tag, then back at me, laughing uproariously. I was dumbfounded.

"Was ist das?" I asked. I really wanted to know what was so damned funny.

Eventually he looked up at me, still smiling. He was a giant of a man, slightly taller than I and wider across the chest and shoulders, with huge thick arms and legs dressed in simple leather armor. There were no identifying marks or colors on him at all, nothing to claim his allegiance to Eisland although that was certainly where he came from. Several runes carved into the blade of his sword bespoke of "protection over Eisland." Besides, there was no mistaking the bright blonde hair, eyes the color of the sky, squarish features – hell, the two of us could have been related. "Ready to die, Tristan Johannes?" he asked in almost perfect Zondrean.

Surprised, I had to think about replying, my mind caught between two languages. Finally, I nodded, and replied in Zondrean, too. "I have been."

This started up a new wave of laughter from the Eislander. "Very brave for a man who spends his days torturing unarmed men. But then again, you people have no regard for life."

"I'm just good at following orders," I said.

Without warning, he whipped his blade around fast and close, and there was nothing I could do but watch it catch the moonlight and dive straight for vulnerable prey. It stopped against my cheek, its feather edge gracefully pressing just hard enough to not break the skin. "I came here to kill you, *Golddrachen*," the man said with a touch of disdain, while I fought very hard to stay calm and breathe. "But, today! Today is your lucky day." I looked up and still, he was smiling, forming deep creases at the edges of his eyes and lips. "I make you a deal."

I had to admit, I was intrigued. "Go on."

The smile subsided somewhat, but the look in his eyes didn't change – he was completely in control of my life, and he knew it. He may have even been enjoying this. "Listen close. You go back to where your people are and go on about your business. On your next patrol you will meet up with a man called Karl. Karl will surrender to you and you will question him as you have so many others. He will answer your questions. You will give your report. You will find what you seek, and you and your men will leave. For good."

I couldn't believe it. "You're just going to hand over what we're looking for?"

"You will not leave empty-handed, but you *will* leave, and you will not return. If you do not follow my instructions, remember that we know where you and your men are hiding, and we will come. I make you a promise – man to man, blood to blood – this is true. So, when you are done, you will go back to the hole you call a city, and forget this place ever existed. That is my deal for you."

My gaze switched between him and the blade, rapidly back and forth. My heart beat so quickly and with so much ferocity that I thought I might not need a sword to end my life. "And if my men refuse to leave? If they're not happy with what they find?"

"I made you a promise, and I am a man of my word. I will keep my promise to you if I have to drink the blood of every *Zondern* who steps foot here. That includes you." The blade slipped away from my cheek and danced idly back and forth from hand to hand. "So you are lucky today, Herr Loringham. You will stay lucky if you do as I tell you. *Verstehen?*"

It took me a long time to answer. I couldn't answer... Was this a dream? Maybe. Perhaps it was a dream, a strange fantasy concocted by an overstressed and overactive imagination, and I would wake soon. But the cold wind, the trickle of blood running out of my nose, the sharpness of the Eislander's blade – they all seemed so real. Surely, I couldn't trust this man, shouldn't have, but his terms were difficult to refuse. We would not leave empty-handed as long as we never came back. That would mean that the campaign would be over. We could go home, perhaps even heroes, and be free of the endless days and nights of patrol and blood and death. Dozens – if not hundreds – of lives would be saved. It was a deal too good to pass up for the likes of a stupid, naïve, desperate fool. A fool like me.

"*Ja,*" I said with a nod.

"Good. We have understanding. I knew you would see things my way. *Wiedersehen.*" He sheathed his sword across his back and left without another word, vanishing into the wilderness and leaving nothing to betray that he was ever there at all. I considered trying to follow, to figure out where he came from, but my legs refused to move, and my body felt heavy and limp. I was trapped – I had to fulfill my end of the bargain.

And I had. And now that same man was standing in front of me again. I wanted nothing more than to rip him limb from limb.

After about ten pulls of the dagger he tossed it over in the air to grab the blade instead of the hilt. It harnessed the tiny bit of light coming from the half-obscured moons above us with a flash of reddish brilliance. "This is yours, I think," he said in his perfect Zondrean with that familiar Eislandisch accent.

"If you give that to me, it'll be in your throat next." I was a bit surprised at my own ability to stay calm, keep a level voice, and not lash out in rage. The pain helped keep me in check – so did the sight of the great sword strapped to his back.

He laughed, a hearty, boisterous laugh. Like the other times I'd heard that laugh, it made me want to kill him that much more, and I'm sure he knew it. "Strong words for a dead man. You look good, by the way. You should not have taken the knife out though. I was careful – you were not."

"Fuck you. Try harder next time."

Again, the big Eislander laughed, this time more of a short chuckle, as if all of this was part of his own personal joke. "I told you, I do not need you dead."

"You also said you were a man of your word." I approached him then, getting close to peer beyond the cloak and get a glimpse at him. It was dry under the overhang, but the rain continued to pelt at my back. No matter, I hardly felt it or the coldness creeping into my bones the more I stood out there. There was a part of me that wanted very much to rip that dagger – *my* ruby-handled dagger, a priceless family heirloom – out of his grasp and just shove it into the darkness underneath that hood as hard as I possibly could. There was also a part of me that knew I was in no shape for that; it would only get me killed.

Of course, that really didn't seem like such a bad outcome, considering.

A bolt of lightning illuminated us in an instant, revealing just for a second those same crystal blue eyes I saw in my recurring nightmares. "I did what I thought was right. What I had to do. You of all people should understand that."

Flashes of the past sprang to life in my mind, mental lightning with no logic behind them, fading away just as quickly as they came. That might have been true, but I wasn't ready for that... any of it. I didn't want to think and wonder how things could have been different. I didn't want to consider what they were saying back in Zondrell, even though, deep down, I knew full fucking well exactly what they were saying. I was thinking the same thing. "What do you want from me?" I asked finally.

"I just want to give this back. I hope you still have your scabbard." He proffered the dagger hilt out for me to take it. Yes, of course I still had the scabbard – it was on my belt when he had rushed in from behind, pulled that blade out and thrust it into my shoulder. "Though, I could have sold it. I thought of this. It would fetch a good price back in Kostbar, *ja*?" There had to be a trick – surely, there was a catch here, somewhere. But as I reached out with my left hand and grabbed it from him, all he did was let go and fold his arms across his chest – nothing more. The trusty little weapon felt heavy and familiar and as balanced as ever before. In a strange way, I was glad to have it back.

"Do me a favor," he said, switching suddenly to Eislandisch. It took a moment for my sleep-deprived mind to make the switch to understand him. It never even occurred to me to wonder why we had switched in the first place, of course. "Do not talk to the Lavançaise. She is... not to be trusted." Doverton's weapon master again – did he know her? What was the connection? Before I got a chance to ask, he continued. "And think about what you will do. You cannot stay here. You need to go back to Zondrell."

I shook my head with a derisive grunt. "Thanks to you, I can't go back there," I said in Eislandisch.

"You can, and you will. Not tomorrow, I think. Go on your own terms. For now, go to sleep. You look tired."

I could thank him for that as well as the terrible pain I woke up with every morning for the past several days. Yes, I was tired. I ached all over. Terrible things haunted me every time I closed my eyes. And this man had the gall to stand there and tell me I ought to go home and rest? Fuck him.

Before I realized it, he was halfway out of sight, slipping off into the darkness far more quietly than a man his size should normally move. "Who are you?" I called after him.

He stopped, considering, perhaps, but not turning back to face me. "Go inside. Rest. We will talk again." Whoever he was, he was gone before I had a chance to protest.

It took a long time to find the strength to move, and the weakness to do what I was told and go back inside. I wanted to chase after him, ask more questions, do... something. What did he mean by going home "on my own terms"? There was no going home for me, anyhow – what did it matter? I began to wonder if anyone had ever been standing there at all. The Eislander who spoke perfect Zondrean was someone I knew, yet didn't know – he was as much a spectre in my memories as he was while standing right in front of me. But yet, if he wasn't there, then I wouldn't have my dagger back in my hands. I thought it was long gone, but there it was, returned in perfect condition, gems intact and all. What had possessed him to return it, I may never know. At that point, I found I couldn't think very clearly about it all, and didn't want to.

As I opened the heavy door to the church once again, I caught another flash of lighting streak across the sky overhead, felt the deep rumble of the resulting thunder pass through me. Wet and cold, shaking and miserable, I considered going back to bed, but I couldn't sleep. Sleep brought dreams, and dreams turned to nightmares... and worse. So, I ambled into the chapel again, sitting down heavily in the first pew, alone, uncomfortable, staring at the altar and the tools of the priestess's trade there, seeing them and yet not at the same time. I thought about everything that had happened, everything that I'd done... Scenes continued to replay in my mind, visions I didn't care to revisit, but they stayed, etched into my psyche as constant, horrible reminders. I even thought about praying, but I didn't expect the Great Lady or anyone else to hear me.

2

I watched the sun rise out of the storms from the night before, the light growing from nothing into a heavy brightness streaming in through the stained-glass windows of the chapel. The images of doves and of the Great Lady grew warmer, more intense, lifelike despite their primitive look, but they weren't comforting. Nothing there was.

At some point during the night, I had tried to read the Book of Catherine that rested in the wall, never daring to pick it up, only turning the fragile handwritten pages from one to the next, searching for some glimmer of something… inspiration, maybe? Hope? An answer, but what was the question? The words eventually started to run together, the beautiful script of the unknown priestess who had copied it during her pilgrimage looking like nothing but scribbles on the pages.

So I sat, in silence, damp and worn, and I prayed. I hadn't done such a thing with any actual conviction in years, and maybe never at all. Prayer had always seemed to me to be the thing that weak men did in desperation, when they had no other options. But I couldn't believe that the gods — if there even *were* any at all — just sat around and waited to answer the prayers of mortals. The world would be a much happier place indeed if that were true. But on the other hand… it was strangely comforting to think that someone, somewhere, cared enough to listen to my thoughts, not answering or judging, just listening with a patient ear. The only problem was, I could not, even with the best my imagination had to offer, convince myself that such a being was out there. I didn't know how to pray "harder" in the hopes that Catherine and her compatriots would suddenly spring into reality.

By dawn, my eyes were so dry they felt as if they were on fire, and I blinked over and over again in the light of the coming day. It gradually grew quite bright in the little chapel, with the sunlight creating interesting colored shadows and shapes on the clean, smooth stone floor. As time passed, the light stretched and morphed itself into new patterns; I watched this happen with great intent for a while, to where I almost failed to notice that I was no longer alone.

"You read too much, and you think too much," came Seraphine's voice wafting from the darkness down the hall. A door closed with a snick, followed by light footsteps.

"No, I'm telling you – I believe it." This was Andella's higher-pitched, pleasant tone, but this morning it had a hint of annoyance, maybe even anger.

"I know you do, and you are my sister so I have a certain obligation to listen to you, but, *I* believe that you read entirely too much. Faith is one thing. Blind, baseless faith is totally different. Besides, nothing's happened yet, which means nothing will happen, so just stop worrying about it."

"I know, but the book says…"

At this they emerged in the chapel, Sister Seraphine with her hands at her rather ample, white-clad hips, and Andella the Pyrelight at her side with her rose-colored lips slightly pursed.

"The book doesn't say *anything*," the priestess hissed as her dark eyes settled on me. She didn't seem entirely glad to see me sitting there, but smiled and said, "Good morning," nonetheless.

"Morning." I knew it took me far too long to answer because they both began to give me a sideways sort of look.

Seraphine smiled but it was an empty one, the sort of smile you give someone when you're trying a bit too hard to be cordial. "And how are we feeling this morning, Mister Loringham?"

"Ah… better. A bit better, thanks."

The smile became just slightly more genuine. "Well, good to see you up and about. At this rate you should be fine in no time." She then turned to her sister. "You're going to be all right while I go up to town? Do you need anything?"

"No, I'm sure we'll be able to manage ourselves – don't you think so, Tristan?" When she looked over at me expectantly, her expression was as warm and friendly as always.

"Sure – of course," I said with a nod.

"All right, then, I'm off." As Seraphine started toward the door, she leaned in toward Andella's ear and said something under her breath I couldn't quite hear. Not that I was trying to listen; their private conversations were their own, but that part of me that had been trained to feed on secrets lingered in the back of my mind, and was annoyed that their voices were just low enough to be imperceptible.

When the great doors at the front of the chapel closed behind the priestess, everything grew very quiet again, save for Andella's bare feet scuffing against the stone. "You're not feeling much better," the mage-girl said, very matter-of-fact. She took me a bit off-guard.

"I… I'm fine, really."

Still walking, she made a slight disapproving little sound under her breath. "You look… you look sad. And you haven't slept at all, have you?" She came to stop right in front of me, blocking some of that light so that it fell on her instead, adding streaks of blue and green and gold to the otherwise clean, unadorned white of her dress. Her long auburn hair was pulled back away from her face, revealing a pale, somewhat sober countenance and sunset-colored eyes.

I stared down at the floor. "No, I don't always sleep through the night. I, ah, have… problems with that. But don't worry about me. I'll be fine." I waited for sharp rebuttals consisting of how I would not heal well if I didn't rest, how I could become ill, and so forth, but they never came. Instead, when I looked back to her, her expression was one of concern, yes, but quiet, sympathetic concern.

"What's this?" she asked, picking up the dagger. She held it up in the light, regarding it with curiosity. I had left it sitting next to me on the pew and hadn't even thought about the fact that it shouldn't really be have been there at all until that moment.

"It was in my things. I was just... I don't know what I was doing, really." By the gods, I was an awful liar.

"It's beautiful." She wouldn't have said that if she knew the action it had seen. But of course, she didn't – she only watched the way the big ruby at the end caught the sunlight, the way the curving of the blade made reflections in it look just a tiny bit off-kilter.

I had the urge to take it away from her, put it away where the light couldn't reach it – in an odd way, I felt like it didn't really deserve to see the light of day anymore. It certainly didn't deserve to be admired. But instead, I resisted the urge. "It was a gift."

Eventually she turned back to me. "I'll put it away with your things so it's safe, then," she said, then darted off to one of the back rooms. I wondered if she had any idea that it hadn't been there in the pile of my bloodied and torn armor and other trappings with everything else. If she did, she said nothing. Within minutes, she was back. "So... didn't you sleep at all last night?"

"I just couldn't. I took a walk."

Her thin auburn eyebrows crinkled in closer to one another. "In the rain."

"In the rain." I suddenly felt rather silly; there was nothing sensible I was going to be able to say to explain that one. "It seemed like a good idea at the time."

At this she smiled, brightening her entire countenance – hell, it brightened the entire room. "If you say so," she said with a shrug. "Not that I would know – maybe a good walk in the rain is good for you. Bad for your clothes, though."

Yes, such a thing *was* bad for clothes. They were just now getting mostly dry, but there were still a few uncomfortable damp spots here and there. At least everything was relatively clean now. I fidgeted a bit with the collar of my tunic and pulled on my sleeves, stretching the cotton back out again to make it just a little bit tight and awkward-fitting instead of extraordinarily so. Not that it made a difference – borrowed clothes are better than none at all, and besides, I wasn't about to impress anyone anytime soon. I looked awful; I didn't even have to look in a mirror to know that, and in fact had been purposely avoiding mirrors for the past several days. No need to find a reason to feel even worse than I already did.

Luckily, none of that really seemed to faze Andella, who continued to smile her friendly, warm, bright smile. As the old saying goes, it was the kind of smile that could bring down empires. "We usually make tea in the morning... I have a garden out back where I grow some mint and chamomile flowers – it's not the best tea in the world, I'm sure, but it's not bad. Would you like some?"

The prospect of a good, proper cup of tea was enough to brighten my sour mood, if just a little. "Absolutely. That sounds great."

"Good! Come on – the kitchen's this way." I rose to follow her, but did it far too quickly for my own good – I was able to take two, maybe three steps before everything started wavering and getting very bright, like I'd looked up directly into a summer highsun. My legs gave out underneath me and my knees crashed into the unforgiving stone floor – at least I had one good hand available to catch some of the weight. I stayed there for a moment, letting this new experience in pain run its course with as much dignity as possible – which, admittedly, wasn't much.

"Are you all right?" She was by my side in an instant, voice and eyes full of alarm and anxiety. Her small, delicate hands pressed gently into my arm and her touch was warm, even comforting. "Are you all right?" she asked again, and this time I responded with a nod, slowly pushing myself back to sit on my heels. I felt like *such* an idiot. "Look, if you don't mind my saying so, you really need to take it easy. This isn't something you just suddenly recover from – it takes time, you know?"

I sat upright and slowly rubbed my temples, feeling a few beads of sweat drip off my brow and into my palm. "I know. But it would be nice if it were sooner rather than later. I'm getting a bit tired of this." I very slowly and awkwardly started to make my way to my feet, and as I did so, Andella firmed her grip, now wrapping one arm around my waist as if she were ready to lift me. Now, this was not really an uncomfortable situation to be in at all, don't get me wrong, but at the same time, it felt somewhat odd, even inappropriate, to accept her aid. I tried to wave her off but she made no attempt to move aside.

"Let me help." Her tone was quite insistent.

"No, you... I can't have you..." I stammered, but this only made her seem that much more resolute. I could see it quite clearly in those strange orange eyes – she was going to help whether I liked it or not.

"I'm stronger than I look. Come on." And she was right – her support was solid and unmoving as I leaned into her, so close I could feel the light warmth of her breath on my cheek, see each little crease in her lips as she pressed them together. She smelled good, too, like lemons mixed with something a bit earthier, maybe cinnamon. "Are you ready?" she asked after a moment, a bit insistent. I had lingered too close for far too long – the words "painfully obvious" sprang to mind. So I steeled myself and let her help me up to standing once again, graciously averting my concentration elsewhere.

"Um... thanks," I said, feeling clumsy as I found my own footing once again.

Andella smiled. "You can't rush getting better. You lost too much blood for that. I'm sure it's not that easy, but you have to give it time." I knew that, of course, but it didn't change my annoyed impatience with the whole thing.

We went to the kitchen together, stepping through the little door to the far eastern side of the chapel, just at the end of an arch of simplistic doves, wings outstretched and heading for some unseen horizon. Inside, it was brighter than I expected – in the center of a cluster of haphazardly arranged shelves and cabinets stood a large, clear glass window. The sun moved higher into the sky, letting in huge streams of warm light, and outside, it glittered against the puddles in the dirt and the drops of water lingering on the grass from the night's storm.

"Go ahead and sit down," Andella bade, going over to the small stone hearth – not a massive wall hearth like many Zondrell homes had, but an older floor one, where a hole was cut in the stone and coals and wood could be placed inside. The heat coming from it was comforting, cheerful, as pleasant as the smell coming from the pots hanging over it. I sat at the little wooden table nearby and watched as she stoked the fire, checked the water, searched around the cupboards for various things. I didn't pay a lot of attention to what she was doing, and might have even been lulled to sleep by the gentle heat of the room for a moment, until a cup full of hot liquid and a plate full of bread and butter and some grapes appeared in front of me.

"I guess we don't have much," she said with a disappointed scowl, "so I think we'll have to wait until Seraphine gets back from Market. She brought these grapes back the other day, though – they're pretty good. I think she said they were imported from Starlandia."

"It's perfect, thank you." The tea was excellent, the bread was excellent – the fact that I could taste any of it with any sense of clarity was really the best part. That, and as soon as I finished something, she brought me a little more.

She smiled weakly through sips of tea. "So, what do you think of life after the Academy?"

I almost choked. Did she really want to know? No, of course not. The hardships of battle and injuries and not seeing your family for months on end did not make for good breakfast conversation. "It's... different. Not quite what I expected it would be."

Her whole countenance brightened. "Yes! I agree. It's like we were in a whole different world for a while. Like the Academy isn't a real place."

I had to laugh aloud at this – she was absolutely right. "That's probably the best description I've ever heard. It's definitely not like real life."

"No, I know! It's great, don't get me wrong, but it's just so much like a fantasy of some kind, you know? You live in this nice place, get regular meals, get to study or train or do whatever all day. Did you start right when you turned eighteen?"

"I turned eighteen about two months after I started. My birthday's actually the day of Autumn Balance."

"Oh, I guess I'm older than you. By a few months anyhow." She smiled, and there was something very hidden in that smile – I wished I knew what it was. "I started just a few days after I turned eighteen. Seems like so long ago. You don't know what you're going to do with your life, then, you know? Well, I didn't, but about halfway through I decided to become a Pyrelight so I could help people, and everyone thought I was so odd for doing that. I come from a family of priests – it was my mum who wanted me to go there in the first place, and she was the priestess here before Seraphine took over. So it made sense. But learning magic and the rites and all of that, and actually doing the job are very different."

"Your job must be very difficult."

Andella shrugged. This was really the first time I'd had a chance to talk with her with any kind of intelligent thought behind it. There was energy in her voice, enthusiasm, as if she didn't get a chance to talk much with people on a regular basis. Well, if I could fill a void for her while getting a chance to listen and enjoy the company of a pretty girl, that was fine. It hardly mattered what we even talked about. "I didn't think it would be until the first time I attended to an actual funeral, if you can believe that. I just thought it would be simpler somehow, I guess. But the first time, I had just come home and I got a summons to go into town. So I went and there was a little girl who had died – some disease or something. It was just awful. I felt so badly for her parents, you know? Some people deal with the loss of their loved ones better than others – at least on the outside – but these people were heartbroken. Who could blame them?" She paused, took another sip, staring into the bottom of the cup for just a moment. "I felt really bad for your friend, too. Alexander? Er, Lord Vestarton, I suppose – right? Sorry. I just don't think... well, I don't think he took his father's death that well."

"Losing his father was difficult for him." To say that my friend was emotional was an understatement. Everything he did, he did with intensity. He *felt* everything, deeper than most people, certainly more deeply than I.

"Do you know he paid me seven hundred Royals instead of the seventy I was supposed to get? I tried to give it back to him and he just told me not to worry about it and walked away. I think... I think he'd been drinking. I just felt so sorry for him – he seemed really miserable."

"He was. He was very close to his father." Heavy drinking was probably the only thing that had kept him going through that time. This was not to be unfair or even dismissive about it – it was simple fact. Everyone has a way of coping with the tragic and the unseen, and a stiff drink had been Alex's way since we first started going to the Silver on a regular basis. Catherine smiles on a man who can smile through the pain, I suppose. But something else was bothering me. "So, wait – you only charged seventy Royals to travel all that way?"

"I normally charge fifty. I asked for a little more because it was so last minute, and far away. I felt bad about that too, but I had to pay for the trip and all. My sister almost fell over when she saw me bring home that much gold. We gave half of it to the big temple in Doverton."

I couldn't even fathom this. Seven hundred gold might have rivaled her entire earnings in the course of the entire year. Sure, their lives seemed simple here in the church, but seven hundred gold was... nearly nothing. I had dropped hundreds of Royals in the course of a single evening back in Zondrell, and I didn't consider myself all that extravagant. Money had a different kind of worth, I suppose, when you already had a lot of it. "I think you would be wise to charge a bit more."

"Oh, maybe. But I'm so new to it, and I don't want to overcharge. People don't have a lot of money these days... well, some people don't, I guess. But, yes, being a Pyrelight isn't a very happy profession, I suppose, but it's important, you know? People need to know their loved ones are going to be safely in Catherine's grace. That is... well, not to say that the military – what you do – isn't important too, of course."

"It has its place." I couldn't help but wonder, what exactly did she know about my work – my *actual* work? Hopefully, not enough. Of course, she likely wouldn't have been sitting there with me if she did know everything, and I wouldn't blame her for it.

"Sure, you all are keeping everyone safe. It's important. I suppose it's difficult, too – more difficult than attending funerals." Her attention dropped back to my shoulder for a moment. "Don't try to tell me otherwise, either. You're living proof of that. I mean, do you realize how blessed you are? A different angle, extra time with an untended wound like that, infections, blood lost – any of a million things could have killed you. But yet, here you are."

"Luck had a lot to do with it." Or something like that.

"Do you remember what happened?"

Even if I did remember every detail, which I didn't, I had no interest in telling her. Ever. This was a nice, sweet girl who retained within her the innocence of simple, honest living. There was no fucking way in Catherine's Purgatory I was going to purposely ruin that. So, I just shook my head and shrugged, non-committal.

"It's okay. Maybe it's for the best, right?" After getting up to refill our teacups again, she tried to change the subject, though it would take me a few minutes to realize that she hadn't really changed it at all. "So, last night, did you walk far?"

"Not really. Barely got further than the door. I just... needed some air."

"Oh. Good. I mean..." She looked down into the teacup sitting between her gently folded, thin hands. "Well, I'm probably not supposed to tell you this," she said, "but you shouldn't go out there by yourself. There are guards on the road." She pointed out the window. "See? You can sometimes see them patrolling."

Indeed, there were a couple of men dressed in the green livery of Doverton on the road at that moment, strolling along with purpose until they were no longer in view. It was hard to make out much in the way of detail, but they appeared armed. Interesting. "They aren't normally posted there?"

She looked across the table almost apologetic, as if to admit that there were guards in the vicinity was quite the insult. "Not really. I just know... well, we were told that you were 'dangerous.'" Her cheeks started to turn a nice rosy pink. "So we were supposed to go find the guards if there were any problems. It's silly, don't you think?"

"Who told you that – Saçaille?" Again, she nodded, so I had to ask the next natural question. "Did she say why?"

"No. That's all she said. She talks to my sister – I don't really talk to her. She's been here every day since you got here, until yesterday. I told her we'd send for her if we needed her. I wasn't very nice about it. I don't know, that woman just sort of... I don't like her that much. I know the King trusts her and all of that. But what do I know? I'm just a Pyrelight."

"Don't sell yourself short." When she smiled, I smiled, but something bothered me – how did the Eislander get past these guards last night? Unless he was working with them somehow? He knew Saçaille, mentioned her even... where did he fit into all of this? I couldn't help but ask, just to see what she might have known. "Tell me something: when I came here, who brought me? Saçaille?"

Her smile faded away, just a bit, and her eyes lit up brightly in their odd way. "No, no. Well, I don't really know who he was. It was... well, he said not to say anything to anyone."

He? Of course. Why he did it in the first place was the better question. I almost – *almost* – didn't care what his name was or even where he came from. But I had to know what she knew. There was no turning back. I reached out and placed my hand on top of her folded ones that she was trying so hard to keep steady and calm. I knew I was making her uncomfortable, but it was too late for worrying about that now. "I really need to know. Was it an Eislandisch man?"

She nodded. "Some warrior, very well-armed. Didn't speak much. Very tall, sort of like yourself. I don't know... Seraphine might have noticed more what he looked like. He burst in just as we were getting ready for bed that evening – frightened us half to death – and literally just sort of dropped you at the door. He told us that we needed to 'fix this' and that we never saw him. And then he left. I have no idea who he was. I mean, I've seen Eislandisch come through here before. You can usually tell if they're soldiers or merchants or whoever, but he had no markings or anything. Just a big sword. Is he a friend of yours?"

"No. But" – and maybe I shouldn't have said this – "he was here last night. I talked to him for a minute. Outside. I was thinking of how he might have gotten by those guards. Are they there at night?"

Her eyes widened. "I think so. Maybe... well, I don't know."

"Do you think he's connected to your sister's friend, Saçaille?"

"Oh, I don't know if 'friend' is a good word," she said, shaking her head. I could feel her anxiety nearly pouring out of her, and I felt bad about it, but I couldn't stop the conversation now. This was too important. "But listen, is this person, um, you know... dangerous?"

I had to think about this. Yes, absolutely. But to her? I had no idea. If he was, could I do anything about it? I'd bloody well give it my best. "No, don't worry about him."

"What did he say to you?"

"He just wanted to know how I was, I suppose. He wasn't here more than a moment."

"Hm, well, let's... let's not say anything to my sister when she comes back. She'll be worried, I think. But I would like to know, too, about Madame Saçaille. I don't know what they talk about, but sometimes she and my sister talk for quite a while. Especially lately. Maybe it's none of my business, but I... I don't really like it."

She looked like she was nearly in tears, making me want to change the subject – fast. I shouldn't have said anything in the first place. "Let's not worry about it for now, yeah?" I fought to look her directly in the eye. I found my next words were not as easy to say aloud as I would have thought. "And... ah, thank you. I mean, I appreciate what you're doing for me. You certainly didn't have to take me into your home and all of that. But I promise you, *I'm* not dangerous."

"Oh, I know that! Seraphine does too, don't worry. I don't know what's going on – it's really probably not my business. But until you get better, well, just don't wander off." She giggled softly, and her entire demeanor changed to a much lighter one, calmer and less worried. Whether it was a front or genuine, though, I couldn't quite tell. "How about you let me take a look at that wound? It's probably time to change the bandage." She scurried off to get her supplies, rushing back nearly as fast as she'd left with a roll of white fabric and a small glass vial.

I did not enjoy the bandage changing ritual, not at all. Her presence and that way she prattled on as she worked, mostly chatting about nothing important, was the only thing that made it survivable. Otherwise, between the awkward way I had to hold my arm up and the yellow, foul-smelling ointment she used to keep the infections out, it was nightmarish. But nonetheless, I dutifully removed my shirt and let her commence the attack.

The old bandage was partially in ruins since it had been wet for so long overnight, but otherwise nothing looked much different than it had the day before, except with a small amount of dried blood scattered around the edges of the wound, thick dark flecks standing out against a canvas of yellow and purple bruising. The few stitches I could see clearly were starting to look withered and worn – they would have to come out soon.

Andella moved her chair to sit at my right, angling to face me with her legs crossed, knees nearly touching mine. We sat so close together that I could feel the heat from her body, and a few stray locks of her long auburn hair grazed ever-so-gently against my skin. I had to concentrate with every possible ounce of will to control my breath, my heartbeat... and all the other reactions that the typical man might get in such close quarters with a girl this lovely. It would have taken nothing, just the tiniest movement, to lean in and kiss her. As she settled in to her work, I couldn't help but watch – not looking at what she was doing, but just watching *her*. She had an intense, focused look on her face, but the pinkish skin around her eyes and the corners of her mouth were smooth, free of the creases that form from stress. And in the bright light of that little kitchen during the daytime, I noticed something about her eyes, something I'd never realized before. Within the pulses of orange, there were flecks of emerald green, nearly the same color as grass in late spring – this must have been her eye color before she became a mage, I assumed. The interplay between the dark, non-luminescent green and the vivid orange was quite intriguing, beautiful, even, in a strange sort of way. I'd never taken a good look at a mage's eyes up close before, especially not a Fire mage. With Water and Earth, the color is unusually bright, but blue and green are natural, everyday eye colors. Even Air mages' white eyes aren't completely off-putting, but orange is never something you see in a person's features. It was bizarre and fascinating.

"You know, if you keep staring at me like that, I may have to say something." She glanced up at me out of the corner of her eye and I instantly felt the hot flush of embarrassment wash over me. With a sharp intake of breath, I turned my head as far in the other direction as humanly possible.

"I apologize," I said quietly. "I was just, um, ah..." Well, nothing I was going to say was going to work out well for me, so I left it at that.

There was a hint of amusement in her tone. "I didn't say it was a bad thing. I don't really get looks like that all that often."

When I turned back, being careful to pay close attention to where my gaze settled, she was smiling. I felt my whole body relax just a little. "I have a hard time believing that," I replied.

Her laughter echoed throughout the room. "Are you trying to be charming?"

My cheeks felt like they were on fire, and it had nothing to do with the warmth of the hearth. "Ah... well... Only if it's working." Laughing, she carefully finished up by wrapping a thin strip of clean cotton around my shoulder, and just like every time we went through this little ritual, having to hold my arm up while she did so was pure torture. I let it settle back down to its normal resting position again very, very slowly, and relief flooded through the entire right side of my body. "Really, I'm sorry," I said. "It won't happen again."

"And I told you not to worry about it." There was that smile again, lingering for almost longer than was comfortable before she spoke again. "You know, oddly enough, a lot of men – *especially* the kinds that go to academies in Zondrell – just aren't too interested in a girl who wants to spend half her time with the dead." Again, her laughter sounded ever-so-slightly like bells ringing within the chapel walls. I had to join her this time.

"Zondrellian men aren't too bright." Myself included – of course, I wasn't quite willing to let slip that particular thought. "You're better off."

Her smile and gaze wandered off, worlds away from where we sat. "Tell me something, do you believe in fate, Tristan?" she asked after a moment.

Shaking my head, I found I could only be honest. "I never really thought about it."

"Not everyone does." She smiled as her attention dropped back to my shoulder, this time to the image of the dragon carved into the skin there. Very gently, she ran her fingers across it; pulsing sensations danced out across my skin in every direction. It was damn near too much to tolerate, and before I realized what I was doing, it was already far too late. I had almost no control over my actions for what seemed like a very long time, but it actually only lasted for a moment, just long enough to taste the slight hint of sweetness on her lips. I think I was even more surprised than she was when it was over.

"I'm sorry." My voice was hoarse and barely audible as I pulled away, looked away into a dark corner of the room. "I... That was inappropriate. I apologize." The kitchen suddenly felt very lonely and cold while I awaited a response – a slap in the face, a terse scolding, something. Instead, she said exactly what I would *never* have expected.

"What's to apologize for?" When our eyes met again, hers were smiling as she gently bit her bottom lip in that way that some women do sometimes when they're waiting expectantly. Compulsion took over – I wanted her, *needed* her. So I pulled her toward me and kissed her again, and to my amazement, she did nothing but reciprocate in kind. When I wrapped my arms around her waist to feel her warmth, her body rose to meet mine. When my fingertips traced along the gentle curves hidden beneath her dress, she only breathed more deeply, held me against her more firmly. Her frame was so soft and light that I could carry her weight, even with just one arm; when I moved to do so, to perhaps find a more comfortable and private space, she never winced, didn't hesitate or ask me to stop. So, I didn't.

I don't believe I need to make clear what happened next; indeed, I'm not sure that I could, even if I were so inclined. The moments passed by in a whirl of feelings and sensations that defied explanation. Flushed and wild exhilaration swept away all of the tension and the pain and the anger that had been collecting in me over the past months, replacing it all with a sense of stillness. I had never felt anything like it before. Lying there with her, with this beautiful and gentle creature that I hardly knew, but yet I felt as if I had known her for years... I was at *peace*. There was no other word to describe it. I could have died right there and then, and would have been happy to endure whatever Judgment awaited me. As it was, when it was over, it took almost no time at all for the persistent steadiness of Andella's heartbeat to lull me into the deepest, most dreamless sleep I'd experienced in a very, very long time.

**

When I woke, the light outside the little window overlooking the bed was fading. I surveyed my surroundings, trying to get my bearings in this new, foreign place. The down-filled bed beneath me was soft and warm and piled high with cotton blankets, so much so that it was one of those beds that you could foresee spending an entire day in. Even my own bed at home in Zondrell didn't quite seem to compare. But, it was still missing something. Lazily, I rolled over – no, definitely missing something.

I was alone.

The normal collection of silly, useless questions started filling my head. I lay looking up at the ceiling for a good several minutes, pondering the various truths and consequences that drifted through my mind while avoiding the different items and trappings of the rest of Andella's small, modest bedchamber. It seemed somehow wrong to investigate her things, to flip through the pile of books spread haphazardly at the side of the bed, or contemplate the humble collection of feminine items like jewelry and perfume resting atop the only other piece of furniture in the room besides the bed itself, a waist-high wooden chest of drawers. Of course, investigating and simply observing were very different things, and I took all of this in as the thoughts continued to churn away, my mind wide awake while my body remained content to linger for a little while longer.

I turned my head to the left and noticed the pile of books – there were actually quite a few, most laying on their sides with the spines facing outward so that the titles were visible, but others were resting against each other in various, off-kilter ways, as if they had been tossed aside in the depths of a sleepless night. Dried bits of candle wax dotted some of the aging leather covers. I couldn't help myself; I had to take a closer look, but just a look, though, certainly not to touch. They weren't mine, after all. Among them were some very interesting things indeed: a very old copy of *Sarabande Rising*, a Zondrean translation of the old Lavançaise love story *Étienne et Larenne*, the long version of *All Love Lost*, a myriad of classic stories, biographies, and histories that any learned Zondrean would be quite familiar with. But there were others there, too – many were religious, with titles referring to gods and souls and so forth, but there was one that caught my eye, titled simply, *Lebenkern*. That was an Eislandisch word – it meant something along the lines of, "the core of life" – and the weathered finish on the cover and antiquated lettering on the spine made me think it was written decades ago. An odd series of circles, enveloped by another circle, was the only other adornment, stitched into the leather below the title. I thought about that word, *Lebenkern*, and it seemed so familiar, but it couldn't be... could it? Besides, what would an old Eislandisch book be doing in a small roadside temple to Catherine, in Doverton, at the bedside of a young Pyrelight?

In the tiff Seraphine and Andella had that morning, they mentioned a book and how Andella read too much. And I thought about the quote from a scrap I read a few weeks ago, while I was reading some papers about the Kaeren that someone had sent up from the city by messenger. *An ancient temple, lost between mountains.* That came from the text that had lured Zondrell up to this area in the first place. The scholars studied it, the King got wind of it, and he knew he had to send out men to look for what could lay here hidden, waiting to be discovered, exploited, leveraged. I had studied parts of that text, too, had pored through pages of script over half a dozen ridiculously cold, sleepless nights, hoping I'd get some kind of revelation from the words... I never did. They were just words, a faery story of bygone times told to children.

Kaeren... kern – such similar words. What if... ? With a very deliberate hand, I reached out to pull the book from its resting place, my fingers briefly tracing the etched letters and the circular symbol. *Lebenkern* – what did it mean? My hands trembled as I opened it, taking great care not to damage the thin, yellowing paper upon which someone had carefully scripted verse after verse. The language was archaic, but readable enough for someone who had some command of written Eislandisch to make sense of it.

"Holy fucking Catherine in Paradise," I said to myself as I read the first few words. For a moment I thought I might still be asleep and dreaming, but this was all very real. Otherwise I wouldn't have been able to feel the cold sweat beading on my forehead, or the coppery taste from swallowing too hard.

Seven elements comprise the energy of this world – the Greater Three are lost, but not gone. They live and wait for a new dawn, this, the dawn of Prophecy. Time stops, half a hero's blood soaks the land to bring forth new Life, bearing with it the Light of a new age.

Seven elements... Greater Three? What did that mean? Maybe it meant nothing. Maybe it was just another story, but there was something about those words. I thought back to all of the other things I had read, which seemed like nothing more than a big blur of information now. Magic had been discussed in some of the texts, but mostly, the things I had read had referred to weapons and warnings – how the world might suffer if things got out of hand. There was some indication that whatever "Kaeren" was had gotten sealed away centuries ago, somewhere in Eisland, or near it, because it was so dangerous. But with danger comes power, and that was the allure. I could just imagine what something like that could do for Zondrell.

I flipped through the book some more, choosing random pages – the further in I got, the harder it was to follow, but I did notice some notes written in the margins here and there in a flowing but hasty scrawl. It looked like someone was trying to translate certain passages, sometimes well, sometimes not so well. At one point, there was a part about some sage taking a trip up a mountain, but the notes said it was a wizard going to a town. On another page, the book spoke of a great "seal" of some kind, but the notes said it was a circle, and there were question marks surrounding it, as if the writer was sure that couldn't be the right word. I wondered who the note-taker was – could it have been Andella herself?

"Ah, good evening." Her voice piercing through the stillness and my own veil of concentration caused me to almost drop the book. I looked up and found it extremely difficult to breathe all of the sudden. "Helping yourself to my books, eh? I didn't think I was gone that long."

Andella set down two small clay cups near a pile of books, making a dulled clinking sound as they came to rest on the stone. Steam poured out over their sides, sending the smell of chamomile in all directions. She then sat down next to me on the edge of the bed, folding one leg gracefully beneath her while the other dangled a few inches above the floor. She was barefoot, wearing only that simple white cotton dress, and while her expression was soft, I could feel the warmth rising from her body, noted the flare in her eyes.

"I just noticed it there. I didn't... I really didn't mean to pry into your things." I stumbled over my words, feeling like a complete and utter jackass.

The glint in her eyes didn't change, nor did her expression. "It's fine. Can you read that? The language, I mean?" Sheepish, I nodded. "Oh. Interesting. I spent a lot of time trying to translate that book when I was at the Magic Academy. It wasn't that easy – I spent a lot of time in the library."

"I used to go there to study for exams sometimes – they had a better collection than our Academy." Of course, I could only get in there during certain times of the week. The rest of the time, the Magic Academy's Great Library was closed to outsiders, and sometimes even to its own students. On those times when I was able to get in, I was only allowed access to a few of the wings, which was a fine trade for the peace and quiet.

"Really?" Her expression softened, and she flashed that lovely smile. "I would have said something if I'd seen you there."

She would have had to. I would never have noticed her or anyone else otherwise. I was far too buried in my studies, especially at that time when exams had started to truly count. I still harbored that fantasy of teaching there someday, too. If you wanted to pass, you had to know your stuff – and I wanted *every* single point. But, she was trying to change the subject again. "Look, this book of yours... it said there were seven elements, something about three being lost to this world. What do you think that means?"

She shrugged, and when she spoke there was – surprisingly – no hint of deception. "I think maybe it means what it says. But, I don't know what would happen if anyone found such a thing." She started to say something else, but just then something made a noise beyond the closed door.

Faint scratchy, shuffling sounds drifted through the walls, and we looked at each other.

"Your sister?" I asked.

She shook her head and stood, smoothing her dress and hair with rapid, nervous movements. "Maybe. If it is, you had better stay quiet and out of sight. I really don't want to talk to her about... us... just yet. It's easier that way. She wouldn't... well, just wait here."

The door clicked softly shut behind her, and I listened intently for more noises. There were many, becoming louder. I realized that these were the sounds of people – several of them. At first, I assumed it was a group of travelers or merchants, but something seemed off about the sounds they made. Metal... These people were carrying or wearing a significant amount of metal, most likely armor and weapons. My heart quickened as the blood turned hot throughout my entire body; I struggled to listen over my own heartbeat. My thoughts jumped to a thousand different conclusions all at once, none of them positive.

And all it took was a brief cough and a muffled question to confirm one of the worst scenarios imaginable. I knew that voice anywhere.

Frantic, my eyes scanned the room. There were no exits here except for the door to the chapel – the windows were far too small to crawl through even if I could break the thick glass. Trapped... completely trapped. A bead of sweat rolled down my forehead, splashed onto my cheek, but otherwise I made no movements at all. I could barely breathe.

More muffled voices, words and identities too indistinct to hear. Could I be quiet enough to get out of bed to listen at the door – and find a modicum of dignity – with my heart racing and my body weak and battered? My muscles steeled themselves for the venture; yes, I could do this, I told myself, the words imprinting themselves on my mind as I rolled to my side, located the clothing that had been quite carelessly tossed aside just a few hours ago, and made my way toward the door. It took an eternity, but I disturbed nothing, didn't stumble, and never even took too heavy of a step.

When I got to the door I leaned against the frame, turning my head to listen through the cracks. I had to close my eyes and concentrate, straining to hear while keeping the swirling voices in my own head at bay. "… you live here, then?" I heard. This was definitely a familiar voice. Victor Wyndham? It could be no other – the air of superiority in his tone was undeniable. But why would he be *here*?

"Yes, I live here, with my sister," replied Andella. She sounded a bit vexed, nervous. The anxiety in her voice just made the sweat on my brow pour down that much more. "She's the priestess. I told you that."

"Right, of course," Victor said. "And neither of you have seen anyone unusual come by in the past week? Someone dressed like one of us, perhaps?"

"You mean a Zondrell soldier? Here?" Andella paused. This was it, this would be the moment. I put my hand on the doorknob but paused. I was not going to let them barge in and take me, kill me, whatever they decided to do with me. I was a man – I could face my fate like one. But even so, I couldn't make myself turn that handle. Not yet.

"No, m'Lord," came Andella's voice again, quiet but confident. It was enough to convince almost anyone that she was indeed telling the truth. "I haven't seen anyone like that. What would a Zondrell solider be doing all the way up here?"

My eyes popped open wide as I drew in sharp, painful breaths. What did she say? Did I hear it right?

Victor cleared his throat. His tone was very slow, calculated, as if he were trying to explain something complicated to a five year-old. "Well, you see, Miss, there's been a bit of an incident, just northwest of here. Some of our men were… attacked, and there were many casualties." The weight of those words and the memories that came with them were heavier than all the iron in Zondrea, resting directly over my heart.

"But," he continued, "the good news is that some seem to have escaped, as well. Injured men may have come here for help, or may have made their way into Doverton. We're trying to find everyone we can. So recently, are you certain you haven't seen anyone like that, maybe someone who's been hurt and looking for healing? Someone even who's come and gone, someone you might have forgotten about?" No one but Victor Wyndham could ask a few simple questions and still manage to sound like such a pompous ass.

"Zondrean, or Eislandisch." This was another voice I knew immediately – Peter Wyndham. That slightly high-pitched, irritating tone could only be one person in this world.

"Oh... no, not at all." Andella sounded even more nervous now, but she made every effort to sound calm, yet concerned at the same time. "The Eislandisch don't come in here too often, unless it's merchants looking to escape bad weather." She paused. "Is Zondrell at war with Eisland again or something?"

"We're not at liberty to discuss our mission, Miss," came Peter's abrupt reply.

"Oh," she said again. "I'm not sure how else I can help you, although I am a Pyrelight. If you take me to the... to the battlefield, I'm sure I can help ease the souls to Catherine's side."

"We've taken care of that already." The pang of bitter sorrow in Peter's tone was unmistakable, and I shared it silently with him. But I also felt relieved – I didn't want her going anywhere with any of those men.

"I see. Well, my sister is up in town, probably at the temple. Maybe some of your people are there."

"Perhaps," said Victor at some length. "If you don't mind, I think we really would like to look around a bit anyhow. We need a moment to rest."

There was a long pause, some shuffling but mostly silence. I could feel the waves of panic gripping my muscles, my lungs, my heart – what was I going to do? Just wait here for gods-knew-what to happen? I had never felt so helpless. Then another voice floated in from the other side of the door, and even though that rich Lavançaise accent sent a chill through my every nerve, I was all too happy to hear it. "Actually, I believe I observed some of your men on the road toward Doverton yesterday. Hurt. But I patrol this area personally, and have not seen anyone in this particular temple other than Mademoiselle, here, and her sister."

Victor's voice dripped with irritation. "And you are?"

"Onyx Saçaille, Weapon Master to my Lord King, Eric Bradenton, of Doverton. I will escort you and your men to the city. I may even be able to get you an audience with the King."

Another pause, maybe some quiet whispers of deliberation. "We need to speak to him, yes. Please lead the way." There was some shuffling of feet, various clinks and clanks, and then a moment of hesitation. Victor cleared his throat again. "You know, you look familiar to me... have you ever been to Zondrell?"

"She attended to my father's funeral." This was Alexander Vestarton, my best friend in the world – I would know that voice anywhere, no matter how hoarse and angry it sounded. There was a part of me that wanted to burst out of there and talk to him, tell him what was going on... and there was another part of me that wished he had never left the safety of Zondrell.

Andella sounded a bit taken aback. "Yes, m'Lord – and I went to Academy there as well."

"Yes, that's right." Victor paused to bask his self-righteous pomposity for a moment. Then, he said, "You know, I find it hard to understand how an Academy-trained mage winds up as a Pyrelight, especially out here."

Now there was a definite hint of venom in the Fire mage's tone. As it was with most people, Victor had managed to thoroughly annoy her. "I help people deal with their grief, and help the dead move on to a better place. There's nothing wrong with that."

"No, of course not, good lady. I'm sure you do a wonderful job at what you do. It just seems to me that someone with your, ah... refinement of skill might be better suited to work at a royal court, or perhaps back at the Academy doing research. Or, even better, serving your country."

"Well, Sir, if you don't mind me saying so, I believe that when finances are not an issue in your family, you can take luxuries like that with your future profession. I, however, do not come from such a family. Now, if you will, I have some cleaning and chores to get done, otherwise I would invite you all to stay and pray. But the temple in Doverton is not too far, and much bigger and more comfortable than this place. I'm sure it will suit you gentlemen just fine."

"Of course." Thoroughly put in his place, Victor's voice became even more officious than before. "Thank you for your time, Miss... ah?"

"Weaver."

"Thank you, Miss Weaver. Enjoy your evening."

I sank to the floor as I heard them begin to take their leave. All of my strength just simply gave out, no longer able to maintain the tension that had been building up within me – breathing was difficult, much less standing. I leaned against the cold wall feeling a hundred conflicting emotions at once. And the questions... there were too many to count.

After a moment, Alex's voice pierced the air once again. His voice sounded strained and fatigued, almost as if he were drunk. "If it's all right, I'd like to stay a bit? Take a rest?"

Andella stammered out a few um's and ah's, but it was Saçaille, cool as ever, who actually replied. "Of course, Monsieur. You will be safe here. I will send someone to bring you to Doverton when you are feeling well."

Just like that? I could feel the hesitation from Andella – and probably Victor as well – from all the way on the other side of the building. As for me, I felt considerably torn between wanting to be someplace else, *anywhere* else, and wanting to rush in and see my old friend. What would he say, I wondered? What was he doing up here at all?

The outside door closed with a considerable, decisive thud, and the place went quiet, save for some shuffling of feet and a few muttered, indecipherable words. Whatever they may have said to each other, I would never know. Hell, I couldn't even find the strength to stand up by myself to go out there and find out.

Eventually, the bedroom door finally creaked open, and Andella found me with my head buried in my arms, staring silently at the hard stone beneath me. I said nothing. What was there to say?

Taking up our cooling teacups, she knelt next to me, leaning up against the wall with her hips resting gently on her heels. Once she'd set the cups down within reaching distance, she rested one warm hand on my arm. I flinched and looked up into eyes that were not quite angry, moist with sadness and pulsing brightly with their own internal light and heat. The orange flecks within her irises almost looked like flames feeding off of fresh tinder, and the color very nearly matched the high color in her cheeks. She said nothing.

I found I could hardly look at her as I spoke. "They were my men. We were ambushed."

"I know."

"Look, this is all very complicated," I began to ramble on, grasping for words. "And, I just don't... um, well you see, I can't... Wait – what did you just say?"

"I said I know. Well, some of it. My sister said there was a battle, and... well, you should come out into the chapel now. It's safe. Your friend's waiting." Her grip grew on my forearm grew slightly tighter.

There is a certain feeling you get when you're disarmed in a fight. Only those who have felt this can truly understand it, but it is a moment of self-doubt and vulnerability and utter fear the likes of which are unprecedented in any other situation. It is the moment that you realize you have lost your protection, the only thing allowing you some control over whether the next breath you take will be your last. I had never felt more like that in that instant, and there weren't even any weapons in sight. "I don't know if I can go out there."

"You can. You need to." Despite what I expected, there was no anger or scolding in her tone or her manner; instead, it seemed like she simply wanted to understand the truth, nothing more and nothing less. She even reached out and placed her hand on mine, and her touch was so soothing... It was a shame I was going to disappoint her so very deeply. I genuinely liked her. I might have even been in love, although I had little idea what being in love felt like.

"What I did... I don't know if I did the right thing," I told her.

The slightest of smiles graced her pretty, rose-colored lips. "It's okay. You still need to talk about it."

She was right. There was no sense in denying anything anymore. Slowly, feeling I was wearing a full suit of leaden armor, I scraped myself up off the floor and followed her into the chapel.

The last light of day was almost gone, but the sconces were lit in the modest temple of Catherine, sending shadowy, fleeting figures here and there around the room. But there was one figure that didn't dissolve into the firelight, sitting far back at the very last pew, partially clouded in a smoky haze. Alex... I wasn't sure I would ever see him again. When he saw me, he sprang up, approaching with a sword raised in one outstretched hand. Maybe this was it – maybe this was the justice waiting for me. Slain by my best friend. Nonetheless, I stood my ground.

"You look like hell, Brother," he said. In the light and close up, I would have said the same about him. His clothes were wrinkled and unkempt, his hair was a wild disaster, and it was obvious he had not slept well in at least a day, maybe longer. But, I could see that familiar glint in his eyes, that sly sort of mirth that was "classic" Alexander Vestarton. There was something else there as well, though. His eyes… well, they weren't as dark as they used to be. There was something strange and cloudy affecting the color of them, turning them from their normal deep brown to a murky silver. I'd never seen anything like it. I was so transfixed by the sight that I didn't even realize that he had turned the sword over, presenting me not with the blade, but with the hilt. "This is yours, I believe. You're lucky I found it."

I couldn't seem to get past the eyes. I thought I might know what it was, but how could that be? It made no sense. "What's… what's wrong with your eyes?"

Now the smile touched his tips. "Save it, Brother. You first."

I took my bloodied and battered sword away from him, staring at it for a moment before resting it against the nearest pew. It was truly the last thing I wanted to look at then. "How did you find me?" I asked.

The smile was still there. "Stroke of luck," he said. "But I'm not here to talk about me."

"I know."

With that, he reached out and gave me a big, gruff hug – the sort of hug that erases the pain of disappointment and shame and misunderstanding. Whatever I was going to say next, I would say amongst friends. I would like to say that such sentiment made me feel better, but it really didn't.

So the three of us sat there before the altar of Lady Catherine and had tea – delicate, fragrant, damned perfect tea. And Alex and Andella listened patiently while I started talking – rambling, really, but at least I did have enough sense to start at the beginning. I wouldn't have known where else to begin.

1

Alexander Vestarton

We arrived late – deep into the night when only wolves and owls were supposed to be awake. We did stop once, for an evening meal and a break, and it had set us back a bit, but night wound up being the best possible time to get there. Seeing that place in full daylight would have been far too much.

The cold was the worst thing, utter ridiculous cold for the time of year. At some point, I heard snow crunching underfoot and realized that, some of the winter snow had not yet melted. Snow, even this early into Spring's Dawn? Bizarre! It wasn't even normal fluffy snow, either, but icy sheets of it, hiding in deep trenches where you could slip or get stuck in it. Around here, you could snap your ankle if you weren't paying attention. And the air – the air smelled so crisp, so vibrant, but it was also a little difficult to breathe. Not that we were all that far away from Zondrell, but being away from the seashore, away from the shelter of the lowest parts of the forest valley, was just enough to change the whole climate within just a few miles. The more we walked the worse it got, but I should have been thankful for the thin air, because it didn't carry odors as well.

"I think we're almost there," Delrin said. He hadn't said anything to me since right after dusk. I almost asked him how he knew that, but I found I didn't have to – I could smell it. It was an evil smell, horrible, like something out of a nightmare. Of course, this one had its own special charms that made it unique – not only was it the stench of death, but of cold death, smothered with the burnt ashes of old wood and cloth and flesh. Eventually, it grew so strong that it was all I could smell – I couldn't take my mind off of it, and no amount of *tsohbac* or torch smoke in the world would cover it up.

Right outside the sign that pointed toward the village of Südenforst, I knelt down and promptly lost everything I had just eaten a few hours ago. I don't think I was the only one, either.

"You all right, my Lord?" asked Delrin, more as a courtesy than out of genuine concern. I nodded and gave up the very last of my evening meal.

Somewhere at the head of the group, I heard Victor shout something, and then some more random men shouted back. What they said I didn't know, didn't care. My mind spun lazily, like I was drunk, yet I wasn't. I *wished* I were. A strong hand guided me to my feet and I made my way toward the sounds, toward the shouting, stepping gingerly along so as not to trip on anything... well, on anything that wasn't exactly a rock. And I didn't have to look down to know they were there, either – how many bodies littered the ground there? There were maybe just a few that hadn't been picked up and tended to yet, but that was enough for me.

The shouting had ended. What had they been doing over there anyhow? But when I got up to what must have been the village's main road – now little more than a stretch of hard-packed dirt covered with ash – I realized it must have been happy shouting because Victor had found what he came for. Peter Wyndham was there, alive and perfectly fine. The brothers were locked in a rough embrace, saying how happy they were to see each other, happy Peter wasn't hurt, that sort of thing. Sure, he wasn't hurt at all – even in the partial darkness, I could see Peter hardly had a scratch on him... the little whelp. He looked pretty bad, though, unshaven and dirty, his black falcon tabard and leather armored breeches all splattered with blood and torn and tattered. There were other soldiers around, too, looking just as bedraggled, milling about even at this time of night, keeping watch over what was left of the place, arranging things, tending to the wounded. Tending to the dead. There was a lot of work left to be done.

"What happened here, Brother?" Victor asked, obviously a bit awestruck by the whole thing as well. His words came out slowly and his voice was weak, cracking at the high points as if he hadn't slept for days on end.

Peter shook his head, folded his arms across his stout chest and appeared to look important. He didn't pull it off very well, though, because his eyes were shiny and quivering, especially noticeable amongst the flickering torches we held. I actually felt a little sorry for him. This wasn't quite the same scheming, competitive jackass I knew from the Academy. Something was different about him now – places like this must make you grow up a lot faster than most young noblemen would like. It was certainly changing my outlook on life as we stood there. I found myself unable to focus on any one thing. There were shadows and movement all around – dark and evil shadows, moving so sad and so slow. I noticed low piles of... something, stacked up not that far away, misshapen and with a sense of density, of weight. I tried very hard not to think about what I knew *that* was. In the faint light of the moons and our torches, I could also see row upon row of tall, thin things sticking up out of the ground, not far from the awful piles I didn't want to think about. They were tall and thin, some almost perfectly straight and others with decorations at the top, and they were all lined up just so, like a row of corn in a field somewhere. But it wasn't corn... no, it had to be swords, the swords of the fallen, far, far too many of them.

"We got fucked, that's what happened," Peter replied, blunt, almost spitting his words out. His use of the Zondrean language had apparently suffered a bit since his departure for this campaign.

Ever one to get right down to business, Victor started firing off questions like arrows. "Shilling and Loringham? Where are they?"

"Shilling's hurt – he's resting on the other side of town... well, over there. He'll be fine, I think." He turned his attention on me then, followed my gaze to the misshapen heavy horrifying pile in the near distance. "He's not in there," he told me – did he even sound a little sympathetic? "Last time I saw Loringham, he was ripping a dagger out of his chest."

That strange bad news sensation took hold of me, but in an entirely new way. It shook me down to the core, through flesh and bone and nerve. I thought I might vomit yet again, but there was nothing left. The cold Eislandisch air gripped me so fiercely that I found myself shivering. Did that mean that... "Is he dead?" My voice was so flat and hollow that I wasn't even sure it was actually me who had said it.

Peter shook his head, ran a dirt-smudged hand through his unwashed, unkempt dark hair. "I don't know. Maybe. He's not here, that's all I know."

Victor cleared his throat. "A soldier from this unit came to the Council yesterday morning, gave a report. Young one, um... Rockbarren or something like that was his name. General Torven sent me up here to investigate."

"Rockwarren. Really, ran all the way home, did he?" Peter turned his head and spat on the ground. "Fucking coward."

"*You* look like you're perfectly fine. Guess the attackers missed you, did they?" I couldn't help myself. I *wasn't* myself, really – didn't feel like it, anyhow. On the other hand, of course, I didn't much care for any Wyndham, especially the men, and they didn't care for me, and that's just the way it was. A small part of me actually wanted to do something violent to Peter, the way he was staring at me with his round saucer eyes narrowed, piercing and absolutely furious. One hand settled on the sword at his belt as he stepped in closer, until I could smell the sweat and grime and fear clinging to him.

"You're a Lord now, aren't you?" he asked, and I nodded. "Well, when you find out what it's like to have people dying all around you, while you're fighting for your own life, you come back and talk to me. Until then, shut the fuck up... m'Lord."

I had a weapon, too. It was just a shortsword and I didn't use it very well, but I had one. I could feel its weight on my hip – cold, comforting, powerful – and I thought about it. I really did. Because I could just envision it, I could imagine what might have happened here. Townspeople scurrying about, tensions flaring, an argument between the officers. Over what, it probably didn't matter. But what would it take to make a cocky, hot-tempered man like Peter Wyndham turn on a comrade, especially one he already didn't like?

It wouldn't take much.

A thin but exceedingly strong hand gripped me by the shoulder, pulling back just enough to make me move with it. I could feel a tiny flare of icy cold, unnatural, transfer through my clothes, down into my skin. The chill burned, if such a thing were possible, and when I glanced up at Victor Wyndham his eyes gleamed like bright blue candles in the dark. "Go have a smoke, Vestarton." So I did, wandering off by myself, but not too far – I wanted to hear what they had to say.

"You're all right, then? Good – I was worried. So, just... Well, the solider who spoke to us, he said there was some fighting between you and Loringham, and then the ambush came. What happened, Peter?" Victor said to his brother, and there was a long silence. Eventually, though, Peter did speak. He started at the beginning.

"We came here on a tip," he began. "Loringham had finally gotten something, I guess. We were supposed to come down here and really start searching. Someone here was supposed to know something, or maybe it was actually supposed to be here... I don't remember. Doesn't matter because it was all horseshit anyhow. There was nothing but women and children here. It's a mining village – all the men are off in gods-know-where, underground mining for gold and gems or some such. But we were told that someone probably knew something, so we rounded them all up, lined them up in the road here. That's when Tristan started taking issue with the way we were doing things – can you fucking believe it? He said we were treating them like prisoners, and we were just there to question them, but I started to wonder... I mean, I don't speak the language, I don't want to, but the tone he used to talk to them was... it was *nice*. Sympathetic. It made me sick. And that's when it hit me – this whole thing's been one lie after another."

Victor's deeper, frailer voice piped in. "You know what you're saying, don't you, Brother?"

"Sure I do. I called him out." The more Peter spoke, the faster his speech became, until his words were almost tripping over one another. "I mean, why the fuck have we been here in this miserable fucking cold, awful place? This is what I asked him, and he says it's because he hasn't gotten the information. Well, what the hell? It's been four months, two bloody seasons in this hellhole, and there was *no* information to be had from *any* of the people we brought in? I can't even tell you how many patrols we went through, and you're telling me that not one of them had even ever *heard* of the Kaeren? It's common legend at least. Are you fucking kidding me? No, it's not possible. It's just not. And then to bring all of us all the way out here to this... *hamlet* and be sympathetic to *these* people? No, something was going on, and I called him on it."

Peter's voice had risen in volume about three times over. Everyone within a three-mile radius could probably have heard him. I hung on his every word, intent, puffing on my *tsohbac* without really tasting it or smelling it or even breathing it in. The simple act of having it was enough. None of those words, unfortunately, seemed to make much sense. Patrols? Information? For the love of Catherine, what exactly were they doing up here?

"All right, all right," Victor said, much quieter. "Just calm down. What happened next?"

"Hey, I know what you're getting at – I didn't do anything. I didn't even touch him. We argued for a bit, until Shilling ordered the men to start burning down these huts, to scare the people and make them talk. Tristan was... well, he was pissed – he drew his weapon. Shilling didn't know what the fuck to do like usual, so he just stood there. I drew. I did. But I didn't do anything. The next thing I knew, some big fucking Eislander barbarian crashes through the underbrush over there and shoves a knife into Tristan's heart, and then comes after me and Shilling. We tried to get out of there, defend ourselves – something – and that's when all hell broke loose. There was blood everywhere, and... look around you. They took us by surprise – there was nothing we could do. When they were done with us they all left us here to watch the village burn to the ground, and those of us still alive stayed to tend the wounded... and do something about the dead."

Victor paused, made a low *hmm* sound at the back of this throat, deep in thought. "But Loringham's gone." Peter grunted in the affirmative. "Well, we're not staying here much longer. It's too dangerous. We'll move out tomorrow morning, go back through Doverton – see if we can find any of our lost men, get some leads."

"You'll lead us?"

"The men'll follow – I'm a captain, after all."

Victor did like to throw around that title, didn't he? I wandered back near them then, so that when I spoke they would hear me. I stared unblinking at them through the haze of *tsohbac* smoke hanging in the thin air around me, formulating my words. It took a lot of effort to do so through the pounding of my heart and the way my nerves quaked and my skin crawled so terribly. "So, wait a moment, go back, Peter – you watched a fellow officer fall like that, and you didn't bother to help him?"

Both Wyndham men seemed to sigh at once. Victor opened his mouth to say something, but his younger brother stopped him. "Look, Alexander, I know he was – is – your friend," he said, idly rubbing his temples as if he had a ripping headache. "And up here, he and I got along, well enough, to the point that even if I'm right, and he really was working with the enemy, I would have helped him. All right? I would have, but he was… there was blood everywhere. I didn't think he'd make it. I don't know if he did. Maybe he crawled off. Didn't look. Maybe they picked him up and they're nursing him back to health somewhere. Or executed him. Who knows? It stopped being important when everyone else here started getting cut apart. If he's going to die, let him die in peace. If he's off with the enemy, then we'll meet again someday and the King and the gods above can decide his fate." Then he did something I never would have expected – he came up to me and put a hand on my shoulder, looked me directly in the eye. "For what it's worth, I am sorry," he said, and I actually believed he meant it.

The two brothers talked some more, but I stopped paying attention. My thoughts were far, far away. There was more business to be dealt with, dead bodies to be identified and sent back to the Great Lady, a plan of action for how to proceed. I still didn't know why they were looking for such a thing. If I remembered correctly, the Kaeren was a story for children about ages long past to let their imaginations run wild while they dream. If there was any truth left to it, if there really was a shining weapon with magical power laying somewhere in the mountains, that knowledge had been lost long, long ago. We didn't know, the Eislandisch didn't know – no one knew. It was lost to history. It was probably better that way. It was all so fucking ridiculous I almost laughed aloud, in spite of myself. How could a stupid faery story could bring about so much death and destruction?

I did finally break down and cry then. I went and sat on the cold ground amongst the rows of bloodied swords and I wept deeply, fiercely, in waves of pain and sorrow that came from someplace deep down inside me – someplace I didn't even know existed. It's not particularly honorable or masculine to cry – I know that, every sodded Zondrean in the world knows that – but I couldn't stop. There were so many things I wanted to do over again, so many things I wanted to say to my friend… oh, by Catherine, how would I tell his parents? How could I tell his mother that her boy was missing, presumed either dead or a traitor, working with an enemy who also just happened to be her own kin? What would I say? Oh sure, by the way, your son's been bleeding out all over the place but the good news is they think he might have conspired with the enemy – oh, didn't you know we waged war on your homeland again? Yeah, we've been fighting with those evil fuckers for a while now, but we sent Tristan in there – you know, your *Eislandisch son* – thinking that that would be a good idea and surely it wouldn't be too difficult for him or anything. Guess we were wrong, sorry about all that.

Eventually I looked up. My eyes hurt, and I noticed the sun was beginning to light the sky golden-purple, just on the far edges of the horizon. What a huge sky, an amazing sky. You don't get a sky like that in Zondrell – too many trees and hills, and buildings. I watched it for a while, watched as gold took out more of the black and purple, gradually growing more and more brilliant, but still not ready for the day to begin just yet. It was truly a beautiful sight, but the brighter it got, the more I wished the sun would go away and never shine here again. But wishing wouldn't solve that problem, and I would have no choice but to look around at the burned out hulk of Südenforst in all its glory. There was blood and unidentifiable bits of people and clothing and all sorts of hideous things all over the place. The grass was charred and nothing was left of civilization here except for some wooden planks and broken pottery strewn around. It was like an angry god had just picked up the entire village and dropped it from five hundred miles up, then set fire to it just in case that didn't do the trick.

My gaze finally settled on one of the swords next to me. Its blade looked like it used to be quite fine, perhaps shaped by an expert blacksmith, but now the edge was pitted with nicks and scratches. Still sharp, sure, but definitely well-used. And stained, too – blackish red remnants of several battles were splashed and smeared all along its length, and even buried into the grooves and jewels that decorated the hilt. Jewels – yes, real jewels, sapphire and ruby, carved into diamond shapes. What normal solider would have a sword like this? Well, none of them – an officer, though, might, and even though it took me a minute, I *knew* this weapon from somewhere.

I stood up and wrenched it out of the ground. I even gave it a little test swing – perfect balance – then just studied it, thinking about how all of those dings and stains and marks had gotten there. This was the sword of a man who went to battle damn near *every day*. But when I last saw it, it was fine, polished, perfect, and hanging on a wall in the Loringham parlor.

I didn't even bother looking up when Peter Wyndham approached me. I didn't want to talk to him or anyone else; all I wanted to do was what I was doing right at that moment. And actually, I didn't even want to be doing that. I wanted to be having a drink and maybe invite a nice-looking girl home with me for an evening. I wanted to be able to wake up in my own bed and look out the window at the stone cityscape of Zondrell instead of the cold crags of mountaintops. I wanted to have a game of cards with my friends – all of them.

Of course, Peter was an asshole and didn't seem to be terribly interested in letting me be, so eventually I said something. "This thing is… it's filthy."

"Yeah, it saw a lot of use," Peter said. "He didn't clean it very well."

"What in Catherine's name were you people doing up here?" I let the tip fall back toward the dirt, where it hit the rocky ground with a metallic ring.

When I finally looked at him, saw him in the light, he really, really looked bad. Peter Wyndham had stripped down to a sleeveless tunic and pants, the stuff you're supposed to wear under your armor, and it was nothing but a giant multicolored stain. Along one of his forearms there was a terrifically wide, straight scar, and on the other side there was a yellowing bruise covering almost the entire area around his elbow. "They didn't brief you very well, did they?" he said, looking at me with a sort of dumbfounded expression on his face, like there was something very important that I was missing. Unfortunately, he was right on target.

I shook my head. "No one briefed me on anything. I just know what I've been hearing. The Kaeren? Really?"

"You're kidding, right?" More head shaking. "You're a Lord – I thought you people were kept informed. Well, let's just say that a lot of people have met their end by that blade you've got there." He paused for a moment, licked his lips, stared down at the rocky ground under our feet. "I don't think he liked it – any of it – but he was really fucking good at it. And they knew that before he ever got here, and they knew he knew the language here, and I hate to tell you this, but no matter what had happened at graduation, whatever medals he got or I got or whatever, he would have been sent up here anyhow. You can blame me if you want, but all I did at that tournament was get my damned nose broken. The only reason I'm here is because I'm a fucking idiot, but they had designs on Tristan ever since he set foot on Academy grounds. I just thought you should know that."

Did he actually think that any of this was making me feel better? Catherine above... he really was an asshole. But the worst part of the whole thing was, I could have done something about all of this, could have kept all of these men alive if I had known... why wouldn't Tristan have told me any of this? For Catherine's sake, I saw him only a little more than a few weeks ago! I could have gone to the Council or the King, thrown some money around, something. That's the power of being the Lord of a major house; you can make your own damned rules. Everybody knows that. So why, *why* wouldn't he have said anything? It was absolutely maddening – I could feel the heat rising in my body just thinking about it. "Some border patrol," I said.

"That's what they told you? Border patrol?" Peter chuckled, a private kind of laugh that obviously wasn't meant for me at all.

My hand clenched tightly around the sword hilt, almost of its own accord. I really wanted him to go the hell away, and I told him so. "Yeah, that's what he told me. Look, do you mind? I'd really like to be alone right now."

"Sure thing, anything you want... Lord Vestarton. My brother says we're moving out once the sun's up. Better try to get some rest." And with that he ambled away, toward the makeshift tents and huts on the other end of the site. I could have followed him, found a warm spot to curl up for an hour or so, but why? So that I could spend even more time with my favorite Wyndham brothers? Catherine help me!

But, as he left, what he said stayed with me. No matter what, Tristan would have been sent up here anyhow. Those words stirred up something – memories, and yet more emotion, but this time it was more than just sadness. Now there was anger there, too, a good fucking lot of it, directed mostly at nothing I could do anything about, including myself.

I picked up a rock and tossed it as hard and as far as I could. That didn't really help, but aiming a few more did seem to calm me, if just a little. Still, I wanted to do something real, something to change things, something to make sense of it all again. A day ago I was running around playing Lord in my estate, set to live a comfortable existence. Now, well... fuck, I had no idea what any of it ever meant.

✸✸

Everyone has their obstacles, their challenges, their... whatever you want to call them. Emotions had always been Tristan's. Whatever was in his heart was destined to stay right where it had wormed its way in. He did not talk about things, he didn't ask for help – he just dealt with it and reacted when necessary. That's just the way it was. In that way, we were about as different as we could be – my heart had generally always been in my hands and out for the world to see, pretty much everywhere I went. After that gods-forsaken, barbaric tournament they put us through to graduate, I actually told Headmaster Janus and the General himself exactly where they could shove their idiotic rules. I thought for sure I would get kicked out of the Academy for that one, but I was compelling enough, I suppose.

Tristan never knew I did this, of course – well, he didn't remember it, anyway. He would have broken a few more ribs of mine if he had. Looking back, though, I should have done more. What, I had no idea, but *something*.

As soon as that tournament was done and we checked to make sure he was all right – which he wasn't, really – he was gone. He'd wandered off to go have his moment in privacy. Hell, if I were him, I might have wanted to do the same, but instead, I was on the other side, me and the rest of the cadets, and most of us were arguing the same point.

"Tristan won that fight, and you know it," I said to Janus once I got a chance to get close to him. There was a lot of commotion, a lot of people standing about not sure of what to do, several tending to Peter Wyndham who was whining incessantly about his nose. Fuck him – half of us were hoping he'd just bleed out.

Janus was noncommittal and unemotional. "There will be a conference with the General, son. Go clean up and get out of here."

"No, wait, I want your word that you'll do the right thing here." This was probably not the right way to appeal to the man who held our futures in his hands, but at that point I didn't care that much. There was a spark in the air that was bigger than anything any of us had ever felt before that day. What was it? It's hard to explain... but this wasn't like an exercise or a sparring match or anything of the sort. This was one-on-one battle, as pure as it got without a few dead bodies lying about, and the paths of our lives were going to be decided here, today, based at least in part on what happened. It was stupid and outdated and made no sense that all of our studies and whatever it was we did for the past four years meant little when faced with one single day, but that was the way it was. It was the biggest day of most of our young lives, and I was not about to see anyone – especially my best friend – get fucked by this jackass who had been dragging us through the sweat and blood and tears of battle training for four miserable years.

"Excuse me?" The sneer in his voice was the same sneer as was seemingly permanently etched on the old soldier's face. "Son, you're not graduated yet. Get out of here before you say something you can't take back."

"Fine, where's the General? I'm going to make sure he realizes that this whole match was rigged from the start."

I did not stick around long enough to hear Janus' response to that, because at that point Corrin Shal-Vesper was dragging me off by the arm. Behind us, I could hear a lot of shouting of questions and various remarks as we made our way toward the Dormitories, the largest of the four buildings that made up the Military half of the Academy ring.

"What the hell is wrong with you?" Corr asked in a hurried, shaking tone. Corr was the morality in our little group. He was the voice of reason – the one who didn't drink too much so that someone could find his way home at the end of the night, the one who made sure everyone studied for exams, things like that. Not that any of this was a problem for Tristan, but it was for me. Tristan typically managed his own business. Me, I needed a bit more nursemaiding, I supposed, to get through the Academy at all.

"It's not right. They can't let him lose, not like that."

Corr shook his head, and some of his sweaty dark hair fell across his forehead. "You don't know if they will. Don't give them a reason to decide against him."

"Come on, man. Tristan was right – he told me they'd call his name first. They did. You've been going to the same school I have, right? You've seen what they've put him through. They're not going to call this in his favor."

"Well…" Corr didn't want to say it, but he did anyhow. And he was calm about it, calm in that certain way he had when things got difficult. Some people got louder when they were upset or angry, but Corr just got quieter. "If it was anyone else," he said, "if it was me up there, or you, I think… maybe they would have just stopped the fight and disqualified Peter, wouldn't they?"

I spat on the ground. "You fucking bet they would have."

Corr made an annoyed sound under his breath and we kept walking, trying to figure out where to go next. Find the General? He could be anywhere by now. Find someone else, one of the Lords, maybe? One of our fathers? We didn't really know what to do; we just kept walking and randomly seeking a direction. There was, however, a bathhouse around the corner and I could hear the high-pitched *whoosh* of water running in. Not much, just a little, like one of the showers was on. Corr and I looked at each other and headed in that direction.

Not everyone had nice running water and proper plumbing in the city, but the Academy certainly did – despite its age they had kept its facilities modern and spent thousands of Royals on making sure the place was as accommodating as it was useful. The Magic Academy, as I understood, was no different. Apparently, the two Academies even used the same sources of heat and water – magical, of course, from some great and mysterious source maintained by the mages. Magical water was not quite the same as the true thing, but it functioned in the same way. It washed away your dirt and your grime, and maybe even your sins if you scrubbed hard enough.

We found a little trail of diluted blood leading into the central drain in the great, marble-floored bathhouse first. The shower part was mostly just an open area where you could go stand or sit on a bench and wash up, do whatever it was you needed to do. I heard the tan-colored marble had come from Drakannya or some such – it was a newer part of this Dormitory, finished about a year ago under the King's direction. Many of us had never even used it yet, since the old one closer to our rooms was good enough.

It was there, though, in a far corner that we found Tristan, sitting quietly under one of the showers with his head in his palms. The water was so hot half the place was awash in steam.

"Hey, Brother, are you all right?" I shouted to him from across the room. No movement. Corr and I looked at each other again. "Hey, Brother? Don't make us come over there."

Finally, I got a hoarse reply. "Go away, please."

Corr spoke up, keeping his voice just loud enough to hear over the water. "Just making sure you're okay, man."

"I'm fine. Go away." That's when I heard it – the hitch in his voice like it got caught on something sharp and unforgiving. That was when I knew what was going on – that shower was masking tears. Everyone cries sometimes, whether you're a tough old soldier or a young girl. It's just the way it is. I've done it countless times. That's not to say that I always wanted an audience, but it was a natural part of life – to me, anyhow. Not to Tristan. But the anger was gone. There was no one left to hurt and nothing left to do but let the tears come.

So, Corr and I did leave, but we didn't go far. We sat outside the door to the bathhouse thinking that we probably ought to take a shower, too, at some point soon. A few people walked past, failing to acknowledge us – they were off on their own business. The halls were deathly quiet for the most part. I wondered if the rest of our class was off packing to go home.

"Oh no," said Corr after a while, looking off down the north hallway. What was his problem now?

Then I realized who was headed our way, boots striking light and efficient taps along the polished stone. A tall gray-bearded man with silver-streaked dark hair and piercing greenish-grayish eyes like stormclouds approached, the various accoutrements of his bearing jingling with him as he walked. There were medals and symbols of office all across the front and down the sleeves of his long black jacket, with a great silver falcon on the chest, wings outstretched and arcing over both shoulders. A glint of silver at his belt shone in the dim torchlight of the hallway, the hilt of the Blade of Zondrell itself. I had only had one other occasion in my life to talk with General Jamison Torven, and that had been in a big room with all of our families and everyone present. It might have been someone's wedding; I couldn't remember. But this! This was a chance for an actual conversation. I couldn't pass it up, and behind me I could feel Corrin trying to will me to stop from whatever I was getting ready to say.

"My Lord!" I said, stepping in front him as he moved closer to us and giving a friendly salute with my right fist to left shoulder. He responded in kind and stopped. Yes, he actually stopped!

"At ease, son," Torven said. Being so close to him, I could see the lines of age and worry and battle etched into the creases of his eyes. How old was he? I had always thought of him as a younger man, I supposed, but really, he was probably closer to retirement than many of us realized. He still had a certain regal bearing to him, maybe even more so than the King himself. Certainly Torven commanded a lot more respect amongst the people of Zondrell. "Cadet Loringham is with you?"

The words caught in my throat for a moment. Why was the General himself looking for Tristan? It could mean only something very good, or something very, very bad. I thought maybe it could go either way at this rate. "Ah... yes, Sir. He's in the showers, Sir. You saw what happened, I assume?"

"Indeed. Quite the performance." With that, Torven moved past us and into the bathhouse. Corrin literally gasped out loud as he did so, and I imagine that he felt the same cold, shaking, nervous feeling that I did. The *bad* feeling. We headed in after him, though, not willing to just let whatever was going to happen go on without us.

"There you are, son. Been looking for you." Torven grabbed a towel and headed toward the spraying water without even taking off that spectacular jacket. Corr and I were stunned.

At first, I don't think Tristan recognized the General. It took him quite a while to get up, put on a towel, turn off the water, all of that. I thought he might fall asleep where he stood. "All right, boy, look at me for a second... Good." Torven was looking him over, checking out the massive bruise on the side of his face. "All right," he said, holding up one finger, "follow my fingertip with your eyes, don't move your head. Can you do that?" Tristan couldn't. He tried – I could see him struggling, but every time Torven's finger moved to one side or the other Tristan's eyes seemed to go the opposite direction. He blinked a lot and eventually shook his head.

"Sorry, I... I can't. I think I'm having a hard time focusing," he said.

"Aye, that's because you have a concussion. It will pass – you'll be all right. You need to get some rest, son."

"What does that mean, Sir?" Corr asked. Clearly he did not remember the terms off of one of those tests we took to learn about battlefield medicine. Amazingly, I did.

"It means he might not remember much from today. Better off maybe, yes? Hm... Well, you are one tough soldier, I'll give you that." He saluted, and acting on reflex, Tristan saluted back. He still didn't quite seem to realize he was talking to the General himself, and that was fine. Three days later he would ask me if we talked to the General after the tournament, because he thought that we did. I told him it was just a dream.

"Sir..." His eyes were searching, darting around. "I wanted to win. I... didn't, did I?" Okay, so he remembered *that* anyhow. Cleaned up, you could see how bad the bruise on the side of his head was, blossoming out of his temple like a purple flower. There were other smaller bruises of various colors all over his body, too. He'd taken a beating, and came out on the other side the victor – he didn't believe that then, or even now, but I did. Most everyone did. How could you think otherwise? The rules were the rules, and the rules said you didn't strike before the match started. It didn't matter if you were Peter Wyndham or Catherine herself, and I still wanted to make sure General Torven understood that.

"Don't worry about that right now," Torven said. "Go get some rest for the next few days, get well. Don't want to miss graduation, now do you?"

More saluting and Torven took his leave, but I was right behind him. Thank the gods Corr was there to keep Tristan on the other side of that door. He didn't need to hear this conversation. It was now or never. I had to say what needed to be said. "Sir, if I may? That contest was rigged. The names weren't pulled randomly."

Torven stopped, folding his arms across the falcon on his chest and furrowed his brow. "And?"

And? What the fuck did that mean? From the look on his face I could tell he was only vaguely interested in what I had to say. I didn't care – I needed to be heard. "And it's not exactly fair. I mean, if you don't judge this outcome the right way... Well, I'm sorry, Sir, but he will never be the same. This meant everything to him."

"Alexander, right?" Amazing – he knew my name! "Alexander, let me tell you something. This place is not designed to be fair. It's designed to build soldiers and officers."

Really? Well, that put things in a different perspective, now didn't it? I felt myself shaking a little as the words just popped out of my mouth without much thought behind them. "Well, you people built the best fucking soldier you could. Do you not realize that?" How cursing at the general of the entire Zondrell army did not get me put straight in the dungeon I'll still never truly know. I'd like to say it was worth the risk.

"I am aware. Look, your concern is admirable, son. My advice is to go help your friend and worry about who gets what medal in a few days." He clapped me on the shoulder, and off he went, fading away down the hallway with his medals jingling the whole way.

That exchange made so much more sense now. When he took his leave I remember thinking that he seemed like a respectable sort. Maybe I'd made an impression. Maybe I even had some impact on the final decision to give the High Honor to Tristan. He hadn't ordered me to the dungeon for swearing at him, and actually came down personally to make sure Tristan was all right. But it wasn't really about concern and respect at all, was it?

No, of course not. Why were any of us stupid enough to think otherwise?

I finally understood, and of all people it had to come from Peter Wyndham. By the gods, I'm an idiot – it sure took me long enough to figure it out. That afternoon back at the Academy, I gave the General the benefit of the doubt because he was the General. But, there was an investment to be protected, wasn't there? They had poured in four years of misery to turn Tristan into exactly what they wanted. It was cold, it was calculating, it was… well fuck, I just witnessed it. I didn't have to *live* it. I should have let him quit when I had the chance, but I didn't know any better. None of us did. We all had the same idea – you get educated, you get an officer's rank, you spend a little time sending privates out to do various crime-stopping and bodyguarding around town, and that's the end of it. You live a good life with good food and drink and women, as much as you want, whenever you want. Maybe you get married and keep your bloodline going, and wait for the next chance for a new social rank. It's the noble's way in Zondrell. Tristan didn't deserve to be denied that, but that's what happened. They decided he was better as a tool to use for their own purposes. A lot of fucking nerve that Torven had… was any of that concern even genuine? I wondered about that as I replayed those moments in my head. Sure, they gave Tristan what he wanted – rewarded him for all that suffering – but that was just to buy his loyalty and make sure he kept performing.

It was really quite disgusting.

**

So I stood there, and my mind raced on despite all of the rage and bad memories, searching for something – a plan? There had to be something I could do, somewhere I could look. I needed answers. And it wasn't a question of whether I would be able to find answers because they were out there – they must have been because I *needed* them. I could think of nothing that I needed more at that point in time. I needed an explanation, a reason why my friend's sword was here and yet he was not, why so many other swords were here while their owners were off to spend eternity with the gods... why this place was destroyed beyond recognition and there was nothing gained to show for it.

I knew what I had to do. Had no idea how to go about it, but that didn't seem like the important part right then. I pulled my shortsword from my belt and drove it down into the ground where Tristan's sword had been. It could wait there. The long slender weapon with the countless battle scars would serve me better – until I was able to return it to its rightful owner, at least. But it wasn't a divining rod, unfortunately, so it couldn't tell me where to go – that, I would have to figure out on my own, unless...

What was *that*?

2

At first, I thought it was just the way the faint dawn light played off of the rocks. But the more I looked, the longer the shadow stood still – it wasn't a shadow at all. It was a figure, a person in a dark cloak, standing at the bottom of the long, craggy slope that led to the main road. Male or female? Definitely male – too tall to be anything else, but with the cloak it was hard to know anything else about him. Had he seen me? Probably not – his back was turned. Perhaps, I could approach, get closer, figure out who this person was. Maybe it was him! Maybe everything would be just fine, and it was all just a big misunderstanding! But, then again…

I started off down the slope, paying careful attention to where I placed my feet so as not to slip on something. I had a feeling that creating a scene would not have been a good idea.

"I told you this would happen." I darted behind the nearest rocky outcropping when I heard the voice, a deep man's voice that held a thick accent, vaguely familiar in its guttural lilt. Eislandisch, but not like Tristan's. More like his mother's, with native inflections. Curiosity kept me frozen in place, straining to hear while leaned up against stone so cold it sent involuntary shivers through my whole body.

"No one asked for your commentary. I paid you to do a job. You have failed." This was another voice, from an unseen woman. She was also speaking slightly broken Zondrean, but with a smoother, more fluid tone. The words almost slurred together... Lavançaise. Interesting. What could they be talking about, especially all the way out here? Was it a coincidence that they were just a few paces away from the former site of Südenforst?

The man was matter-of-fact. "I did exactly what you asked."

"*Tch.* Then why are these people here?"

"It would not have mattered. They would be here regardless. I told you that."

The woman seemed quite petulant, and the more she spoke, the louder and harder her tone became. "The girl did her part – you could not have done yours just as simply?"

"The girl?" There was a pause heavy enough to crush stone. "You *paid* her?" I didn't know who they were talking about or what that meant, but the man was clearly disgusted by this realization. I could only imagine what people like this may have paid a girl to do. Or perhaps, maybe I couldn't imagine it, which was even worse. My imagination darted around as they continued.

"There was a job to be done, and she was paid well. I thought you understood how that worked."

Another long pause. "I hope it was... a life-changing amount."

Impatient, the woman made another *tch* sound, clicking her tongue against her teeth in annoyance. "I told you to remove the threat. They are still here – in fact, there are *more* of them." *Them*... did she mean, us? Zondrell? There was little room for doubt. This was getting quite interesting indeed.

"I believe the situation is a little more... complex than you think. These things take time to develop."

The woman audibly scoffed. "I do not recall paying you to come up with elaborate plans, and yet here you are, still creating them. Is your young friend part of your grand plan, Brin? Maybe I *will* kill him, just to prove a point."

"You, *Fräulein*, are a liar." Whoever he was, this man "Brin" had no problem saying what he wanted to say. "Besides, what point would that be?"

She ignored his question entirely, which I found interesting. I could only guess as to the reason. "Your plan is not working," she said after a long pause. "It has failed. You have failed. You were paid for a service, and I assumed you capable. Yet, the threat is still here. If you had done as you were told, this situation would be ended."

The man spoke again, but now a bit softer, and all I could discern were growls and hisses. I tried to angle myself to get a view of them, maybe get a little closer to hear what was going on... And promptly tripped over my own feet. A few rocks crashed together making just enough noise to stop all conversation. I froze and gripped Tristan's sword a little more firmly. What I intended to do with it I wasn't certain yet. I really wasn't thinking much at that moment, which was probably a good thing, because thinking too much would have been the death of me.

The next moments were a flash. The man said something sharp and foreign, and then a dagger hurtled end over end in my direction, aimed directly for my left eye. I didn't have a chance to close it or flinch. But instead of lodging itself in my skull, it did the strangest thing. It paused in midair, dangling just within an inch of my face.

I was as shocked as they were. "Of all the..." was the woman's annoyed retort. The man simply laughed, truly amused, apparently, by their turn of fortune. Or mine. Or what, I don't know. What I knew for sure was that a weapon previously hurtling at a high rate of speed had now stopped its momentum, and was sitting there, patiently defying the laws of physics just for me. It actually took only a minute for everything to click but it certainly felt like forever as my mind grasped for the only possible explanation. Within my veins, my blood roiled as the skin enveloping them crawled mercilessly.

✳✳

You see, that's the feeling one gets when working with magic. Well, I don't know if everyone feels it the same way, but that's how it feels for me. That's how it always felt, painful and hideous. Maybe if I'd practiced, the feeling would have gone away over time, but that was certainly not going to happen. I hadn't had a real choice in the matter.

One thing I knew for sure when I first walked through the gates to the Zondrell Military Academy for acceptance was that I was not going to be going into the Magic Academy instead. That happens sometimes, often much to the dismay of the boys' fathers. I knew it would be devastating to my own father, but there was a chance. There was magic in our family, far, far back in the bloodlines, which presented a constant looming threat that other young Vestarton men would have it somewhere down the road. In my family, magic was looked upon as more of a scourge than a benefit, and my father had said often that he would be mortified if I grew up into a "magic-tossing coward" like Victor Wyndham. Where the Wyndhams were proud to have a male mage among them – known to be far more rare but also much more powerful than the average female mage – the Vestartons just simply would not be happy with the only male heir being untrained in the art of real combat. It just wouldn't do – bad for appearances and all that.

I shivered just thinking about it. The thing they called The Box used to keep me up late at night. I was terrified of it. That was the last part of Registration Day, and for weeks beforehand, I had nightmares about it. Rarely had I ever feared anything quite so much before, but as the day came closer and closer, I could think of little else. I tried to imagine what it looked like, what would happen when I walked into it. Would it swallow me whole? Would I wind up on a different plane of existence or something? But, the most important question of all: would it keep me out of the Military Academy? There was a small chance, but it was there, and my father reminded me of it regularly as the big day approached. So I sat up late every night dreading the moment when I would enter The Box. The Box did not lie – The Box would find me out. The Box would turn me into an embarrassing disappointment.

They make you wait in line and watch the other cadets take their turn in The Box before you. It's just a big block of obsidian – at least, that's what it looks like on the outside. A young lady wizard sat at a nearby desk with a big stack of papers and some sorts of tubes and gears on it, took each registrant's name and some information, and then they walked in. What happened in there? I had no idea before it was my turn, but everyone who came out said, "Nothing." None of them had the gift, and that was fine with them. Their fathers were all like my father, no doubt.

And then it was my turn. I swallowed hard. I didn't want to go in. "Alexander Xavier Marcus Vestarton, yes?" the young lady with the papers said, her Earth-magic green eyes glowing with a light all their own. Bizarrely beautiful, infinite in their brilliance... and quite impatient. She said my name one more time, with a bit more emphasis.

I nodded. "That's me, although actually, it's Alexander *Marcus* Xavier – you've got them turned around," I said weakly.

"Hm, yes, sorry. Go on in, then. Stand and wait – The Box will react if you have the potential for magic study. Wait at least a few minutes for something to happen before you come out, all right?"

Again, I nodded. I stepped into The Box nervously, and my heart jumped as the door slid shut behind me. There was no light at all, not even coming in from around the door edges. Utter darkness and a heavy feeling enveloped me—I folded my arms across my chest as if I felt a chill, even though there was none. In fact, it was rather warm inside. I didn't know how long I would have to stay in there, but it felt like I'd been standing there for quite a while, even though it was only a few moments. As I was about to turn to the door, perhaps to knock on it or try to push it open, the oddest thing happened.

Whirling white and silver lights started to circle around me, rising up from the floor and eventually finding their way to the ceiling, near my head. I reached out toward one and it dodged my grasp. I took a deep breath to try to blow them away from me but instead inhaled strange heavy air, air that tingled and sparkled. Eventually the lights circled faster and faster, then stopped in place, went back around the other direction. They sped up and slowed down, did all kinds of odd things. Obviously, this was what they meant by a "reaction." I tried to close my eyes, ignore it all, hoping I would wake up in my bed and it would turn out to be just another dream. But when I dared to look again, I was still there.

I suddenly began to feel very ill. I clawed at the door trying to get the hell away from there, perhaps to save myself from my fate, but it only opened on its own, when it so chose. The lights whipped up into a real frenzy, changed colors, stopped and started, went fast and slow – it seemed in an instant that a million years had passed, and in another, that I could count every tiny fraction of a second. The hair on my entire body stood up, and the crawling began, running around under my skin like nothing I'd ever felt before. No hit of bittergum or any other recreational substance could have prepared me for that feeling. No recreational substance had ever made me want to cry out and roll around and otherwise find ways to escape that horrible, dreadful feeling before. I believe at some point during the next few seconds I prayed to any god that would listen that I would never, ever do anything wrong ever again. I might not have held that promise, but a few seconds later the door did finally yield to my clawing and pushing.

I almost fell out of The Box. The green-eyed Earth mage regarded me with a raided eyebrow, then looked back to her paperwork and strange instrumentation. "Did you observe anything, Mister Vestarton?" she asked.

I barely missed a beat as I flicked a strand of hair off my brow. "No, madam, not a thing." Thank the gods I'm a remarkable liar... or that this apprentice mage was fantastically stupid.

Either way, lying got me into the Military Academy and I never looked back. Except, of course, to figure out how to keep the magic from touching my eyes. That was thanks to Zizah. I met her in the Market that afternoon, as I was wandering about "getting some air" and trying desperately to find a mirror. I knew it. I could feel it, and all I had to do was stop and peer into a jeweled Katalahni mirror to learn the truth – my irises were already beginning to turn strange and sort of vaguely luminescent. The magic was released, and everyone would know. It was only a matter of time. I was completely ruined... or so I thought.

"You look distressed," she said from the front of her little storefront, in the midst of the bustling Zondrell bazaar. Even though there were probably a million people walking around, at that moment it was just her and me standing there, regarding each other. She smiled an enchanting dark smile and I had no choice but to return the favor.

"Well, Miss, it's a bit of a long story," was all I could come up with for a reply.

"I have time. Especially if you buy something at the end of the day." Shrewd and beautiful. I always was a sucker for the exotic ones, and she was that if nothing else. Gorgeous skin that was almost mahogany in color, dark almond-shaped eyes with just a hint of a sparkle to them that didn't quite seem natural. She knew things, this otherwise average bazaar merchant from a distant land. What did she know? I soon found out as I told her my story over a cup of jasmine tea. Why not? Who would she tell, after all? For some reason, I had to tell someone, and it was not going to be someone I knew. Not even Tristan. No one in the Zondrell nobility could ever know this secret.

"You have a problem, *Habibi*. But I think I know how to fix it. The price is steep, however."

"You don't know who I am, do you?"

She smiled. That was all I needed to say. She herself was a mage but she knew the secret, an old Katalahni secret that was not known to many. In the desert, I found out, keeping one's business to oneself is a way of life, and being able to conceal magic can mean the difference between life or death there. It was all in the *tsohbac*, of all things! I just had to smoke when I felt the "urge" – that awful skin-crawling sensation. If it got worse, smoke more, she said. That's all there was to it.

The problem was, the longer you needed to hide, the more you had to smoke. It took only about six months before I became a serious addict – I could, on a given week, go through two entire boxes, which was an awful lot of *tsohbac*. My friends complained, and it was beginning to singlehandedly fund Zizah's little merchant operation. Even I had to get used to it. But it was worth it; no one ever found out.

⁎⁎

Until now, however. The secret was out, at least amongst two total strangers, and it had also just saved my life. Instinct or not, it didn't really matter. All I knew was that magic was keeping a blade from cutting a path to my brain, and I had to be thankful. Very fucking thankful.

Gradually, I gained my composure. My breathing steadied. If I had been able to look in a mirror I am certain that my irises had gone from chestnut to some kind of brilliant alien something in an instant, because I could feel the sharp burn, a flintstrike right behind my eyeballs. I reached out and plucked the simple steel dagger out of its stasis, then casually adjusted my collar.

"Now," I said, slowly and deliberately, "let's try to keep this civilized, shall we?" I faced my two opponents with a hint of a smirk, suddenly feeling quite confident. It was either that or feel dead, because confidence was the only thing keeping me alive for the time being and we all knew it.

The woman, tall and well-muscled and very, very angry, moved for the blade strapped low across the small of her back, but the Eislandisch man held a hand out to stop her. In the low light of dawn, he really did look like Tristan. It was uncanny. I'm not one to say that "they all look alike" – no, this man really looked like he could be related to Tristan somehow. The high cheekbones, the square jaw, even the way he carried himself reminded me of Tristan in many ways, but this man was certainly not him. He was older, battle-scarred and even more imposing, with a scruffy beard and a hint of something wild behind crystal blue eyes.

"Civilized, eh?" he said. "So, you are just here for *Morgentea* then?"

"Would you believe me if I said I was?"

At this the man laughed out loud, but his companion was not amused. She never took her black – yes, *black* – eyes from me, examining me with a contemptuous, almost hateful and unblinking stare. Her whole demeanor, clothes, everything was black. I had never seen a Lavançaise woman look so mean before, and I hoped to never see another. She obviously could rip me into shreds without a second thought, and the only thing keeping her from doing so was my magic. For whatever that was worth. Of course, she didn't have to know how untrained I was, now did she?

"Get your people out of this land. Today." She was definitely not making small talk, but I had something to quell her – or at least throw her off track.

"Oh, I'm sorry – you think I'm with them, up there? Oh no, I'm not really." I was impressed at my own ability to think fast, and talk even faster. "I mean, I'm an independent investigator, actually. I'm here looking for someone. Perhaps you've seen him?" They glanced at each other quickly, then back to me, waiting for elaboration. "He's Eislandisch, but not really. Got a Zondrell accent. Sort of tall, blond, blue eyes, as you might guess. About twenty-ish, soldier-type... you can't miss him. Big tattoo of a monster right here." I pointed to my right shoulder and as I did so, both the man and the woman seemed to wince, ever so slightly. They knew, and at once they knew that I knew. Neither seemed pleased.

At length, the Eislander said, "Sounds like an interesting man you seek. Why do you think you will find him here?"

"He's a friend, and he's missing."

"Have you checked with the *Zondern* up on the hill there? Many of them aren't talking though." At this the smirk turned into more of a grimace. Remorse? Disgust? It was definitely one of those but I wasn't sure which.

I began to fidget with the borrowed dagger, rolling it around in my palm, trying to appear casually irritated. I had no idea if any level of bravado was advisable, but as far as I could tell, I still had the upper hand. "He's not among the dead, if that's what you mean," I said, very curt. "Don't tell me – you don't know much about that either, do you?"

At this, both of them were silent, but only for a moment. She began to say something, but he interrupted her immediately. "Fräulein," he said, condescending to the core, "go back to your side of the border and let the men talk, will you?"

Her fists clenched at her sides. "*Pardonnez-moi*?" Her words dripped with pure hatred.

"Maybe it is my accent. Or yours. But I said..." She put up a hand, and with that, turned to the east and headed down the road, moving with intense purpose. If there had been anything in her path, it would have died. I sure as hell didn't want to go that way without some serious protection just in case she decided to turn around and come back.

When she was good and out of range, the man's posture loosened. Not in a relaxed way, really, but in a way that suggested some relief had settled in. He regarded me carefully, eyes searching for something. But what? Was he just looking for the right place in which to drive a sword? His expression was unreadable, so I remained on guard, still fussing with that dagger. I hoped to Catherine that it was his and not the Lavançaise's. Magic could only protect me so well for so long. Eventually, though, he did answer that question because he snatched it out of my grasp, too quick for me to even react, and slid it into the side of his right boot.

"Your name is Vestarton, *ja*?"

I was taken aback. I think my mouth dropped open. How did he know that? I had my signet ring but it was just a stylized "V"… Who *was* this person?

"You look like your father did, when he was your age." I said nothing, so he continued. "The stance, the curve of the jaw, that nervous look – he was like that, too. Always searching for something."

Funny, I never saw my father as the nervous type. Perhaps he lost some of that after the War. Wait a moment… "The War of the Northlands. That would have been more than twenty-or-some-such years ago. You knew my father then?"

The big man nodded slowly, the amused smirk returning. "During the occupation of Kostbar. He is a good man, your father."

"Was. He died a few weeks ago."

His brow furrowed a bit with a look of compassion. It was only there a short time, though. "May his blood reach the gods. He was one of the few *Zondern* I would not have killed, given the chance."

Interesting compliment. Things were starting to make sense, even though the coincidence was almost too amazing to believe. Of all the people in Eisland, how was it that the first one I ran into just happened to be around during the war, in the city of Kostbar during the Zondrellian occupation where my father and Tristan's father had served as army captains? That would explain the nearly perfect use of the Zondrean language – he looked to be the right age, probably pretty young, impressionable, when it's easy to pick up languages. And who else was there at that time, but... "You wouldn't happen to know the names Jannausch or Loringham, would you?"

At this, his blue eyes narrowed to slits, and I knew I had struck a nerve. Or maybe, those names stirred up unpleasant emotion. Again, his expressions, or lack thereof, revealed very little about what he actually felt. Now, there was absolutely no doubt – he was definitely related to Tristan if that's the way he carried himself. "You and I," he said, "we should take a walk." As he started up the road toward the west, further into Eisland, I hesitated to follow suit. Where were we headed? I didn't know, but I wasn't sure I wanted to find out. After several steps, he turned back to me. "Your people are not far, and we have some things to discuss, I think – without them – and the light comes quicker now. They will not be interested in discussion if we wake them."

"No, I don't believe they will." And so we walked, not too fast and as promised, not too far. It was more of a stroll really, and it would have been leisurely if it hadn't been so tense and, honestly, a bit surreal. I did not think that I was trudging off to my death, but at the same time, I didn't feel safe either. But, what was better – talking to this man who possibly knew where Tristan was, or dealing with the Wyndham brothers and finding the truth slipping further and further out of reach?

As we walked, the wind whipped through the valley a bit, sending odd sounds all throughout the land. And as the sun came up more, I could see how striking the resemblance was between this man and Tristan. Whoever this person was, his last name was almost certainly Jannausch. After a time, he spoke. "Your friend... he's fine. Well, not fine. But, not dead."

Oddly, this was somewhat comforting. "How bad? What happened?" I could actually hear the tension in my own voice.

"Bad enough, but he will recover. I was careful."

"*You* were careful?" What the hell did that mean?

"Herr Vestarton, when you are in the heat of battle, you must act quickly, make important decisions. Sometimes, those decisions must be very, very... what's the word? *Genau.* No. *Präzise.*"

"Precise?"

"*Ja*. That. I made a decision to keep your friend alive, and that is what I did." Brin paused, considered his words. "It was not an easy decision."

"But he's related to you." At this, he turned and glared at me, but did not stop walking. I returned his cold look with one of my own. "It's rather obvious. But you still haven't answered my question – what happened? Back there, in Südenforst? Did you kill all of those men?"

"By myself?" A slight chuckle, a bit inappropriately placed. "Of course not. I will let him tell you all of that. He knows as much as I – maybe more."

I took a step in front of him and stopped short, attempting to make him stop and look me in the eye. All this actually did was get me damn near run over by someone who was about a foot taller than I, and quite a bit broader. Magic or no, this was not someone who was easy to bully about – also a family trait. "Look, I want answers," I said sternly, holding up that longsword I was still clinging to and waving it about a bit as I spoke. "Why are you even talking to me if you're not going to tell me anything?" For just a moment, I glanced past him, at the big weapon hanging off his back, at the mountainous countryside behind us. We hadn't gone that far – I could see glimpses of smoke up on the ridge where the town used to be.

There was something in his crystal gaze that I couldn't quite explain, a mixture of emotion, experience – the wisdom that can only come from years on a battlefield. "That woman back there hired me because I owed her a favor," he began. His words very nearly tumbled forth. "I was supposed to kill your friend. And I almost did. But I like to know my enemy… and he is related, as you say. He is my sister's son." Amazing. Gretchen's brother – older? Younger? Hard to tell, but I leaned toward younger. Probably too young to have much say over whether his sister was to run off with a Zondrean officer when the war was over. "Blood spilling blood – that is not the way we do things. So, I changed the plan, but it was not, apparently, to Fräulein's liking. Now, I am here, with you. Destiny."

I shook my head. "I don't believe in destiny. And I don't understand. I… shit, man, I don't understand much of anything right now."

Another one of those strange, sly smiles. "This is what must happen. You will go back to your people. They will want to go to Doverton, to speak with the King. It is almost... what's the word? Obligatory. They will have to. Take this same road back east, toward town. Near to the other side of the border is a very small church for your goddess. It is very old, but there are people inside. Your friend is there."

It was almost too much to take in. So many questions whirled around my brain, but few made it into coherent sentences. And to top it all, he started to walk away. Just like that? I made a few weak sounds of protest, and he actually did stop, about ten steps down the road. But, he didn't turn around at all, just called over his shoulder.

"Oh, tell the women there that Onyx sent you. They will know."

"That Lavançaise – that was Onyx? Who is she?" The Eislander grunted in response, and said nothing, so I pressed on. "What's in it for you, then? Why are you telling me this?"

"We will see each other again." He blended into the rocky landscape within minutes, leaving me standing there, watching the light creep slowly into the western sky. I had to get back to the campsite... where I would say *what*, exactly? Hey guys, let's go past this church and you all just drop me off? Hell, I'd have better luck convincing them I'd just seen the earthly form of Catherine Herself in the mountainside.

That is, of course, unless you believed that destiny gibberish. By the late afternoon, I was actually starting to.

✳✳

We didn't get moving until later in the morning, which actually worked out well because I managed to get a few hours of sleep. Exhaustion had finally taken its toll and quite honestly, I was terrified of anyone getting too close to me. There were no mirrors around but I *knew* that the magic was crawling its way through me, beginning to touch my eyes. The very last thing I wanted to do was attempt to explain to Victor Wyndham – Captain of Magics – exactly why and how I had cheated my way past entering the Magic Academy. Lord or otherwise, such a discovery would have certain repercussions that I had no interest in ever facing.

As the Eislander had predicted, Victor planned to spend some time in Doverton and gain audience with the King there. About twenty of the men accompanied us, leaving another handful behind to continue cleaning up, dealing with the dead, and so forth. Captain Shilling stayed back as well, since he couldn't walk, leaving Victor – Catherine help us – in command. Even with twenty or so soldiers, we were a small enough band that they'd be able to rest in Doverton's guard barracks without interfering much with their daily operations. Throwing some money at Doverton officials would probably help ease any uncertainty and make our men welcome there. Not that I cared about any of this, because I had no plans to join them.

And again, as if on cue, the church appeared a few miles past the sign marking Doverton's border. We hadn't even gone that far, really, as the sun was still up – somewhat, anyhow – by the time we got there. Small and very old indeed – it hardly looked like much at all from the outside. The stained-glass windows depicted the goddess Catherine and her symbol of the dove, but they were stylized, almost primitive. Definitely not the kind of artwork seen in modern temples. I wondered why someone had built such a thing outside of the city limits, but then again, it had probably been here first.

"Should we stop?" I asked innocently to Victor and Peter, who were, of course, walking at the head of the group. I had made it a point to not engage them or anyone else in much conversation, so as not to attract unwanted eye contact. Since I was smoking *tsohbac* at a steady clip, it wasn't that difficult to pull off. I was actually lighting new ones from the previous one – fuck that whole business of waiting and striking a flint.

Peter shook his head but Victor overruled him with a wave of his hand. "Survivors might have come here for healing. Bring a few men with us – come on."

Inside it was quiet and dark. Perhaps this was a good thing. The Wyndhams and their handful of armored men all immediately began snooping around. One lit a torch to see better, since the ancient stained glass really didn't let the light in that well. Another went up to the altar and started pawing at the things there for healing and praying and whatnot. Even from a distance, it was obvious that it had been used recently-– the incense still smelled quite strong. For my part, I rested in a rickety old pew, in the last row by the door. I really just wanted them all to go away.

That's when destiny walked into the room – almost literally. I could hardly believe what I was seeing, but I would know that light-footed, lithe form just about anywhere. I had watched her send my father's corpse to Paradise not that long ago with such care and purpose. I couldn't remember her name... Weaver? Yes, it was Weaver, couldn't remember the first name. Something unusual. I'd only spoken to her for a few minutes, right before the funeral. I did remember thinking that she had been phenomenally pretty and young for a Pyrelight, but what the hell did I know about such things? I also knew that she had been from Doverton because she told me so right before I handed her a lot more gold than what she'd asked for, mostly because I was too wrapped up in misery to sit there and count coins. But I had asked for Academy-trained – I wanted the best Pyrelight money could buy. That's who they sent. But how was it that she was here, now, where a strange man named Jannausch had sent me just a few hours ago? Coincidences like that came once in a lifetime, if you were lucky.

Words were exchanged. She seemed quite unhappy to have us there, even though it was a church and doors weren't barred or anything. Everyone is welcome in the house of Catherine – or they're supposed to be. Victor grew increasingly convinced that there were people hiding out in the temple, and oddly enough, he was correct, but he never found that out.

The dark Lavançaise barged in not a few minutes later. If she didn't just have one outstanding sense of timing, then she must have been watching from some corner somewhere. She took a brief glance at me, knowing and intimidating at once, and took over the situation. The men were to be escorted to the King personally, by her, since she was his Weapon Master, after all. How or why the King of Doverton managed to hire this woman to be his Weapon Master, I could only imagine. No matter. Within moments, Victor, Peter, and the soldiers were being whisked out the door, and they all could have cared less that I asked to stay behind and "rest." The whole thing worked out as if it were scripted – I might as well have had a front row seat to some sort of stage play. Destiny certainly was an amazing thing when it was working for you.

When they were gone the Pyrelight turned to me with a sideways glance. She studied me. Maybe she didn't recognize me? "So, ah, call me Alex, yeah? Nice to see you, Miss... Weaver." I was stumbling over my words as I reached into my pocket for another *tsohbac*. "Is this all right?" I asked her, holding it up and getting ready to light it. It had been almost ten minutes since the last one – definitely time, even though my pocket was nearly empty now. What would happen after I was out? I had no idea. Didn't want to even think about it.

She managed a meek smile. "It won't help you forever, you know. It's already not enough."

"W... what do you mean?"

"I mean your magic's showing."

That was bad. And it wasn't like I could tell her she was seeing things. I found that my hands were shaking as I lit and inhaled deeply. She was probably right – it wouldn't work forever. Zizah had told me that same thing. And now that I had actually used some of that power welling up and squirming around inside, it was only a matter of time before the whole cover was blown entirely. Damn it all.

"It's all right," she continued. "But... you can't deny who you are for much longer." What did that mean? She was staring at me in a way that would have been quite interesting if it wasn't so unnerving. Was there something wrong? Did anyone ever tell her it was rather rude to stare like that?

Instead of asking, though, I changed the subject. Pleasantries had to end. "So, he is here, right? Tristan Loringham? Onyx sent me."

Yep, the pleasantries were *definitely* over, as she put her hands on her round, white-clad hips and the fires in her eyes flared just a little. "She did, did she?"

"Yeah. We, ah... ran into each other early this morning. Look, I'm not with those cretins. Tristan's a friend of mine; I've been looking for him. I have to know what's going on. Please."

Maybe it was because she had met me once before. Maybe it was the pleading and fraught tone in my voice, or even the way she had been staring into my eyes as if she was seeing something she'd never seen before. Or, this was all part of the script – if one were to believe in such a thing. Whatever the case, she relented, and after a little time, Tristan emerged from the shadows. And for all of the wondering and worrying I had done, words failed me at first.

He looked… awful. Beyond awful. My heart sank and I felt that cold, bad-news feeling again. This was damn near a different person than the one I'd known before, than the one who left Zondrell just a few months ago. Even during the worst times at the Academy, even when he had come back for my father's funeral, he hadn't ever looked this battleworn, beaten down. His Eislandisch uncle might as well have been his twin in that moment. Tristan held one arm close to his body, and his voice was gravelly and harsh, but it was – somewhere in there – still him. Still the guy who used to casually count cards during games of Five Star until I'd catch him and then he'd give me my money back by continuing to cheat, just making himself lose instead of win. Still the guy who'd go out of his way to open a door for a woman even if she didn't thank him or look him in the eye. Still the guy who made sure that I made it out of every drunken brawl I almost started at the Silver but could never finish even on my best day.

I handed him his sword back, treated him like the brother that he was to me, and this seemed to take him off-guard. What else was he expecting? Despite it all, despite anything that had happened before and what would happen next, I was still happy to see him.

PART TWO

There was nothing worse than leaving the temple angry. She hated arguing with her sister, but also hated arguing about silly things. That argument was unlikely to go away when she returned home, so Seraphine Weaver decided not to go back there right away after buying a few things in the market. Instead, she spent the majority of her day at the big temple, in Doverton, helping to copy Peaceday prayer cards and saying little to any of her colleagues there. It was a good day to concentrate and stay absorbed in tedious work. At least she was getting something accomplished – for the past few days she had felt rather restless sitting about and making sure their guest had what he needed. Andella had been a big help, but that was only because she didn't have any requests to travel for a funeral at the moment. She also suspected that Andella liked him a bit more than was appropriate or necessary, but that was a battle for another day. One thing at a time.

She felt awful for Mister Loringham, she really did. He seemed like a nice young man – a bit... edgy, perhaps, but polite and well-spoken. The fact that he came from money was reflected in his bearing. But, as the big Eislander had told her that fated night, "Some accidents are hard to avoid – especially when they are not accidents." He had laughed so casually about that as he left the church, and the next morning, when Madame Saçaille barged in unannounced, she was beyond solace. It didn't take long for Seraphine to figure out that Madame would have preferred that this "accident" had taken its course a bit differently. She had even gone so far as to suggest that they simply stop treating him and let him bleed out – luckily, Andella had not been in the room for that. She would have had a fit far worse than Seraphine herself did. It didn't matter if these Zondrell boys were out of control with their lust for battle – or whatever was going on. No one deserved that. To Onyx, Tristan was to be treated like a prisoner and a criminal; to Seraphine, the poor boy was just in an unfortunate situation.

And then there was Andella and her Prophecy.

Oh, hogwash! Impossible. She could believe lots of things, and have absolute faith in things she had never seen with her own eyes. Otherwise she would never have made a good priestess. But to believe the prophecies described in some old book were actually coming true? It just didn't make any sense. The Book of Catherine held no such prophecies, just revelations and instructions on serving and living in peace. Even if there were prophecies in there, she would have been hard-pressed to believe such things; the Book was written by men after all, and men didn't know the future. But yet, Saçaille also believed the Prophecy – they had debated its existence many times. If she were so worried about it coming true... No, it made no sense, and it continued to make no sense as she flipped these ideas around in her mind, over and over again, throughout the day. With each new prayer card she wrote, each time she dipped her quill into the inkwell, she thought of this and how odd the whole thing was. It gave her a headache.

"Huh, would you look at that," came a voice off in the next room, one of the acolytes. Seraphine looked up from her cards.

Another voice piped up. "That's strange. I wonder what they're doing here? Rather a lot of them."

By then, Seraphine felt she had to go and see for herself. Several of the young girls that kept the temple clean and organized – priestesses in training – were at a small window that looked out into the main street of the city of Doverton, the one that ran from the main gates directly to the palace of the King.

"What are you all looking at?" she asked casually, even though she felt a tremor of concern deep in her heart. She didn't know why, exactly, but any unusual sights seemed quite unsettling nowadays. You never knew what could happen.

One of the girls turned to her, then pointed out the window. The light, Seraphine realized, was weaker than it should have been. How late was it? She must have spent all day with those cards. "Look, Sister," the acolyte said. "There's a bunch of soldiers being led up the street. What colors are those? Black? Who wears black? Zondrell, right? What do you suppose that's all about?"

Zondrell soldiers? That was not the sort of news that was going to ease her mind or help her headache. "I... well, I have no idea," was all she could say, but in her heart all she wanted to do was run out of there and find out more. She wondered about her sister, about Tristan, about her temple – was everything all right? Was Andella safe? Of course, if she had just run out of there, the girls would have known something was amiss, and questions would be asked. No one was to know what was going on at her temple. This was the agreement she made, and one she would stick with. She had to be smart about this. So, she went back and finished her last card, collected all seventy-eight cards she'd done that day, and brought them out to the priestesses in the main part of the temple in a nice, perfect little stack.

"I think there's enough for the festival now with these," she said, trying to keep her tone even, pleasant, normal.

Priestess Veronica smiled brightly with her big round face and pleasantly plump demeanor. Her dark eyes sparkled as the creases around them grew deeper. The old gal had a way of making anyone feel good, feel welcomed. Seraphine supposed that was what made a great priestess. Did she have that same quality? She rather doubted it now, but perhaps someday. "Thank you so much, Sister! You are truly a blessing," Veronica said.

"Oh, it's nothing. I'll stop by again in a few days to see you. Send word if you need me sooner. Peace be with you, Sister – now if you'll excuse me, I just realized how late it was. My own sister will be expecting me." She gathered her things and hurried off without another word, and no one seemed to be the wiser.

But instead of going toward the gate, she moved toward the palace, walking quickly, dodging people along the way. Doverton was not a huge, sprawling city, not like Zondrell or Starlandia. Far from it. Its streets were simple grids, with a distinct northern, southern, eastern, and western district and the King's castle at the center. From one end of one of the four main streets, you could see clear across to the castle and even a bit beyond, due to the gentle rolling hills upon which Doverton lay. Its proximity to the mountains and the Eislandisch border had made it a strategically valuable location for centuries, being well-protected from almost anything that would come to threaten it. There were also the mines – Doverton had several different types of gems and ores that it could rely on for revenue and trade, putting it in a strong position amongst the other Zondrean city-states despite being the smallest of all of them. Being so small and so secure, it rarely saw much military action at all – even during the Rift Era, when the once-unified cities started warring amongst each other and eventually became separate states, Doverton was hardly touched. In fact, if the history books were right, Doverton's people merely decided to become independent when they heard everyone else had split away from the capitol in Zondrell and there was a war going on.

No wonder so many people were wandering about on the street, even with the sun now hanging so low in the sky. They were looking around, whispering to each other, trying to remember which city wore black and silver with the falcon symbol on the front. Not that seeing twenty or so soldiers being escorted calmly through the middle of town was a foreboding sight, but most of the time, Zondrell barely acknowledged the existence of Doverton. To see several of their uniforms at the same time was a sight unseen by most – probably even including the King himself.

When they stopped in the middle of the street, everyone else stopped too. Or pretended to, at any rate. No one wanted to be accused of spying or butting in on what was going on, but it was clear that something interesting was happening. Seraphine pushed her way through the growing crowd until she finally got close enough to see some of their faces. Tristan was not among the group, nor was her sister. In fact, the only ones she recognized among them were a couple of the King's Honor Guards and a very, very annoyed Onyx Saçaille. It was no particular secret that the King's weapon master had a distaste for most Zondreans. Her patience was short with many people, especially nobility – save for the King himself. Why she lived and worked in Doverton, no one was really sure, but there was much speculation about her relationship with the King. King Eric IV, of the Bradenton House, was a practical man, and his wife had passed many years ago. Why not take up with a pretty woman who could also serve as the Weapon Master? Most people in Doverton thought little of it because they generally liked their King, and perhaps surprisingly, they liked Saçaille, too – who wouldn't like someone who, within just a few short years, had turned their modest little fighting force into one of the most efficient and elite in all of Zondrea?

"I think we should be allowed to go to the palace first," said one of the men. He appeared to be the leader of the group, a taller, slender man who even at a distance, struck Seraphine as headstrong and arrogant. As she moved around to get a better view she realized he was also a mage, a Water mage with bright, pulsing blue eyes. "Some of our men could use a rest."

"You may rest at the temple. The King is indisposed at present," Onyx sneered through a clenched jaw and drawn lips. She had tried so hard to be pleasant and welcoming, but had nearly reached the end of her ability to be remain civil with these Zondrell jackasses. The mage was especially irritating, and he would simply not stop talking and asking questions. Too bad no one seemed to outrank him to shut him up.

"Fine, fine. But we don't have all day."

Faced in public with twenty sets of eyes staring her down, looking for a favorable reply, Saçaille relented. "Have it your way." As they turned back and started toward the temple, Seraphine moved as fast as she could to beat them there. She felt compelled to know what was going on, and what better way to find out than to stay close to where the action was?

The brisk wind and anticipation of what might be to come made her walk a tad faster, her feet aching just a bit more than usual in their simple leather shoes. Someone said hello to her, and she waved back without looking. She couldn't look – she was focused too much on her destination, and she needed to get there quickly. This same focus was what made her bump into someone so hard her sack shot forward and parcels of wrapped cheese and salted meat scattered themselves all over the gravel.

"Oh dear, I'm so sorry," she said, kneeling down to grab up her packages. A large, strong hand on her forearm made her stop.

"Allow me." It was a very tall, wide-shouldered man in a heavy, dark cloak, and once she realized what she was looking at, she instantly knew him. She didn't even have to see his face, although she could see those clear blue eyes staring back at her from under his hood. The large Eislandisch man carefully picked up all of things she had gotten at market, made sure they were not damaged, and placed them back in the sack while she watched, not really sure what to say or do.

"Thank you," was all she could manage once he presented her with her goods.

"Bad things are about to happen," he said, matter-of-fact. "Can you feel it?"

"What are you talking about? What things?"

He pulled the hood back to reveal a bit of a cleaner version of the face she remembered from the night he dropped poor Tristan at their door. In fact, they really rather looked a bit alike now that she had a good look at him in what was left of the daylight. His eyes were shaped a bit differently, his skin just a bit lighter and more ruddy than olive, and of course, he was much older, but they could certainly have been related somehow. "You… do not feel it?"

"No, I'm sorry – I don't understand."

"Then maybe I was wrong."

"What? What are you talking about? Look, Sir, I have to get going."

She started to push past him, then, but stopped when she felt a strong hand close around her elbow. "When you see her, tell your sister not to fear the coming storm," he said, then released his grip. As she turned around, confused and rather shaken, he had already started to melt into the crowd.

Her round cheeks were flushed and her dark, reddish hair mussed about in several directions by the time she charged through the door of the temple for the second time that day. Its hinges creaked and groaned with the excessive exercise – not too unlike the joints in her knees – and she was met with several inquisitive looks.

"Is something wrong, Sister?" Veronica said, rushing up to meet her. She took her sack from her and set it aside, holding Seraphine's arm with her other hand to guide her into the safety of the church. "Did you see what was happening outside?"

"They're coming this way," Seraphine said through deep breaths. She hadn't run quite like that in ages and was surprised at how quickly it took her wind right out of her.

"Not those Zondrell soldiers?"

"Yes, they want to rest here."

Sister Veronica shrugged and motioned to some of the acolytes, who scurried off to do things like make tea and make sure there was somewhere appropriate for guests to sit. Of course there was – the main chapel was enormous compared to the tiny little church that Seraphine ran, and there were smaller chapels for private ceremonies like weddings and funerals on either side of the main one, as well. Everything was perfectly pristine and ready for visitors at any time, day or night. But yet, it wasn't every day that a contingent of soldiers from another city – and the King's Weapon Master – walked in unannounced.

Saçaille and the two Honor Guards led them through the large double-doors, filing them in one or two at a time. Mostly young lads, heads down, quiet, fatigued. Some looked unhappy to be there, others just simply looked unhappy, while a few more seemed thrilled at the prospect of getting inside and into a warm building for a little while. The clanking of metal and the thuds of heavy boots on stone accompanied them, creating a raucous chorus that echoed across the great chapel's chamber.

"Who's in charge here?" asked the Water mage, who apparently only liked speaking to other people who were "in charge" of something. Now that he was just a few feet away, Seraphine could see that his features seemed to match his character. He was striking, but not in the way that made ladies swoon over him. They might have swooned over other things he had to offer, like money or prestige (and based on his jewelry and the cut of his jacket, he had plenty of both), but this man had the features of a hawk – sharp and gaunt and all-together too severe to be attractive.

"I'm the caretaker here," Sister Veronica said, setting forward and offering her hand in friendship. The young Water mage took it briefly, an empty gesture devoid of feeling. "Do you gentlemen need something?"

The tone in Saçaille's voice was pure fake courtesy. "They are here to rest. They wish to see the King for an audience."

"When can we see the King?" the mage asked.

"The King does not take visitors during the dinner hour. You may speak with him later. As I told you before." The Honor Guards behind their Weapon Master looked at each other with a silent smirk at this – they knew exactly how many times this nobleman mage had asked this same question. It was getting to the point of passing for comedy, even amongst some of the Zondrell troops.

Sister Veronica did her best to keep the mood light, motioning to the mage and his men to come in, relax, get comfortable. "Please, rest, have some tea and a warm meal. We have plenty to share."

Most of the men did just that, and were happy to do so. They took off sword belts, settled in on pews, chatted amongst themselves. They didn't even wait for the mage to give them a command – perhaps he wasn't their true leader at all. Everyone looked, to Seraphine, like they were trying very hard to gain a semblance of normalcy, but something was off. It seemed that at any second they would jump to the ready, to put those swords back on and use them. Only one of them, a shorter lad, younger, with a nice round face and hardened, dark eyes, stayed exactly where he was, near the shoulder of the mage. Despite the fact that they didn't resemble each other that much, Seraphine guessed that they were cousins or maybe brothers, given the same way they carried themselves, and the same way they frowned as they surveyed their comrades attempting to enjoy themselves.

"Go sit for a bit," the shorter one said.

The mage's eyes flared brightly with magical light, and his tone was as cold as the magic he possessed. "Not until we get an audience."

"What the fuck difference does it make, Victor? We're not in a hurry."

"We are not here to waste time, Peter." With that, the mage called Victor did move, but not to rest anywhere. Instead, he started walking around, surveying the chapel, poking his head into the darkened smaller chapels that flanked the great one on the north and south, looking behind the altar to look for... well, something. Seraphine had no idea what, but when she happened to glance over at Saçaille, it did not appear that his activity was to her liking. Her arms were crossed tightly against her chest, an effort to keep herself from reaching for her sword. Seraphine would have guessed that the Weapon Master wanted very much to send this haughty wizard straight back to Zondrell – in pieces on the back of a shield. After a few moments of watching him pry into other people's things, she too began to stroll about, her footsteps making light strikes against the marble floor.

As she passed in front of Seraphine, she whispered, "Say nothing." Seraphine felt her heart speed up. This didn't sound good. What was going on?

"Captain?" Onyx raised her voice so that it carried across the chamber. "Are you looking for something… specific?"

"As I told you before, we're looking for men of ours that might have been lost." Victor turned to Sister Veronica with a piercing gaze. "Has anyone come through here in the past few days who might have been from Zondrell?"

"This place sees many visitors from day to day, my lord. You'll have to be more specific," the old priestess replied.

"Someone in uniforms like we have, perhaps? He might have been injured, looking for treatment? Even without the uniform, he'd sound like he was from Zondrell when he spoke, even though he might look Eislandisch. Does this sound like anyone you've seen?" Veronica shook her head. "No? How about any of you?" The mage started to pace the room again, to see if he could make eye contact with any of the acolytes. All of the girls shook their heads too, some with wide eyes and looking half scared out of their wits.

When he finally got to Seraphine, she felt frozen in place. He might as well have set some of his ice magic upon her, and the air truly did grow cold in his presence. This was not a man to be trifled with. A most unpleasant feeling of fear and distrust and confusion all muddled together at once. Who was this person? Should she say something? Should she hide the truth? Of course, in reality, it was easier to simply not say anything than lie, like she did when it came to answering her sister's questions about what she and Saçaille talked about behind closed doors. But here, now, with this man standing before her expectantly, she found that lying was much more difficult than she even thought possible.

She almost said something. She almost said that yes, she knew that man they were looking for. Why was he asking, anyhow? But, that would only be something said by someone who truly didn't believe the Prophecy. She didn't… but then again, maybe she had her doubts. All of this fighting, all of these machinations – Saçaille had done this to these men. It was she who had turned them into this sad group of wanderers they saw sitting in the temple at Doverton, searching for whatever it was they thought they were looking for. Seraphine knew this in her heart, no one had to tell her. No one would, even if she'd asked. She just knew that her temple was "safe," and that the "threat" was being taken care of. That's what Saçaille kept telling her, though if she had to sit and ask herself, she never truly knew what she was being kept safe from. Now she knew, because she was staring right at him – and he wanted answers. If she said something now, perhaps this whole nonsense would end and she and her sister could go back to their lives as they had been.

If, of course, that silly Prophecy wasn't starting.

"No, m'Lord. I've not see anyone like that," Seraphine muttered, shaking her head and looking down at the floor. For the moment, Victor seemed satisfied and turned away from her; the relief she felt was something beyond words. She wanted to run off and make her way back to her temple as quickly as she could, but that might draw suspicion. With the way her pulse rose and the sweat began to make her robes cling to her, she had a feeling she was already doing a poor job of hiding any secrets.

Victor went back to stand before Saçaille, hands clasped behind his back. Even being taller than average himself, he still stood a few inches shorter than she, but this was not a man who was intimidated easily. "So, how is it that there can be a battle less than ten miles away and you've not seen any of our men? Surely they'd come over here for healing."

"Perhaps they became… lost." The emotionless way she said those words made Seraphine's stomach turn. "You still have not said why there was a battle so near my border at all. Answer my question, and I will answer yours."

He wasn't going to. Instead he stalked off, clearly irritated, with the other one – Peter – not far behind. They spoke in hushed tones at the back of the chapel, avoiding the rest of their group. For their part, the rest of the men didn't seem too affected. They wanted nothing to do with Saçaille, and most really didn't want to be anywhere else but at home in a warm bed. Seraphine's heart silently wept for them – some of them looked so young, boys being led around by other boys to do the work of men. Prophecy or no Prophecy, it was the kind of work that led to ruin.

After several hours of waiting, watching, and helping her Sisters with food and tea and wine for their guests, Seraphine decided she had to leave. The sun was gone, the tension in the temple was increasing by the minute, and she wanted to get back to Andella, to try to tell her what was going on. She picked up her things and moved to the door, but Saçaille was there to block her path. "Going home?"

"Yes, it's getting late."

Onyx lowered her voice to barely a whisper, leaning in so close that Seraphine could smell the sweet scent of her heady, spiced perfume. Yes, even warriors sometimes wore perfume. "You had best wait here."

"Why? What's going on?"

"Here it is safer." The Lavançaise shot a dark glance at the Zondrellian men, seeking out the mage to keep him within view. "Stay and wait."

Safer? What did that mean? What kind of trouble was waiting for her at home? Was her sister safe? She certainly hoped so. She didn't *not* trust Tristan, but at the same time... well, no, it was true – she didn't really trust him. Just like she didn't really *not* believe in the Prophecy. Seraphine found herself feeling quite light-headed, and the color vanished from her cheeks. "Are bad things happening?" she muttered.

"That depends on who you ask, Mademoiselle."

1

Tristan Loringham

Two days – they'd given me all of two days to enjoy my earned freedom from the Academy. But that's the way it happens sometimes, or so they told me when the three well-armored guards came to inform me I had until tomorrow evening to pack my things and say goodbye to my friends and family for a while. How long, they weren't sure, but the journey would be short by horseback, and I would be at my destination by morning.

"Isn't there a briefing or something I should be getting?" I asked the eldest of the guards, the one who had been doing most of the speaking.

"No, Sir," he said through partially clenched teeth. "Not now – you will receive your briefing when you arrive. Be ready by sundown, and sure to get some rest as we won't be stopping along the way." And that was it. They turned around and left as quickly as they had arrived, leaving my parents, and me, quite bewildered. Of the three of us, my father seemed the least surprised; maybe he knew something was coming. He might have even known where I was going, and what I would learn when I arrived – I will never know if this is true, but I wouldn't be surprised. It's not like he would have done anything about it. I think, when it came down to it, he believed it was a fitting punishment to send me off far beyond the comforting walls of Zondrell after what happened during the graduation tournament.

"You really should have declined that last match," he would tell me over and over again after it happened. He was embarrassed, and something in me understood that, perhaps even agreed with it, but at the same time, his lack of support upset me to no end.

All I could say in reply was, "It got me the Medal, didn't it?"

Somehow, amazingly, in the end they had decided to reward me with what I had worked so hard to achieve, and I was, for a while, quite pleased with myself because of it. No one in my family had ever received a High Honor from the Academy before, even though the Loringhams had been military men from the beginning of time. They were good soldiers, sure, but not great ones. *I* was great – or so I wanted my father to believe, and he did, I think. My mother believed it, too, but convincing her wasn't difficult. In fact, she was so pleased with that Medal she had a special shelf built in the sitting room specifically for it, just a small display, nothing too ostentatious, but something that allowed it to stay in at least partial sunlight most of the day, so as to capitalize on the luster of the pure silver from which it was carved. I thought about taking it with me when I left, for luck or some silly notion, but something made me leave it where it was.

Mum was, of course, *most* displeased with the news of my imminent and near-immediate departure. I don't think I had seen her so angry since I had accidentally broken the good tea set when I was seven, but this time the anger was directed squarely at my father. She pulled him into the parlor and shut the door, but privacy was futile the way she yelled, her sharp accent punctuating every word and sending it out through the entire house. "They cannot even give the dignity of more than a few days of warning? This is insulting! Tristan has spent years in that *place*, and now they want him to go away again? They will not even say where?"

My father maintained a sense of stoic calm, as was his general nature. "This is the Zondrell military, my dear. These things happen sometimes."

"There is no need for them to treat us this way. They do this to avenge the boy at the tournament."

"Probably, Gretchen, but what do you want me to do about it?"

"Say something to someone. That boy started the fight. They should punish *him*."

"Who says they're not?"

I stopped listening. Father was not going to say anything to anyone on my behalf, and honestly, I didn't want him to. I could accept my fate – it couldn't have been all *that* bad. The land was generally at peace, there were no great wars raging in any of the nearby city-states… nothing terrible or dangerous could possibly be awaiting me. Of course, when you're young, you're stupid; you think you're invincible, immune to death and pain and suffering, so I went on about my day with my thoughts fully entrenched in that invincible haze. I assumed I might be gone a few days – a week at the most – and that I would return as if nothing interesting had happened, going on about my business of staking my claim as a young nobleman in Zondrell society. I still find it hard to fathom just how wrong about that assumption I was.

That last day in the city went by far too quickly. Alex, Corrin, and I went down to the artist's shop outside Center Market to get our tattoos – as was tradition, all Academy graduates get something, somewhere, usually a family crest or something inconspicuous, yet meaningful in some way. No one knew how the tradition started, especially since the art of decorating someone's skin was not at all a native Zondrean skill, but somewhere along the line, it became the most popular thing to do to signify that you had graduated from an Academy. The place off of Center Market – Three Sisters Curios and Artistry – was where many went, mainly because of the fantastic work that was done there, but also because the three Katalahni sisters themselves were quite lovely and easy to get along with. In addition to tattooing, they also created and sold various goods from their homeland, including customized jewelry, which had lately become *all* the rage amongst the finest ladies of Zondrell.

Corr got the Shal-Vesper crest, an elaborate white "S" and a red "V" intertwined against a teardrop-shaped field of black, emblazoned in the center of his back, small enough and placed well enough to stay out of sight most of the time. Alex and I had a harder time choosing something – this was permanent, after all, and that fact was not lost on either of us – so we flipped through the tattered book of sketches the sisters had on their front counter.

The eldest of the three ladies, a tall, svelte brown-skinned woman with her shiny black hair always put up in multiple tightly-wound braids, leaned over the counter to observe and help us choose something. "You are a romantic, Mister Vestarton – or so says my sister. You should get a flower." She smiled and across the room, I noticed Zizah blushing noticeably, in spite of her dark honey-colored complexion. Not everyone knew about Alexander and his occasional evenings with Zizah, but it was certainly common knowledge around the sisters' shop.

Alex considered the currently open page for a moment, filled with several images of different kinds of flowers. Some were smaller, some larger, some a bit more feminine and delicate in the way they were drawn, while others were sharper, with crisper lines and subdued colors. "All right – you pick one off this page for me. Put it right here." He pointed to the left side of his chest, just over his heart, a sly sort of smile on his face. "If you're going to be called a romantic, you might as well own up to it, right?"

Zizah's strangely accented lilt had a slight air of annoyance in it. "Well, if you must let all the girls see it, be sure you let them know who put it on you, at least."

And then it was my turn. I flipped a few more pages – nothing. A few more – still nothing. Then, almost at the end, an interesting sketch, unusual, the only one on that particular page… "You know what that is, don't you?" the tall sister asked.

"Of course," I said. "You drew this?"

"Yes, that was one of mine. It is supposed to be gold, from an old Katalahni story. Such a thing would suit *you* very well, Mister Loringham. You should get that." In the Old literature, the gold dragon usually represented strength or courage, something that was fearsome and yet was also to be respected. Gold dragons were neither good nor evil, and in the Katalahni story she mentioned, they also could not be killed. The hero, reckless and foolish, had gone to slay one, only to fall to fatigue when he realized the battle couldn't be won. The moral of the story? Sometimes the beast to be slain is what's in a man's heart.

"That's the one," I told her without hesitation. "Put it where I'll be able to see it." She chose the meaty part of my right shoulder – my swordarm, of course.

The whole thing took just about an hour to complete. Art was in the sisters' blood, and tattooing was invented in the sandy dunes of Katalahnad, so they knew exactly what they were doing. More often than not, people prefer not to watch what's going on, instead shutting their eyes to think about something other than the pain, but fascination with how they worked kept me fully entranced the entire time. The device they used was truly amazing – it was more or less a knife, a very thin and very sharp little instrument that cut just beneath the surface of the skin. The interesting part came in the thing affixed to the top of the knife — just between the handle and the blade sat a small cup resembling a writer's inkwell. Occasionally, the sisters would reach to a nearby table and pour some colored dye into this container, which had a small hole at its bottom just big enough to allow the water-thinned substance to glide down a groove in the blade and seep into each incision. When guided by a practiced hand, it could form patterns in much the same way as a painter might use his brush on a piece of canvas; it took a great deal of skill to ensure that each line was drawn so thin and so perfect that it would close without scarring, leaving behind only the picture, immortalized in brightly-colored inks. Of all of the dyes, the gold one had burned the most, sending all of the nerves in the right side of my body alight at once, but I never twitched or flinched, not once. Rivulets of blood tinged with gold and black pigments trailed down my arm, collecting in a sizable pool on the floor. The cuts had to be deep enough, of course, or the dye wouldn't go far enough into the flesh, so bleeding was expected, and after some time, I grew accustomed to the cool sensation every time a new rivulet formed and flowed.

When it was over, we each had fresh bandages covering our artistic new wounds, but not before taking an opportunity to review our finished products. "It's good," I told the artist as I peered into the little mirror hanging on the wall in front of where I sat. Although the flesh around it was bright red and there were still some spots in the design that seeped small amounts of blood, it looked as if it belonged there, as if it had always been there.

We paid the ladies for their work and spent a good part of the rest of that day at the Silver, drinking, talking, enjoying the time we had left together. Various people floated in and out of the place, had a drink with us, and left. By the time the sun grew low and heavy in the clear sky of early fall, it was just me and Alex, taking out the last of our third bottle of wine. "So how long will you be gone, do you know?" he asked between sips.

I shook my head. "They wouldn't say. I don't even know where I'm going."

"That's a fucking joke. What is this then, punishment?"

"My father thinks so."

"Your father *would*." Alexander downed the rest of his drink and lit another *tsohbac* stick from the candle burning in the center of our table. The smoke ebbed and flowed around us, filling our immediate surroundings with that thick, rich, slightly sweet sort of odor that can only be found in the best tobacco. Personally, I didn't see what the allure was, but lots of people smoked the stuff quite regularly, and Alex... well, he probably did it a lot more than the average person, but it did give him something do with his hands. Before he took up *tsohbac*, he could often be found fiddling with the buttons on his shirts, adjusting his jewelry, running his fingers through his hair, whatever it took to keep him occupied.

"It's all right – whatever it is, it can't be all that bad," I said at length, at the time still believing it... or perhaps just trying to convince myself.

That whole day, I had a general sense that I was somehow looking on, observing life as it happened in a surreal sort of trance. Perhaps I could blame it on the excitement, the trepidation of going somewhere else, someplace perhaps far from the city I knew. Or, maybe it was just the wine. Either way, before I knew it, it was sundown, and I was saying goodbye to people as three regular troops and a very irritated Peter Wyndham waited patiently in the street. The prospect of traveling with him didn't appeal to me much, but his presence did confirm one thing – this was *definitely* some kind of punishment. I resigned to it with a bit of a sigh while Alex, in his ever-optimistic way, insisted that we'd be right back at the Silver in a couple of days, nothing to worry about. Both of our mothers fought back steady streams of tears. But it was my father who most surprised me – he wished me luck and insisted I take a good weapon, not the simple, cheap thing I had been using for practice and everyday carry at the Academy. So he gave me the one on the wall, the one that for many years as a boy I was forbidden to touch, the one with the three jewels embedded into the hilt. Before I started at the Academy, he'd promised it to me, but we kept it there, safe on the wall all that time. This had been his blade when it last saw battle, decades ago, but now it was polished and brand new once again – it flashed even in the dim light of torches and Sarabande, the Early Moon.

I put up my hands at first, refusing to take it. "I can't take that," I said. But all he did was press it more forcefully into the silver falcon crest stitched into the front of my uniform.

"Yes, you can. Just bring it back before summer's out. You'll need to be back by then if your application's gone through."

"You know about that?" I had no intention of telling him I had put in to teach at the Academy unless they were to actually accept it – and I had little faith that they would. But then again, news travels fast in the tight circles of Zondrell nobility.

"It's a good idea," Father said, pushing that sword on me just a little harder. So I accepted it, replacing the simple steel one at my belt with the much grander piece of craftsmanship. Looking back, I wonder if he would have given it to me if he'd known the kinds of things it would soon bear witness to.

After that, all I could do was say a final goodbye and mount up. There was no reason to prolong it any further. Besides, I could feel Wyndham's hateful glaring behind me. He said absolutely nothing to me until we were well clear of the city, the walls of Zondrell getting smaller and smaller behind us as our horses trudged dutifully along the wide dirt road, what they called Dover Pass, the long path that curved from Zondrell in a north-northeast direction toward the city-state of Doverton, and beyond that, into the mountains that separated the Zondrean states from Eisland. I only knew this because I had seen it on maps – I had never experienced it for myself. I had never even been so far beyond the city gates before, for that matter.

"Do you know where we're going?" Peter asked about two miles into the journey, breaking the general silence that characterized our little group. Our accompaniment did not acknowledge him.

"We'll find out when we get there," I replied, my voice seeming to come from far away. Didn't I want to know where we were headed just as much as he did? Yes, a part of me definitely did, but it was a small part; the rest of me really couldn't have cared less. The sooner we got there and did whatever we were supposed to do, the sooner it would be over.

Peter made a *humph* sound at the back of his throat. "Well, this is… this is totally unacceptable. Haven't I been punished enough?"

"Shut the fuck up, Wyndham." When I said this, one of the soldiers snickered.

"Fuck you. This is your fault. Do you know you broke my nose in two different places? It really hurts." I looked at him, then, really looked for the first time, and indeed, he bore a rather colorful collection of bruises across the bridge of his nose – a nose slightly less straight and a bit wider than it once was.

I pulled the reins hard to the left and stopped my horse directly in front of his, forcing him to stop with a jolt. The horses thought little of it, seeing the opportunity to dip their heads in search of something to eat, but Peter's round eyes were wider than the twin full moons. "I could try for three." When he couldn't come up with anything clever to respond with, I continued. "Or, you can be quiet and we can travel in peace. It's your choice."

He chose wisely, and no one said anything else for the rest of the journey.

**

We arrived at our destination somewhere around midmorning, just as the sun was beginning to find its peak. We had already watched the sunrise, but this wasn't just any sunrise – the Dover Pass had taken us high into the wilderness, up into the foothills and eventually into the rocky, harsh swells that led to the white-capped Mountains with Two Names. The ground had become uneven and unreliable, our horses carefully stepping along half-eroded, ancient paths. In fact, we were far enough from the low-lying forests and coastal grasslands of Zondrell that the air had become a little difficult to breathe, but the views... in all directions, everywhere I looked, the views were nothing short of spectacular. It seemed as if you could see forever, and that the sky was a thousand times bigger than it looked over Zondrell. The moons and the stars seemed closer to the ground here, as if you could climb just a tiny bit higher and reach out to touch them. And when the sun began to creep out from the east, it lit off a firestorm of colors – purples, blues, oranges, golds – the likes of which I had never seen.

"Welcome to Eisland," said the man who was waiting to greet us. I knew him mostly by reputation, although he had spoken at a few lectures at the Academy a couple of years ago. Captain Cedric Shilling was a serious figure, a stout gentleman of about fifty or so, who had made the Army his entire life. Very few men of his social standing would still be running campaigns and actively participating in military affairs at his age, but by all accounts, Shilling was no typical Zondrell noble. His elder brother, Alastair, held the seat of the House, and there were many children to carry on the family name and wealth; there was little need for him to do the same, and he had no desire for it. Women are notoriously difficult to order around, anyhow, and children, doubly so.

Peter and I saluted, fists to shoulders, standing straight and tall and looking straight ahead. A similar return gesture, however, never came; instead Shilling just waved us off.

"At ease, gentlemen, please," he said, and we relaxed. Just a little. "So how long did it take you to get here?"

Wyndham shrugged. "We left before sundown. Probably could have gone a bit faster than we did, but I guess there was no hurry." He shot a sideways glance at our escorts for just a moment.

"No, not particularly. Although, now that I have you here... Lieutenant Loringham, come with me for a moment, would you?" I started to follow him as he barked a few additional orders back over his shoulder toward the soldiers, something regarding getting our things and placing them somewhere. We climbed a small ridge that then led down into a clearing amongst the haphazard forest of tall thin pines, where dozens of canvas tents and simple cloth bedrolls lay clustered together around cooking gear and smoldering firepits. There really weren't that many men there – perhaps a hundred or less – and they all looked like they had been there for quite a while. Many were not even awake just yet, but those who were barely acknowledged us as we trudged through the center of the campsite.

"Been doing a lot of watching for the past couple of months up here," said Shilling. I walked about a pace behind him, taking in the surroundings, getting used to the idea that this place could very well be my home for just as long as it had been theirs, if not longer. I still had no idea why they were all there in the first place, though.

"'Watching,' Sir?"

When he stopped, I stopped. He turned around to face me, his hands clasped behind his back and his gray-flecked dark eyes searching, looking me over – assessing me. "Yes, patrolling, getting a sense of who comes through here, how often, where they come from... you know, observation. They do teach you about that at the Academy still, do they not?"

"Well, yes Sir, it's just that I, ah..." I struggled for words that wouldn't make me sound like stupid, or worse, that I was questioning him. "I'm sorry. Please continue."

Something like a smirk formed deep creases at one corner of his lips, adding to his weathered appearance. "How tired are you, Lieutenant?"

I shook my head. "I don't know – I haven't slept since yesterday, if that's what you mean, but I'm all right." This was an outright lie. My body felt like it was made of lead, and even though I was indeed awake and coherent, I was starting to have trouble focusing my vision. "May I ask why, Sir?"

"Got a job for you. There's a patrol we know about that comes through near here in the morning hours. Go with Sergeant Delrin and his squad – we'll talk more when you get back. You won't be gone long."

"Aye, Sir." He and I both knew that it was highly inappropriate for me to question him at that point. I had just been given an order, and regardless of how tired I might have been, that order was going to be carried out. I could only hope that he had something similar in store for Wyndham.

"Good lad." He tapped me on the chest. "You're wearing your armor under that, yes?" I nodded; even though I didn't think I'd need it so quickly, I had put on my entire cold weather set before we set out – wool shirt with long sleeves and leggings to match, followed by thick leather plates strapped around me at various strategic places, and then topped off by the black and silver livery of Zondrell in coarse linen. Many men, especially officers, wore steel instead of simple leather, but I always preferred to have the luxury of moving around unhindered. Fighting becomes quite difficult when you're weighed down with sixty pounds of metal.

"All right then," Shilling said with that same smirk on his face, "get after it. Delrin will fill you in – over there. Be careful." I nodded and set off toward the edge of camp where Shilling directed me with a weak nod and not another word.

Delrin did not "fill me in" as much as quietly lead me and other men with us, a rough group of soldiers who greeted me with little more than inarticulate grunts. The Sergeant seemed to know exactly where he was going, cutting a careful path through the wilderness and taking care to stay mostly within the shade of the trees. Given the weathered look of his skin, the way the age lines crawled across his face, the way the close-cropped hair turned to salt and pepper the closer it came to his temples, I assumed he had walked similar patrols many times before in many different places.

"Do be careful we don't mistake you for one of them, Sir," was all Delrin said to me during the entire half-hour trek, sometime after we left sight of the camp and but directly before he turned and spat on my boots. I could have had him for insubordination but we weren't in the middle of the city –

this was the open wilderness, and the formalities of the Zondrell Military didn't really mean much to these men. Rules just got in the way of business, and besides, this was one of the senior men around here – to confront him would have brought on the fury of the entire group, if not that of every solider back at the camp. So, despite my instincts to the contrary, I did the smart thing and kept my mouth shut.

The cold thin air was so strange to me, and not only was it hard to breathe but it made everything seem a little off, disorienting. The more I tried to catch my breath and get my wits about me, the worse it seemed to get. We moved cautiously through the wilderness for about a half an hour before there was a crackle of dead branches breaking underfoot, somewhere up ahead. We all paused, and a hush fell over the woods. Several of them looked at me for a signal. A signal – what signal? I couldn't even see anyone. The trees and the rocks cast shadows everywhere I looked, and there were places here where sunlight had probably not shone in centuries. I didn't know what to do, but I wasn't going to let them know that. I peered deep into the spotty gloom and eventually I did see something, a lighter spot in a clearing about fifty feet ahead of us, with shadows moving around within it. I moved closer, as silently as I could, to get a better look. I barely took a breath, and my heart was pounding to the point where it was all I could hear. My limbs shook so much I was sure that I would trip and fall, alerting everyone in a two-mile radius to our presence.

There were five of them, a small band of men in the blue and silver livery of the nation of Eisland. Delrin had not spoken out of turn – I could have been mistaken for any one of them. They were all tall, broad-shouldered, blond and blue-eyed, pure-blooded Eislandisch to the core. And they were armed, too, with longswords on their belts or strapped across the back. Five of them, ten of us… surely the advantage was with Zondrell. I wished, though, that I'd had time to think about *why* we were out here, why we were getting ready to attack, because then maybe things would have gone differently. As it was, though, my legs eventually did give out a bit and I stumbled in the dead branches and leaves of the forest floor.

The battle was effectively on, whether I wanted it or not.

Almost as soon as the first Eislander peeked his head into the woods, my men were on him, and he was dead before he knew what hit him. The rest of them were smarter, though, and they scattered into the darkness to gain some advantage. For a split second I froze in place, not sure what to do with myself. I'd never drawn actual sharpened steel with the intent to kill another person. And never, not even through all the training at the Academy, did I ever imagine I would be in such a situation. It's just not something I thought about. They always told us that the "grunts" would do that sort of thing for us. But here I was, and there were live people out there that wanted my blood… and the grunts weren't exactly there to protect me, either.

I heard a metallic noise to my right and instantly ripped my sword off my belt. My heart leapt into my throat and I felt lightheaded – far from quick-to-react. I just barely dodged a swing that would have taken my head clean off. I remember feeling off-balance and halfway on one knee, looking up at the Eislandisch soldier trying to kill me, and I thought it was odd that we should be fighting. After all, we might be cousins somewhere down the line – who knew? But, he didn't seem to have the same reservations.

It was a fast fight, a furious one, something I'd never experienced before; there was no calculating what to do next, where to strike, no conversation and certainly no holding back for fear of hurting the opponent "too much." But in spite of this, my body knew what to do and moved fluidly, of its own accord. Thinking was only going to get in the way… or get me killed. Even when I got the upper hand and thrust forward, sending my sword deep into his stomach, hearing the gurgling and tearing sounds as it went in and watching the leather and cloth around the impact point blacken, I didn't stop to ponder what I'd done – there was no time. I didn't take a moment to reflect on the fact that this was probably the first time in years – if ever – that the ornate sword my father had given me had tasted blood, and that now its fine polish was ruined.

Before I even had the opportunity to loosen my weapon from its deathgrip, I felt something to the left, a presence, a figure, something threatening. Then I felt wind from a blade against my cheek. On my hip I had a dagger, that good silver one with a red jewel on the handle that my father gave to me when I was sixteen years old. I'd never really used it or carried it before, but for some reason I had grabbed it before I left home. And I was glad for it because it saved my life that day. With my left hand I pulled it out and jabbed at my unseen attacker without even looking back. I didn't have to – my hand knew where to go. The next thing I knew I felt something warm and wet spray across my arm, the whole side of my clothes, my face, my hair. It took a few minutes for me to register what it was I was covered in and what I had just done. Time stood still as I watched the light fade from the eyes of the man who was still impaled on my sword. I couldn't look away – hell, I couldn't even move.

"Well done, Sir," one of my men said, sort of quiet as if in disbelief. His voice started me, and I pulled my weapons in quickly – too quickly, in fact. Bodies slumped at my feet and the sickening sound of them hitting the ground made me jump back a step. I looked down at them, and at my hands with white knuckles gripping those blades with all my might. A tremendous amount of self-control was the only thing keeping me from crying or vomiting or the gods knew what else.

Someone poked me in the shoulder and I wheeled about to face him. It was Sergeant Delrin, eyes narrowed and brow furrowed. He cleared his throat and gestured to an Eislandisch soldier, injured but still alive, struggling in the grasp of two of my men. One of them applied pressure to the small of his back and he fell to his knees with an angered grunt. "Sir – you want this last one then?" When I cocked my head, not sure I heard him right, he repeated himself. "Do you want this one? To take back to camp?"

With the back of my left hand, I wiped my cheek and felt the warm crimson smear across my skin. My hands trembled mightily, but I managed not to drop my weapons. I'm not sure I could have if I'd tried. "Take him back?"

Delrin clapped me on the shoulder, and there was a different sort of glimmer in his dark gray eyes then, something I couldn't quite pin down. "We do more than just scout... well, we do now that you're here."

I didn't quite know how to respond to this, but I also didn't want them to figure that out. So, I said in the most authoritarian tone I could muster, "All right then. Let's head back," and turned to go back the way we had come. However, I only took a few steps before I heard the sounds of scuffling, of twigs breaking underfoot and rocks scattering across the ground.

"Hey, get him under control, will you?" shouted one of the men as I turned back to the group. Another made an attempt to subdue our captive with the butt of a sword to the gut, but it didn't do much good. The Eislander was tall and stocky, built like a stone tower, and had no intention of simply surrendering to us. A large number of foreign obscenities streamed from his lips.

"The more you fight, the worse it will be," I told him in his native tongue. I didn't even know what that meant. Maybe he knew that, too, because he looked at me with more hate than I had seen in anyone's eyes, ever.

"Fuck you, *Halben*," he said in Eislandisch, every syllable sending forth a spray of spittle. "Let me go or kill me now. I will not help you people."

I hated that word, *Halben*. I knew what it meant because I'd heard it before, many times while walking through Market Square and some of the places in Zondrell where merchants and travelers from other lands tended to gather. It was a slang term for someone who was half-Zondrean and half-Eislandisch, and was among one of the nastiest things you could say to someone in the Eislandisch world. My mother almost had the Guard called on her once for yelling at someone who had called me that on the street – even though I was only about six, I remembered it vividly. She had been beyond furious, almost wild in her anger.

The calm demeanor I was working so hard to maintain faded; it had become damn near impossible to take a normal breath or keep my limbs from shaking, but I stepped toward him anyhow, stood nose to nose with him and looked him directly in his sky-colored eyes. "You'll do whatever we want you to do," I said to him. "Now, walk." For almost a full minute, he considered me, the weapons I held, what his options were and what the consequences might be – I could almost see all of these thoughts moving around through the window of his eyes. But eventually, he put his head down and relaxed, and with that, we were on the move once again.

I spoke to no one else the entire trek back to camp. I hardly looked at anything but the ground under my feet. The only thing I wanted to do was to get into a bedroll somewhere, go to sleep, and never wake up again. Better yet, perhaps I would wake up and find myself in that bedroll, and I would realize that the past few hours had been nothing more than an unusually creative dream. The Academy prepares cadets for the inevitability of battle, of death and gore and all that, sure – I knew that someday I would probably have to take another man's life. I had accepted that a long time ago, just like every other cadet who had come before me, and all the others who would come after. It's just the way of things. But it had been so *easy*. It was as easy as walking or breathing, and that... well, that was terrifying. Some people are good at different things, like music and art and so forth, and I always envied people with such talents. I had never been much for art, couldn't play an instrument or sing, couldn't write a poem or make something that might benefit someone else. So, did that mean my only talent was death?

When we made it back to camp, Peter Wyndham was there near the central tent, having tea with Captain Shilling. It couldn't have been good tea, as it couldn't have been more than some lemongrass stewed in an iron pot for a few minutes, but the Captain did have a full silver tea service. It must have been one of the few things available to remind him of home.

Peter's round eyes grew even bigger as I approached. "Wow... you look, ah... What happened?"

Not for a second did I think he cared about my welfare. There was a good chance that soon he, too, would come back from a jaunt out in the woods covered in blood. I ignored him. "M'Lord, we have a captive, Sir," I said to Shilling with a stiff salute.

"You do? Excellent." That smirk with the hint of sinister intent crossed the captain's lips once again as he pulled a folded piece of paper out of his breast pocket. "Here take this – translate that and ask him those questions. Take him into that tent over there for some privacy, yeah?"

I only realized after I had taken the paper and opened it up how badly my hands were shaking. I wondered if anyone else had noticed. "Ah, Sir... I, um, I'm not certain about this," I stammered as I read the words scrawled across the page once more.

"What's the problem? I thought they told me you speak the language. You *can* read and translate, can't you?"

"Yes, Sir, it's just that... um..."

Now the smirk was replaced by more of a sneer, an unhappy one. "Spit it out, boy. I don't have all day."

I didn't know quite how to say it. Maybe this was some kind of bizarre nightmare. "You're asking me to ask him this?"

"Yes. What's the problem?"

I read them over one more time. *Have you ever seen an ancient temple in the mountains or forests near here? Have you ever witnessed any unusual activity in this area, such as flashes of light or unexplained magical effects? Do you have any knowledge of the Kaeren? Do you know where the Kaeren is located?* "I'm sorry, Sir," I tried so hard to put it delicately, but the words just didn't come out quite right, "but this has to be the strangest collection of questions I've ever seen."

Shilling leaned back in his seat and took a sip of tea. I thought for sure that he was quietly planning my execution, but instead, he chuckled. "Yes, I know that. But the scholars at the Magic Academy have convinced the King that this *thing*, whatever it is, is here, and it is now our job to locate it. The King has made it clear that it is extremely important that we find it and bring it back to Zondrell, and we can't go home until we do. So, whether you like it or not, you *will* do what you're told. Are we clear, Mister Loringham?"

"Yes, Sir." As I turned to carry out my orders, I noticed Peter out of the corner of my eye – all of the confidence and swagger in him was gone, replaced by a pale blankness, the kind of look a man gets when he's utterly confused and has nowhere to turn for guidance. I knew how he felt.

When it was just me and the Eislandisch captive staring at each other in the empty tent, I did what I was told to do – I asked each question in turn, in Eislandisch, pausing for an answer after each one. The man said nothing, so I asked them again. Still nothing.

"You do understand me? You understand these questions?" I asked him.

"I understand," he replied, more calmly than I would have expected. "I know nothing about this thing you ask about, and I have nothing to say to you, *Halben*." He flexed his shoulders a bit, straining against the ropes that bound him, but otherwise stood perfectly motionless before me, not frightened, not even nervous. But he was so young; he couldn't have been much older than me. I wondered how anyone in such a situation as his could be so composed; I even envied him for it. But then again, my mother had been able to do the same thing – she could turn her emotions on and off like the flame in an oil lamp. Maybe I could learn a lesson or two more from the Eislandisch yet.

I searched his eyes for some hint of a lie, some sort of weakness, but there was none to be found – nothing *I* was going to be able to uncover, anyhow. So I told him I would be back, turned around, and headed back to Shilling.

"Why are you back so quickly?" the captain asked, visibly annoyed.

"My Lord, he doesn't seem to know anything. He couldn't answer any of these questions."

Shilling stood so quickly he almost knocked over the entire tea setting. "Come over here," he said as he grabbed my shoulder – quite hard – and pulled me off to a quiet corner, just out of earshot of Wyndham or anyone else. "What about this assignment do you not understand, boy?"

My heart began to race; was I being scolded? "I'm sorry – I thought I was supposed to ask these questions. I've done that."

Shilling's dark eyes rolled up toward the sky for a moment while he composed himself. I could tell he was quite close to yelling at me, or worse, but his tone remained even, yet as sharp as any blade. I could only just continue to stand there and listen, trying to figure out what I was doing wrong. "Yes, but this isn't Academy Fun Time, boy. This is real, and you have real orders and I expect real results. Now, I realize that they did not brief you well before you came here, but you were sent here highly recommended. I was told that you had all of the skills that we need to carry out this mission – that you had the language, the fighting, and the disposition, to handle this. Now, as far as I can tell in the few hours that I've known you, son, I would say that if I had to pay for you to come here, I'd want my money back."

I looked down at my hands and my clothes, still splattered with someone else's blood. He might as well have slapped me across the face like a misbehaving kid. The 'disposition'? For what, exactly? "Sir, I..."

"Stop yourself right there," he hissed, cutting me off. "Listen to me, and listen carefully. You have one of two choices to make here. One, you may choose not to carry out this mission, and I will send you home. When that happens, I will send along dishonorable discharge papers, the contents of which will be carried out immediately upon your return to the city. You will be stripped of your rank, your medal, everything you have spent most of your young, privileged little life working toward. At that point, more than likely your father will disown you – I know for a fact that he wouldn't think twice about it – which leaves you homeless and the gods know what else. I mean, the last time such a thing happened to someone, he was kicked clear out of the city.

"Or, you can do what I have ordered you to do – get my answers. By any means necessary. I have spent far more time in this miserable, cold, disgusting hellhole of a country than I would have liked, looking for something that everyone seems to think is not here. But I have been tasked with finding this thing, and I do not like to return home from any mission empty-handed. It looks bad. The General and the King do not appreciate failure, but they like success – quite a bit – and they *do* reward dutiful service. So, do you understand your choices here, Lieutenant?"

The captain crossed his arms across his chest and looked at me expectantly. And by his harsh glare, I could tell that he meant every word he said. Misery or glory – choose one. It couldn't possibly have been more clear. All of the blood felt like it had drained right out of my body, and a chill settled in, making me so nauseous that I wasn't sure if I would make it to another complete sentence. Yes, I understood my choices. Yes, I understood what he wanted me to do. But I didn't like it – I didn't like any of this. The Academy trains soldiers, leaders, honorable warriors, not thugs and murderers. Maybe I wasn't cut out for the military after all; maybe it would have been better if I had quit that first year. At least then I would have been able to gather a few things before I found myself nameless and cast out on the streets. But then again, if killing on the battlefield was so easy...

"You said, 'by any means necessary.'"

Shilling smirked again. "Yes – do I need to elaborate on what that means?" In a lightning movement he pulled the jeweled dagger off from my belt and held it up to the light. It was still glistening and sticky. "Or are you not as stupid as you look, and indeed as smart as your exam results have indicated?" With a nonchalant toss, he handed the weapon back over, hilt first.

"I understand, Sir," I said softly, taking back my blade.

"Good. Don't come back until you've got what I need, or he's dead. I don't have time for bandying about." He stalked off, presumably back to his tea, but I had no doubt that he was watching me out of the corner of his eye as I made my way back to the empty tent.

I had a job to do.

Inside the tent, the growing gloom of afternoon had cast much of the light away and replaced it with shadows. "You return," the Eislandisch soldier said. "What do you want now?"

I could have sat down and planned it all out, thought about everything I was going to do, how I might... well, *do* it. But I couldn't even bring myself to start. It isn't like they teach interrogation tactics at the Academy. Not that it was something that needed a formal explanation; honestly, if I already knew how to hurt people on the battlefield, what made this any different? I could treat it like any other battle – the only difference was it was one where I was in complete control.

And the other man didn't have a weapon.

And he was bound and helpless.

My grip tightened around the dagger resting in my palm, much like the way the muscles and tendons had begun to constrict in my throat. If I was going to do it, I had to just get it over with, not think about the details. "I have orders to kill you," I said very quietly, very calmly. It didn't even really sound like my own voice. "But if you can tell me what I want to know, I might be able to spare you."

"Go ahead – get it over with, then. I know nothing." The soldier looked in my direction, but he wasn't looking directly at me. It wasn't until I walked in closer, until I stood face to face with him and could look into his vacant azure stare that I realized he wasn't devoid of emotion at all. On the contrary, he was positively terrified. The vein in his throat thumped fast with the beat of his heart, and there was a faint sheen of sweat covering his brow and cheeks. The muscles in his jaw quivered just the tiniest bit – so little that it was nearly imperceptible – and he could not, for any amount of money or fame or freedom in the world, look me directly in the eye.

Fucking hell – he was lying.

I grabbed him roughly by the silver-trimmed collar of his tunic and held my dagger to one side of his face, pressing just enough so as to make its presence felt, but not so hard as to break the skin. Not yet. "Are you certain about that?"

His entire body seemed to tense all at once. No, he wasn't certain at all; he didn't even need to say anything. But he still tried like hell to remain calm, and his voice was low and smooth, unstrained. "I told you, I know nothing. I am not afraid to die."

For one tiny frozen moment in time, we stood there like that, waiting each other out. As my blade continued pushing into his cheek, I could see that vein pumping that much more wildly, could feel the heat and tension rising within him that much more. "One problem – I don't believe you," I said as I quickly pulled the dagger downward, cutting a thin, bloody line across the side of his face from brow to jawline. The surprise of the action and of the pain he no doubt felt was enough to make him stagger backward a step, his eyes growing wide as they settled on drops of his own blood trickling down the length of the weapon in my hand. I once heard at the Academy that a man is far more likely to be frightened by the sight of his own blood than by the sight of an attacker or even the pain of injury. No, it's that initial wave of fear that sets in when you see your own blood splattered and dripping that makes you start to panic, to let your guard down, to make mistakes. I knew then I could use that to my advantage, especially since the flesh of the face and head is thin, and it bleeds and stings quite a bit when cut.

Again I held the blade on him, with the point aimed directly for his heart. "What do you want from me? What are you?

Some kind of mercenary?" he asked through shuddery breaths.

I pushed a little harder on the blade, enough to cause quite a lot of discomfort. "No, not a mercenary. And I told you what I want. Answer my questions."

"Fuck you, *Halben* scum. Eislandisch blood is too good for the likes of you." He spat on me again, and this time I didn't hold back any retaliation. He received a cut on the other side of his face to match the first one for his insubordination.

"Wait," he growled, grimacing as the blood rolled down his cheeks and neck. "This thing you talk about – Kaeren – I know nothing of it... I am just a common soldier."

Still lying. It was too obvious, and I was sick of this. I was tired; I was so tired I could have fallen asleep on my feet. I wanted it to end just as much as he did, maybe more so. So I punched him across the face as hard as I could, with the dagger still in my hand to give it a little extra force. The crunching sound it made as bones and cartilage gave way was enough to put him on his knees. "Why do you patrol here, in this area?" I asked as he coughed and struggled to breathe in air and not blood.

"I have orders," he replied, now angry, almost shouting. The stalwart veneer was gone. "Why are you asking me these questions?"

"Because I have orders, too. Answer me." I reared back to hit him again but he shook his head violently.

"No, no, please – look, I only joined the army about a year ago. I patrol here because I am from this area, from Reichlich. It's just north of here."

I made sure he saw my fingers clench tightly around that dagger. "I know where it is. But that's not why you patrol here."

"Look, I have a wife, and a new baby at home. Please..." He was damn near groveling now – the very mention of his family seemed to change everything. He was no longer a solider but a young man, barely more than a boy, wishing he could go home and see his loved ones one more time. It was now I who could not make eye contact.

But I still had a job to do. "Why do you patrol this area?" I asked again. When he shook his head and said nothing, I hit him again. More sickening sounds, more blood dripping onto the floor of the hut and sprayed across my knuckles. I became aware of an intense energy swirling around within me; it was like the heat of battle, but at the same time, an entirely different feeling all together, and indescribably unpleasant. The Eislander hunched forward with a groan, but I had no intention of letting this go on much longer – there was no time to allow him to sit there and absorb his suffering, or worse yet, go unconscious. So I grabbed a handful of blond hair and picked his head up, made him look at me and at the point of my blade now positioned within inches of his right eye. "Why do you patrol this area?" I asked once more.

"My orders... just that," he said through spitting out wads of blood and lost teeth. "Lots of patrols – maybe dozens. They never said. Just patrol, in groups of four or six."

"Patrol for what? Are you protecting something?"

He looked up at me and managed a slight shrug. "Possible. Our orders are to question or kill on sight, especially *Zondern*. That's all I know." He didn't even have to ask me to believe him – I could see it in his eyes. I let him go and he slumped into a defeated, bleeding heap.

"What did he say?"

The voice was gruff and harsh and speaking Zondrean... Zondrean? It took me a moment to process it, but when I realized who he was and what he'd said, my heart almost stopped. How long had he been there? I turned around to face Captain Shilling with the dagger still gripped so tightly I thought I might never be able to get it go.

"Young man, I said, 'what did he say'?"

It took a moment to gather my thoughts. What had he said? Anything useful, anything worth reporting? How did it all translate out? Should I tell him word for word? In the end, though, I only told him the parts I thought were most important. "Sir, he said there are many patrols, perhaps dozens, and that their orders are to question or kill anyone on sight."

Shilling nodded. "We know there are plenty of patrols out there. Anything else?"

"He's just a common soldier – he doesn't seem to know anything more that would be useful to us."

"And you believe that to be true?"

I glanced behind me at the Eislander and the little pools of blood and spit all around him. The way he sat there, dazed and broken and dirty, spoke more for his current state of mind than any words could. "Yes, Sir."

"All right, kill him, then." I must not have been able to mask my distaste at the order, as he narrowed his gaze on me then, the gray flecks in them standing out like flashing steel swords. "Lieutenant, it is neither practical nor wise for us to be looking after prisoners here. Either you do it, or I do it, but this boy is not leaving here alive. Do you understand me?" His weathered hand went to the sword on his belt, but I put my hand up.

"No, it's fine. I'll do it."

"Good. When you're done, I'll need a report, word for word of what was said between you and our friend here. Then you go rest for a bit, yeah? You've earned it for the day, I think."

When he was gone I turned on the solider – the young Eislandisch man whose name I didn't even know – sheathed the dagger and drew my sword, still smeared with blood and dirt from the earlier battle. "Stand up," I said to him, and he did, moving slow. He knew what was coming and unlike before, there was genuine terror in his eyes now. He was indeed afraid to die, after all.

There was only one honorable way for an Eislandisch warrior to die – at least, according to the books I'd read over the years about my mother's homeland. The Eislanders believe that all souls swim along a river of blood, a great astral river that runs through the entire universe, through all places and all things. When something is born, its soul steps out of the River and takes on whatever form that is called forth – person, plant, animal – and when it dies, it returns to be born anew another day. The cycle is endless, the River unaffected by time or the elements. And, to respect and commemorate it, the Eislandisch warrior strives to die with his lifeblood pouring out of him, flowing just like that great River where he will soon return.

I slit his throat from behind so that I didn't have to look him in the eye, nor did I watch while he bled out onto the dirt. I couldn't – I'm enough of a man to admit my cowardice. But for what it was worth, ensuring that that young man died with honor was the only good deed I would perform that day.

2

Both Andella and Alex had listened very patiently the entire time, never interrupting, hardly even stirring. She was, in fact, riveted; Alex, maybe less so. His expression was grave and almost bereft of emotion. Was it the things being said, or just a lack of sleep? I couldn't tell. Not that I am a master storyteller by any means – quite the opposite. At first, I could barely speak in coherent sentences, but as the events grew sharper in my mind's eye, the words started to tumble forth, sometimes with awkward pauses from one thought to the next. But it was all there, every detail... for better or worse. I didn't *want* to tell this story, didn't have any desire to revisit the memories that lay in the darker recesses of my mind. Saying it all out loud made it that much more real. At the same time, it also felt... somehow liberating? I didn't want to give a voice to this tale eating its way through my heart and mind – I *especially* never wanted Andella to have to hear all this – but at the same time, I did need to let it out.

Eventually though, Andella took advantage of a break in my carrying on. "So," she said, "did they – did you – keep looking? For the Kaeren, I mean?"

I nodded. "We did the same thing over and over again for months."

"They made you do... that... every day?" Just from the way she said it, I knew how she felt. And I couldn't blame her – I was just as disgusted with myself.

"Not every day; a few times a week, maybe. Sometimes even less when the snow was heavy. Didn't always amount to much more than a stroll through the woods. Sometimes, though..." For the first time in several hours, I looked away from the floor and up at her, her incandescent eyes seeming even brighter in the evening's darkness, and glistening with moisture. "But we never learned anything new, never found anything. I studied the Kaeren – read everything I could get my hands on. Never got me anywhere. I doubt it even exists at all."

At this, Andella did something very curious: she blinked. Not once, but several times in rapid succession, something she had not yet done to any noticeable degree. People, I've learned, tend to have little gestures, little unconscious things that they do when they're uncomfortable. And when they're lying. I wondered what it meant – it could have been nothing, but then again, maybe not. I thought about the book, *Lebenkern*, sitting there by her bed with those strange ancient words in them, and wondered... What secrets did they hold?

I tried to push those thoughts out of my mind for the time being. "It got to a point where I realized I could have just copied the first report I wrote over and over," I continued. "I might as well have. I used to think about telling Captain Shilling that whole thing was a wash, that we should let it go and go home."

Alex interjected. "Why didn't you?" The strange new lights behind his eyes bored a hole into me.

Good question. Not that I hadn't *tried* to say something; I had, on many occasions. The right thing to say, the courage, the manhood, whatever you wanted to call it – it was just never quite there. When it came down to it, I was a coward... a stupid fucking coward. I wasn't even man enough to be able to say it aloud. All I could do was look at them both with a vacant stare, and dreadful, heavy stillness settled over the room.

"Seriously, you should have said something to me. At the funeral. Why didn't you?"

"And say what, Alex?" I shook my head and looked away. "It's... there was nothing to say that would change anything."

Alex leaned back and folded his arms across his chest, looking ready to read me a lecture or something. This was about the last thing I needed, but I was willing to endure whatever was going to come my way. His jaw clenched up in anger, and his words sprang out in half-yelling, staccato phrases. "But this is wrong. What are we now, barbarians? This is not what civilized people do. *We don't do this kind of thing.* Did you actually see Südenforst – or what's left of it? Holy hell, what happened there?" I just shook my head weakly. "You're fucking kidding me? This is bad... this is really bad. What are we going to do? What about this Brin Jannausch person? Where does he come in?"

I felt like I'd been hit over the head. "Who?"

At this, Alex got up for a moment, as if inspired with a thought, then sat down heavily in one of the pews once again, and I could see then how haggard he looked. His dark hair was messy and unkempt, there were dark circles under his eyes, and it looked like he had slept at least one night in the clothes he wore. And those eyes... so odd, unnerving even. How could he have simply "become" a mage? And what kind of mage was he? The more I looked the more he seemed unlike any Air mage I had ever seen. Everything was off – the color seemed off, they were silver, not white – and there was just nothing simple about the luminescence there. There were glimmers and swirls deep in those eyes that made no sense whatsoever, as if he had quicksilver swirling around in his pupils. I couldn't figure it out, and honestly, I wasn't sure I wanted to know. All in all, he looked almost as bad as I did, and I'd never seen him like that, ever – not even at his father's funeral did he look so miserable.

Hands shaking slightly, he reached into his shirt pocket only to pull out nothing. Must have been fresh out of *tsohbac.* "There was this Eislander... I saw him this morning. Early, like right at dawn. He was with someone, that Lavançaise – Onyx?" He looked over at Andella and she nodded, confirming. My confusion must have been quite evident. "They were talking... she said something about him failing, that she'd hired him and he failed. I overheard them, then they found me out. Almost fucking got me killed, but I talked my way out of it."

I said nothing, just stared at him, not sure where he was headed, or even if I was hearing him right. He pointed at my shoulder. "He told me. He told me about Südenforst, about you. That's how I knew you were here. And you know what? His name was Jannausch. He knew who I was – said I looked like my father. Because he was in the war, during the occupation of Kostbar, where he knew my father and your father because he's your mother's damned brother! Can you believe it? And apparently he's the reason you're still alive right now. He said he was paid to kill you and he couldn't do it."

"Brinnürjn." Yes, my mother had a brother. She'd only mentioned him once or twice, if that, in my entire life. She had not seen him in many years – all she said was that he was a madman and had deserted the family as a youth. I never knew for sure, but I imagined that she regretted whatever had happened to make him leave.

"Yeah. That Onyx woman called him Brin. So your mother *does* have a brother?" I nodded, and he continued talking, loudly, hurried, as if he had to get the words out or they would get lost forever. "Well, she's got to – the man looks just like you, only older. He said he took you out of that battle – on purpose, I guess... I think he felt bad about it, too. It was a really strange conversation, but I could see, there was something there. Like remorse, you know? So what the hell happened there?"

My stomach felt like it was about to just drop out and land on the floor. "He never told me his name."

"What did you *do*, Brother?"

What did I do? Good question. What didn't I do? I didn't do my duty, didn't follow orders. But I did know what I was doing, the whole time – and I did it anyhow.

"I fucked up. That's what I did. I fucked up."

✳✳

Everyone breaks eventually. After three months up there in the borderlands, this was one of the most important things I had learned. That, and the more you think, the more you feel, and too much thinking was not going to help the job get done.

It was all about following orders, accomplishing the mission, and to that end, I had grown skilled at what I was doing. My whole life centered around one thing, and one thing only, and even though we continually failed to get any results, Captain Shilling was pleased because I was performing well, to the apparent best of my ability, and so he was happy to waste all the time in the world out there in the mountainous woodlands, even in the snow and the cold of winter. We would work through the same routine day in and day out for years if we had to – the mission was just too important, and we were too close to just give up. So I did what I did, I did it well, and I tried not to think about it or question it.

That is, until they brought in the girl.

Sonja was her name. They brought her in late – I was almost asleep when the entrance to my tent ruffled open, instantly sucking out all of the heat. "We've got one for you, Sir," one of the troops barked at me. From the way his eyes lazily scanned everything, moving back and forth without focus, he looked a tad bit tired, maybe drunk. I barely acknowledged him, just got up and started to get dressed. "Better watch out for this one – she's a biter."

I paused as I fastened my belt. "She?"

"Aye, Sir. Wandering out alone in the woods. We... ah, we softened her up a bit for you." I looked past his mischievous, evil little smile and moved out of the tent without another word.

I found her huddled in the corner of the Small Tent – we couldn't come up with a better name for it, so that's what we called it – sitting in the shadows where the light from the single torch just barely reached, hugging her knees to her chest and crying softly. They'd left her with nothing but the tattered remains of her dress to cover herself, and there were black and blue bruises running along her back, her arms, the backs of her thighs. Her flax-colored hair was sweaty and matted against her neck, little strings of it falling down around her shoulders here and there. I had half a mind to turn around and find the animals among men who thought this kind of thing was acceptable behavior, but leaving her there alone would just prolong her agony further. I could deal with the soldiers later.

When I folded the entrance to the tent closed, she picked up her head and looked at me, genuine horror in her eyes, eyes like little drops of pure water. "No. No more," she whispered in staccato, clipped Zondrean. Maybe she thought I didn't speak her language, but she wasn't really speaking to me – it was more of a general plea to anyone who would listen.

"Take this," I said to her in Eislandisch, pulling off my tunic and handing it to her. Cold though it was in the midst of a late winter's night in Eisland, I hardly felt the chill on my exposed flesh. When she didn't move, I said it again, with a little more force, and then she did take it, snatching it quickly from my hand as someone might do when taking a favorite bone away from a particularly irritable dog. Respectfully, I turned while she slipped it over her head – it was large enough on her to almost be worn as another dress, but at least it was warm and new and clean.

After I stopped hearing movement, I turned back around, staring down at the shivering, frightened little girl – how old could she have been? Fourteen? Fifteen, maybe? She had stopped watching me and stared unblinking at the dirt floor. "*Stehen Sie*," I ordered, but when she didn't stand up, I said it again. Still nothing. So I knelt down, ready to physically pick her up from the floor, but the moment I touched her arm she screamed with unexpected ferocity, the kind of scream that makes your blood curdle like rotten milk in the sun. I almost jumped to get away from the sound, and it ceased as soon as I backed away. She crossed her arms, holding herself, burying her face into her chest as far as it would go – I noticed a single new tear streak down her cheek.

I took a long, deep breath, let it out slowly, trying to control the deafening sound of my heart beating, louder and louder. I could actually feel the blood pumping through my veins, raging through, pulsing through my chest, my throat, my head. This was not what I wanted to be doing. I didn't want to be here, didn't want to look at this girl, didn't want to have anything to do with any of it. But outside, I heard the occasional footstep, a chuckle or a snippet of conversation. I knew what they were expecting. I was here for a specific purpose, with a specific duty to fulfill. It had to be done.

I knelt down before her again, close but not too close, keeping my hands where she could see them, as casual and non-threatening as possible. She didn't move, but she didn't cry out, either. "I need to talk to you," I said to her.

It took a long time for her to respond. "They said that the lands near the border have been dangerous lately... now I know why." Her voice was so quiet I strained to hear.

"I need to ask you some questions. And if you answer them, I can let you go." At this, she looked up again, regarding me very carefully, searching, evaluating. Did she know I was lying? Her gaze settled on my shoulder, on the tattoo of the gold dragon, forever prowling.

"I have nothing to say," she said. This was not what I was looking forward to hearing. Not at all. Now I had no choice but to turn away from the normal, rational side of myself and toward a much more unpleasant side that I didn't like at all. I didn't even like to think that I had such a side. But it was there, and it was getting easier and easier to invoke every dark, damnable day.

Slowly, I pulled my ruby-handled knife from my belt, letting it make a bit of a clanging sound as it left the safety of its sheath. I hadn't kept it particularly clean as of late; all along the shiny steel blade, droplets and streaks of reddish-black dried blood absorbed the torchlight. I casually twisted it back and forth in my palm. "I can make you speak. You do not want me to do that." By the way her eyes widened, I was sure she believed I meant every word. "Tell me your name."

Another long pause, as if she had to think about it. The entire time, her eyes followed the movement of the dagger in my grasp, every once in a while stealing a glance at me directly. Her lower lip quivered ever so slightly, as if struggling to hold back a flood of tears. Finally, she said, "Sonja. My name is Sonja."

I nodded. "Good. Sonja, what were you doing out there alone, in the wilderness?"

"Walking."

"To where?"

"Doverton, to get some things for my mother. It is closer than Kostbar, and the spices and vegetables are cheaper. Is it a crime to travel this way now, is that it?"

"I will ask the questions," I replied curtly. And I did – in fact, I berated her with questions, The Questions, the ones I always had to ask. Sometimes she said things, sometimes she didn't.

Very little of it was getting me anywhere. The whole thing was so... so ridiculous, so awful, so *stupid* – *we* were stupid for being out here, carrying out this ill-fated, ridiculous mission. People were dying on both sides, and for what, exactly? The more I spoke with Sonja, the more that feeling grew, like a painful void getting deeper and darker with each passing second. Maybe she knew that, too, because at some point, she reached out and grabbed me by the forearm, tight with fear and panic.

"I don't know any of these things you ask. Please don't hurt me, please... I'll do anything. You have Eislandisch blood – you *must* have a soul. Please I beg you, let me go home!"

A soul? Did *I* have a soul? I looked at my stained blade, the flecks of rust-colored dried blood under my fingernails, and back to her, shaking my head. Leaving prisoners alive... it wasn't an option, but I couldn't find the words to explain. Not that there was anything I could say that would be of any comfort. No, we both knew what my assigned duty was, and luckily I didn't have to say anything at all. She just started sobbing again, the cry of someone whose spirit has been crushed.

For the love of the gods... what was I doing? What the fuck was I doing, terrorizing a young girl – for what? What good would it do? Even if she did know something, even if the mission would be over that night if she had one good piece of information... it suddenly just didn't seem worth it. For the first time in my life, I failed to follow my orders. It was no mistake – I knew exactly what I was doing. And I'd surely go to my pyre early because of it, but there in the confines of the Small Tent on that night, the one that stunk of blood and sweat and fear, I didn't care about the consequences.

I reached out and gently – but firmly – held her by the chin, picking up her head so that she couldn't look away. Her lovely blue eyes were rimmed and crisscrossed with crimson. "Sonja, listen to me. Those people out there – the Zondreans – they can't understand what we're saying, but they expect you to be dead when you leave this place. You can't sneak away. But, I can get you out, alive. It will be painful... it has to look convincing."

She became very quiet; she stopped sobbing, stopped moving, hardly even breathed. "I can go home?" she whispered. I nodded, and she didn't hesitate. "Then, do it."

My knife was a lead hammer, heavy and dead in my hand. A part of me very much wished she had said no – hadn't she been tortured enough? "When they take you from here, and leave you outside the camp, you must wait until they're gone before you head for home. If they see you still live, we're both dead. Do you understand?" She did. And so I took that knife and did what I knew, what I did well, all the while imagining I was somewhere else, *someone* else. The human body, even that of a young girl, can withstand a great deal of pain and suffering. It can be cut, it can be bruised and scarred and beaten, but with just the right amount of restraint – of premeditation – it can teeter on the brink of life and death for quite a while. When it was done, the blood on my hands was thick and warm, and her cries would echo in my nightmares. But, she would live.

I tried to go back to sleep afterward, but couldn't. I wasn't so sure I'd ever be able to sleep again after watching them drag her bloodstained body away, after thinking about what I'd done, what the consequences could be. I knew what could happen. She could easily run back to the first Eislander she saw and give away our position, how many of us there were, anything she could about who we were and what we were doing there. She might have been young, but certainly not too young to know the colors and symbol of Zondrell, and that Zondrell soldiers were not supposed to be on the wrong side of the border. The question was: *would* she reveal us? Or, would she decide to stay quiet because her life had been saved? The solider in me hoped for the latter; the man – the human – in me, however, secretly hoped much darker things, things that would likely not just affect me but every man there. I might have just made a terrible mistake – I might have just signed my entire company's death warrant. Only time would tell for sure, but in the meantime, I found I could do nothing but lie there wide awake until well after the first light of dawn, when it was time to get up and do it all over again. A different day, the same routine. It never ended.

**

Except when it did end, it ended with a mighty crash. And it was all my fault. "Some three days later, he found us – Brinnürjn. Caught up with me when I was alone. I made a deal with him." I had to stop and find my words for a moment. It felt so horrible to even say them. "I trusted he was going to keep his end of our bargain and… he set us up. He sent us to Südenforst because we were going to 'find what we were looking for.' Didn't even matter to me if it was actually anything to do with the Kaeren or not. But instead we got ambushed. And why not? They knew where we were and where we going to be – all because I let that girl go. I made it easy on them. I fucked up. Bad. I thought I was doing the right thing, but I can't lie and say I didn't know what I was doing."

Andella and Alex were both stricken silent – I wouldn't have expected anything else. I couldn't even bring myself to consider what they must have thought of me. I took a deep breath, a feeble attempt to cleanse the evil from my soul. "My men were killed because I couldn't do my job anymore. I found an easy way out and I took it. I thought… I really believed we were all going to go back home victorious, but I'm just a fool. And a traitor. That's what they're saying, isn't it?" I'd never said it aloud before even though I had thought about it many times recently, and the words actually hurt. Maybe it was the just way Alex returned my questioning look. I don't know. But a *traitor* – hadn't I worked hard for my country? Hadn't I done everything I could to serve Zondrell to the highest degree? Of course I had… but the rule is a constant, and it holds true for everyone: we all break eventually. "You know what the worst part is? I don't think I'd do it differently. I can't see how I would have… if I had it to do again, I'd do it the exact same way. What kind of person am I?"

Continued silence was my reply, but only until Alex came up with something to offer. Catherine bless him – he was doing his best. "It makes you the kind who doesn't slaughter defenseless little girls. I think you should take a bit of comfort in that. I do."

"Was her life worth all of those others?"

"I… don't know, man. I don't know." Alex shook his head, struggling with the question just as much as I was. Perhaps it had no answer. "Here's what I do know. People are going to say lots of things, Brother. But there's what people say, and what the truth is. You know, before I tripped and almost got a dagger in the face, that Jannausch and Onyx were saying something else. He said something about a girl getting paid – for what, I don't know. He seemed really upset by it but Onyx didn't think it was all that important. I think maybe… maybe they were talking about your Sonja." Alex paused, his voice growing quieter and quieter. "I think you were set up, Brother. That's defensible. We could go to Council with this."

For a moment, I could hear nothing but the vague sounds of the breeze outside in that chapel. I looked off into the darkness, watching shadows that may or may not have really been there. What he was saying changed everything. It made me feel sick to the very core of my being. I felt lightheaded and yet so heavy I couldn't move. Who would do such a thing? Why indeed would Doverton – another Zondrean city-state, and an ally – attack Zondrell without a really, really good reason? And to go to such ends, hiring scouts and assassins, for what? Why? It made no sense, unless…

Unless they were hiding something.

Maybe we were too close, or closer than we thought. I thought about that book again, and the things it said in that first page I'd turned to. It seemed like something from a faery tale, but what if it were true? What if there *were* other types of magic, locked away and hidden? If it was not just a story, but something more than that, maybe "kaeren" or "kern" or whatever it was meant something very different than what we all thought. Maybe it wasn't a weapon or a thing at all, but something else entirely. A place? A person? Maybe.

Or, I was just grasping and would have been better off giving myself up.

"Did you hear what I said?" Alex asked.

Yes, I heard him. I just suddenly didn't care that much. I turned my back to them and moved toward the bedrooms, holding the walls for support as I went. I felt as if the whole world was going to come crashing down around me, or perhaps that I would simply crumble like a piece of burnt parchment. I was weak enough – I probably would. And they were the last people I wanted to see that. They'd seen enough already. "I need to get some rest. I can't think right now."

"No, wait," Alex called behind me, "we need to talk about this. We need to come up with a plan, or... Hey, are you listening to me?"

I wasn't. I pretended like I didn't hear him and kept on going. There was more conversation, but I didn't listen. I couldn't. I crashed into the nearest bed and I slept, dreaming of things that were better left unspoken in the waking world.

When I woke up later, it was still dark, and the only thing I felt like doing was... well, nothing. I lay there, couldn't go back to sleep, then finally sat up to stare at nothing for a while. It seemed to be something I was good at. And I cried, frustrated, angry, weak tears of pointless self-pity. The more those feelings enveloped me, the more they took hold and grew roots into my soul. It didn't matter how many times I tried to give myself excuses, or how many ways the story could be twisted to see the "positive" side. Maybe there was no right answer, and maybe there had been a setup. That didn't excuse anything. It always came back to the fact that I stupidly, recklessly – *selfishly* – gave up one life for dozens of others.

When the door quietly opened and Andella glided in, my only concern was getting rid of those tears as fast as possible. But she sat by me and put her arms around me and didn't say anything for a while, and that was all right. I could give in to a bit of comforting silence.

"I've been thinking," she said after a time, a mix of trepidation and excitement in her voice. "I think... you know that book I have? I think the Prophecy in it is coming true. And I think that book is what you've been looking for. Or what your people have been looking for, at any rate." I looked up at her and the only thing I could really see in the dark were her eyes – those fantastic swirling eyes of rich color. "I know, it sounds crazy. But the more I think about it, the more I believe it. And your friend... he can – it's amazing. He can make time stop."

"What? Are you talking about Alex?" Sure, he had something going on that I couldn't explain. But to think that Alexander Vestarton, of all people, was the herald of some grand ancient prophecy was a bit much to take in. He didn't like magic, had no interest in it, and I loved him like a brother and all, but this was the same friend I had damn near dragged home from the Silver weekly for the past four years because he was too drunk to make it on his own. For Catherine's sake, if it weren't for Corrin and me, he wouldn't have even passed half of his exams at the Academy.

"I saw it. Just now. There's no other explanation. It's got to be... Time magic, just like the book says. Seraphine had always said that book was just a story and nothing more, even though our mum said hundreds of years ago some grandfather of ours many times over had been able to heal the sick and raise the dead with just his own two hands. Do you know what that is? That's Life magic. What else could it be?"

I felt like perhaps I was still dreaming. None of what she said seemed to make much sense, but then I thought about the few little passages I had read in that strange, fated book. And it still made no sense. "You're saying that whatever magic Alex has come across can actually stop time?"

"Yes. I saw it with my own eyes. And something else." Her voice grew softer and softer as she spoke, as if she was unsure or nervous or fearful. "I was thinking about that next line, where it talks about 'half a hero's blood'? Maybe there's more to that line somehow. I mean, I've thought about it ever since you got here. It just seemed like maybe... maybe it made sense, even though I don't like it. I have such a bad feeling about it, but I can't stop thinking that it might be... well, you know."

Now that... *that* was absolutely ridiculous. I chuckled in spite of myself. "I'm no hero."

"But..."

"Please. No one in their right mind would mistake me for such a thing." Heroes did noble things, honorable things, important things. They didn't follow orders blindly until it hurt so bad they did something unbelievably stupid. They sure as hell didn't do the kinds of things I had found myself doing over the past four months. "Look, I would go anywhere with you and do anything for you. But that idea? I'm sorry, it makes no sense. Let's not talk about it anymore, okay?"

She pulled my big rough hands into her tiny soft ones, looking deep into my eyes again in that special, soul-seeking way she had. But along with gentle concern there was something else there staring back at me – fear. If she could see so deeply, how could she not see that what she was suggesting was just... *insane*? "But you don't know what might happen in the future."

I shook my head. "Don't you get it? There *is* no future. Not for me."

"I don't know that you're the one who gets to decide that. We don't make our own Fate." On this, I had to agree, but I wasn't ready to say such a thing out loud – not yet. I just found myself wanting to look away into the darkness, but she had me transfixed. "You said you'd go anywhere? I'm worried about my sister," she said. "All of this talk... I'm just worried. This isn't like her. Will you go with me to the city to find her? I mean, I don't need you to, but I would just... I don't know. It'd be better if you were there. Can you make it?"

Of course I would go. Without question. Not because I was some madman's idea of a "hero," but because I was a guy in love – yes, I said it – with a girl who had the uncanny ability to make his pain just a little more bearable... The only girl who had ever – and would ever – see him cry.

1

Alexander Vestarton

Some people liked to have someone nearby to share in their misery, to hold them up and make them feel better in difficult times. My friend Tristan was the complete opposite of that. On those few occasions where I actually saw emotions get the best of him, they came up as anger, not sorrow. That was how people got beaten up at the Silver after we'd all had a few too many and things were said that shouldn't have been. That's how Peter Wyndham got his face bashed in during the Graduation Tournament, and that was how I got myself bloodied trying to be a good friend. It was only in the rarest of moments that his pain was expressed in actual sadness. I could only think of maybe two times in our whole lives when I'd see him shed a tear, and I think we were about seven years old for one of them. I had never, though, seen him quite like this. This was beyond the kind of pain you cry about; this was the kind that leaves you just… empty. Who am I to even try to put words to it? I knew nothing of that kind of agony, really; maybe I never would. The moment I told him what I'd overheard about them paying that girl, that was it. There was nothing there. In retrospect, I shouldn't have said anything at all.

Sergeant Delrin was right. No one – not even Tristan Loringham, Zondrell's best and brightest – was built to go through all of that and not come out of it a bit broken. Disturbed. Whatever you wanted to call it. He really was like a different person. I did have a hard time believing that the same man who had decided to commit himself so completely to his military service would have done everything Tristan just told me he'd done. But you know what? I didn't blame him. Not in the least. If this were a Council court, I'd defend him to the death, and not just because he was my friend. I wouldn't have killed that girl, either, no way, no how. Even if it was the right thing to do, it *couldn't* have been right. We're officers and nobles – gentlemen of a royal court in a modern age. Slaughter like that is... well, it's the same thing we accuse the "lesser" nations of doing all the time. Except those so-called barbarians weren't who we thought they were after all, were they? In Zondrell, we send our best boys – our wealthiest, most privileged, and supposedly smartest and strongest – through *four years* of schooling on everything from ancient history to modern battle tactics to breed officers and soldiers that understood both war and how to prevent it. They used to stress to us constantly to conduct ourselves with dignity – *dignity*, this was the word they used. There's nothing dignified about killing defenseless little girls, burning down towns, and everything else in between. This was not what we signed up for. Tristan *should* have said something weeks ago. I could have done something – paid someone off, called the Council to task for this idiotic behavior... something, anything. What could I do now that the damage was done? What could anyone do? The gods themselves would have a hard time getting him out of this predicament.

One thing I was sure about was that I knew my friend well enough to know that he did not want me or the girl around while he tried to make his peace with whatever he needed to make peace with. He'd already said far more than I think he wanted to. I had even tried to stop him a couple of times but it didn't do much good. And once I let go of the idea that we were going to solve this problem right there, that night, I decided it was fine – go, Brother, rest and brood or think or do whatever you need to do. Just don't go fall on your sword. And yes, I did worry about that kind of thing. This was also the same man who once stayed up overnight training nonstop for one of those big sparring matches where we all got evaluated on points, and then after that, promptly holed up to study for our next written exam for the next five hours. Sure, he got every point there was to get and then slept for about twelve hours afterward, but anyone who can push themselves like that seemed quite capable of suicide in my mind. Just the five hours of studying alone would have driven most normal people to it, anyhow – that was why I never studied past a couple of hours a day and got piss-poor marks. In the end, we all graduated on the same day.

"Will he be all right?" Andella the mage-girl asked, voice trembling. I wondered if she was thinking the same things I was.

"I hope so."

"I hope so, too. I just don't understand how all of this could happen. I think... I should go say something to him." She started to get up, but I shook my head.

"Don't. Leave him be right now. Trust me." From the half-worried, half-annoyed way she bit her lip as she relaxed again, I learned one very interesting thing. She cared for him. It was obvious. Interesting – but good for him. He sure as hell needed *someone* to care about him. "Look, you want to know how this happened? People are obviously scum and no less willing to do sick fucking things to each other than they were hundreds of years ago. *That's* how this happened."

Our eyes met for a moment, and in dim torchlight and the outside light nearly gone, I could see the pulses and whirls in her eyes very clearly. I suppose with the color they should have reminded me of a candle flame fighting against a strong wind, but all I really noticed was that they seemed to pulse in time with her breath. Did my eyes look like that, too? I thought briefly to go find a mirror but then again, I really didn't want to know. What I wanted more than anything at that moment was a drink. This seemed like a more acceptable expression of the mix of emotions I was feeling than, say, breaking something that wasn't mine or finding someone to scream at for an hour. Andella certainly appreciated that, I would imagine.

I had a pack somewhere, with a flask of Drakannyan brandy in it. The good stuff – the thousand-Royal a bottle kind. When I was throwing things together to leave, I thought maybe I would need it – you know, for an emergency. This evening definitely qualified. But was it here? Did I even bring it with me? I got up and tripped over my pack not too far away, near the temple door. Oh, thank the gods. In it I found my large silver flask and one – just one – *tsohbac.* That was it. I was out. My pockets were empty, and so was the little tin in my pack. Whatever my eyes looked like, well, everyone was going to have to get used to it, including me.

I decided to just sit there on the floor, resting my back against the wall, and hit that bottle with full force. The warm liquid slid down my throat trying its best to soothe the terrible crushing weight of... well, everything. Even with the added effects of the *tsohbac*, the comfort they could provide was short-lived at best. I still felt that life as I knew it was over. What am I saying? That wasn't just a feeling – it was true.

"I hope there's more alcohol around here?" I asked between a pull from the flask and another from my *tsohbac* stick.

"There's some wine in the kitchen. Um... please, help yourself." Andella's voice sounded so far off that it was almost dead. I couldn't imagine what she was thinking, and to some extent, I didn't really care that much.

Ah, except that I did. Or felt like I needed to. Doverton was an ally, and that Lavançaise woman worked for the King. And she was the one who hired Jannausch, and apparently some poor young girl, as spies and assassins to work against her own allies. Why? By the gods, who knew what role little Andella here was playing? Sure, she seemed nice and all, but trust was getting harder and harder to come by all of the sudden. My mind was quickly putting together a variety of odd little schemes and scenarios – none of them had happy endings. I imagined that any minute now Victor and his men were going to come trudging back here with Catherine knew what kind of news, or what kind of taste for blood. Or maybe they'd go to Doverton and get themselves killed, and we'd all be in the middle of some kind of new war – no one would even know why or what started it. As the brandy settled in and ran its course, the scenarios got more and more wild and disjointed, which certainly didn't help.

I took a long pull from that flask and it tasted like beautiful molten gold. "So, tell me something. What does Doverton have to do with all of this? Why do they want our people dead?"

"I… I wish I knew."

Now *that* was hesitation if I ever heard it. I crushed out the very last precious bit of *tsohbac* and pressed on. "All right then. What do *you* have to do with this?"

I couldn't see her from where I sat, but I could hear her get up and walk toward me. She came to stand over me with her hands clasped together, then gradually she sank to the floor, sitting on her knees as if in prayer. "Nothing. Nothing – I swear to you. But Alexander – Lord Vestarton – I think… I think maybe my sister does." She swallowed hard, and there was genuine fear in her eyes. "She's the priestess here, except she's not here right now – she should have been home a while ago. She went to town, just to Market and maybe to visit at the Great Temple. But she talks to Madame Saçaille. I don't know what they talk about, but they've been talking more lately. And now this… Please, I don't know what to do, but I don't want anything bad to happen to my sister."

Even through a faint haze of *tsohbac* smoke and flickering torchlight, I could see the tears welling up in her eyes. One or two slid down her cheeks the longer I sat there silent. So, I did what was probably the wrong thing and pressed on with my questions. "You have no idea what they talk about?"

"Not really. My sister tells me not to worry," she said, shaking her head with a sniffle. "When Saçaille comes by, they leave the room – I never thought that much about it until today. I told Tristan about it. I mean, I never felt like Saçaille was all that trustworthy or anything, but I always thought she was just checking in on us, making sure everything was all right."

"Because there's something here that's worth the time of a King's Weapon Master?" It seemed like a logical next question, but it got a very illogical response. I thought perhaps I hadn't said what I thought I said because the brandy was getting to me. Whatever the case, she burst into a torrent of tears, leaning into her hands and doubling over with each powerful sob. "Hey, wait – what did I say?"

I let her carry on that way for several minutes until I found the good graces to move in and put a hand on her shoulder. I'm certain it wasn't much comfort. Truth be told, I didn't want to comfort her – sweet as she seemed, I just wanted to know what the hell she was so upset about. No one cries like that without a good reason. Lucky for both of us, her tears subsided enough to speak within a few minutes, well before I lost my patience.

Her voice was quiet, excited, nervous all at once. "There's a book here. An old book – it's always been here, I guess. It talks about things… magic, a lot of things. I've been trying to translate it because it's in some kind of Old Eislandisch. I never got that far but I did figure out how to read some of it when I was at the Academy. I was interested in it, you know? They say our great-great-grandfather could heal people by just touching them, and my mum said he learned it from that book. My sister always says I'm mad for even thinking about this – she tells me to forget about the book entirely. I think… well, I don't know, but I think people believe that the secret of what people call 'Kaeren' is in that book."

I took another sip of brandy, and another after that. I was trying so hard to be calm, rational. It wasn't working, because this surely was not what she actually said. Of course it wasn't, because what I heard was something insane. "I'm sorry, I must be really quite drunk already. You didn't just say there's some book about the Kaeren here in this church and that's what you're all upset about… right?"

She almost smiled as she shook her head. "It's not a faery tale. At least, I don't think it is. Otherwise why would everyone be killing each other over it?"

"Because they're idiots? I don't know." This, by far, was officially the most bizarre conversation I had ever had, or perhaps would ever have in my whole life. And yet I felt compelled to find out more. "You really think this thing is real?"

"Yes. Look at you – your magic is… there's nothing else like it. I think the Prophecy did come true."

"Oh, there's a prophecy too? Great. Has it been sealed in a cave for two hundred years and only the oldest faery in the forest can find it? Come on, lass – I've heard this story before. Besides, what does my magic have to do with anything? It's useless. I don't even want it." My magic was hideously uncomfortable to live with at best. What kind of prophecy could this be – someday there will be a man who will be annoyed and tortured with magic he doesn't want and that'll bring about the end of the world? What the fuck kind of ridiculous thing… I almost laughed aloud at the thought.

"Have you looked at your eyes?"

"No. Why?" If whatever felt like it was slowly burning a hole in my soul was showing itself in my eyes, then I really didn't want to see. Ever.

"It's like no other magic I've ever seen."

"Oh please, that's ridiculous. Let me show you what this co-called magic is all about." Did she really want to see this amazing, terrible, prophetic magic? Fine. I found I couldn't sit still any longer anyhow. I had to get up, move around, let some of this evil whatever-it-was out. The worse I felt, the worse the skin-crawling got, to the point where it almost burned. So I stood up, I concentrated…

And nothing happened.

I tried again. Something should happen, right? I didn't know what, exactly. I didn't quite know how to control it or make it happen, either. If I was an Air mage, shouldn't I be able to summon a whirlwind or control the weather or some craziness like that? But I couldn't seem to manage even a tiny breeze. Maybe I wasn't an Air mage, even though I'd seen it for myself – white was the color of the Air, and that's what color my eyes had turned that first time, after I stepped into the Box. At least I thought that's what I saw, and it was something I'd tried to stave off for years. A bit too late for that now. A part of me did want to see what I really looked like, if I looked as strange as I felt. Then, the other part didn't want to know, didn't want to see it, and didn't want anything to do with it.

Maybe… well, what *had* I been able to do? I had kept that dagger from hurtling into my skull – that was it. So, maybe I could float something else, something small like a coin, if I concentrated on it? Easy enough. I pulled a hundred-Royal out of my pocket and flipped it into the air. Without much effort at all, I found I could make it stay there, suspended, frozen in place. It took a few tries, but with some practice I could get it to stay there for minutes at a time. The bizarre feeling of terrible things crawling inside my veins grew much more intense, but now, I was focused on what I could do, less so on the feelings it produced. I found it wasn't that bad. I could manage it, live with it even, if I could just not pay it so much attention. Really, making that coin hover was a fun bit of a diversion – I could stop it when it was high in the air, or when it was almost back in my hand. It was a good way to cheat at any coin-flipping game, since you could choose when, where, and how it would land. Provided, of course, that they weren't watching you manipulate things.

I got so engrossed in this little activity that I almost forgot about the fact that I was being watched. And not only watched, but stared at in abject wonder, like some sort of oddity on display in a museum.

"It's not that interesting. That's all I can do."

She shook her head. "You have no idea. 'Time stops, half a hero's blood soaks the land to bring forth new Life, bearing with it the Light of a new age.'"

None of this made an inkling of sense but I knew this must have been her prophecy from the way she spoke, as if reading those words right out of that magical book of hers. "So what does that mean?"

"You just made time stop."

Clearly, this girl had gone insane. "I did not."

"You just saw it for yourself. What kind of mage do you think you are?"

I flipped the coin a few more times, considering. It was getting easier – I could even talk while I did it. "You know, I don't think I am one." Coin up. Freeze. "I'm not trained. I could have gone to the Magic Academy, but I lied to them so that I wouldn't have to. Fuck magic – no offense. But I don't really *want* to be a mage." Coin down. Flip, and back up again. "But whatever I've been… afflicted with here, it's obviously Air magic. Right? I mean, what else would it be? My eyes turn some odd kind of white when I don't want them to, and I can float stupid things in the air for a really short period of time. My blood burns and my skin crawls every moment of every day. It's getting worse all the time. And I *hate* it. I hate it with a passion. I don't know how you people don't just want to fall on a sword at the nearest fucking opportunity." The coin dropped heads-up into my waiting palm.

"But what if I told you it wasn't Air magic? That it was something more than that?" My only response was a terse laugh. She was certifiably mad – I was certain of that. Maybe I was dreaming and we weren't even having this conversation. "Fine, if it's Air, then blow out that torch over there," she insisted, pointing at the nearest wall torch.

All right then, if it was a challenge she wanted, so be it. I was just drunk enough to find some humor in the whole situation. Sure, if I could float a stupid little coin in the air, I could blow out a torch. Why not? Shouldn't that be child's play? I walked over to the torch, concentrating on it. Nothing happened. So I tried waving my hands about a little, like the silly way many mages did when they wanted to make it look like they were doing something important. Still nothing. At this rate, I was losing interest fast, but I did feel some of that burning-awful power deep inside, rising up to the surface.

I closed my eyes and when I opened them, I could barely believe what I was seeing. Was there something more in that flask than just brandy? The fire was still. Not "out," but still. Motionless, like a painting. I looked at Andella, then back at the fire as if it were an alien thing. It was even still hot – I put my hand over it and there was heat there, but it was steady, no fluctuations. The temperature was captured along with the flames. Both of us stood fascinated by the bizarreness of it until whatever crept into me to be able to do that in the first place lost its grip. The fire resumed its normal function, flickering away like nothing had ever happened.

"That's not natural," I whispered the only words I could come up with.

"I'm no expert – I've just read parts of that book – but that's not Air magic. It can't be. It's got to be Time."

I emptied the flask and prayed it would refill itself again. Sure, I could *stop time*, but of course I couldn't make alcohol materialize. What was having some unusual type of magic good for, anyhow? This all must have been a bad trick played by a very angry god. "So fine, let's say you're right. Let's say your little prophecy is real. What now?"

For a few agonizing minutes, she was silent. Finally, she said, "I don't know. All I know is that there are three lost magics, according to the book. *Zeitkern*, *Lebenkern*, and *Lichtenkern* – Time, Life, and Light. So, if we find the other two, then... well, that's the part I don't know. I'm scared. Life won't be the same anymore, will it?"

"Yeah sure, for me it won't."

A hint of a tear sprang back into her eyes as she folded her arms across her chest as if a sudden chill had struck her. "I wish I knew why my sister wasn't back yet."

"Maybe she'll be back in the morning."

"What if she's not?"

"Then... we can go look for her." Sure, why the fuck not? Go look for the lost sister – sounded better than staying here and waiting for Victor and Peter to come trudging back out to bring us our fate. The girl started to speak up again, but I waved my hand. "Look, you said there's wine in the kitchen, right? I'm going to go find that, then go to sleep. In the morning, if we're lucky enough to wake up without any of this having happened, that would be great. But I'm going to go see if I can at least forget about it for a while. You do the same. All right?" I honestly didn't care if she had anything else to say; I was too tired and not drunk enough for that. I just wanted to curl up somewhere and wake up back in my own bed at home. It wasn't going to happen, and I knew this deep down. So I did what any self-respecting young Lord would do in this situation – I marched myself into the kitchen, drank a bottle and a half of cheap Rose River Red and passed out cold on the kitchen table.

It was the best sleep I'd had in days.

✳✳

I dreamt of strange things that night, disconnected fragments of memories that didn't make much sense and didn't stick around very long. But one of those little fragments did – so much so that it would be branded into my memory forever.

I was in the wilderness, mountainous, a little desolate – but peaceful. Didn't seem like it was all that far from where we were, and yet it also felt many miles way. I didn't recognize the area, but it was definitely a real place, not just some dreamworld. Of that, for some reason, I was certain.

Despite the quiet, there was something amiss. At first, a feeling, then it became something more than that. I could see it – blood, everywhere. All over the ground, splattered on the rocks, just everywhere. Where did it come from? And a better question – whose was it? I couldn't see anyone though, just the blood and mountains. So I moved forward a bit, not sure where I was heading. I hardly knew where I was, much less where to go, and the blood... I didn't want to step on something I shouldn't, that was for sure.

I hardly took more than five steps before I met up with something... someone. A victim? What had happened here? I knelt and looked down to see what was lying there at my feet. Maybe it was just an animal. Was this a hunting expedition? Yes, perhaps I was on a hunting expedition – that wouldn't be such a bad dream to have.

Sure, hunting would have been a fine thing to call it, if it was normal to hunt people. Because it was a person on the ground and all of that blood must have belonged to that person. The closer I leaned in, the more I realized what I was seeing.

It was Tristan. Deader than dead, blood everywhere, just... dead. And for some reason the only thing that was going through my mind was that I was too late. Something had happened, and I was too late to do anything about it. The worst part was, I was not just powerless, but hopeless, like something else, something more important, had died too. I couldn't describe it but the feeling was so stifling and so real that when I jerked awake, my breath came in short, sharp gasps.

What the hell was that all about?

I looked around. I had almost forgotten where I was, or that I had fallen asleep sitting up. My back had never ached so much – same thing was true for my head. Little food and mixing brandy and wine like that really hadn't been the best idea I'd ever had. Thank the gods that the sun had not quite come up yet, as the only light that funneled in through the big window facing east was soft and pink and relatively harmless. I could hear a faint pounding noise coming from somewhere – was that my head? – and I noticed the warmth of a fire somewhere by my feet. A half-empty bottle resting on the rickety wooden table in front of me came into focus, from which I reached out and took a few sips. Gradually, it felt less like someone was driving an axe through my skull and more like my brain was being crushed very slowly. Much better.

Looking down, I realized I was a living, breathing disaster. Dirty jacket and tunic full of sweat and grime, stains on my breeches – I hadn't even pulled off my boots and didn't want to, either. The last time I had gone so unkempt for so long, I was probably three years old. I hadn't shaved in a couple of days, either, and it was catching up fast. Gods, I had to look awful. Amazing how all of one's efforts to keep up with appearances can go straight to hell in less than three days.

Mirror, mirror, there had to be a mirror somewhere. Women lived here, after all; didn't they like to keep mirrors around? Well, these women didn't, at least not in their kitchen. They did have that window, though, and maybe it would provide enough of a reflection to at least figure out if I'd be willing to be seen in public. I didn't even think about what else I might notice when I found a spot of glass and just the right angle to view my unfortunate reflection.

"Holy hell." What else was there to say? I had never in my life seen anything like it. The parts of my eyes that used to be a nice deep brown were all wrong. They looked like silvery molten metal, and they swirled and pulsed of their own accord – they reminded me of tiny stars on a clear night. I touched my face, touched the window, just to make sure they were real things, that what I was looking at was indeed part of this world. Maybe I was dreaming again? Sure, it was possible. I definitely *wanted* to be dreaming again. I wanted my chestnut-colored eyes that ladies seemed to like so much back. I wanted to be back at home, clean, warm, and safe, and I wanted to pretend like none of this ever happened. I would have been happy to go do another few years at the Academy if it meant not having to be there, at that moment, looking at my own grizzled image with awful, strange, fallen stars wedged into my eyeballs.

If I had been just a tiny bit closer to stone drunk, like I was a few hours ago, I would have smashed that wine bottle right through that fucking window. But... why let so much good alcohol go to waste? Actually, it wasn't very "good" at all, but it was good for something. So I did what any sane person in my situation would do – I grabbed that bottle up and indulged in a few more comforting gulps.

Outside, a few puffy clouds floated high in the sky, and for no particular reason I imagined I could see the wind carry them along. This, of course, was silly and impossible. But there it was all the same – all of the little particles of dust and moisture were out there, moving slowly in time to their own rhythm. I could shut my eyes and open them again, and they were still there, doing their dance. Even when I moved my hand in front my face, I could see how the air parted to make way for it. I might as well have been moving through sand or water. Even more bizarre, if I focused on a cluster of particles just so, they would speed up or slow down, moving independently of the others. By the gods, what was in that wine? All I knew was that this was far stranger than the time Corr and I mixed bittergum and Birrizi *d'trulo* during Peaceday Festival our second year in the Academy. Tristan really missed out on that one... but to his credit, he also didn't fail his math exam because he was spending the next three days trying to decide if the universe truly existed or not.

Well, the universe could stop existing anytime it felt like it. I closed my eyes again, shut them as tight as I could, and when I opened them, everything was still again, normal, the way it should be. My happiness with this was short-lived when I saw that reflection of my haggard face starting back at me with those swirling little pots of quicksilver in my irises. Yes, the universe definitely had permission to just stop anytime it was ready – I was done.

I thought to make my way out of the kitchen but something outside, beyond my reflection and beyond the glass, caught me. There were men out there, out on the road that stretched between Doverton and the Eislandisch border. There were maybe seven or eight of them, what looked like two small groups coming together, just ghosts and silhouettes against the faint light of dawn. The group that had just run in from the city to the east seemed excited about something – they gesticulated wildly while the others at first seemed unaffected, then they got excited too. They were too far away and it was too dark to figure out what might be going on, whether this was even a happy kind of excitement or anger or what, but it was definitely something important. After a few moments of this, they all started rushing off back to the east until they were out of sight. Somehow, I doubted this was normal behavior, so I grabbed up the rest of my wine and made my way out into the chapel.

The torches had all flickered out, except for the two larger ones near the door, but I could see well enough. A pretty place – peaceful, especially at this hour. This wasn't the kind of chapel where you went to Peaceday morning mass and pretended to pay attention. This was where you went to cloister yourself up for a few days because you'd done something very, very bad and were looking for a free pass into Paradise. The way the dim light filtered in through those simplistic stained-glass images of Catherine and a bunch of doves flying around made me think that somehow, you could feel like you were closer to the divine there – at least, just a little. Too bad the goddess didn't seem to be waiting around to listen to prayers much lately.

Nothing was touched – my stuff was still sitting by the door, the altar and the things upon it were still neat and tidy. Not that I expected anything to be different, but yet… I couldn't place it, but something seemed off. Was there a breeze? Yes, it was damn cold, actually, but that couldn't just be due to some torches going out. Actually, it probably had a lot to do with the door being open, just enough to let the wind blow in. Who would go and leave the door open like that, I had no idea, but it never occurred to me that this was suspicious or even odd. It should have, but that's what happens when you drink a whole flask of Drakannyan brandy and almost two bottles of Rose River Red in the span of a few hours. No, instead I thought little of just shutting that door all the way, never realizing or caring that it had previously been locked.

I should really have cared about this, though, because the next thing I knew I was on my knees, bent over a shattered bottle, wondering what the fuck just happened. A tremendous pain shot out from the back of my head and wrapped itself around every nerve it could find… and what was that, blood? I touched the place where it hurt most and yes indeed, there was something thick and crimson matting up my hair back there. How did that get there? I looked around for an answer only a second or two away from getting turned into a piece of meat on a skewer.

The person with the sword hilt that had tried to crack my skull open was turning the sharp part of his weapon on me. My addled brain could not even begin to think about who this person was, but it was certainly a sobering enough sight to make some part of me react. Just as the blade came down, aimed for my unarmored chest, I rolled over and out of the way, trying to make my way to my feet. This was not easy, but luckily, time was on my side – quite literally. I realized that my attacker looked to be moving rather slow for someone trying to kill someone else. He almost looked like he was moving through water – even the bits of dust floating around him were slowing down, sort of like they had done outside the window a few minutes ago. It didn't last long, but it was long enough for me to pick myself up and start moving to the other side of the room, tripping over pews as I did so.

There was a sword in here, Tristan's sword… where was it? I knew it was here somewhere. And it was, where he'd left it, resting against a pew near the front of the room – it might as well have been in Starlandia. Somehow, even with this strange murderer chasing me and being so clumsy because I couldn't see straight, I managed to get to it. It felt dead and heavy and cold in my grip, but it was enough to parry the next blow that was coming down at my skull. The man made an annoyed grunt and continued with his onslaught – and unfortunately for me, he was no amateur. He came at me from every direction and every angle, hitting really fucking hard, much harder than anyone had ever done during Academy sparring sessions. I had never really been in a fight that wasn't a spar, of course, and it did not take long for him to figure that out.

This guy could overpower me. This guy could kill me. These were the only things running through my mind – everything else I did was based on instinct alone. We went back and forth across the chapel, dodging pews as we went, making various clangs and battle noises that rang throughout the entire room, echoing against stone and glass. At some point, I put a gash into one of those old pews that I'd later feel terrible about. I parried, I blocked, sometimes I even fought back, but the most important thing was the magic. Without the magic, I would have already been dead and bleeding out. No, I could be man enough to admit that any semblance of skill with a blade that I had was of almost no consequence. What I could do was slow him down, change his rhythm, make him take the occasional misstep. He had no idea what was going on, but the confused expression on his weathered face told the story. It didn't happen all at once, but rather in bursts of energy – inspiration? Call it what you will, but that awful burning horrible stuff was strong enough to keep me alive, and keep this man guessing.

Right up until it ran out.

It felt like something was leaving my body, like I'd already been stabbed. But no, I looked down and saw no wounds... yet. There would be one in short order if I didn't do something, but it was the *doing* part that had gotten rather difficult. As I stepped back to avoid another slice I stumbled and fell over a pew, landing half on it and half on the floor in a heap of stupidity. I had managed to keep ahold of the sword, but it felt so heavy. *I* felt so heavy – every limb felt odd and disconnected and uncoordinated. All I could really do was look up at the gracefully curved shortsword bearing down at me.

I'm going to die here. This was all I could think. I'm going to die in some backwater place, looking like a peasant, and I never even had a chance to get married and have an heir. It was such a ridiculous thing to think. Instead, I should have been thinking about why the killing blow seemed to take so long, but that might have been because the man had a dagger lodged in the side of his throat. He started to make these really strange gurgling noises that I'd never heard anyone make before. Yep, that was probably it.

My attacker toppled over just like a tree that's been cut down, landing just in front of me, coloring everything around him a rich shade of crimson. I had never seen so much blood coming out of someone like that. It spilled out over the front of his nondescript tunic and down his arm, began to soak the floor beneath him, spreading out further than I would have thought possible. It was only once it touched where my hand was trying to prop the rest of me up into a sitting position that I tried to move – it was warm and viscous and just so very wrong.

"I think I'm going to be ill," I muttered as I failed to get my feet under me once again. Catherine help me if I was going to fall into that pool of blood. Lucky for me, there was someone there willing to keep that from happening.

"Are you okay?" asked Tristan as he helped pull me up with the same hand that he just used to cause the grotesque mess now at our feet. He was shirtless, blood splattered right across his chest, but it bothered me far more than it seemed to bother him. Being so disturbed by this, it didn't even register with me right away that he was wearing his boots and his uniform breeches, the kind with the hard leather pads built into them to serve as armor. He'd shaved and washed his hair too – were we going somewhere or something?

"Yeah, I just, ah, he just hit me back here." I felt the back of my head again to see if it was any more damaged than before. It wasn't anything except a bit stickier. "It's... this is not like Academy training at all, is it?"

"Not in the least." There was nothing to read in his expression.

My head hurt so badly, and I felt a little like I was floating. Everything felt disconnected and odd, but it wasn't the alcohol. No, I was sober enough now; this was something far less pleasant. "I am having the absolute strangest morning."

"Yeah, I can see that." Tristan turned his concern to the dead man. "Did he say anything to you?"

"No, he was just... there." Right? No, everything had happened so fast, but I was pretty sure he didn't say anything. "I sort of – well, I came in here and the door was open just a crack, you know? So I closed it and didn't think much about it and then, *wham!* That was it."

As he knelt down to look at the body more closely, I couldn't help but notice how much he favored that right shoulder, how awkwardly he moved. He had a fresh bandage over it, covering part of the golden monster tattooed there so that all it could do was peek out from underneath. I had a feeling it was a good thing that he didn't have to do any real fighting himself, although to be honest, Tristan with just his left hand and a dagger was still a better fighter than me with all of my faculties intact in full battle gear. I also couldn't help but cringe at the thought of rifling through the dead man's clothing and pockets the way he was. I'd have to take out another bottle of wine to feel up to doing that, but... well, maybe you get used to it.

"He doesn't really look like a highwayman or something, does he? Where's he from?" I asked, trying to ignore the ripping headache that was starting to spread over me.

"He looks Zondrean, but there's no identification, no colors, nothing. If I had to guess, though, I'd say Doverton."

"He is from Doverton. I recognize him." Andella's voice was so small I almost didn't hear what she said. When I looked up Tristan was already on his feet, moving to shield her from the grisly scene.

"I told you to wait back there," he said, sounding more sad than frustrated, but definitely a mix of both.

Her eyes were wide and glassy in a way I didn't think was possible for mages. The Fires within them hardly moved at all. She held a frayed, fading cloak tightly around her shoulders. "I know, but I was worried. Why... why is there an Honor Guard dead in the middle of the chapel?"

"We were just wondering that ourselves," I said. "Wait, what's the Honor Guard? King's men?"

As she spoke, she seemed to realize what she was saying – her words sort of slowed down and faltered the further she got into each sentence. "Right, it's the King's personal guard – the best of the best. I recognize him; I don't know his name but I know I've seen him before. They're the only ones who train personally with Madame Saçaille."

"So you're saying that crazy bitch sent assassins out here to kill us?" What the hell? The longer I was here in this church the stranger things seemed to get. Magic, prophecies, assassins – it was all getting to be a bit too much. At any moment, surely someone was going to pop out from behind a corner and tell me how this was all one very elaborate practical joke. That moment could not come along quick enough.

"Or just you." Me? Why me? "I think it makes sense now. I think... Madame Saçaille doesn't want to see the Prophecy come true."

The Prophecy again? Unreal. "Wait, she knows about this too?" I asked. "Is this like common knowledge or something and I'm the only person who doesn't fucking know about it?" A glance at Tristan told me he was thinking something along the same lines, but he said nothing.

"Like I told you, she talks to my sister. That book and this temple have been in my family for so many generations... I don't know. Maybe she's protecting it in a different sort of way, you know?" At this, she turned to Tristan, looking up at him with that same glassy stare. "Please, we have to go."

As she started away toward the back room to get her things or do whatever she needed to do, I couldn't help but ask after her, "Go where?" Even though I thought I knew the answer, everything seemed like a surprise this morning. Who knew? Maybe we were getting ready to run away and hide in the mountains somewhere or something. That didn't sound like a bad idea.

"Doverton. If this is all true, then her sister might be in danger." Or she might be dead. This is what I thought Tristan would say next, but that probably wasn't a good idea – at least not while the girl might be within earshot. I still didn't have a good understanding of *why* this sister might be another target, but Andella had said something about three magics. Even in my addled state, I did remember that part. Maybe she thought her sister had one of these other so-called special magic powers? Then again, maybe she and everyone else had all gone mad, including me. That possibility was still on the table.

"Did she, ah, talk to you?"

Tristan nodded. "Yeah. We talked."

"And?"

"And I..." He trailed off. Hesitated. If he'd believed the entire thing about prophecies and whatnot without question, I would have assumed that he'd lost it completely. Sure, that Andella was pretty, but still. It was comforting to see a bit of confusion and disbelief cloud his features. There was some anger there, too – plenty of that. A lot of blood had been spilled over this apparent ages-old and valuable knowledge, far more than I even understood. "Look, I don't know. I do know she believes it, and maybe she's right. I saw you – I saw what you can do."

Every shake of my head sent waves of pain through everything from the neck up. The more I moved, the more it hurt. "It's a party trick. This is not some great revelation or gifts from above," I said. And yet, people were conspiring and killing each other over this? It made me mad – really fucking mad, to the point where I could feel that horrible, strange power bubbling back up to the surface, ready for another round where it could fizzle out just when I actually found some use for it. Stupid, maddening, useless power. "Fuck... we shouldn't even be here, man. We should be home, asleep in our own damned beds. I should have a hangover from Montagne Prince Bleu, not that cheap Rose River swill. And I *certainly* should not be standing over a dead fucking body. What the hell is going on? We don't deserve any of this."

His eyes narrowed in a gaze that might have been a fresh take on the old favorite are-you-stupid look, but if it was, I was really, *really* stupid. "You stop asking that after a while. It's not really worth it."

"Fuck that. I should have just gone to the Magic Academy after all and sat in that damned library of theirs for the last four years. That way my father would still be alive because he wouldn't have been able to die knowing his heir was a good-for-nothing mage." I got a very puzzled look in response, so I kept going. The secret no longer needed to be secret. "Yeah, you know how they make you get into that Box when you register at the Academy? Well, I lied. And I never told anyone because I didn't want it getting out – you know, because of my father and all. Maybe I should have said something, but it didn't matter, you know? I was never going to use it. I didn't want any fucking magic, and I still don't. This whole thing is insane."

For a while, Tristan said nothing. Not that I really expected him to say anything particular, but he seemed almost dumbstruck – or angry, I couldn't tell which. Eventually, he came back with one simple phrase, a line from something but I forget what it was: "'Accept the path you walk.'"

"Really? Do you really believe that? I mean, come on. Since when do you just give up like that?" My voice had reached quite the shrill pitch, but I didn't care. The fact that I began to feel the tingling of that magic rising from deep within me somewhere made me even more furious. I wanted so much to just knock over one of those pews or break a window or something, but looking at Tristan made me think twice. His demeanor was the complete opposite of mine. If there had been anything to see beyond the wall of stoicism he'd put up, I wasn't going to see it that day.

"Acceptance isn't the same thing as giving up."

In another state of mind, I might have agreed with him. Maybe... well, probably not. I wasn't ready to accept anything that wasn't me sleeping it off in my own warm, clean bed, then getting up and thinking about how to spend a few thousand Royals. And then there was that dream I'd had – was *that* the kind of path we were supposed to walk? Following a trail of gore to our deaths? I sure hoped not. "So what, you're just giving in to this ridiculous Fate business, chalk it up to the gods and whatever else you think is out there? No – you know what? No. Fuck that."

"How do you know that if we'd done anything different, we still wouldn't be sitting here, right now?" Looking down at the blood pouring out over the stone, he shook his head. "You don't. You can't. All you can do is whatever you think is right."

I shrugged. By the gods, my head hurt – the rest of me didn't feel that great, either. "Well if that's true, then Fate is a stone-cold bitch."

He tightened his grip on that jeweled dagger of his and started back toward the bedrooms to finish getting dressed. "Just... just get yourself together – we need to get moving."

And he left me there, full of bound-up rage with nothing good around to break or throw. Why did Fate have to be so bloody concerned with us, anyhow? Fate... I didn't care if you could fight it or not – I just didn't want to have anything to do with it.

2

The walk to Doverton took less time than I thought it would. This was good because I had decided at the last minute to borrow the assassin's sword, and the ill-fitting, cheap belt it was on allowed the scabbard to bang about all over the place with every step I took. I'd have a bruise the size of Center Market on my thigh by the time we got to the city. We approached the gates just as the sun was growing big in the eastern sky, shining over flowers and grass that was just starting to come to life. The ground was surprisingly fertile up here for being so rocky and close to the mountains, but it did seem to hold moisture quite well. It was nothing compared to the lush hills spreading out around the south and east of Zondrell, of course, where the mountains were just a distant thought out on the horizon.

Very little was said in those two miles or so that we walked, and that was fine. Believe it or not, I was out of things to say for a while. I had nothing on my mind but one question: what were we going to walk into? Victor and Peter had taken troops up there into the city… and there was enough uncertainty and anger there amongst all of them to fuel a *lot* of things. Even with only a few men, with Victor's magic and his brother's temper they could do some damage if they felt like it. But, how likely was that? Surely they were smarter than that. For all I knew, they were already gone and on their way home. Of course, if that were the case, wouldn't they have come back to the church to get me? Maybe. Or maybe Victor took the opportunity to get rid of me and hope I'd get lost finding my way home. Oops, sorry everyone, we don't know where he went – hey, do you think anyone would mind if we poked around in his coffers since his estate's been vacated? I could see it now.

As we neared the gate I noticed there were a lot of guards standing around – many more than I would have thought normal for a city as small as Doverton. It seemed like they had a whole quarter of their army on guard there. "What's all that about?" I asked Andella, who was staring at the scene up ahead just as intently as I was.

"I don't know."

"Do they always have that many guards at the gates?"

"No, never."

She started walking faster, and Tristan and I followed her lead. When I looked over at him, he had that same stoic lack-of-expression on his face. I will never know what he was thinking during that morning – he had never been the kind of person who was easy to "read." None of this was new. But for maybe the very first time in our lives, that fact really bothered me.

When we got to the gate, we were greeted with many more bared weapons than I cared to count. I couldn't even see past the wall of green and steel blocking our path. "No one is allowed into the city at this time," several guardsmen barked in unison.

"What's going on?" Andella asked, hands on her hips in a certain brand of defiance that would have been cute had it not been so serious. Tristan put his left arm out in front of her, protective but for the time being, also silent.

"No one is allowed in or out, Miss Weaver," one of the men said. I found it quaint that it was a small enough town where people knew each other by name. That almost never happened in Zondrell unless you were important. "There's been an incident."

An incident? There was no way my worst feelings were actually on the mark, was there? That *bad* feeling washed over me more like a tidal wave than like a gentle cold shower.

"What do you mean?"

"Just go home. Everyone is safe, but we need to make sure before we open the city back up again. The Guard is handling it." Someone leaned over and whispered in the one guard's ear, and as he did so his expression changed from friendly concern to downright stern. "Miss Weaver, are these men with you?" Andella nodded. "All right, can you stand aside for a moment?" As four or five of them started to move toward us, she stood her ground, though it didn't do her a lot of good. They just ignored her as they moved in on Tristan and I.

"Hey, can we go see your boss?" I asked, trying to downplay the fact that I wasn't feeling too good about any of this. "I have a few things to discuss with her."

They were, however, much more interested in Tristan and could have cared less about me. Well, of course – he *was* standing there wearing black and silver. Well, it wasn't that easy to tell because of the rips and bloodstains, but the style of the tabard and armor was still difficult to mistake for anything else but Zondrell. Despite everything having been laundered, his uniform was still in horrible condition. The tunic was a mess, the leather plates of the armor had rips and gashes all over – why he didn't just wear steel like most people interested in their personal safety, I'll never know. Too restrictive, sure, but it kept people from putting holes in you, like the kinds of holes these Doverton guards looked like they wanted to put into us.

They kept their steel trained on us for the intimidation factor, but I was willing to go as peacefully as Tristan was. They motioned for us to start moving, but Andella, on the other hand, wasn't so patient. "Wait – where *are* you taking us? I wanted to make sure my sister's all right. She hasn't been home in a day. What's going on here?"

"Your sister's fine. All of the girls in the church are fine. But... you, ah, can't go there. You can stay here or go home, ma'am, but..."

"I will not!" Those hands went back on those hips. "I'm coming with you."

The façade of authority and knowing what they were doing was starting to fade. I could see it in their dark eyes – some of these guardsmen were downright terrified. Why, I had no idea. Andella continued to protest but it wasn't getting her anywhere, until Tristan leaned over and said something to her in a voice too low to hear. Whatever it was, she calmed down considerably, but still, she wasn't taking no for an answer. And at some point, they gave up and relented. "All right, then. All of you, come with us," one of them said with a sigh as we were led through the gates and within the high cobblestone walls that surrounded Doverton.

Funny, I had always known it was a small city, but actually being there made me realize what that meant. The streets were wide, but lined only by gravel and whatever natural stone was already there. There were no cobblestones set in neat little rows, as you saw in many parts of Zondrell, nor were the buildings pushed so close together that you could hear what happened in your neighbor's house. Even in the nicer parts of Zondrell, that usually held true and in fact, here, you couldn't really tell which were the "nicer parts." At least, not from where I stood. Everything looked sort of the same – tiny little homes, the occasional inn or general store. No massive fountains, no bazaars full of fabulous wares with shops that never closed, no spectacular church or palace. By comparison, Doverton was as simple and, well, *boring* as a town could get.

Too bad I wasn't going to get a chance for the full tour. We were led by four men, the one who seemed to speak for the rest at the front, with two flanking and another behind us. As we headed down what appeared to be the main road, I wondered where everyone was. There was almost *no one* on the streets at all. No one, except for a rather tall fellow in a dark cloak, making his way up the road toward us. It couldn't be…

Oh, but it could. "I will take these to Saçaille," Brin Jannausch said to the guards, coming to stand about ten paces in front of us with his arms across his chest. Everyone stopped, and I heard at least one of the guards huff in annoyance. Or maybe that was Tristan.

"That's *Madame* Saçaille to you, Sir," our leader said. "And that's all right, we'll take them."

"You have a gate to guard, do you not? No one in, no one out, *ja?* Otherwise, I would not be here right now."

"Sir, if you'll just step out of the way."

"You could just go around me. Unless, something is stopping you?"

The four guards looked at each other with a nervous glint in their eyes. They looked at us, then back at Jannausch. Whatever experience they might have had with this odd Eislandisch character, I could only guess, but it didn't seem to be all that positive. "We'll, uh... we'll be right behind you."

Jannausch chuckled as the four guards stepped away, eyeing us as they gestured for us to move on ahead. I had no idea if we were getting a break or a death sentence, but either way, we seemed to have little choice in the matter. Well, unless we wanted to start a battle in the streets, which didn't seem to be the wisest idea. Even Tristan, as much as I could see the seething rage in his eyes beginning to boil over, stayed as collected and cool as ever. As we continued on with Jannausch in the lead, Tristan said a few things in Eislandisch I failed to understand.

The Eislander laughed – whatever Tristan had said, it must have been quite amusing. "Stay your hand, *Jüngling.* Everyone here is on edge. Besides, the person you should be complaining to is not me. I have been... how do you say? Let go. Sacked. I have done my last job for Fräulein there."

"Doesn't matter," Tristan replied. "Next time, tell her not to send amateurs."

"It is hard to reason with one who believes death is the answer."

Death – an answer? To what? "What does that mean?" I asked.

The big Eislander stopped and turned to me, and for a fleeting moment, I saw something not unlike shock – or maybe fear – in his expression. "Herr Vestarton, she believes what many might – that this world is not prepared to handle people like yourself. Power of a different nature scares people, makes them do things that are... irrational."

"Not this again." Almost as if it didn't like it when people talked about it, I could feel the magic in my veins rise up and begin to slither.

"Many men have died, and more might still. It is not hard to find evil in a prophecy like that. Everyone must do what they think is right – you, your Zondrell brethren, even Onyx Saçaille. Fate decides who makes the best choice."

"So what about you?"

"Me? I will stand on the side of Fate."

At this, Tristan snorted derisively and kept on walking, with Andella right along with him. "They said something about the church, right?" Tristan asked. "That's where we're going?"

"Your men are there," Jannausch said as he and I hurried to catch up. "Fräulein, I tried to warn your sister but she stayed. Not the wisest decision." When she looked to him with big round eyes full of concern, he continued. "As I understand, an audience with the King did not go so well. There were threats; a man died on both sides. That Water mage that they have with them is quite... strong. They all found refuge in the church."

"What?" Tristan and I said it almost the exact same time.

"The army can do nothing as the priestesses have been... ah, how do you say? *Geiseln genommen.*"

A bit of color drained from Tristan's face. "They took them as hostages? Seriously?"

Jannausch nodded. "I must say, I was as surprised as you. Even for *Zondern*, they are fools."

For her part, Andella had heard all she needed to hear. She started walking faster than any of us, moving with drive and purpose.

"Hey, ah..." I started to say after her, but couldn't find anything to end the sentence with. Neither could Tristan, who had a look on his face that reflected my own confusion and fear. This was just amazing. No, ridiculous – unconscionable! I knew that Victor and Peter Wyndham were total asses of the highest order, but would never have believed them capable of threatening a bunch of priestesses and holding them prisoner – never. Not even for personal gain. This was too much. I wondered what they possibly could have said to the King of Doverton to start something like this in motion in the first place. Sure, Victor was arrogant and Peter liked to talk way outside his boundaries, but this was another city, another set of rules. Everyone knows you don't just waltz in and make demands or throw your weight around in another man's town unless you know what you're doing. Well, unless of course you think you can just make up your own rules.

"Fools" wasn't a strong enough word for them. I couldn't even think of a nasty enough word, and that was really saying something.

We started walking a little faster until we got to the center of the city, where the spires of the temple of Catherine rose high into the sky, obscuring the sun as it continued to make its daily ascent. It was nothing like the grand temple at Zondrell, with all of its gold trim and massive wings that were bigger than most people's homes, but it was still magnificent enough to hold the words and deeds handed down by the Goddess. How ironic that a place with images of doves stained into all of its windows would be the centerpiece of what was probably the most violent thing that had happened in Doverton in decades. The goddess of peace was no doubt furious with every last one of us.

Across the street, gathered near the entrance to a storefront of some kind, was a small collection of green-clad troops. Not that far away, posted at different corners around the church, were similar contingents, all of them looking very tense and very unhappy. Each time they spoke to each other you could see the unease in their gestures, the way they carried themselves. I wondered how many of these men had ever even seen a battle that didn't involve a couple of drunkards at the neighborhood tavern. Not that I was any sort of veteran myself, but it wasn't like Doverton had a military academy of its own. These men were just soldiers, there to keep peace and order. If this had been Zondrell and twenty foreigners had decided to hole themselves up in the temple like this, they would already have been dealt with. Of course, Zondrell had battlemages in its ranks – obviously, Doverton did not, otherwise they would have been able to handle a few tricks from the likes of Victor Wyndham. Or, maybe Victor really was that strong. I had a hard time believing that, though.

Jannausch led us toward the group in front of the store, and there was the lady herself – the King's Weapon Master, clad in proper Doverton livery now, complete with armor. But, to say that she fit in with the rest of the regular soldiers would be a vast understatement. The metal plates at her shoulders, elbows, and knees gleamed bright in the morning sun, and even from a distance I could see that all of the leather bits were freshly oiled. Well, one thing was certain about her – she took care of her things. She did not, however, take as much care in paying attention to her surroundings at that moment, because before she had a chance to react, she had a hand around her throat.

I had to admit, I was impressed. I did not think it was possible to be so calm with some thirty swords pointed at you, but there was Tristan nonetheless – he did not even blink. Now, what would have prompted him to test his nerves in that way, I had no idea. I wished I'd been a bit more prepared for it. What the hell? If this was his idea of a "plan," well, I'd hate to think of what he'd come up with if he'd had more time to think it through. I glanced at Andella and Jannausch and they both appeared to be about as surprised as I was.

"If you want to kill us," he snarled as he clenched just a little bit tighter, "you'll have to do it right now in front of all of these witnesses. And when you do, you'll have seventy thousand troops on your doorstep by dawn. Is that what you want?"

Saçaille considered, her ebony gaze scanning everything and everyone. She could have easily reached for the blade sheathed low on her back, but she didn't. In fact, she didn't even flinch, except to put up one hand to stop her men from making decisions on their own. Through a few light sputtering coughs, she said, "I take it my… scout is not coming back."

"You'll have to do something yourself for once. Or, you accept my offer."

An offer? We didn't talk about any offers. Was it really wise to try to deal with this woman – which also meant dealing with her entire fucking army? Besides, let's be fair, his track record on bargaining with hostiles didn't seem that strong. I started to speak up, but he just shot me *that* look and shook his head. Okay, fine, sure. Go ahead and get us killed. That's all right – I was tired of what this life had turned into anyhow. Holy hell, what was he thinking?

At least she was going to give him the chance to actually explain whatever this offer was. "Speak."

"I'm going to go over to that church and give myself up to those men – they're here because of me. You know that as well as I do. But, once I go over there, we go from this place in peace. If your soldiers so much as breathe wrong in our direction, you'll have a war on your hands."

"And if they kill you?" This was exactly what I would have asked. Clearly, my friend had lost his mind if he thought that the same people whose reaction to a bad day in front of the King was to go and take a bunch of innocent priestesses hostage were going to talk reason and sense with someone that they blamed for having to be here in the first place.

"Then you still have a war to deal with. Do you think that Zondrell will let its men die by Doverton's blade and not retaliate?"

Well, that was a good point. He was right – Zondrell wouldn't stand by quietly once this incident saw the light of day. And even if they killed every Zondrellian within five miles of the city, the news would still get back. People talked; they gossiped and fretted and wondered aloud all the time. There would be a war within weeks, if not days, if things really went wrong here. And it didn't matter what kind of training these Doverton troops might have had – there just weren't enough of them to put up a fight against the giant that was Zondrell.

Nearby, Jannausch leaned back against the store building. "Zondrell loves blood, Onyx," he said. "Perhaps you should listen. You would not want to be on the wrong side of Fate, would you?" Around us, some of the troops began to murmur similar things. They knew – they weren't stupid. Hell, a single, *injured* Zondrell solider had their leader overmatched and at his mercy right in front of their eyes.

Well, maybe not entirely overmatched, but she made no move to fight back, even though the longer they stood there like that, the whiter her skin got around the points where Tristan held her. It felt like an eternity before she finally relented with a half-breathless, irritated, "Fine." He loosened his grip and stepped away, leaving her with bright red marks along each side of her neck that she casually massaged in between stifled coughs. Some of her men lowered their blades, too, but not all. "I admit, I admire your... bravery."

"I want you to swear that these men can leave in peace," he said.

"I give you my word."

Tristan shook his head, and I didn't blame him. This woman had not proven herself to be all that trustworthy – the whole trying to kill us thing had a nasty way of sticking in one's mind. "That's not good enough."

"All right." With more grace that I'd ever seen anyone do just about anything before, she reached down, grabbed up her blade, and swept it across the palm of her other hand before sheathing that curiously short, shimmering sword once again. She held out her palm as the blood dripped off of it and down to the ground below. "You have my blood. Where I come from, blood is an oath not to be broken. If you do as you say you will, your men walk free back to Zondrell. Even this one." Her dark gaze turned on me. "Though I should think *your* time may grow much shorter. This world is not ready for what you hold."

Yeah, I'd heard that before. But the more I thought about it, and the more I felt that magic boiling and writhing around inside, the less I was willing to succumb to anyone's threats, hers included. "You know what, darling, I can take care of myself pretty well," I said.

The black of her eyes was colder than a thousand winters. "You will need an army bigger than Zondrell to keep your enemies at bay. You will see."

Tristan stepped between us. "Just keep your word." With that, he took a deep breath and turned to face the church.

That dream, the one where he was dead and bleeding all over the ground in some unknown place, came rushing back. I didn't like this, not one bit. What if that was more than just a dream? The sense of utter hopelessness that I felt in the dream had been so strong – I felt it again, a pang deep in my gut that made my heart beat way too fast and the magic swirl around under my skin like an angry snake.

"Wait! No, wait just a minute," I shouted. "This is a bad fucking idea." I looked over at Andella and she nodded in agreement. She looked like she was about to break at any moment, tears welling up to quench those orange flames in her eyes.

"I don't like this," she said. "Please, think about what you're doing."

But instead of listening to us, or wanting to stop those tears from falling, Tristan just kept walking. I reached out and grabbed him by the arm, pulling hard enough to make him stop and turn back. Again, I must have been pretty fucking stupid to get a look like that. "I owe it to them. Besides, there is no other choice."

I could understand that – sure, he thought he was making up for something. But how did he know they would see it the same way? "Are you kidding? We can turn around and go home. We can go somewhere else. We can tell these people to all get fucked for all I care, but what you're doing is just... it's suicide, man."

"You don't know that." No, actually, I thought I did. People were already dead – once the first blood was spilled, it got easier. I wasn't sure of much, but I was pretty sure of that. "Besides, you wouldn't just walk away any more than I would, and you know it." Maybe, but that's beside the point. I didn't have any dreams about *me* dying. "This is the right thing to do, and..."

I couldn't take it anymore and cut him off. "Yeah, yeah, don't start waxing philosophical, Brother. This is reckless. Idiotic. Let Doverton handle Doverton's problems. They might kill you the minute you walk over there. How many times did you hear them tell us in training – desperate people do desperate things. You can't trust them to act like reasonable men. If they were anywhere close to reasonable, we wouldn't be standing here having this conversation."

He breathed out a heavy sigh. "It's a risk I'm willing to take." Oh dear Catherine, did he just say that? I started to shake my head and protest some more, but he wasn't going to give me the chance. "Look, Alex, just tell me you'll do one thing for me. All right?"

Sure, I promise to keep telling you you're an idiot until you drop this. But fine... I couldn't not hear him out. The time for talking reason and sense was apparently long gone. "You know I will."

He looked over at Andella, then back at me, his blue eyes like stone, unblinking. "Just promise me you won't let her out of your sight. No matter what."

My initial reaction was more anger. "Tristan, this is insane. You realize that?"

"Just fucking promise." He wasn't willing to say it, or maybe he couldn't put it into words, but I knew what he meant, and I knew that there was no other answer I could give. If I didn't, I had no right to call him Brother. So, I grabbed his outstretched hand, and said what any good brother is supposed to say.

"Right. I promise." I turned to Andella, who had turned quite still. Stricken was maybe a better word. "You heard the man. Stay close."

And of course, the tears got bigger and started rolling down her pale cheeks. I couldn't blame her – I sort of wanted to cry too. But now I had a promise to keep and had to keep myself together. Stay sharp, stay focused. If something was going to happen, I wanted to be ready – had to be. The blood felt like it was just falling out of my body as that terribly bad feeling gripped me by the soul and shook. I could only *imagine* how Tristan felt as he went to her and just held her for a moment, resting his forehead against hers so that they could share a gaze that was just for them. I think he said something, but those words weren't for me to hear. It was perhaps the single most tender, sincere gesture I'd ever seen him make toward anyone, and it was enough to both bring more tears, and calm them down. By the time he started off across the road toward the church, Andella and I were both quiet, standing shoulder to shoulder, ready as we'd ever be for whatever was going to happen.

Behind us, I heard Jannausch mutter, "The right choice. *Gute Reise.*"

✶✶

He didn't even get that close to the door before voices floated out telling him to stay back. Tristan, being Tristan, ignored this and kept walking, until a sheet of ice about three feet wide fell out of the sky and landed right in front of him, shattering into a million pieces onto the ground. My heart leapt into my throat – no wonder these Doverton guards were keeping a healthy distance.

Both Wyndham brothers and a few other Zondrell soldiers stepped out of the darkened doorway then, with wild looks in their tired, sunken eyes. Even from a distance, I could see the desperation I expected to see there, and if they hadn't been so insane as to take hostages in a church the way they did, I would have felt sympathy for them – a lot of sympathy. But what the hell were they thinking? Did they think that someone was going to rescue them somehow, or that Doverton would simply have a change of heart and let them leave? Even if they would have before, they wouldn't now. You don't just take over a church and hold the priestesses hostage without expecting some unhappy retaliation.

"I knew it – I fucking knew it! So you're working for Doverton *and* the Eislandisch?" Peter's tone was full of arrogance and derisive shock, but there was some stress and fear in that shouting, too. "You just might be the boldest traitor in history, Loringham."

Tristan folded his arms across his chest, standing his ground without trying to look threatening. "You have no idea what you're talking about."

"Yeah? Enlighten me."

"Remember that girl they found in the woods a few weeks ago? They brought her to me. I didn't kill her." There were some whispers and hushed murmurs among some of the men standing nearby at this. No one looked upset as much as confused, maybe nervous. "I couldn't do it. It wasn't right – we're not animals. So I let her go. But she was a spy; they already knew about our position. They already knew what we were doing up there. They manipulated us – me – right up until they had us where they wanted us. Maybe I was wrong, but I thought I was doing the right thing, protecting our mission and my men. I'll stand by that until I die."

From the look on his pallid, round face, I couldn't tell what Peter thought. He seemed at a total loss for words. Imagine that – Peter Wyndham, without anything to say.

Tristan continued. "I don't ask for anything – do whatever you want to me, I don't care. But don't do it here. Let these people go, leave this city in peace. The army will allow it; I talked to them. They just want us out of here."

Peter was still speechless, but unfortunately, his brother wasn't. "No one pays you to think," Victor snarled. "No one pays you to make decisions. Do you even have any proof of what you're talking about? Probably not. Doesn't matter. You're here to carry out the will of the King – period. And you couldn't even do that right. For Catherine's sake, you're as much a disgrace as your father. Marry a sub-human Eislandisch and this is what you get. Unbelievable."

What a miserable ass. But Tristan took all of this with grace, staring straight ahead, never even moving. A most stunning display of restraint. He didn't even so much as flinch when Victor continued on his tirade, his voice growing louder and more forceful by the minute. People three blocks over could hear him carrying on.

"No one told you to have your own morals, Loringham. No one. You do what you're told. You didn't even have to fucking *find* anything. You just had to do some scouting and keep those people distracted, thin their ranks. It's about strength, superiority – something you wouldn't really know anything about, would you? If Doverton thinks that they have anything on us, they're sadly mistaken, and they can be the first to fall. Zondrell will be the capitol of a new unified Zondrea someday, you know, and when that happens... well, there's no room in this world for people like you. There's no room for judgment calls from low-ranking officers from disgraced families who think they know better than everyone else."

Peter shook his head, big round eyes full of a mix of fear and surprise. "Victor..."

But Victor wanted to hear none of it. "Shut up, Brother. Go back inside and let me handle this." So Peter did – he backed up a few feet, turned around, and headed for the shadows of the church entrance. I could hardly believe his absolute, unabashed cowardice. If Victor were my brother, I would have hauled off and beaten the piss out of him. And a unified Zondrea? Were they mad? Of course, bringing the city-states under one banner again, like it was hundreds of years ago, would bring a lot of money into Zondrell's coffers. If a great war was the best way King Kelvaar could think up to fix his gold problem, then... well, there just wasn't a lot of hope left for Zondrell this dynasty, was there? I wondered how long this idea had been bantered around at the Council meetings over the past few months – or maybe years. I certainly knew how I'd vote if it came up again. We didn't need a unified Zondrea. We just needed some simple fiscal responsibility. Not that hard, really, and this is coming from me. I love to spend money as much as anyone, but fuck... *not* spending it is just not that difficult.

Tristan's voice remained as even and calm as his stance. I, on the other hand, wanted so badly just to leap out there, sword at the ready to wipe that arrogant, self-aggrandizing attitude of Victor's right out of existence. The only reason why I didn't was because of that promise. "You have twenty men and they have five thousand, Victor. Now is not the time to start a war. I'm not asking for anything but for us to leave this place in peace. It's not that much to ask."

No, it wasn't. At least, most sane people didn't think so. I used to think Victor Wyndham was just a prick, not crazy. I *used* to think that, anyhow.

Victor took a few steps toward Tristan, then a few more, until they were standing eye to eye. "So that's it?"

"Yeah."

For several minutes, Victor said nothing. He started to walk a close circle around Tristan, looking over to me briefly as he did so. It was too far away, but was there a flash of something there in his eyes? I couldn't tell, but a chill shot through me nonetheless. "One problem," he said, lining his words up very carefully. "Justice like that takes time – I didn't come here to waste time. And quite frankly, these people you claim to have a deal with *attacked* us. Just like you did."

"I did not. I just told you…"

"Shut up. Why should we trust you – of *all people*?"

It might as well have been a scene on a stage somewhere, and I was in the audience, just watching from afar without any say as to what would happen next. Standing at Tristan's back, a wink of light appeared in Victor's hands – nothing very big, just this razor-thin and bluish-white thing. And the next minute, it wasn't there at all, gone not because it vanished, but because it was buried in blood and flesh and bone. There wasn't even any time to react. It was just there, and in a moment… gone, sending Tristan to his knees.

"There's no room in this world for traitors, either," said Victor, folding his arms across his chest.

For a moment, all I did was stand there, staring in utter disbelief as Tristan struggled to get back to his feet, but couldn't. What just happened? Did I just see what I thought I saw? I felt as helpless as he looked. What an idiot – couldn't I have done something more? What was wrong with me? But I felt frozen, disconnected, like I was observing everything – even myself – from some faraway place. It was only when Andella cried out and started running that I snapped out of my trance.

I chased her for maybe twenty feet before I heard lots of yelling and movement and the rings of swords leaving scabbards. And then the cold hit – bitter, powerful cold, worse than any cold of any winter. It was like running into an invisible wall. You could see your breath form clouds of smoky frost in the air. The strangest thing, though, was the snow. Yes, snowflakes had started to fall, sprinkling down from a clear, sunny sky in the middle of Spring's Dawn. As one of them sparkled in the light when it landed on my cheek, I felt the strangest sense of foreboding that I had ever felt in my life. This couldn't all be from Victor, could it? Perhaps he was a lot more powerful than most people gave him credit for, which was already quite a bit. You don't get to be "Captain of Magics" for nothing, I suppose.

"Don't come any closer, Vestarton. You at least still have a chance for a trial for now… if you play your hand right."

Fuck that – the more it dawned on me that my best friend was unmoving, bleeding out on the ground just out of my reach, I wanted to tear Victor's eyes out. Civility was dead and gone. Everything we grew up knowing and learning was a lie. None of us were any better than common highwaymen and barbarians, and I was very close to joining Victor in following my baser instincts.

It was lucky, in some ways, that Victor was focused on me, because if he had been paying closer attention, things might have been a lot worse. Even as it was, those snowflakes quickly got bigger and bigger until they had turned into sharp arrows made from ice, falling out of the sky with quickening force. More sounds – scrambling, screaming – came from all directions. I dared not look. I didn't want to know. All I could think was that I was breaking a promise already, hardly more than five minutes after I'd made it. The girl had darted off and I was supposed to protect her and now there were ice spears all over the place and people were getting hurt and…

And they stopped. I took a moment to clear my head, look around. All of them, glittering and hovering as if they had formed there, perfect icicles attached to nothing at all. You could walk in between and pick one out if you liked. The entire intersection in front of that church was just... *still.* Behind us and in front of us, a number of confused and pained voices said things I didn't hear or understand.

Victor was nonplussed. "Impressive trick, Alexander. Where did you...? Never mind. You know what? It doesn't matter. You have no training. You don't even know how to control that power, do you?"

No, of course not, but he didn't need to know that. I had no idea how that great stirring in my chest, under my skin, deep in my veins, translated into controlling the fabric of time itself, but it didn't matter. All I knew was that in fits and flashes I could see all of the particles that made up that fabric – I could watch them dance and move and I could make them do what I wanted, even if the longer I held the ice in space, the more it hurt. It felt a lot like I imagined getting struck with lightning must feel like. Nonetheless, I could even make the ice start going back up the way it came, each little spear dissolving into the sky like it had never existed. I only hoped that my own utter fascination at this wasn't evident on my face. "Maybe you shouldn't underestimate me," I growled.

Victor spat on the ground. "I'm not going to just give up, Vestarton. One more Zondrell soldier is dead, and you're as guilty as any of the Doverton scum over there. Or your friend." He turned around just in time for a great flash of fire, followed by a girlish yelp, to spring from nowhere. Surprised, he let out a girlish yelp of his own and stumbled backward, almost losing his balance.

This would have been a commendable move on Andella's part. Fire, after all, is the natural enemy of water and ice – that is, if the two magics are of equal power. The problem was, they weren't. Not in the least. I knew this, and it was a good thing because the spear of ice meant for her throat instead paused just long enough for me to dive over and pluck the thing from the air. I wouldn't feel the horrible pain from the cold of it for at least a few minutes later, though, because I was far too busy wielding it like a two-handed sword. I swung out with every bit of strength I had, seeking any vital organ I could find as long as it belonged to Victor Wyndham. Even earlier that morning, I just didn't want that assassin to kill me – when I struck, I had no intention of killing him. But there with Victor, I wanted nothing more than to lodge a blade into his skinny little frame and twist.

Too bad I missed.

Well, not exactly. I did hit him, but put little more than a gash of red right across his gaunt, arrogant face. But when I returned with the backhand swing to give it another go, the little pillar of ice in my hands turned to liquid, falling to the earth in a harmless puddle. Oh, what the fuck? Did he really just do that? Of course he did. And he was laughing about it.

"Vestarton, you're an even worse swordsman than you are a wizard. Your father would die twice more if he could see you right now."

Maybe, but I had a real sword too, and wasn't afraid to give the whole killing thing another go. I pulled the curved blade from my belt just in time to fend off another of those deadly icicles, a smaller one that shattered in two as it hit the flat side of my weapon. I lunged in with another strike meant for something soft and vulnerable but instead chopped right into another stupid ice pillar. How the hell was he creating these so quickly? All he had to do was think about them and they appeared. Perhaps there was something to be said for a bit of training.

Fuck him. Fuck him and his magic and his orders and his idiotic belief in a Zondrea unified under fear and blood. Fuck him and his underhanded, cowardly tactics. I refused to believe in any Fate where Victor Wyndham played an important part in anything. But, every time I lashed out, I got nothing I wanted. I struck again, and again, and only found myself chipping away at pieces of ice.

And he was still laughing – oh Catherine help me, I wanted so badly to watch him suffer. "You do realize that the more you do this, the less likely you'll ever make it to a trial for your treason?"

Behind him, I caught a flash of something brilliant and purple-blue. What was that? I had no idea. I didn't care, because I was too busy trying to either kill or not be killed. "And trying to start a war on your own without the King's order *doesn't* constitute treason? You're delusional, Wyndham."

"Ha! I'm delusional? You're the one who seems to think you're going to walk away from this."

The thing was, I wasn't going to win. Not alone. I could slow things down, I could stop crazy things from flying at me, but I could not swing that sword fast enough. I couldn't stop *him.* I tried – Catherine help me, I tried. But Victor was right – I was neither the wizard nor the swordsman that I needed to be.

Luckily, I wasn't alone, and he forgot that part. So did I until I heard a sickening sound – a wet, gory, horrible sound that I never wanted to hear again – and Victor suddenly fell forward. He attempted to catch himself, reaching toward me as he fell, but didn't succeed. No, instead he just sort of crumpled there on the ground like a piece of withering old parchment. What happened? I stood dumbfounded until I noticed the dagger with a ruby set in the handle buried in his back, just left of center. I would hear that strange alien wheezing sound he made in my nightmares for the next few days, but yet, I had never been so happy to witness something so hideous.

Bailed out of a losing fight twice in one day – no doubt I'd be getting teased about this for months yet to come. And I *wanted* to hear about it, as often as possible, because if that was the case, then that meant we were both alive.

But blood... blood, there was so much blood. Not Victor's though. It was splattered all over the gravel and earth – just like my dream from that morning. A smear of blood led to a widening pool where Tristan had dragged himself up, gotten that little knife out and gathered his strength for one well-timed thrust. Everything across his midsection was wet and dark, especially the spot just below his heart where his armor was torn beyond repair. It was the same blood that was all over Andella, too, on her hands and ruining her dress while she knelt there at his side. A smudge of crimson on her cheek became more of a streak as it mixed with a few stray tears. She looked up at me with fear in her eyes so deep that it had seemed to quell the fires there. Her eyes were no longer orange – or maybe I was just seeing things. Did it matter at that point?

"I can't..." she started to say. "I don't know."

I tossed the sword down – it wasn't needed anymore. "What do you mean?"

Her words came in between fighting hitches and sobs of frustration. "I can't do enough. I don't know how."

"Don't know how to do what?" But I knew what she was going to say next, didn't I? Because there was a Prophecy, right? I wondered if she knew what was going to happen this whole time, and if she had, why didn't she have the good sense to keep it from happening in the first place? If I had been a different kind of man, right about then I would have slapped her.

"This is it. Life. *Lebenkern.* And I can't do it right." She looked down at her small, thin hands, bloodstained and trembling.

That flash — whatever that light had been, it wasn't Fire magic. It was that other thing, this *Lebenkern*, this power I didn't understand and didn't quite believe existed. And yet, what choice was there but to believe? "Holy hell," I whispered as I knelt down, reached for Tristan's broad neck to feel for a pulse. Catherine's luck — it was weak, but it was there. Shit! What now? I wracked my brain for an idea and... wait. I had it. It would have to be so careful and subtle — things I wasn't good at — but I could do *something*. As Fate would have it, I had magic that could help in a way no other magic could. It was about time for it to start being useful.

"Can you do this, ah... *Lebenkern* thing if you had more time?" I asked her.

"I don't know. What do you mean?"

"I can slow the bleeding down." Yes, I could see it, every cell, every droplet, every pulsebeat, and if I just concentrated hard enough, and in the right way... "But I can't stop it because, well, I don't know if that would be a good idea. And I can't slow it forever. I don't even know how long it'll last, but..."

"Do it. Please."

We had to. It wasn't just the right thing to do — it was the only thing we could do. Because suddenly, it didn't matter that half the town was watching us. It didn't matter that Victor Wyndham was gasping for air a few feet away from us, or that his brother Peter was shaking and nervous as he came out with his sword at the ready and pointed in our direction. All that mattered was my friend — my brother-in-arms, a man who'd just put his life on the line so that a few others could live... even if they neither appreciated it nor deserved it. If that's not the definition of a "hero," I'm not sure what is.

1

Tristan Loringham

I thought my eyes were open, but I could see nothing. I reached out, tried to grab at something, but I felt nothing. The air itself seemed to have no feel, no resistance. Even the smell of dirt and gravel and sweat and dewy spring grasses was gone, the air left stale and empty in its wake. The only thing I heard was a strange sound, a loud but dull roar, not like an animal or even any sort of creature. Water... that's what it sounded like, like a river streaming down through the mountains, tearing its way through rock as if it were parchment. But where was it coming from?

Of course, I didn't know because I couldn't see, and I couldn't get up or move around or do anything. All I could do was listen to the sound of this rushing water, and think. Except I couldn't even remember how I got there – wherever "there" was – in the first place. What was I doing before?

Oh yeah... Victor. Something happened, didn't it? Something bad. I remembered not being able to catch my breath, and the way the strength felt like it had been wrenched out of my body by an invisible hand. I remembered a flash of green light, the electric tingle of magic all around. I saw Alex fighting things that weren't there (or were they?), and I had felt so tired. And so terrified – I couldn't breathe right, like something was pushing the air out of my lungs too fast. The last thing I could remember was a sense of mounting panic and the heavy, familiar weight of that silver dagger of mine.

None of that was there anymore. Not the pain, not the light, not the magic, not the people – everything was just gone. I didn't know where it went, and strangely, I didn't know that I cared. Thoughts would come and go, but there was nothing weighing them down, no emotions – no happiness, no pain, no fear, no regret. They were just free to be there, drifting along on a current all their own. *Free*. It was the only word I could find to describe what I felt. But there was no sense of elation that went along with that. It wasn't free in the way a bird flies through the air, but more in the way the wind goes wherever it chooses on any given day. There is no thought there, no sentience. The wind just does what it does, and my thoughts were the same.

Wind... did I feel a breeze? Maybe it was just my imagination. It was still dark, except for something that seemed so very far ahead in the distance. I could barely focus on it, but something was definitely there, faintly pulsing, like a single star in an endless night. And within the span of a few moments – or maybe a few hours – it grew bigger and brighter and more real until it wasn't really just a light at all, but a place.

Yes, I was *somewhere*, but as shapes and colors came into being, I didn't recognize anything there. It seemed to be nothing but a field, some countryside somewhere, with green grass growing as high as my knees. Bright red, pink, purple, blue, and orange flowers grew in patches that became more and more plentiful closer to the edge of what appeared to be a river – the source, no doubt, of that roaring, rushing sound. And this was no ordinary river, either. I had never seen one like this before, stretching across the land for miles and miles in either direction. I could see neither its start nor its end, and a row of willowy trees obscured whatever might have been on the other side.

I turned around, realizing suddenly that I could move again, and as I looked around, I saw that the field also stretched on for miles and miles, appearing to dissolve into the still yellow light of the day. No roads or paths were there to point the way toward anywhere, and every once in a while the breeze would wash over it all, turning it into a grassy sea of sorts. The wind fluttered through my hair, too, and I reached up and realized that it wasn't quite as long as it was before. My face was freshly shaved, too, and as I looked down, I realized that I was in my full dress uniform, every thread from tabard to cuff cleaned, pressed, and perfect. The falcon symbol across my chest stared up at me, and I realized I hadn't worn this uniform since graduation. In fact, it was still hanging in my room at home. The uniform I was supposed to be wearing was the normal, everyday one, with the armor that was starting to wear itself apart, and bloodstains in the cloth that would never, ever come out even though she had said she'd spent the better part of a day trying to clean it for me.

Andella. "Everything will be all right. I'll believe if you believe." It was the last thing I had said to her. There were other things I might have said, but the words weren't there. Now, it seemed petty to think about going back to try to say them over again, to do or say something different. But I remembered feeling like I was in such a hurry, that I had something important to do, that nothing could stand in the way. *I'll believe if you believe* – it felt like I had said those words ages ago. And maybe I had. When I turned back to the river, I noticed that the sun never seemed to change its position in the cloudless sky above, and that the river, as great as it was, never seemed to change its flow. It marched on, relentless, outside of time, and as it did so, I could almost hear voices in the roaring of its waters.

I wanted to get a closer look. It wasn't so much a conscious desire, but a compulsion – I *had* to approach the river. I wanted to see the water, feel how cold it was, maybe even reach in and get a drink. So I walked toward the river's edge, feeling the soft sponginess of the earth underfoot even though each step made no sound whatsoever. The closer I came, the softer the ground became until it was more like a rich, thick mud, fertile enough to support the most unique and colorful and delicate of the flowers here. I took great care not to step on them as I passed through, until I came across a spot that grabbed onto my boot, holding me in place for just a second. When I broke free I noticed a pool gathering inside my bootprint... but this was like no water I had ever seen. It was bright red.

In front of me, the river yawned and stretched and groaned its way across the land, and I realized that it too, was as crimson as the petals on some of those flowers along its banks. The sunlight sparkled in a strange sort of way on its surface, much like the way light is caught by polished metal. I started to kneel down at the shore, thinking to just get a better view, since surely, I was just seeing things. Water is not red, after all.

"Don't."

What was that? Startled, I jumped up and spun around, looking for the owner of the voice. But, the field was as empty then as it was a moment ago. Perhaps my mind was playing tricks, since all I could really hear was the steady flow of the water. But as I returned to the river, I heard that voice again.

"Don't."

Don't what? Don't get too close? But I could be careful – the riverbank stood just a few inches above the waterline. I wouldn't have to reach far and I just wanted to see... Ignoring the voice, I knelt back down and reached in this time, just letting my hand skim the surface. My fingertips came back wet with what could only be one thing, and it wasn't water.

It was blood – crimson, slightly viscous, pure untainted blood. But instead of being horrified, as I expected myself to be, I was enthralled by it. How could it be that this river existed at all? Maybe it didn't, and yet, I was there. I *knew* I was there. I could *feel* the breeze and the tickle of the grass and the way the blood began to dry into a sticky smear on my hand. I could *hear* the rushing of that water, and I could *see* this land in all its colorful glory... this land, that didn't seem to have any smells to it even though it should have been alive with the scents of all of those flowers, all of that fresh, beautiful, green grass. I opened my mouth to speak – to say what, I wasn't sure – but found no sound could come forth. I felt like I could speak, but there just weren't any words there.

Shaking my head, I peered down into the water again, this time not to touch it, but just to watch. What else was there to do, except...

"Step in." Another voice from nowhere, this one distinctly different from the other one I'd heard. A deeper voice, somewhat familiar. "You must be here for a reason. So, enter."

A reason? What reason would that be? I still didn't even know where "here" was. But as I continued to stare at the water, I realized that I could see deeper, beyond just the surface. Past the odd glimmer of the sunlight, there was movement underneath, not just the ripple of the current, but something else. Looking deeper still, I realized what it was.

It was people – men, women, children – all floating along with the undercurrent in quick succession, too fast to make out details. Sometimes I noticed animals, too, horses, dogs, cats, all sorts of creatures. Who were all of these beings? Were they all… dead? Well, they had to be, but if they were dead, then what was I?

"Go on."

A body floated by slowly enough that I could make out its features, and even though it did not seem to speak, I heard that voice, clear and distinct. It wasn't speaking Zondrean, either, even though to me it was all just words; the lines between language seemed to have melted away. It was the voice – and corpse – of that young Eislandisch soldier that I had killed four months ago. The first man I'd ever had to interrogate, the one who'd had a wife and a new baby at home. The one who had gotten an honorable death by my hand because I didn't have the courage to do anything but follow orders given to me by men who didn't hold the same value for life as others did – as I should have.

An honorable death… wait. This place couldn't be… it just couldn't be *that* river. That was where people came to die – if you even believed in it in the first place. But I was raised in the church of Catherine, where people went to the Lady's doorstep and were welcomed into Paradise. There was no goddess here, that much was certain. Just this river, perhaps The River of Eislandisch belief, its blood-waters moving so quickly, carrying these souls, or whatever they were, to their next destinations.

The soldier was gone, but the voice remained. "Go on, get it over with."

I could have easily done just that. The water was right there. I could reach out and touch it. I could let the current pull me down into the depths and find out just exactly where it would take me. Or maybe I would just float along there forever, without pain, without regret – *free.* And just as I started to move closer yet to the water's surface, I saw another familiar face float past. I had to blink – could it be? It looked for all the world like Lord Vestarton, Alex's father. I didn't have to stare into the river to picture him – handsome, dignified in his later years, and vibrant and always smiling back when we were kids. Sometimes stern, yes, but never without cause. When we did dumb things, we heard about it, but the lectures he gave always came from a place of wisdom, and of compassion. Unlike my own father, Xavier never seemed to forget what it was like learning how to become a man in a place as strange and ruthless as the noble society of Zondrell.

I thought perhaps I would hear Xavier's voice, like I had heard the Eislandisch soldier. But there was nothing except that low, thunderous roar of the River. And yet, as my gaze followed him until he was out of sight, I had the sudden urge to step back. Maybe I wasn't supposed to be here. I didn't know why I felt that way, but the compulsion to enter and let the blood wash me away was no longer as strong. Still, it was there. I felt... lost. What if I sat here forever? What would happen to me? I didn't know, but I felt a growing sense of dread that I hadn't felt before. It pulled at me, weighed down my thoughts, clouded my vision. I eased back and sat down in the mud there, not worried about the uniform, and continued to just stare into the water. Images of various people floated by, people I knew, people I didn't know, people I wanted to forget. Hundreds, thousands of images, all forms of life from all walks of life. The depths of that river knew no bounds, and there I was, waiting on its banks – for what, I could not explain.

"You have to get up." There was that other voice again, the first one. A woman's voice, delicate but urgent. And she seemed familiar too, but this wasn't a voice from the river. I didn't know where it came from – carried on the wind perhaps. I kept staring into the crimson waters.

"Please don't go." Now I did look for someone, something, squinting to see out into the distance as far as I could. I looked because I wanted to tell this person what I felt – that maybe I *had* to go. But even if I could have spoken, I could say it to nothing except River and grass and flowers, and a sun that never seemed to move.

"Please, you can't go." I damn well could do whatever I wanted. And if I wanted to sit here for the rest of time, then I would. And if I didn't want to... well, I supposed there was only one other option.

"This is not your path. Accept the one you're on." Who's to say? Does everyone really have a "path?" Was it that soldier's "path" to get his throat slit by a stranger before he'd even had the chance to live his life? Was it my "path" to serve as his executioner? What kind of god creates a path like that? I didn't have an answer for any of it. Maybe no one did – at least, no one in this place.

I found my way to my feet, turning my back to the River for a moment. Each time the voice spoke, it got louder, clearer. I wanted to know where it came from. Maybe if I just started walking back the way I came, I could find something, so I started off, following the footsteps that had brought me to the river's edge. I found myself feeling more and more anxious the further away I got, though. Was this wrong? The riverbank had seemed so... inviting, in its way.

When I ran out of footprints, I found nothing but knee-high grass and pink flowers – no different from everywhere else in this place. "We need you," said the voice, and here, I felt something, a presence. But I still couldn't speak, and I couldn't see anyone, and the sense of dread was getting more and more tangible. It wrapped itself around me and I felt the ground being pulled away. I wasn't floating off – no, the ground was literally being ripped away from where I stood, even though the sky stayed exactly as it was, with the sun hanging high in a cloudless spring-blue sky. Somehow, I became aware of a torrent of sensations that had been blissfully absent before, various waves of different types of pain that I couldn't even quite make sense of, or even register as pain. I just sensed them, didn't feel them. What I did feel, though was this presence wrapped around me, growing tighter and tighter, yet comforting all the same. Warm, gentle – safe.

✳✳

The brightness of the sky overhead assaulted my vision, but this wasn't the same sky as before. At the River's edge, the sun held none of the warmth that I could now feel against my cheeks and forehead. I reached up and felt for that presence, and my hand landed on a head of soft auburn hair.

"Oh! You're..." Andella looked up and half her face was smeared bright red. It was in her hair, too, forming sticky, dark crimson snarls. Her eyes were so strange to me at that moment, and all I could do was focus on them, and the feel of her arms wrapped tightly around me. Unfortunately, that moment didn't last very long.

The rush of the water was gone, replaced with a bevy of other noises – voices, shouting, movement. And there were smells too, the smell of something not unlike stagnant water, of wet dirt and gravel, of blood. I could taste blood, too, that unmistakable taste like salty liquid copper, a whole lot of it, building in my chest and throat, choking me so much that I jerked over to one side into sort of a fetal position and started coughing, uncontrollable painful coughs that brought with them disturbing amounts of crimson-colored spittle. I might as well have been vomiting up a River of my own. And when I looked – really *looked* – at the ground where I had been laying, I realized that there was a lot more blood already there, soaking into the ground, staining every small rock it came into contact with.

"Holy fuck! Talk to me, Brother. Oh, fuck, I can't believe that worked. Come on, talk to me." When I finally stopped coughing long enough to pick my head up and turn to Alex, his expression could only be described as one of sheer amazement mixed with glee. Sweat poured off of his forehead, and his eyes were alive and glowing and completely of their own world.

Magic. Oh, no – I started to remember.

I tried to pull myself up to sit, but everything felt so weak. My whole body shook and trembled, but stronger hands were nearby to help, though one of the few clear-thinking parts of me didn't want them there. I wanted to be able to do move on my own power – I was so tired of feeling so wretched. The entire weight of the pain crushed down upon me, worse than it had ever been.

"Victor… where?" This was as close to speaking as I could get without hacking up more unpleasantness.

"Yeah, ah," Alex nodded behind us, "he's not well."

Sprawled out on the ground with his own pool of blood a few feet away was Victor Wyndham, with his brother and a couple of other soldiers hovered around him without much of a clue about what they ought to be doing. I could hear vague wheezing sounds and some unhappy growling noises emanating from Victor, but instead of trying to do something helpful about it, everyone seemed to have the same wild look of fear, panic. Of course, he would have been worse off if I had been trying… if I hadn't been half-dead and thinking only that I had to do *something*. I could have accepted what he'd done to me; that was fine. Almost to be expected, in fact. But hurting friends, innocent people, no – not even if he somehow had a right to do it.

Peter had a firm grip on his blade and he eyed us with all of the pent-up fear and frustration he had to bear. "What sort of demons are you people?" he asked, voice breaking like a pubescent boy's.

With an angry grunt, Alex got to his feet, using that sword he'd taken off the assassin from Andella's church as leverage. He leveled the blade squarely with Peter's throat, but his words were just as sharp. "*You're* the ones who came in here looking for a fight. You wanted one? You got it. And you lost. Now stop pointing that thing at me unless you want it shoved through your eye socket. For fuck's sake, why don't you help your idiot brother before he dies like the dog that he is?" Better words could not have been chosen.

"But you…"

"But what, Peter? Catherine-on-a-pike, man, you're lucky you're still standing right about now. One word and all of those guys in green over there will come over here to finish you off. We're the only things standing between you and death right about now, and from where I'm standing, you don't fucking deserve it."

Alex was right – the Doverton guard was everywhere. I could see green uniforms all around us, holding steady for at least a little while longer. Still, Peter refused to let his guard down. Despite everything, this was still someone I had fought alongside more than once or twice. Where Alex could not, I could at least summon a modicum of respect – and maybe even sympathy – for him. I knew, for instance, that he idolized his big brother Victor and had sometimes wished that he had been able to go to the Magic Academy, too. Maybe then, he would have been able to be as powerful and important in his father's eyes. So that's why I struggled to stand up then, getting some help from Andella despite her whispered warnings telling me not to try to move, and even though everything spun around like I'd just downed an entire case of wine.

"Stay back," I bade her, and in response her eyes narrowed. I knew she was probably sick of hearing things like that, but I was serious – I hated the idea that she had been in danger so many times today, and that I was powerless to do much about it. My own safety mattered far less to me than hers did. I hoped that a look alone would convey that, and after a time, it must have because she took a few steps backward, cautiously looking back to Saçaille and her men and back to us again. There was much commotion back there, and all around us, with people shouting and running about, but for the moment, I was most worried about what was right in front of me – a very angry, partially crazed Peter Wyndham facing off against an equally irate Alexander Vestarton.

In trying to unsheathe my blade I almost fell back to my knees again. At least I – somehow – had enough strength in my right arm to hold it properly, even if I did have to lean heavily on Alex with the other arm for support. "This has to stop," I said, wishing there were more force behind those words.

"Fuck you." Peter spat on the ground. So much for respect. "You're a traitor, and… and some kind of demon, and… I don't know what else."

"I just want to do what's right. This is wrong. Everything that's happening here is wrong, and you know it." If he did or not, he made no indication either way. He didn't move, but he didn't back down, either.

"You shouldn't be standing right now. I should have killed you myself a long time ago. I should have known better." Those words, the way he said them, they felt like poisoned arrows, but I said nothing. Let him think what he wanted –

nothing I was going to say could change that. Besides, there was a little part of me that still didn't disagree. All of the rationalizing and attempts for redemption in the world weren't going to change the fact that a lot of men were still dead.

Then he did something I should have expected, but didn't. He tightened his grip on his weapon and lunged at me with all his force, thrusting with controlled accuracy to ensure he was indeed going to hit me and not Alex. And he would have succeeded, too – I had neither the reflexes nor the strength to parry him. What I did have, though, was a little magic on my side. Peter seemed to move in slow motion; I could see each breath he took, each contortion of his features as he moved in. It was the strangest thing, but while I could move freely, he seemed mired in unseen muck. At my side, Alex yelled something, but I didn't hear him. All I knew was that this was the best opening I was ever going to get.

So, I did what came naturally, and without even worrying about how much it would hurt to do so, I stepped to the side and let my sword find the hilt of his. It was a maneuver I'd learned a long time ago, something I'd practiced over and over again because you had to be perfect to get it right. If you weren't, you'd hurt your opponent, but this was one of the few times where pain was not the goal. Instead, all you had to do was reach in, catch the underside of that hilt, and pull.

Peter's weapon flew out of his hand and landed about three feet away with an empty *clink!* as it hit the gravel. A string of curses flew out of his mouth, accompanied by Alex's sudden peal of uproarious laughter. Even though it felt like something was tearing at my arm and most of the rest of my torso with flaming claws, I held my sword at the level of Peter's heart, and there was little he could do about it except freeze in place and try to think of a way to regain the upper hand. His eyes darted around, searching, and Alex chuckled, "Go ahead, Wyndham. Try it. I dare you."

We might have stood off like that for a long time if someone else didn't approach, stepping out from the shadow of the church with his weapon out, but lowered, almost dragging along the ground, in fact. He came to stand at attention before me, turning his back on Peter and Victor and all of the rest of them. "You said we could leave in peace if we surrendered?"

said Sergeant Delrin. I was so surprised to see him there I almost didn't pay attention to his words. I thought for sure he had gone home – maybe he'd come back up with whatever contingent Victor had brought with him to hunt me down.

"I… I'll swear to it on all the honor I have left." And that was the truth. If I had to hold back the entire Doverton army by myself, I still wanted those men to go free, to go back to Zondrell alive – even Peter and Victor. Too many of them had already fallen as it was, and the only thing that could happen if they didn't go in peace now would be war. I saw no other future there. It would be bloody and it would be brutal, and it might even become the next great Zondrean Civil War. No one here truly wanted that, whether they knew it or not.

In that way that he had that I'd seen more than a few times before, Delrin's dark eyes searched me. If I could have focused better, I would have noticed his expression soften, the lines in his face contorting from frown to smile. He looked back at the church, at Peter, and then again turned to me, sheathing his blade at his waist. "Right, Sir. We'll go on ahead then." His right fist came to his left shoulder in salute, and he started off down the road.

"What are you doing? Hey, that's insubordination! I'll have your rank for that," Peter called out behind him, but he never turned back. And one by one, others came out of the church to do the same thing. Each man, many of whom I knew, stood in turn before me and Alex, gave a salute at attention, and marched off after Delrin. I could hardly believe – or understand – what I was seeing. By the time all but one was gone, Peter's protests had turned to whimpers.

The nineteenth man – the last of them to emerge from the church – turned his attention first to Peter. "Do you want help, Sir? This is your last chance."

"Last chance?"

Alex seemed unable to stifle his laughter at this young kid – a new recruit, barely out of his teens, Fellsmith I believe his name was – giving his lieutenant an ultimatum. "You better take him up on it, Peter. Get your brother the hell out of here and don't look back."

And he did. After a few minutes of contemplation, Peter's eyes grew empty and devoid of the anger and fear they'd once held. His heart wasn't here, in this fight or whatever it had become – I knew it, he *had* to know it. Quietly, blindly, he followed the boy's lead when it came to figuring out how to stabilize Victor enough to get him ready for travel. He didn't even know what to do with himself when Fellsmith presented me with the weapon that had caused all of Victor's current problems in the first place.

"This is yours, Sir." The parts of the ruby in the handle not smeared with blood glinted in the sunlight. I let my sword fall to the dirt as I accepted that dagger, and when he saluted, I saluted him back. Even as they slowly began to move away, shouldering their burden of a gaunt-faced, misguided Water mage between them, I continued to hold that salute.

At my side, Alex breathed a heavy sigh. "You did it."

No, not me. I didn't do it alone. I'd be dead and this place would be a wreckage of bodies the likes of which the streets of Doverton had probably never seen before if it hadn't been for him, and for Andella. But I didn't know how to say that to them. All I could do was just accept their help as they started leading me toward the doors of the church. I could feel Andella's heartbeat grow quicker as she pressed against me, holding me up on one side while Alex did so on the other.

We didn't get that far, until we heard voices and the rattle of men in armor behind us. There, Onyx Saçaille stood with a great wide gash in the side of one leg, a few inches below the hip. It didn't look like a sword strike, though – Victor's magic? Must have been. The light armor she had there was dented and torn aside and despite a makeshift bandage around the wound, blood still seeped out to turn the green-dyed breeches underneath an off shade of black. "You would truly stand before my army for those men?" she asked, standing in an awkward, pained way. None of her troops nearby offered her aid, although I doubted she would have accepted anyhow.

"Yes."

"*Oui,* I believe this. And I will keep my oath – do not worry." I caught a hint of something in her black eyes, something I couldn't quite place. "When you wish to know about the Light, do let me know." The way she said that word, "Light," I could hear the capital L there. What it meant, I wasn't quite sure.

Andella drew in a sharp breath. "Do you know about... ?"

"Another time." She started to turn away in the most graceful way possible.

"Can I, um, help you, Madame?" Andella offered, but Onyx waved her away.

"I prefer a more... natural way. But I appreciate the offer, Mademoiselle. Go. See your sister."

Natural... no, what happened back there was not natural. But it happened. Somewhere, whoever had written those words in that book all those years ago was smiling, for his prediction – his Prophecy – seemed to have come true. *I'll believe if you believe.* And I did, but I'm no hero; I never wanted nor claimed to be one. I just wanted to do what was right. I had to admit, I was glad I finally had my chance.

2

It was late in the day when I awoke again, in a fluffy, down-filled bed that was just a bit too small for me to move around in comfortably. Amber light shone in from the sagging sun outside the western windows. Where was I? It took a minute for me to get my bearings, and it was eventually the smell of the incense braziers that helped me remember. The church – of course, where else but another church? Earlier, it had been full of activity, with priestesses and acolytes talking and running all around, lots of hugging, a little crying. None of them even had a scratch on them, but the relief of being free from their captors had been no less powerful. Andella finally reconnected with Seraphine, and they had a lot more to share than one might think after just a day of being separated. Seraphine seemed happy yet sad at the same time, and thanked Alex and I many times over for keeping her sister safe.

And there were a million questions, too. *Do you think Victor made it?* I don't know. *What are we going to do now?* I don't know. *What if Zondrell decides to come back up here and start something?* I don't know. I wished I had answers, but I was just too tired to think. All I knew for sure was that something very important happened that morning, and that our lives were not going to be the same anymore. How they might change, each of us could only speculate, but for me, it was all getting to be a bit much. As everyone continued to talk around me, I found I could hardly keep my eyes open, let alone listen and pay attention. Graciously, the head priestess there led me to a room where I could get some rest, and my consciousness shut down within minutes.

Now everything was quiet – gone was the clamor of the voices of a dozen priestesses, punctuated periodically by loud statements and insistent questions from Alex. I sat up slowly, looking around at the sparse little room without much thought behind it. On the table near the bed was a tray with some bread and a bowl of warm broth that smelled full of rosemary, along with a scrap of parchment with familiar flowing script written on it. I sat up and grabbed the note.

> *T –*
> *Went to the palace to talk to King Eric. This should be good. Gave your girl and her sister 200R to get out of here and go to dinner. I think they'll be safe.*
> *AMXV*

In a small town like Doverton, two hundred Royals could probably buy you enough to eat for a week. I doubted there were too many high-luxury taverns or inns here, and I further doubted that the Weaver girls would even think to go eat at places like that – unless, of course, Alex had insisted. That seemed like something he would do. They couldn't have left that long ago, either, since it wasn't even dark out yet.

The broth I'd been left was good – damn good in fact. It wasn't much more than a simple chicken broth, but with a rich, salty taste and a perfect, smooth texture. Then again, maybe it had something to do with the fact that I hadn't eaten much in quite a while. At any rate, it was gone in a matter of minutes, leaving me to ponder something else: I felt *good*. I wasn't ready to run a race or anything, but I felt less pain than I had felt in days – weeks even. Both of my arms even worked properly again, more or less. Breathing didn't hurt anymore. It should have – my logical mind and my memories told me that it should have. But this all rather defied any sense of logic. I should have been on my way to the pyre, and yet, I was very much alive, like something out of an old legend somewhere... or some ancient, dusty book sitting on a shelf in a forgotten little temple, nestled in the Mountains with Two Names at the edge of the Eislandisch border.

I swung my legs over the side of the bed and came to the realization that I wasn't wearing much to speak of. This wasn't that surprising, since my last recollection of my uniform and armor included a lot of rips and tears and bloodstains. Some of that damage had left scars to remember it by, including a star-shaped one being guarded by the gold dragon on my shoulder, and another jagged one near the breastbone, not more than a few inches off-center. Any further the other way and it would have been directly over my heart. Both of them were bright pink and shiny as the skin was just starting to mend itself and settle there. It was almost too much to believe; it was certainly too much to understand just yet.

The same person – whoever it was – who had thought to bring me some chicken broth had also thought to leave some clothes so that I could cover all of those scars. They weren't tailored of course, but they were close enough, with rather dour gray breeches and tunic made of good, soft cotton. The simple leather boots even fit, which was a bit of a surprise. Without a mirror, there wasn't much I could do to ensure I looked civilized enough to be amongst other humans, but I did the best I could to smooth back my hair before putting on the last item – my sword belt. I may not have needed it, but I did need its reassuring weight, as the instant I strapped it into place, I felt a sense of ease. Sad, perhaps, that this was the only thing that made me feel comfortable, even in the safety of a church, but nonetheless, it couldn't be denied. I did, at least, unfurl and tie the scabbard's red peace bond around the hilt, letting any onlooker know that it wasn't there to be used. The silk ribbon stood in stark contrast to the rest of my attire, clean and perfect since it had never seen the light of day. As they say, there's a first time for everything. Without another thought, I opened the door out to a small, bright antechamber.

"Oh! Hello there, Sir," said a young girl in a simple white dress, dark hair pulled up into a bun. She dropped the book she had been reading on the altar at the front of the room and came up to me with a friendly, but questioning, look.

"Good afternoon." I looked past her through the windows lining one wall. The stained glass there depicted a scene of nondescript people watching the goddess descend from the sky, sitting on a ray of sunlight that matched up just about perfect with the actual light from the setting sun outside. It made for quite the display. Even though this temple was smaller than Zondrell's, it was every bit as lovely, I had to admit.

"Are you all right, Sir?"

Considering the past day or so, yes, I thought I was doing pretty damn well. "I'm fine, thank you."

"Oh good! Well, your friend, Lord Alexander, got summoned up to the King's palace about an hour ago. And you just missed Sister Seraphine and Miss Andella – they went to the Laughing Cat. It's an inn just across the street and at the end of the block if you're looking for them." She gestured over at the hall leading out into a much larger room, which must have been the main chapel. "Your other friend was out there in the last pew the last time I saw him. He might still be there if you want to catch him."

"Other friend?"

"Yes, Sir. The Eislandisch man?"

Of course. How could I forget? And there he was, resting comfortably in the last pew with his eyes half-closed, staring up at the vaulted ceiling and its various painted figures and patterns. Brin Jannausch made no move at all when I approached, except to say, "Have a seat." I did – I didn't even think about it that hard. My curiosity for what he might say was too great, and my anger with him had all but washed away. I didn't necessarily want to welcome him to our next family holiday meal, but at the same time... perhaps I just understood him better than I once had. "How do you feel?"

"Like I've been run over by a herd of wild horses. But otherwise, not bad."

He offered a gruff laugh. "People in the streets are talking about a miracle. It is all over town."

"I'm sure." A miracle – good word. I couldn't think of a better one.

My mother's brother continued to look skyward, a pensive expression carving deeper lines into his face. "I do hope you understand the importance of what happened here today."

"I think I do." Did I? From the look he gave me when he opened his eyes and turned, I started to think perhaps not. At least, not in the way that he understood it.

"Tell me something," he asked at length. "Who did you see at the River's edge?" I'm sure I showed far more surprise than I had wished to, but I said nothing. I really didn't want to talk about that, especially not with him. "You have the look of a man who has seen the River."

I continued to say nothing. This was absolutely the last thing I wanted to talk about. After a few minutes I almost moved to get up, but he spoke again. "I saw my parents – your grandparents. My father, of course, I knew. He had been dead since I was a child. Mining accident. But my mother... I had not known until that moment."

At any other time, I would have been willing to pass off my experience – or whatever you wanted to call it – as nothing more than a very vivid dream. But, after seeing the way his blue eyes grew so distant, looking well beyond me and into some other version of reality, it was much, much harder to deny. "That would have been maybe six or seven years ago," I said. "I remember that. We got a letter and some things delivered to the house, and the next thing I knew, my mother was devastated for weeks. She wouldn't talk much about it."

"Seven years, three months, and ten days – to be exact. I was in Lavancée at the time. No letter would have found me. But Gretchen was very close to our mother. She should have been devastated." The way he said it, I knew better than to inquire any further. That past was theirs, not mine.

Instead, I had a different question. "So, what made you turn away?"

At this, his lips curled back into a smile. "A woman. It is always a woman, *ja*?"

Something like that. I couldn't help but return his expression with a slight chuckle. "She wasn't Lavançaise by chance, was she?" I couldn't help but ask.

"You... think you are very perceptive, do you not? I am not here to tell stories." Now we both laughed, for a good long while. For someone who conveyed such an enigmatic and untouchable air, he wound up being just as human as me or anyone else after all.

After a time, the room grew quiet again. "It really was beautiful there, though," I said. If I closed my eyes just right I could see the vibrant lushness of those flowers at the River's edge in my mind's eye anytime I wanted. Even if I didn't want to remember much else, I hoped that vision, at least, would be one that never faded.

"You will have your chance to go back. We all will. But you have been given something – you understand this?" I nodded, even though I wasn't sure that I did. "Nothing gives without expecting something in return. Fate has plans for you."

I couldn't imagine what that meant, but I wished someone would just out and tell me – get it over with. But, from his simple responses and the careful way he spoke, I couldn't figure out whether Jannausch was the one who could do so. "How do you know so much about all this?"

"Because I took the time to listen. And to accept the path before me. It took much longer for this than it will take for you, I think. My path has taken some… diversions." I could not, in my wildest imagination, think of what he must have encountered on the path he had taken through life thus far. I didn't have to, though – it was all written into the lines of his face and into the tiniest flecks of blue-white in his eyes. "But, I am glad. Blood against blood is not how we do things. So I am glad I put faith in you. Do not make me regret this."

"Why me?"

"Why? I do not know. Lucky, I guess." The smile on his lips grew tenfold as he rose to his feet, adjusting his cloak again as he did so.

My rise was quite a bit slower, but eventually I was able to stand eye-to-eye with him once again. "What, in a hurry?" I wasn't about to beg him to say more, but he was hiding something, and it bothered me.

"Go home. I told your mother I would send you home. I do not intend to break that word. You need to go back to Zondrell first."

First? Before what? Then again, maybe I didn't want to know just yet. I could be content to just let Fate take its course. Things do take time – there was little arguing that point. But, there were too many unanswered questions. I hardly even knew what I was supposed to do when I got home, provided I even made it there in one piece. For all I knew, there could have been a contingent of troops waiting for me halfway between Doverton and Zondrell. And after what happened this morning, the gods only knew who might be quite interested in a couple of mages that people said could perform "miracles." I shuddered at the prospect.

Sensing my unease, Brin shook his head. "You will know more when you are ready. You are not there yet. Here – take this with you." From a pocket somewhere under the cloak, he produced a piece of parchment rolled into a small tube and tied with a simple black ribbon. "It may help. You will not do much for anyone from the end of a rope," he said, holding the item out for me to take.

And I did take it, although I found my heart race a little at the idea of opening it. "What is this?"

"My *Zondern* in writing is… not that good. But good enough, I think. Read it." Even though I still didn't want to, I unwrapped and unrolled the note at his request. The handwriting was legible, decent even, and at the bottom was an embossed gold-foil seal, a seven-pointed star with the phrase, "Glory from sea to sea, mountain to mountain," written in Eislandisch in a delicate circle around it.

> *King and Council of Zondrell:*
>
> *My name is Brinnürjn Jannausch. I am brother to your Lady Gretchen Loringham, and my sword is claimed by the King of Eisland, Keis Sturmberg. On 42 Winterherz my men found the Zondrell camp hidden in the forest south of Südwald and Kostbar. From there they attacked many men on routine patrol. This violates the Second Treaty of the Northlands on Grounds 7, 8, and 10.*
>
> *On 3 Frühlingsmorgen, I sent a spy to learn of Zondrell's secrets. This spy, a young girl trained very well, was caught and questioned, but learned nothing new. We knew already what we needed. We organized new offensives so that on 18 Frühlingsmorgen, Zondrell would meet its fate at*

Südenforst. Your men were led there by lies. They knew no recourse.

I speak for Keis Sturmberg and my word is his word. It is best for our two countries to forget this battle, or more will follow. We stand ready if you choose to violate the Second Treaty once more.

– Brinnürjn Jannausch, General of the Seventh
Army of Königstadt

"Is any of this… true?" I asked, still not sure what to make of it after two readings. I was getting ready for a third when he started laughing again, so loud that it reverberated throughout the chapel.

"If you think I am a general then you must also think the sun is black, *Jüngling.* But if Zondrell asks, Keis Sturmberg will tell them that I am. He will say what I have said. That seal and violation of the Northlands Treaty carries more weight than your word."

Carefully, I rolled the letter back up and replaced the tie. Whether it was helpful or not, I wouldn't know until I got home. But the fact that it had been written at all – and that he had seemingly gone to some trouble to write it – made me smile, just a little bit. To some extent, it might have been the least he could do. On the other hand, it might have been far more than I deserved. "Thank you."

He extended his hand out to me then, and even though I hesitated, it wasn't for very long. I'd like to think that it would have brought my mother some joy, or at least some peace, to see me shake her brother's hand. "Walk the River's edge, Tristan Johannes."

"You do the same."

Even as he left, a million questions formed and swirled around in my brain, but couldn't make their way to the surface. Not yet, maybe not ever. For perhaps the first time in my life, I had the sense that the future was not only unknown, but also filled with possibility. It was not, all together, that bad of a feeling.

✳✳

The Laughing Cat Inn reminded me of the Silver – small, warm, comfortable, not too noisy, filled with the smells of good food and good drink. A simple wooden staircase in the corner led up to what I could only assume were rooms for travelers, although from the trappings in the place I had no doubt that any traveler staying here had to have more than a few coins to their name. It was appointed quite well, a place where tapestries decorated richly painted walls, and where good silk and fur trim adorned every man and woman. This was apparently where the better half of Doverton society whiled away their hours, and I felt a bit out of place as soon as I walked in the door. It hadn't even been that long ago since I'd been doing the same things they were all doing now, but when I walked in, I felt their gazes on me in a strange and unnerving sort of way. It certainly wasn't the first time I felt like I didn't belong somewhere, but for some reason, it bothered me more than it ever had in the past. With only a few tables in the place, though, it wasn't that hard to find what I was looking for. Ignoring everyone else, I pulled up a chair, and Andella and Seraphine nearly spilled their drinks.

"Oh! You're up! We were just getting something to eat. I didn't think you'd be up so soon, otherwise we would have waited." Andella looked at me with big, lovely eyes full of concern and apology and... something else. What was it? Something was different. "Sorry."

"Don't worry about it." When I smiled, she smiled, and visibly relaxed.

"How do you feel?" asked Seraphine. The priestess shared that same look of concern that her sister had, but hers was more of a motherly kind of concern – warm, not as complex. Dark circles rimmed her eyes, and she looked like she was about ready for a nap of her own. She'd had an interesting day, to be sure, and I doubted all of her questions were answered. "Are you up to eating? Our food is almost ready."

I nodded. The more I sat there amongst all of the rich smells of that inn, I realized I could have eaten half my weight in meat and still would have been hungry. "I feel all right. Better than a few hours ago."

"Well good. See, I told you, Andie." The women exchanged a glance that I couldn't quite interpret.

"I was... um, practicing, earlier. It's funny. It's like I have to learn magic all over again." Then I realized what it was that was different about her – her eyes were no longer orange. Now, they were a distinctive lavender-blue, but not bright like that of a Water mage. No, this blue had deep, rich undertones, like the color of lapis or a clear sky right before dawn, yet the flecks of white and lighter purple within dominated, pulsing and swirling around in that way that mages had. The effect changed her whole countenance in a way that could hardly be put into words, save to say that just looking at her made a lot my pain seem to just melt away.

Seraphine scrunched up her nose in a sort of disapproving frown. "You need to take it slow, that's all." I didn't quite know what that meant, but I had heard of students at the Magic Academy practicing so much that they'd simply drop over and faint where they stood. If that was what had been happening, we would need to have a serious talk. I didn't want anyone hurting themselves on my account – *especially* her.

Before Andella had a chance to say anything else, the barmaid come over with a platter, including roast beef, some turkey, potatoes done in a few different ways, some bread and cheese – it all might as well have been served by the hand of Catherine Herself. It took a surprising amount of willpower to not just tear into everything there in a most ungentlemanly manner. However, I could not help myself from pulling the barmaid aside before she left.

"Can I get you something, sir?" she asked.

"Yes, ah... do you happen to have any Drakannyan brandy back there?" The way her brow furrowed, I couldn't tell if I'd just asked for the impossible or not. Surely an establishment like this had at least a bottle or two somewhere.

"Well, I think so, sir. I'll have to ask the owner." The young girl – who had a figure that probably gave her a terrible time with the drunken men later in the evenings – hurried off, disappearing into the room behind the bar for a moment. When she emerged she had a cylinder-shaped silver bottle in one hand and a glass in the other. She seemed quite pleased with herself.

"Leave the bottle," I bade her as she poured out a generous dose of the golden liquid. Drakannyan brandy was a favorite of anyone who could afford it and anyone who enjoyed a good strong drink. The serving girl hesitated, but didn't choose to argue; we must have looked enough like we could pay the tab at the end of the night. Perhaps only people who knew to ask for such a thing were given such a nod in the first place.

When she was gone, I took one small sip, just enough to get that flavor on my tongue. Alex used to call it molten gold, and that was an apt description, although to me, it tasted more like hot coals doused with honey – and that evening, it had never, ever tasted better. I offered some to the sisters. "Better drink up before Alex gets here. This won't last long."

Seraphine shook her head, but Andella took a brave, dainty sip from my glass. "Oh my, that's strong."

"It's Paradise in a bottle." I filled the glass back up and had another go, laughing to myself at what I'd just said. Paradise... I sure didn't see anything to drink there. "So, Alex went to the palace, right?"

"They came and took him," said Seraphine between bites.

As if trying to reassure me of something, Andella piped up right away. "It seemed friendly enough, though. Our King is a good man – I'm sure he just wanted to chat, you know? It's been rather an... exciting morning. They asked me to go too, but..."

"But you need your rest." The priestess' big-sisterly scowl ended that line of conversation. Instead, the conversation turned to lighter things, talk of the inn and how popular it was, and how they'd never been there before because normally, it was too expensive. But Alexander had insisted that they take what they thought was far too much money over there to "have themselves a nice time and not worry about anything for a few hours." And so, that was exactly what they did, although they hadn't been sure where to start with the food so they just ordered everything that was on special. Not a bad strategy – I would have done the same thing.

By the time Alex did get there another hour or so later, the inn did indeed live up to its popularity, with people sitting or standing all about, someone playing a lute on the stairs, and extra barmaids trying very hard to meet everyone's needs. It was just like the Silver at sundown – I had to admit, I loved every minute of it. The bottle of Drakannyan brandy was about half gone, too, leaving me in quite the good mood.

As Alex found himself a chair and settled in between Seraphine and me, he looked back over his shoulder. I noticed he'd gotten a chance to clean up and get some fresh clothes for himself as well, although he still wore his short, black wool jacket that he liked so much. It had seen better days, but at least all of the buttons were still there. "Fucking pricks," he said – rather, whispered – and I realized he was talking about two green-clad soldiers heading back toward the front door.

I filled up my glass with brandy and handed it to him. "What happened?"

"Well, let's see." He downed the liquor without hesitation. "Oh by the Lady, that's better. We need more of that. All right, well, do you want the good news first or the bad news?"

The women almost both said the same thing at once. "What bad news?"

"Ah, well," he pulled some papers from inside his jacket with some official-looking stamps and writing on them, "these are passes to a caravan to leaves tomorrow morning. We're to be on it – no exceptions. This King here is not a man to mince words, let me tell you that much. They really don't want us in their city drawing all sorts of attention and whatnot."

"Where is this caravan going?" I asked.

"To Zondrell." The hitch in his voice was unmistakable. But, to his surprise, this was probably the best news I'd heard all day.

"Fine, that's where we were heading anyhow."

Surprised, his quicksilver eyes widened. "Since when?"

"I think we have to. I have a letter here – when we get back I'll take it to Council. Try my luck, I suppose." I pulled Brin's letter out of my pocket and let him read it, with Andella peering over his shoulder behind him.

"Isn't this the seal of Eisland? Where did he get this from? Wait, he's no general, is he?"

"No, but he said that seal is legitimate. You'll help me bring this forward, right?"

"Well, yeah, but Brother..." He trailed off, collecting his thoughts as he read through the letter again before handing it back to me. "I have a letter too, and even so, it's risky. You realize that?"

Of course I did, but I was willing to let Fate do the guiding. "What does your letter say?"

From his jacket he produced another document, this one on better parchment, rolled and sealed with wax and an ornate imprint. "I don't want to unseal it until we get it in front of the Council, but the King read it to me before he signed. It's all about our 'heroism in the face of conflict' and how much of a service we did to Doverton in 'quelling an unfortunate misunderstanding.' It's a good letter. So, that's the good news – we are not dangerous in the eyes of Doverton law or anything like that. They just want us the hell out of here. And by the way, there are three passes." He turned and looked at Andella, and I could see the color drain from her cheeks just a little.

"The King wants me to leave too?" she asked in a small voice almost too quiet for the raucous inn. From her worried expression, though, I could fill in the missing words just fine. To my right, I heard Seraphine take a deep breath.

"You're part of all this attention, too, my dear. He's got a point, though – you don't want to see what happens when people find out they might be able to go to the little church down the road and get healed of their ailments." He poured himself another drink, the bottle now almost gone. "You know, Saçaille isn't wrong. People are going to... well, I don't know what they'll do when they figure us out. It won't be pretty."

"People tend to be attracted to miracles," I said, and I could tell right away that this was a banned word in Alex's vocabulary already.

"Don't call it that, man. Just don't. It's great and all, don't get me wrong – I'm glad we're not dead, you know? But I'm not ready for that kind of talk." Honestly, I had serious doubts he ever would be, and that was all right. All of it was all right – I felt like I could shoulder the burden for all of us. The more we talked and ate and drank, the stronger this conviction grew in my mind.

We made it through half a second bottle of brandy before realizing how late it was, and that there were things that Andella needed to pack. She was clearly not happy about the forced trip, and her sister even less so, although she never once said anything against it. On the contrary, she must have realized, as Alex did, that to go back to that church and continue life as usual was not an option. But, when it was finally time to go for the evening, she hardly said much more than a simple thank-you. I had a feeling she would blame us – more specifically, me – for everything that had happened to her sister and their way of life for many years to come, and that was to be expected. She had spent years ignoring and actively refuting the whole idea of any sort of Prophecy in the first place; to have it rise up and claim her only family in the world showed just how cruel Fate could be. A stone-cold bitch, indeed. If I had been able to find the right words, I would have apologized before we left. But as usual, I could never quite find the right things to say at the right times – not when it counted.

"One thing," Andella said. "I wanted to say something to you." We were standing in the street outside the inn alone, Alex and Seraphine already well on their way back toward the temple in the woods. After seeing the rather exorbitant bill he'd paid on our behalf, it seemed that Seraphine had warmed up to him, at least enough to tolerate his half-drunken ramblings on the way home. She wasn't his type, otherwise I'd worry a bit for her... ah, personal safety. But on the other hand, I was fairly certain that a plain, down-to-earth kind of woman like Sister Seraphine could put Alexander Vestarton squarely in his place on any given day without blinking.

"I... um, I was going to say something to you, too. You first." There were, in fact, lots of things I might have liked to say. The brandy helped make some of them tangible enough to actually speak aloud.

Even in the darkness, her smile no longer had a spark to it, but something else, something gentler but no less beautiful. "I just wanted to tell you that I'm glad we're going to Zondrell together. I didn't want you to leave – you know, on your own."

"I don't know that I would have. Look, I..." Taking a deep breath, I *knew* I sounded like a complete clod, but the alcohol encouraged me to keep going. "I just want you to know that ah... well, what I mean is, I wouldn't be here right now if it wasn't for you. I believed, and I'm thankful – eternally thankful. What happened today was a miracle, and I don't understand it, and I don't deserve it, but I wouldn't give it back for anything. Not now."

"I believed, too, like you said." She shook her head, looking down toward the ground. "But it could have been better, or at least different. I'm just not that strong. I wish I were stronger. Now, I can't even use Fire anymore, and I just… I'm sorry you had to suffer like that, because of me."

I put my arms around her small frame and felt her shaking, just a tiny bit. It did feel good, though, to be able to hold her properly, with both arms. "What? No! No, you don't need to be sorry. Are you kidding? And you don't have to be scared." What I wanted to say next was that I would protect her until I really did meet my end, but I couldn't quite get the words out. She knew that part, though – she had to.

Her eyes were as luminescent as the moons as she looked up at me. "I know. But you know what I want?"

"What's that?"

"I want you to teach me how to fight, too. I want to be stronger, like you."

Not sure if I heard her right, I didn't respond right away. Maybe I was too drunk and was hearing things. But when she continued looking up at me with that hopeful gaze, I realized that she had in fact just asked me to teach her the sword. And intellectually, I could support her in that desire – I considered myself as progressive as anyone, and if a woman wanted to join the military or learn to fight, that was her business. Many did every day, although it was far less common amongst the Zondreans than in Lavancée or Eisland. I just didn't know that I necessarily wanted any woman in *my* life to do that. I learned to use a blade because it was expected, and it was one of the few skills I proved to be good at in my young life. But up until recently, I had not thought much about the fact that it was also a life-threatening pursuit. Now, that was all I thought about. "I don't know. We can talk about that later."

"Promise?"

"Sure. I promise that we'll talk about it."

"Fair enough." She laughed aloud, that lovely, tinkling little laugh. "You'll come and help me pack, right? I don't know what to bring."

Even though everything still hurt, and I wanted very much to curl up and go back to sleep, all I could do was nod. "I can't think of anything I'd rather do."

EPILOGUE

A day had not gone by in months that Lord Jonathan Loringham had not thought about his son. He wondered what was going on, where he was, whether he was in pain. He thought about himself at that age, and how during the War he had often found himself pushed by that same desire Tristan seemed to have – to serve, and be recognized for it. When Brin had come to house about a week or so ago, he also remembered how easy it was for those off the battlefield to forget that there are few "right" decisions in war. There is always another side, another choice with its own consequences. Almost twenty-five years ago, he had chosen not to kill the fifteen-year-old brother of the Eislandisch girl he'd fallen for when he'd had the chance. Killing a kid like that was wrong, even if that same kid was something of a menace to his contingent for their entire six-month occupation of Kostbar. Not that long after they were finally pushed out of the city, Brin would become one of the War's most decorated soldiers – Jonathan lost track of how many times he'd heard about his promotions. He might have even been promoted to General by the end. That kid, they'd say – wasn't he too young to even be in the army? Of course he was, but Eisland had a man ready and willing to serve with everything he had; by that point in the War, Zondrell would have been so lucky to get men like him in their ranks. They weren't stupid. Jonathan and anyone else who'd spent time in Kostbar and followed the career of the "boy warrior" knew that without him, the tide of war might have gone another direction. Those same people might have had Jonathan's head on a pike in Center Square, if they knew that he'd had a chance, and pulled back at the last minute.

Sitting at his desk with a set of ledgers he should have been working on in front of him, Jonathan shook his head with a sigh. He should never have agreed to let Tristan go to "the north" – whatever that meant – to assist in the search for some faery story, the legend of Kaeren. But the King himself had asked for this, was convinced that now was the time, and had promised a great deal of fame and accolades. Tristan might even make General someday himself – he'd heard those words from Kelvaar's own lips. And yet, he had never felt right about any of it. He wouldn't find out why until it was far, far too late.

He should have known better. Brin was right – he truly was a *Dummkopf*. But he had trusted Kelvaar, and General Torven, and now he had to face the fact that his son might be dead somewhere and the entire city seemed to think the worst about him. The things he'd heard – whether rumors or fact, no one seemed to know for sure – was enough to bring any father to his knees. To make matters worse, his wife had all but stopped speaking to him.

"My Lord? Someone's at the door for you." Frederick, his loyal butler, stood quiet but expectant at the door to Jonathan's study.

"Who is it?"

"It's a soldier, m'Lord. Says his name is Sergeant Delrin and he served with our Young Master."

This got his attention – anyone else, and he would have sent him away. He rose from his seat and pushed aside the accounting ledger that should have been filled with rows of figures, but instead had remained blank for the past two hours. "Bring him in."

A few minutes later, a rather bedraggled-looking man stepped into the study, coming to stand at perfect attention in the doorway. The silver falcon on his chest was obscured by dust and grime and years beyond his actual age played out in the lines of his face, but his grayish, dark eyes were steady, unblinking. "My Lord," he said in greeting.

"Sergeant, what can I do for you? And please, be at ease."

The soldier didn't move. "My Lord, I just arrived from Doverton. There was an incident there, and I want you to know what happened."

Jonathan's vision seemed to blur and he felt like he might become ill. Clumsily, he sat back down. "Go on, Sergeant," he said, but the news he steeled himself to hear did not come.

"I want you to know that yesterday morning, Lieutenant Loringham risked his life to save myself and eighteen of my men from... a very difficult situation." He paused, cleared his throat. As he continued, though, his words came faster, more confident. "It is because of him that I am here right now, and I wanted you to know that. People will say things – different things, I think – because a lot has happened. But any of us who served with him and were there yesterday know the truth. He risked his life for us, and that wasn't even the first time. He's still alive to tell about it because the gods saw what I saw – your son, m'Lord, is a hero. And... I just wanted to come by and tell you that."

The room fell silent, Jonathan at a complete loss for words. He wanted to know more, to ask many questions, but something about this soldier told him not to. This man had said everything he was going to say – he had nothing more he was willing to offer. "Thank you, Sergeant. I appreciate you coming here."

He showed Sergeant Delrin out personally, still itching to ask questions that he kept to himself. What exactly happened? Where was Tristan now? If he was still alive, was he coming home? Jonathan prayed to Catherine above that he would – perhaps Vestarton would have enough sense to force him to come home, if they'd even been able to meet up. He would spend most of the rest of that day in silence, thinking, wondering, until just around sundown, when his answers would come with a knock at the door.

**

When the sun began to go down, the merchants of Zondrell's Center Market began to pack their wares away, with most of their customers going off to find their homes, or the nearest inn, to eat and finish their days. Zizah al-Shallal was no different, taking each of her jewels and bits of finery and placing them one by one into a special cushioned box she'd had made just for storing them. After all, a scratched bracelet or broken necklace was worth nothing more than a headache.

Today, it was lucky for the street children who played nearby that there was extra food left, too. In fact, looking into the brazier she realized she still had several meals there that had not been sold. Surprising, too, since it had been such a nice day and there had been many people wandering the market. She had already counted her gold – four hundred and twenty-nine Royals, not bad for the middle of the week, although more of that came from merchandise than tea and spiced meat. Someone had bought a copper ring with an emerald set in it and a pair of matching earrings, and another had bought one of the better silver bracelets, the one with the serpent's heads at either end. She would have to remind herself to find more of those bracelets, as that was the last one and they seemed to sell well enough.

As she put the last jewels away and began to put together a dish for the children, she did not even turn around when someone approached her booth. "I am sorry, we are closed for today," she said.

"That's all right. I just came by to say hello."

Now there was a voice she did not expect to hear. Her red lips formed into a smile. "People have been talking today, *Habibi*. They are saying many interesting things."

"I'm sure. Don't believe everything you hear."

"I have kept that in mind. But they did say you were the one who hurt the Army wizard that came back today."

"Me?" He clicked his tongue, and she didn't need even look to know he was wearing a smug sort of half-smile. "*I* hardly touched him. Besides, he got what was coming to him."

"No doubt." Now she did turn, facing a figure with a heavy blue cloak pulled over his head so as to hide as much of his face as possible. Such a shame – it was a pretty face to hide. She leaned in to look closer, but hid the surprise she felt when she saw his eyes. Perhaps the things she'd heard, particularly earlier that day, had some validity. "You are not feeling well, *Habibi*? Too bad I am out of your *tsohbac*. I am waiting for my shipment. It was supposed to come... yesterday, I think."

"Actually, I think I'm going to quit."

Now this was rather surprising. She raised one dark eyebrow. "If you quit, I will need to find other things to charge you for."

Alexander – now Lord Alexander, she had to keep reminding herself – reached out and kissed her by the hand in that certain way he had that she rather liked, and his smile was almost as bright as the strange silver whirling in his eyes. "I was thinking about that. How about magic lessons?"

"From me? *Habibi*, I am no teacher. Besides, I... what kind of magic do you have?" She had never seen anything like what she saw in him; perhaps it had something to do with years of a constant *tsohbac* habit. But yet, she had known men who had stopped after much longer who never had the look that Alexander had then. She herself had stopped once, just for a few days during one of those Zondrell holidays when the markets had to stay closed, just to see what would happen. Certainly, her eyes never, ever looked like little maelstroms; they had just turned blue, nothing more.

"I'll show you." From a pocket he pulled out a gold coin, showed it to her, then flipped it up into the air. Just before it landed, right in front of her eyes, it ceased to move. It might as well have been a painting of a coin, but it was there, as solid as ever. She could even reach out and touch it, pulling it from its frozen descent. "What do you think?"

Zizah considered the coin – it seemed normal enough, nothing odd about it, no hidden strings. But how did he get it to do that? Intrigued, she gazed back to him, tilting her head just slightly to one side. "You have quite the trick. Does it get better?"

"It does. I can't control it very well though. And I think the time has passed for going to school. So, do you want to see more?"

"As long as it is you bringing the magic and the gold, I do, *Habibi*. But I do wonder," she rested her elbows on the wooden stand so that she could get an even better look at him, "where does all this come from? You are gone for a few days and come back with special tricks – it is very strange, I think."

He continued to smile but shook his head. "Another day. I just wanted to stop by and see you before you closed. I need to head home – just got back, after all." Before she could say anything else he did the hand-kiss again and she felt her question melt away. "Why don't you come to the house tomorrow after you've closed up shop for the day?" And of course, she said she would, and she let him kiss her one more time, this time on the cheek, and she wondered about him long after he had gone away into the evening shadows. Those eyes, that magic, were so intriguing. Waiting a whole day to find out more seemed like too long.

Candles everywhere, set in beautiful silver candelabras. Tapestries and paintings and mirrors on every wall. Servants tending to her every need… these were the sorts of things she expected to find in a palace, not in someone's private home. But then again, she'd never had a chance to see how true nobility lived. All of the finery around her made Andella Weaver feel dreadfully out of place, and she wasn't doing a good job at hiding it.

"So, there's a blue dress here, and a purple one. Hmm, purple's more your color, yes? Yes, I think so. Looks good with your eyes. And I think the Young Master will appreciate this more anyhow." Lissa, the Loringhams' longtime maid, gave a broad, pretty smile. Tristan had entrusted her to Lissa when they walked in the door, and at first Andella had felt awkward going off with a stranger, but Lissa was perhaps the kindest, most gentle-natured person she'd ever met. And, she supposed, it would have been more awkward to be in the middle of what was sure to be a bit of family drama than to have someone help you get washed up and size you up for clothing.

"Is that his favorite color?" Andella asked, gazing at the two garments Lissa held up for her in fascination. They were beautiful things, made from silk and ornate lace – she would have guessed that each of them cost more than she'd ever spent on a year's worth of food. It also struck her as she said it that she didn't know something as simple as his favorite color. So much yet to learn... she wanted very much to know more.

"I believe it is. Try it on. It looks like it should fit – for the most part. We might have to hem it up in back. My Lady's a bit bigger on top than you are, my dear."

Andella reached for the dress, then paused. "Wait, this is Lady Loringham's?"

"Well, it's certainly not mine, dear," the maid replied with a laugh, her lovely dark eyes bright and merry. "My Lady has plenty to spare, don't worry."

Plenty of dresses just like this one... to *spare*? Of course she did – simply amazing. The whole concept seemed quite alien to Andella, and she felt just that much stranger putting on something that belonged to a woman she hadn't formally met yet. Nonetheless, the way that silk touched her skin was like nothing she'd ever quite experienced, and when she looked at herself in the mirror, she was entranced by who she saw there. The girl staring back at her was dressed like some princess, with eyes that sparkled with an indigo hue – not the color of the sea but more like an early evening sky, with the stars coming out and lavender fading into deeper night. She was not yet used to that color, not in the least, and it still felt like something was *missing*. The magic she had spent four years trying to perfect was gone, and in its wake was something very different, something that might take another four years or longer to master. Practicing the concentration – visualizing bringing the energy up from her heart to the surface, just like they taught her at the Academy – helped quite a bit, and most of the ride to Zondrell she had done just that. But she still felt weak, a beginner just learning to make the magic bend to her will. Surprisingly, it didn't bother her that much that she'd never be able to act as a Pyrelight again, although she had no idea how she'd support her sister and the temple in the future. What would they do for money? Tristan and Alexander had both told her not to worry about any of that, but she did nonetheless. She had no interest in becoming their charity case.

Behind her, Lissa tugged a bit at the dress's open back, startling her away from getting lost in her own thoughts. "Yes, that's very nice. Just about right. A little longer than I thought at the bottom, though, yes? We'll find you some taller shoes."

"I feel so different in this."

"I'm sure we can have some things made for you that'll fit better – I'll look into that tomorrow at the tailor."

Andella shook her head. "That's not what I meant. I..."

"I know what you meant, dear, and I understand," Lissa interjected, gently starting to pull Andella's auburn hair back to tie it with a simple matching ribbon. "But you couldn't have picked a nicer family to stay with. These people will simply not let you run around without proper attire. Trust me on this one."

When the hair was sufficiently secured, she ventured to look again at the girl in the mirror who was her and yet not. "Thank you," she said, voice soft.

"Not necessary, my dear. I'm here to serve. Now, let me find some things to go with that." The maid started off out of the dressing room, but was stopped short by the tallest and most elegant Eislandisch woman Andella had ever seen. Her long blonde hair was pulled back into a series of interwoven braids, not a strand out of place, and with her long, black silk gown trimmed in white fur, she reminded Andella of the Snow Queen from that old children's faery tale. Everything about Lady Gretchen Loringham seemed absolutely perfect and lovely, even though her cheeks were wet and glistening.

"Everything all right, m'Lady?" Lissa asked, giving Gretchen a knowing, wise sort of look, the kind of look that could only be shared between women who had been friends for many years.

"It is good." Her accent was rich and deep and intriguing. "I wanted to come and meet this girl who helped my son come home."

"Oh, I... well..." Andella stammered, not sure where to start or what to say. "What I mean is, I'm happy to be here. I'm happy I could help, and, ah, thank you for letting me into your home."

"You are an honored guest." Gretchen regarded her, evaluating the choice of apparel. It seemed to meet her approval, but something was missing. "You need jewelry. Lissa, find something that will look good, *ja*?" Lissa hurried off to do as she was asked, returning moments later with a silver necklace with bright purple jewels on it larger than a horse's eye, and two matching bracelets.

"This is what I had in mind. What do you think, m'Lady?" As Lissa fastened the necklace at her throat, Andella could do nothing except look in the mirror and continue to disbelieve what she saw.

"I don't really know what to say," she admitted, brushing her fingertips across the surface of one of those huge gems.

"There is no need, *Herzchen*. You brought my Tristan home – this is a greater gift." A note of something not quite like sorrow crept into the Lady's smiling expression. "He talks with his father now. We will eat in a few hours. I hope you are hungry?" Andella nodded graciously. "Good. So, tell me, you were the girl who ran Lord Xavier's funeral, *ja*?"

She looked down at the floor, surprised that she was remembered at all. "Oh, yes, m'Lady. Alex – er, Lord Vestarton – asked for an Academy-trained Pyrelight, so they got me."

"Hm. It was very nice," Gretchen said with a wistful sort of smile. "But you come from Doverton, Tristan said. I used to go there sometimes with my father when I was a very little girl. He was a miner... we used to trade for things that we could not get in Kostbar. Are there still many Eislandisch traders there?"

In just a short time, Tristan must have told them quite a few things about her. That was all right – she wouldn't know where to begin if Gretchen just asked her "about herself" anyhow. Starting with Doverton made sense, so she told her how yes, the Eislandisch still came there a lot, but she herself had never been up as far as Kostbar, though she'd heard it was lovely, especially in the summers. Instead of doing much traveling, she had always lived with her sister at the little church, and she told Gretchen how she had been able to go to the Magic Academy in Zondrell after passing a test that let her enter without having to pay for the full tuition. It had been a gamble to come all that way and possibly not be able to enter at all, but her sister had insisted and it had been her mother's greatest wish for her before she'd passed away. She had been very lucky to be amongst the top ten students who were admitted that particular day. All that had seemed like a very long time ago, and the more she tried to hide her uncertainty with telling her story, the more awkward she felt, even though Lady Loringham listened with such great interest. Andella kept prattling on and on, about the Academy, about Doverton, about whatever came to mind, until some noises coming from downstairs distracted them.

A door opening and closing. Light, staccato footfalls on the wooden floor. Then men's voices, one stern and one officious, calculating. In the upstairs dressing room, both Gretchen and Andella felt their hearts quicken.

"General, what can I do for you?" This was the stern voice, someone who was most displeased to see whoever had come to visit.

The other voice maintained as pleasant a tone as possible, but there was no mistaking friendliness for weakness. "Jonathan, I have something here – a full pardon signed by the King himself. You can read it if you want. All we need is some information."

"Keep it. We'll go before Council."

"Jonathan, you do understand what this means, don't you? A *full pardon*." A long pause. Andella wanted very much to run down there and see what was going on. After a time, the man they called the General spoke again. "Surely, boy, *you* understand? This kind of an opportunity doesn't come every day, especially considering what you've done. But all that could be forgiven. We just want to know what you know – we want to hear about what happened the other day at Doverton."

Tristan's voice was hoarse, soft, yet like the General's, far from weak. "As my father said, Sir, we'll go before Council."

"Are you daft, boy? Do you have any idea how important this could be to Zondrell?"

"I do, and I'm sorry, Sir – I can't help you."

The General's patience was crumbling. "You're not making a good case against a charge of treason, boy, I'll tell you that much. Just come and talk to me, and you can make all of that go away." Palpable silence was the only response. "You're making a mistake – a huge mistake. Such promise, wasted. Are you really that much of a fool?"

That other voice, the stern one – Tristan's father – broke in more loudly this time. "Jamison, you heard him. We're done here. And don't bother going across the street – Vestarton won't talk to you either."

"Hm. Good day to you then, gentlemen. I'll see you at the next Council. In the meantime, you may want to be careful who you talk to around town." More shuffling, then the slamming of the big, heavy front door. Masking her fear with action, Lady Loringham glided out into the hall then, and Andella followed her to peer over the balcony railing to the first floor below them.

Tristan stood across from his father in the hall, arms crossed before his chest and staring a hole through the closed door. When Lord Loringham put a hand on his shoulder, it seemed to startle him a bit. "Son, go get yourself cleaned up, take a rest, like I told you. There's plenty of time to talk about this later," he said, then turned to the butler waiting patiently at their side. "Frederick, make sure we've got twelve settings for dinner, please? The Vestartons and the Shal-Vespers will be joining us. Use the silver and the good plates, yes?"

"Aye, m'Lord." Frederick went off to do what he was asked with a bow.

Lady Gretchen motioned like she was going to say something, but Tristan was already making his way up the stairs, taking slow, deliberate steps. The tired and anxiety-ridden look he'd had in his eyes for most of the day – at least, ever since they'd gotten into that carriage early that morning –

was gone, though. In its place was a sort of... resolute clarity. Andella could think of no better term to describe it.

Without a word, Tristan wrapped one arm around his mother's shoulders and kissed her on the cheek. Then he turned to Andella and did the same thing. "Tell me something. Do you trust me?" he whispered into her ear, and she nodded. She was certain – there were no questions left. There hadn't been for some time. "You have no idea what that means to me." When he pulled away from her that same clarity continued to brighten his countenance. "And ah... you look absolutely stunning."

She felt her cheeks grow warm, but in a good way. He had no idea what that meant to her – all of it, in fact, the entirety of the past two weeks. It wasn't how she had envisioned her life, to be sure, but Fate had other plans. She was most thankful that she would not have to walk this strange new path alone.

The End

Tristan and Alexander will return!

In the meantime, please check out Halsbren Publishing LLC's other great fantasy titles available at Amazon.com, or anywhere fine books are sold.

www.AuthorJayErickson.com
or
www.zelda23publishing.com

If you enjoyed this novel, please take a moment and review it favorably. Every bit helps.

Thank you.

Anastasia M. Trekles
Author

ABOUT THE AUTHOR

 Dr. Anastasia Trekles is a clinical professor at Purdue University. She also works with several professional non-profits to support educators and writers in Indiana and the Chicagoland area. Dr. Trekles has an extensive background with education technology, including design and pedagogical strategies as well as the effective integration of various technologies into teaching. She has taught a wide array of undergraduate- and graduate- level courses in these areas, both in classrooms and via distance education. While she might not have graduated from the Zondrell Magic Academy, she has spent a fair amount of time around schools.

Dr. Trekles has a personal passion for all types of fantasy fiction. The world of M'Gistryn is a world completely her own, but she can trace her inspiration of it to everything from Final Fantasy to Star Wars, from Harry Potter to the Sopranos, and from Ancient Rome to feudal Europe. To Dr. Trekles there is more to M'Gistryn than magic and prophecies – it's a world full of real people, struggling with real situations and real emotions.

In her debut novel, *Core*, she explores issues of war, coming of age, and the fulfillment of our life's purpose.

Dr. Anastasia Trekles currently resides in Northwest Indiana.